Collateral Damage

Nina Verona

Ebook ISBN 978-1-950093-49-6

Paperback ISBN 978-1-950093-50-2

Cover Design by Natasha Snow Designs

Editing by Cassie Mae at Cookie Lynn Publishing Services

Published by Addison & Gray Press LLC

*This book is dedicated to the kind of love
that teaches you how to walk again.*

PLAYLIST

Champagne Problems - Taylor Swift

I Know It Won't Work - Gracie Abrams

Can I Be Him - Games Arthur

Eyes Don't Lie - Isabel LaRosa

Waiting Room - Phoebe Bridgers

Killing Me - Dylan Matthew

Now That We Don't Talk - Taylor Swift

Party 4 U - Charlie xcx

Run For The Hills - Tate McRae

Do I Wanna Know? - Hozier

The Beach - The Neighborhood

Back To Friends - Sombr

Nirvana - Eliana

Scream My Name - Thomas LaRosa

Ruin My Life - Zara Larsson

Hideaway - Cigarettes After Sex

Loved By You - KIRBY

Daylight - Taylor Swift

Collateral Damage is recommended

for adult readers only.

.

Please be mindful of your triggers

before proceeding.

This book contains content including but not limited to depictions of
sexually explicit encounters, childhood trauma, alcohol abuse,
adult drowning, bodily injury, loss of limb, and death.

A NOTE FROM NINA

Dear Reader,

This book is a standalone romance and the second in an interconnected series. I recommend reading *Crushed by Love* first, Ethan's story, before diving into *Collateral Damage*, Cooper's story. The twin brothers' lives are deeply intertwined, and reading book one will keep you from missing out on epic plot twists and a beautiful love story. That said, you can read this book as an enjoyable standalone if you wish. I hope you love Cooper and Sybil as much as I do!

-Nina Verona

PREVIOUSLY IN THE SERIES

Spoilers ahead for book one, Crushed by Love.

Fresh out of the foster care system, eighteen-year-old Arden Davis lands a summer housekeeping job at a billionaire family's Nantucket estate, only to find herself living alone with twin brothers, Ethan and Cooper King. Sparks fly with both men, but her contract is abruptly canceled. With nowhere safe to go before college, she stays in the empty beach house until a hurricane forces Ethan's return.

Trapped together, they fall hard and fast, but when Arden finds a photo of Ethan's ex—who looks eerily similar to herself —she realizes she's a rebound and ends the relationship.

Starting college in Boston, she's blindsided by trespassing charges from Ethan's family. Unsure what to do, she's intercepted by a mysterious couple—her long-lost aunt and uncle, the Laurences—who welcome her into their family and end her legal troubles. The real shock? Ethan's ex, Sybil, is Arden's cousin.

Two years later, Arden is thriving with the Laurences and

returns to Nantucket for vacation when she collides with the Kings. She learns the families are sworn enemies due to an affair between her uncle and Ethan's late mother. Despite mounting tensions, Arden and Ethan rekindle their love in secret, but when Sybil warns Arden will have to choose between the families, things spiral out of control.

At the height of the feud, a boating accident leaves Arden's uncle dead and Cooper's right leg severed below the knee. Heartbroken, she walks away from Ethan, having realized their families are too toxic for them to be together. When Ethan is unfairly charged with manslaughter, she begs the Laurences to help him, but they refuse—until a buried family secret changes everything.

Arden's uncle knew about her existence all along, and her guilt-ridden aunt wants Arden to be happy, encouraging her to follow her heart. Arden does exactly that, reuniting with Ethan after the manslaughter charges are dropped.

Six months later, at a New Year's Eve party, Cooper and Sybil cross paths, leading to an explosive confrontation between old friends who have now become enemies.

Things between Sybil and Cooper are about to get interesting...

PROLOGUE

A girl stands inside an aging gazebo overlooking her favorite beach, strawberry curls tangling in the summer breeze. She imagines the crashing surf below is orchestra music, and the mostly bare vines climbing the gazebo are covered in flowers. Between small hands, rests a massive bouquet of hand-picked white magnolias and blue hydrangeas—her favorites. Her dress is also white, of course. She's getting married today. She wishes she had a real veil, but for now, the pillowcase tied like a headband will have to do.

Across from her stand two boys. Her favorite boys.

Lots of favorites today.

Their mom made them bring suits to the beach house this year. The boys said the suits were for fancy dinners. *Perfect.* They're nice enough outfits for today, but the boys wear them uncomfortably, saying the itchy fabric is a million-and-one degrees. The best grooms do *not* act so annoyed and certainly don't scratch under their suit jackets.

"Cooper, stand there," the girl instructs, moving the boy

with the brown eyes to stand in front of her. "And Ethan, you're over here. You're the minister, so you have to marry us."

The boy with blue eyes stands between them, a cheeky grin on his six-year-old face. "Whatever you say, Valentine," he teases.

He thinks this whole thing is one big joke, but the girl doesn't mind too much, not when they call her that. She rolls her eyes whenever they use her nickname, but her lips turn up in a smile.

"Remember what we talked about?" she says to Ethan. "You can't call me Valentine for the ceremony. It won't count. You have to use my real name. Sybil Laurence."

Ethan nods solemnly.

"Can we hurry?" the groom whines. "It's too hot."

Sybil eyes the way his cheeks have gone red. He's complaining, but he's right. It's scorching, and everyone would rather be swimming, but Cooper agreed to get married after a harrowing game of *rock paper scissors*, so there's no turning back now.

"Do you want to marry me or not?" Sybil challenges, her green gaze narrowing into tight slits. The boy nods, mostly because he wants to get this over with, but also to beat his brother and collect his prize. When Sybil said she wanted to hold a pretend wedding, the twins both wanted to be the groom. That wasn't going to work. There can only be one groom.

Sybil straightens her spine and motions for Ethan to proceed.

"Our dearly beloves," Ethan says, and Sybil almost corrects him but decides better of it. "We are gathered here today—"

Despite the heat, Cooper takes Sybil's hands and squeezes, holding tight to his girl.

The happy couple proceed to get married, complete with an innocent peck on the lips. It's their first kiss, but it might be their last. Not ten minutes later, Cooper pushes Sybil into the pool, and she comes up sputtering, demanding a divorce.

Cooper laughs it off when Ethan, always the hero, says he'll marry her instead.

"I accept," she replies haughtily, shooting her now ex-husband a dagger-glare from where she floats like a cupcake in the water. He could've waited for her to change into her swimming suit! "We'll get married another time, though. Maybe tomorrow. I'm *done* with weddings today."

"Yes, maybe tomorrow," Ethan agrees. "I'm going to get changed."

He sprints off, but Cooper stays, staring at the girl for a minute—his bride, his valentine, favorite person, best friend, and now his ex-wife. He fought so hard to win that game, and he messed it up. In his defense, he only pushed her into the pool because Ethan teased them about the kiss. He was trying to push *Ethan* into the pool, and she got in the way.

"Well, what do you have to say for yourself?" she demands, hands on her hips and water dripping off her upturned face.

"I meant to push Ethan, not you," he confesses desperately.

She rolls her eyes. "Yeah, right. You just don't want to be married."

Rejection hurts. Anger seems appropriate.

"Not to a drowned rat, I don't!"

Cooper can't even say the truth. She won't listen. She's like that sometimes. Stubborn as a mule, her daddy says, not that Cooper knows what a mule is.

"You're the rat!"

He hides his embarrassment by cannon-balling into the pool and soaking Sybil all over again.

PART ONE

> *"Not that I loved Caesar less,*
> *but that I loved Rome more."*
>
> William Shakespeare's Julius Caesar

ONE

S ybil
     Present - Age 26

"I'm sorry, could you repeat that?" I ask my cousin, sounding like a deranged hyena, because there is *no way* she said what I think she said. Not my sweet baby cousin. Not the woman who lived with me for two years. Not the person I know to be cautious and reserved and, most of all, guarded.

"We eloped!" Her smile is sunshine radiant.

Yup. That's the word: *eloped.*

I try to fake a smile, I really do, but I can tell she's already caught my pure horror.

"How... e-exciting," I manage.

She lifts a hand to show off a diamond ring, and I nearly fall out of the chair. We're having a boozy brunch together in midtown, and it wouldn't be the first time I fell out of a chair during a boozy brunch, but it would certainly be the most memorable.

Her diamond reflects off the sun streaming through the window we're sitting by as the winter cold battles the quirky Soho restaurant's insufficient heating. I shiver, wishing we were tucked into a dark corner. I'm entirely too exposed right now.

I'm supposed to say congratulations and fake sincerity. If I were totally sober, I might be able to pull it off, but I'm two large mimosas deep, and the truth slides out of my mouth just as easily as the alcohol went in.

"But... *why*?"

Her expression drops, those big brown eyes glossing over.

"Don't get me wrong, Arden," I backpedal. "I'm happy for you and Ethan. I'm just... surprised."

Truth be told, I *wasn't* happy for them initially being together, so I don't blame her for thinking I hate this announcement. But the thing is, Ethan King was *mine* first. He was my everything for years—my best friend, my boyfriend, and even my fiancé.

And then he was nothing.

So, when Arden first confessed her love for my ex, I freaked out, and admittedly, I treated her like shit. I've spent five months making it up to them. Ethan and Arden suit each other. They're crazy in love, and he and I have been over for years. She deserves to be happy, and so does he, even if I wanted to hate him.

But marriage? They've only been official since August.

It's January.

She's still in college, for Christ's sake!

Ethan knows better.

And I swear to God, if he were here, I'd kick him in the shins, right here underneath this table. But no, it's only me and my sweetheart cousin today. She asked to get together as soon as she returned from her Maldives holiday with Ethan—a beach trip that apparently turned into a whole lot more than frolicking in the sand.

"Why *not* get married?" Arden challenges, her eyes glistening with starry-eyed emotion. "We're in love."

"Umm... because you're so young."

"So what? I know what I want. Besides, lots of people get married young."

Yeah, and lots of people get divorced, too.

"It's just... why did you guys feel the need to get married so soon?" I ask. "You could've been engaged for a while first."

Like normal people with *families* they care about do. While this is ultimately their decision, they took a wedding away from the rest of us. It's an unmistakable stab of betrayal. While I only met my cousin a few years ago, she's quickly become one of my best friends.

This elopement? It hurts. It's like a knife to the chest, both shocking and painful, but I know this isn't about me. I need to deal with that knife all on my own—don't make it Arden's problem.

"I know what you're thinking," she says, placing her hand on top of mine. At least it's not the hand with the rock on it. "You're hurt we did this without inviting anyone."

I nod once.

"But please try to understand that Ethan and I got married for *us*. Not for anyone else. And with all the drama that's happened between our two families, can you blame us?"

"When you put it that way..." I grumble.

"And now nobody can try to break us up. We're more than a dating couple; we're a married couple. We're legally committed to each other." She sighs wistfully. "Forever."

I roll my eyes but give her hand a squeeze before returning to my omelet. "Why do you have to be so cute?" As much as I might hate this for me, I love it for her. She's happy. That's all I want.

The Laurence family and the King family hate each other, but these two? They're our own little Romeo and Juliet, except they get a happy ending. Maybe it's destiny, maybe they were truly supposed to end up together. I don't know, but I *do* know they've found the kind of love I've only dreamed about.

I let out a sigh. "I'm happy for you, and honestly, you probably did the right thing to avoid the drama."

She smiles. "I knew you'd understand. That's why I wanted to tell you first."

I give her a pointed look. "If you expect me to be the messenger, I'm not cut out for that shit."

She takes a long drink of her plain orange juice. No mimosa when the woman is still shy of twenty-one. Ethan's about to turn twenty-seven. *The cradle-robber.*

"Don't worry, Ethan and I will tell everybody," she promises. "But we're hoping to have a nice reception to celebrate. That way, the families can still have a way to share in our happy news."

Well, good luck. A party with estranged families is bound to have drama, even one celebrating people we mutually love. My heart aches every time I think of the undoing of two happy families that once shared everything. I'm not sad about losing Ethan. It's obvious we weren't meant to be, but it hurts that I lost *all* of the Kings. My two best friends, Ethan and his twin brother Cooper, their parents, who were like second parents to me, especially Victoria King. When she passed, it broke all our hearts.

But more than any of that, the pain is the worst when I think of my father and the horrible way we lost him last summer. His anger was so deep he couldn't let it go. He let it harm the Kings and kill himself. When I think of Dad, my heart doesn't hurt... it *bleeds*.

That man was my idol.

He was enigmatic and wonderful and my biggest fan. But he was a cheater, a liar, and had a temper that got him killed. He destroyed so much, but despite everything, I still love him, and I always will.

Even now, my smile feels cracked and jagged, hiding the true me underneath: the girl who lost the ones she loved...

"A reception is not the same as a big wedding, but it's the closest we're going to get. I know Amelia will appreciate it," Arden continues.

My mother loves a party, especially one centered around her family. Two and a half years ago, when we discovered Arden existed, Mom took her in like one of our own. Arden grew up in foster care, something my mom feels terrible about. Arden's mom was my mother's little sister, a troubled woman who died of drug addiction and hid her baby from the family.

It was only after Dad died we learned how much he knew. Dad was aware of Arden all along. Social services tried to place her with us, and Dad told them to leave us alone. Dad's not here to defend his actions, but that was the betrayal that finally broke Mom. She gave Arden and Ethan her blessing.

"Let me help with the planning?" I ask, surprising us both.

Arden's eyes widen as she tucks a strand of loose auburn hair behind her ear. Sometimes looking at Arden is like looking in a mirror. She and I are *so* similar in our features, but she's more petite and has brown eyes instead of green. That and she's six years younger.

"You'd do that for me? Are you sure?" She twists her bottom lip.

"Unless I'm overstepping? Maybe you and Ethan want to be

in charge of everything. I'm only offering in case you need help," I ramble. "Maybe I shouldn't? This is *your* thing."

She snorts. "The reception is for everyone else. If it was for us, Ethan and I wouldn't have eloped in the first place."

"True." Visions of a gorgeous reception run through my head. "I'd be happy to help." I give her a faux-dramatic look, like we're in a job interview. "Event planning is one of my strengths."

She laughs but she gets that I'm being serious. I graduated with a business degree from Harvard. My emphasis is in marketing and public relations, and now I work for the Laurence Foundation. I fundraise and spearhead events to support our philanthropic efforts, so I've got party-planning connections up the wazoo and Pinterest boards filled with ideas.

"How soon are you thinking? Is two months okay? A March event is possible, though it won't be easy. Venues book years out, but I could pull some strings."

She laughs. "Tell me when and where, and I'll be there."

The server takes our plates, and while we're waiting for the check to arrive, I lean across the table, giving my cousin my best conspiratorial grin.

"About this elopement... you're not getting out of here without telling me everything."

Her eyes sparkle, but she holds her excitement in. "It's not too weird?"

"What would be weird about you marrying the guy I was engaged to?" I deadpan, then we both laugh. "Of course, it's weird, but I don't care. I want to know how this happened, and don't you dare leave out any details."

She spends the rest of our brunch gushing about how it unfolded, from the way he proposed spontaneously as they were about to fall asleep, to how they woke up the next morning and he asked again, to her saying yes and the ring shopping they did that very same day, to the local priest who agreed to marry them on the beach with little more than a photographer as their witness.

By the time she's done, we're both a blubbering mess.

"So yeah, I'm a married woman," she gushes.

"Gah, I'm so happy for you." I clutch my heart with genuine happiness for my sweet cousin, and her lips curve in a smile she couldn't fight even if she wanted to.

The entire affair sounds ridiculously romantic.

And... I'm a little jealous. Not jealous because she ended up with Ethan, but that she has something I don't believe I'll ever experience—unconditional love and trust, and unwavering faith that her relationship will last.

I don't think that's possible for me. Not that I'm cynical enough to think it's impossible for everyone, but I'm smart enough to recognize its improbability. I've been through too much, *seen* too much. I've trusted the wrong people. I've loved and lost and lost again.

I've got the kind of issues that make a girl recoil from anything beyond casual sex, and that's never going to change.

Just like my history won't change either.

Two

C ooper
Past - Age 18

They're kissing, and I think I might die.

Any possibility of ever being with Sybil Laurence is officially gone. It's over. She's my dream girl, and now that dream will stay locked away in my imagination.

While I can't say I'm surprised—I even feel a sense of vindication at being right—I'm fucking *shattered*. A knife lodges into my pathetic heart and twists, but I can't even be mad about it. They're Ethan and Sybil...

And I love them both.

I should've talked to my brother about my feelings. He wouldn't be kissing her if I had. Or not. Maybe he would've anyway, and things between my brother and me would've become awkward.

But the fact remains, nobody saw her first or called dibs. Maybe that's where the trouble started. If you like a girl, you tell your brother, so he doesn't make a move. It's a simple rule, but an important one. My twin and I are competitive as fuck, except for when it comes to this. Contrary to the rumor mill, we don't share. Dating the same woman is a line we've never crossed and never will—one we drew in middle school when girls started getting hot and we started noticing.

But Sybil Laurence? She's different.

She's not a sister, but she's family. She's been around since the beginning. Hell, our birthdays are only a month apart. Ethan and I were born in January, and she came along in February, just in time to be her parents' Valentine's Day present. They even used to call her Valentine when we were little—a nickname Ethan and I adopted and Sybil never corrected. I think she secretly likes it, though she'll never admit it.

I saw that girl go through the awkward braces stage, a year of bad acne, and a gangly growth spurt. She looked like a giraffe, and when Ethan told her as much during fourth-grade summer, she stomped around the beach house for a week. I'll never forget when she had her first puppy-love heartbreak at twelve over some idiot she "dated" for two days. Ethan and I laughed about that one behind her back. We knew better than to do it to her face and risk pissing our moms off.

All this is to say that Sybil Laurence is not a romantic option. Not even now that she's grown into a gorgeous and sophisticated woman. Not even now that she's the kind of person I'd be expected to date and someone my parents already love. And not even now that she's got a maturity about her that makes her seem so much older than eighteen, like everyone else our age is trying to catch up to things she figured out long ago.

Bottom line: Sybil Laurence is off limits.

Ethan knows all of this, and I thought he agreed. It was understood. An unspoken rule. Don't date Sybil.

But did Ethan and I ever have this conversation? No. We fucking didn't. And that was a big mistake on my part.

Now they're making out in the pool like they belong together.

"Are you alright?" the girl sitting on my lap purrs into my ear. I think her name is Tracy. Or maybe it's Lacy. Stacy?

Whatever her name is, she's straddling me in the hot tub, the overly chlorinated bubbles swirling around us. We've been making out on and off for the better part of an hour. I was into it, too. *Really* into it. Even though we barely met a few hours ago, I'd already made mental plans to get her naked tonight. Things were going perfectly until I came up for air, ready to ask Tracy/Lacy/Stacy to go somewhere more private, and I saw them.

Sybil and Ethan.

And now I can't even remember this girl's name anymore.

There they are, bodies pressed against the side of the pool, arms wrapped around each other. Sybil's lips—her perfect cherry-red lips—are currently working against my brother's mouth like he's the love of her fucking life.

Shit.

Ethan's got her against the side of the pool like he's ready to do her right there, despite all the people around. PDA is not usually his thing, but it's as if he's forgotten there's a party happening around him. What's worse is she seems to have forgotten everyone else as well. It's them and nobody else.

I'm part of that *nobody else*, apparently.

My entire body heats from more than the hot tub, and one thing is painfully clear—I've never been more jealous of Ethan than I am right now.

"I need a drink," I mutter to Tracy/Lacy/Stacy and peel her off my lap before she can protest.

She falls back with a pout, her cleavage bouncing in her

bikini top. Normally that would keep my attention, especially since she's the sexy vixen-type with her long jet-black wet hair, beads of water on her soft, tanned skin, and lips puffy from kissing. Under different circumstances, I would take this as far as she'd let me—most likely with my dick buried in her as she screamed my name. But I can't. I'm too... pissed? Flustered? Confused? Angry?

I don't even know what to call what I'm feeling. It's more than jealousy. It's hurt and fear and so many other emotions I want nothing to do with.

"I'll come with you?" the girl asks, sucking her bottom lip into her mouth. She probably thinks this is the part where we find a room and lose our swimsuits.

What is wrong with me? Wouldn't fucking her make me feel better? I already know the answer to that is a big fat *no,* and I hate it.

I've got to get out of here.

This party isn't happening at our beach house, and thank goodness for Perry Hargrove and his constant parties and many available bedrooms. I don't know what I'd do if I had to attempt sleep while Ethan fucks Sybil in his room across from mine.

Are they going to sleep together tonight? Looks like it. But maybe this will become a one-off drunken mistake that will lead to nothing.

Ethan knows better than to go after Sybil, let alone actually date her. He knows better than to take this big of a risk.

Or maybe he knows better than to let Sybil fall for someone else, losing his chance with the most beautiful girl he's ever laid eyes on.

Ethan's always been smarter than me. I shouldn't be surprised he's smart enough to want the woman he also considers his best friend. Who wouldn't want to date their best friend when she's gorgeous and intelligent and funny and kind and gets you in ways other people don't?

I wouldn't be so jealous if she wasn't my best friend, too.

I might be in love with the girl, but my true best friend isn't actually Sybil.

It's Ethan.

My brother.

My twin.

I must be loyal to him above all else.

And that means supporting him with her.

There are three of us in our trio, but there's only room for two to fall in love, which means one has to go.

I guess that not-so-lucky one is me.

THREE

S ybil
    Present - Age 27

How much does Cooper King hate me? On a scale of one to ten, I bet it's eleven, and I don't even blame him. He's certainly let me know how angry he is every time we've run into each other.

But I'll be honest, Cooper was on my mind as I planned Ethan and Arden's reception. I'll have to spend a whole evening with my ex-best friend that hopefully doesn't end up in another screaming match. I'm genuinely sad our friendship will never see the light of day. Things are cordial with Ethan, and that's good enough for me. But with Cooper? They're still broken.

Peering around at the reception, pride swells in my chest. I can honestly say I've done a job well done. We were able to snag the ballroom at one of Manhattan's swankiest hotels by picking a weeknight, and the gold-hued space has been decorated in shades of blue, per the bride's request, to "match Ethan's eyes," she'd said—gag me with a spoon but also... *awwww*. Everything has been meticulously planned and executed, from the gourmet food to the band to the guest list.

Now all we do is sit back and enjoy.

I'm trying to do exactly that, but my analytical brain hasn't been able to switch off event-coordination mode.

I'm currently standing against the far wall beside the bar, double checking we're not running low on champagne, when familiar voices catch my attention. It's Cooper King and his father, Conrad King. Conrad used to scare the absolute shit out of me, and from the way my body tenses, that might still be true. They're around the corner in the nearby hall, having what they probably think is a private conversation. I shouldn't stay here and listen, but my body stays glued to the spot anyway, my ears prickling.

"Are you going to make the announcement, or am I?" Conrad King asks his son, and my hackles rise.

"You are." His voice is cold and heartless, lacking the warmth I took for granted for so many years.

"You don't want to gloat?" Conrad questions, sending a shiver of unease down my spine. I swear, if they do anything to ruin this special evening for Arden and Ethan, I'm going to lose my shit.

"Something like that," Cooper says. "I'm not really the gloating type."

"Fine, but remember, the end goal here is King. Always King."

"Always has been and always will be."

My stomach hardens. I have half a mind to interrupt them and demand answers.

"Go talk to her," Conrad adds. "You know what you need to do, son."

"I don't want to talk to her. They're all rotten. The entire

Laurence family," Cooper snips and my ears burn. "Except for Chandler and Arden. But the rest of them are rotten as far as I'm concerned."

"Make *amends* with Sybil, or you'll regret it," his father insists.

My entire body goes numb.

"I was ready to make amends before her father cost me my leg," he growls. "I still have phantom pains that will most likely never go away. Do you know what that feels like?"

"Everyone has pain, son."

Flashes of that day return like a never-ending nightmare. He's right; my father drove our speedboat into Ethan's sailboat. I was there. It was the single most terrifying and horrible day of my life. I lost my dad that day, but I also lost so much more...

I lost my sense of trust.

And Cooper lost his leg.

"And don't forget the way they treated Ethan," Cooper continues. "The media shitstorm nearly destroyed us, and Sybil *willingly* participated in that."

My cheeks heat, shame burning through me. When my father died, I wanted someone to blame. Even though I knew Ethan was innocent, I didn't stop the police from charging him with manslaughter. Luckily, the charges were dropped, but only after our family almost lost Arden for good. She was livid with us.

"Don't forget Gregory's actions that day cost him his life," Conrad reminds.

"I don't care. It's unforgivable."

My heart aches, and I can't listen to anymore. I peel off the wall and stumble into the throng of guests, focusing on everyone's glamourous cocktail attire and fitted designer suites.

"Hey, you. Let's dance," my old pal Perry Hargrove says, catching my elbow and stopping me in my tracks.

Perry can be an idiot-ass at times, same as all my guy-friends, but he's a good person. He tried to date Arden last summer and ended up making a fool out of himself and Ethan over it. They had a fight and everything, but they're fine now. Not wanting to cause a scene, I nod and let him pull me in for a slow dance.

"Are you okay?" he asks, his dark eyes shining with concern.

I have to look away. "I don't want to talk about it."

"The reception is going well," he says, changing the subject. "And I look great in this new suit, if I do say so myself."

I smile, taking in his fitted black suit and the way the white collar of the shirt contrasts against his skin. He's a gorgeous African American man, so he looks great in anything he wears, but this particular outfit is lethal.

"You do look good," I muse. "And I look good, too, don't I?"

He whistles low, taking a tiny step back to make room for roving eyes. I'm in a shiny yellow slip dress, my ode to Andy in *How To Lose A Guy in Ten Days*. My favorite romcom. I've watched it a hundred times, and it still makes me laugh.

"Amazing as ever."

Just then, Cooper strides up to us, his face set in a determined expression.

"Mind if I cut in?" he drawls.

Perry gives me a sheepish look, his gaze jumping between me and one of his best friends. I widen my eyes at Perry in a *don't you dare* expression.

"I don't know, man," he says.

I turn on Cooper, glaring daggers. He's faking this charm. He doesn't want to talk to me, let alone dance. He's only here because of his father.

Not happening.

Cooper somehow manages to channel so much fake charisma that I want to vomit as he grins at me with a devil-may-care smirk. "Come on. One dance with an old friend? For old time's sake."

I shake my head. I'm not falling for his bullshit.

"Don't want to dance with a cripple?" He raises his eyebrows.

The blood drains from my face. It's a low blow to get what he wants, but it works.

"Fine," I grumble, nodding at Perry to step away.

Cooper grins like he's won some kind of prize, but I know his grins, and this one is fake.

"Please be careful with me, baby," he says as he pulls me into his arms, and I get caught on the way that casual *baby* rolled off his tongue. "I won't be able to feel it if you step on my right foot."

The guilt over his leg is all consuming and my face flames.

He chuckles. "I'm joking. Relax, Valentine."

"Don't call me that."

"Oh? You like being called *baby*, then? Is that it?"

Actually, him calling me baby definitely did something, namely to the heat in my stomach, not that I'll admit it. "Don't call me anything."

With a knowing smirk, he tugs me closer until our bodies are pressed together. At least I don't have to look him in the eye anymore, but feeling his broad chest against my breasts sends unwanted shivers through my body. What the hell is wrong with me? The music is too slow and sultry. He's too close. That's what's wrong. Nothing more.

I catch sight of Ethan and Arden dancing and let that relax me, remembering what this is all for. Those two are currently lost in their own world and having a great wedding reception—all worth it.

Coop and I don't talk, and I wonder if his "making amends" directive is out the window. Whatever. I don't care. But not talking presents another problem. Specifically, the way our bodies fit together well as we dance. He's taller than me, which is good; I'm taller than most guys. His build is exactly the kind I prefer—athletic and broad without being too bulky. He's grown into quite the man. Too bad he thinks I'm vile.

"Could you relax and let me lead?" he gripes into my ear, his mouth a little too close for comfort.

I pin him with my gaze. "Maybe if you did a better job of leading, I wouldn't have to make up for your lack of dancing skills."

His eyes narrow. "Are you determined to be a pain in my ass, or does it come naturally?"

That's rich coming from him. "You were the one who asked me to dance. I was fine with Perry."

He tugs me in tighter, and I try not to think too hard about the way my breath catches in my throat or the hard plains of his broad chest. He's bigger than I remember.

"There's something I need to discuss with you," he says. "You're not an easy woman to get a hold of."

True. I've been screening his calls.

"Do you blame me after the way you behaved on New Year's Eve?"

"That was..." His hand twitches against the small of my back. "I'm sorry. It was my first night out with this new prosthetic, and everyone was staring like they expected it to fall off. I got drunker than I should've, and honestly, I don't remember much, but I know I embarrassed myself, and I'm sorry."

I blink, a little shocked by the confession and apology. It's enough for me to dance longer, but not *much* longer.

"What do you want to talk to me about? You only have about a minute left in this song, so make it quick."

FOUR

S ybil
   Present - Age 27

It's obvious and heartbreaking Cooper is not the man he used to be. Not even close. Every time I think I can see the Cooper I used to know underneath this new version, he does or says something to remind me the boy I adored doesn't exist anymore.

New Year's Eve was the perfect example.

Thanks to Arden and Ethan, we all ended up at the same party. After a botched attempt at checking on him—in which he bit my head off—I had spent the night avoiding Cooper, catching up with old friends and making new ones. By the time midnight rolled around, I'd been cozy with an attractive man, my New Year's kiss for the night in the bag. I can't remember the guy's name now, but he was sexy and single and funny and safe and exactly the kind of guy I like to hook up with.

The countdown was about to begin, and I was locked in on

this man when Cooper grabbed my wrist and tugged me to him, claiming we needed to talk. I knew exactly what this was. He was trying to ruin my evening.

He did exactly that.

I told Coop to fuck off when the guy I was interested in found someone else to kiss at midnight. Cooper laughed at me, said I was predictable and needed to have higher standards. We ended up in a heated, embarrassing argument, I stormed out, and Arden and Ethan took Coop's drunk-ass home.

That can't happen again. Not here. Not tonight.

"What do you want, Cooper?" I demand. "Spit it out."

"Have you received your trust fund yet?"

I blink once, then twice. Why would he ask that? I haven't talked openly about my trust fund with anyone. What's done is done.

"My finances are none of your business."

Truthfully, my inheritance was released to me after my father's death. He was lost at sea, but enough people witnessed him going into the bloody, shark-infested waters that the state of Massachusetts released his death certificate. The lawyers and trustee took care of the estate, and I was given more than enough. I'll never have to work again if I don't want to, but that's not me. I love my work with the foundation, and I studied at Harvard for a reason.

A frown pulls at the corners of my lips. "I don't want to talk about this, Cooper."

"Can you humor me for a minute? This is important."

I sigh. "Fine."

"Were you given ownership in Laurence International?"

I blink. "My father's equity was divided among the children. We own the majority of the company, yes."

"But it's a small majority, isn't it?"

We own fifty-four percent. It would've been more, but

Father had to sell much of the equity years ago. When he stepped in as CEO, the company was in trouble, and he did what he had to do to bring it to the thriving conglomerate valued at billions of dollars it is today. Laurence is in many industries, thanks to my dad's leadership.

Cooper grins with a boastful expression that is unfamiliar to me. More proof that Cooper isn't the sweet, loving guy I remember. "I'm right, aren't I?"

My eyes narrow. "You sound like your father. What does any of this have to do with you?"

He steps back, steel walls guarding his emotions.

The unmistakable ding of someone making a toast rings from the front of the room. That's weird; we already did the speeches. I turn to see the devil himself standing at the front of the room, gaining everyone's attention, and my stomach drops.

Conrad King.

"Ladies and gentleman... Friends, Romans, Countrymen, lend me your ears," Conrad booms. The music has quieted, and everyone has turned to him, several chuckling at his stupid joke. He's quoting Shakespeare now? Give me a break. "It's with great pleasure I stand before you today to celebrate my son, Ethan, and his match to the beautiful Arden Laurence."

I snort, and Cooper side-eyes me.

"What?" I whisper. "You know that's not how he really feels."

Cooper shakes his head. "You have no idea."

"With the union of our families comes a new lease on life and an opportunity for peace," Conrad continues, taking complete attention as he speaks into the microphone that was definitely *not* intended for his use. I make a mental note to talk to the band about that one.

I peer around, trying to get a sense of where the rest of my family is. They're all up front, and Cooper and I are in the back.

Maybe I should edge my way over, but as I start to move, Coop grabs my elbow. "You don't want to interrupt him."

He shoots me a charged look, and my nerves skyrocket.

"It's no secret that the late Gregory Laurence and I had a falling out some years ago," Conrad continues. "My only regret is we couldn't repair our relationship before his passing."

Bullshit.

The crowd stirs at this, and I'm sure I'm not the only one who thinks his lies sound forced. These men *hated* each other; my father had an affair with his wife—something that didn't come out until after her death. It blew up our lives and dismantled a lucrative business partnership. My parents nearly got divorced over it. I lost Ethan and Cooper in the process of choosing my family.

"I truly believe Gregory is looking down on us now, grateful for this union between our kids."

A few people clap, and a sly smile transforms Conrad's face into something that appears charismatic, but I know is sinister.

"Years ago, when we were raising young children, Gregory and I signed a contract."

I freeze, and everyone in the room seems to do the same. Cooper's hand is still on my elbow. He squeezes once before letting go.

"A marriage contract."

Confusion washes over my body. What does that even mean?

"The terms were simple. If a King heir were to marry a Laurence heir, an exchange of company equity would take place."

I dart a glance at Cooper, but he's stony faced. Rage roils through me—so *this* was why he asked. He was confirming intel.

"The King's would gain ten percent ownership of Laurence International, and ten percent in King Media would go to their family. We thought of it as a mutually beneficial partnership; not only would the children be tied together in matrimony, but in business as well."

I feel like I'm sinking into the marble floor, my body heavy with questions I'll never have answers to. Why would my father agree to a contract like that?

I take a deep breath and think this through. Marriage contract or not, King Media and Laurence International *did* end up doing a lot of business together, but as far as I know, actual ownership never exchanged hands. It doesn't seem like something my father would've agreed to, but then again, he did a lot of things I never thought he was capable of doing.

"Alright, that's enough." My mother climbs to the stage, visibly ruffled, and I bite my lip. My mother is the poster child for grace and sophistication, and my role model. A knot of worry twists in my stomach, tightening quickly. I hope Mom's okay.

"Aren't you pleased by this union, Amelia?" Conrad repeats, and instead of my mother having to pry the mic from his hands, he passes it to her as if she is next in line to make a speech. She already gave one an hour ago.

"Very pleased," she quips and turns to the guests. "Thank you all for coming. We're blessed to have so many wonderful friends and family who are happy to share in our joy. Now please, enjoy yourselves."

She hands the mic to the band behind her, and the singer takes over, but it's too late. The party is ruined. Oh, not for everyone. The guests are definitely going to enjoy themselves; this is the kind of gossip New York City's elite lives for. No, the party is ruined for those of us who want to know what the hell is going on. One glimpse of Arden's horrified face and Ethan's angry grimace, and I know I've failed them.

I turn on Cooper. "You knew he was going to say that?"

"Yes," he says, wearing a mask of indifference.

"And you didn't think to warn us?"

"If I'd have told you, I wouldn't have had the satisfaction of seeing your face right now."

He's. Fucking. Gloating.

My rage comes quick, like a flash of gasoline to a flame, and I slap him clean across the face. He steps back, his hand traveling to the spot I made contact. My own hand rings with pain and betrayal, but I don't regret hitting him. Not even if it added more gossip for our guests to spread.

"Who are you?" I hiss, glaring into Cooper's dark eyes.

"I'm exactly who you made me to be." He turns and walks away, his gait slightly changed from before the accident. But his back is straight, and his head is high, as if he doesn't have a care in the world. As if he already won. Maybe he did, even if I'm still not sure what I lost.

FIVE

It only takes a few minutes for everyone in the Laurence family to gather in the chef's kitchen that's adjacent to the ballroom. Mom cleared the staff out for a family meeting, and apparently, this was the only place to do it.

"What's *he* doing here?" Hayes growls in Ethan's direction, and Arden straightens her spine protectively.

"I swear I didn't know about any of this," Ethan says, holding up his hands, and I know him well enough to know he's being honest.

"Your twin knew," I announce, and his face pales.

My jaw is locked so tight I feel my teeth might crack. Where the hell is Coop? Probably mingling among the guests somewhere, smug as hell, despite his father ruining what was a perfectly respectable wedding reception.

Arden turns on my mother. "Aunt Amelia, please explain what this marriage contract means?"

"It's *nothing*, I promise," Mom replies, her voice strained. "Yes, there *was* a contract made, but it doesn't apply to nieces—only to Gregory's biological children and Conrad's biological children. There's nothing to worry about since Ethan didn't marry Sybil."

Ethan and I exchange a sheepish glance. Guess we *really* dodged a bullet there.

"But the stock prices..." Mother's voice trails off. "That could be a problem once this news gets out. Shareholders don't like scandal."

Our company is publicly traded, and King is not, which basically means we're beholden to our shareholders and—especially—our board. But King? Barring legalities, they can pretty much do whatever the hell they want. Conrad has a company board at King, but they don't own him, he owns them. He's the primary company owner, creator, and the CEO. He steers the ship, and nobody complains because he's damn good at his job.

And ruthless as hell.

"Why would Conrad say all that in front of everybody?" Arden's voice is meek, but the rest of us know Conrad King better than my cousin ever did. None of this surprises me in the slightest. He hates our family, and if saying stupid bullshit to get a rise out of us, he's going to say stupid bullshit, even at the expense of his son.

"This night was supposed to be about you and Ethan," I reply, giving Arden my most apologetic look. "I'm so sorry that happened."

Everything was going so well, too.

"I should've known something like this was going to happen," Ethan growls. "Don't blame yourself, Sybil. You did a good job."

Did I? "I should've planned for this somehow. Obviously, the microphone was a bad call. I could've had someone running interference."

Ethan and Arden's only main request for tonight? No drama.

Damn it.

"Conrad wanted one last chance to get revenge on your uncle," my mother says, patting Arden on the shoulder. "I'm so sorry about this. Let's go out there and enjoy the rest of your night, shall we? If anyone asks about the marriage contract, you say it's a good thing you're Gregory's *niece* and move on to another conversation."

"Why does Uncle Conrad want to get back at Dad?" Chandler asks from where he's been leaning against one of the industrial refrigerators, and my heart sinks.

We've kept so much from my brother. Even though he's an adult, he has the heart and mind of someone much younger because of his Down Syndrome. He doesn't need to know about our sordid family history.

Mom frowns. "Oh, sweetie. Once we get home, you and I can talk about it privately."

He steps forward, and Mom pats him on the shoulder.

"Tell me now. I want to know," he demands, voice cracking.

Fuck. My heart has already taken a beating, but right now it's about to go through another ten rounds. Of course he's known we've been hiding things from him. Chandler is not dumb, contrary to what people may think.

Mom opens and closes her mouth, the color draining from her face, and I know she's about to confess the truth.

But before a word comes out, the door flies open, and Cooper stalks in, followed closely by his scummy father.

Cooper's earthy-brown hair has grown since the accident, hanging around those dark eyes. He looks so much like his father these days. The smug eyes. The clenched jaw. The air of confidence that boarders on arrogance. It's apparent they've come here to gloat, not to apologize or explain.

"What's going on here?" Ethan's voice is laced with venom, which makes me happy for Arden. This is a man who is always going to put his bride first, no matter the circumstance, and Arden deserves nothing less than complete devotion.

"I think it's time we talk about some things," Conrad says, and my chest tightens, as if a band of anxiety is squeezing my ribcage. Somehow, I know that whatever is about to happen is going to make my world spin upside down.

He slides into the center of the kitchen like he owns the place, pulling out an envelope from his inside suit jacket and presenting it to my mother. "You know I've been meaning to speak with you about Arden," he says. "Don't act so surprised."

Her eyes grow cold. "How dare you."

"How dare *I*? I've been trying to set up a meeting with you for weeks, but you refused to see me. I tried to warn you, Amelia. I really did."

My mother doesn't say a word as she snatches the envelope from Conrad's hands and tears it open. My heart pounds against my ribcage, increasing in tempo when Mom's face goes from incredulous, to shocked, to resigned in the space of a long, drawn-out minute. Her backside hits the edge of the nearby countertop, her entire body defeated, and tears form in her eyes.

"What is it?" I breathe, stepping forward. I try to take the paper, but she shakes her head.

"Arden, this is for you," she says solemnly.

Arden's cheeks go bright red as she strides forward and takes the paper, her eyes scanning the contents. She passes it off to Ethan, who looks it over, his face hardening to steel.

"Would someone tell me what is going on here?" I turn to

my old lover, my old friend, the boy I count on to always tell me the truth. "Ethan, what is it? Tell me."

But he doesn't say a word.

"Please tell us," Chandler says, and Hayes folds his arms over his chest, appearing equally frustrated. My brothers are twenty-three and seventeen. They're still young, and especially young-at-heart, but they can hold their own.

Ethan tucks his arm around his wife and glares at our father, but he's as speechless as the rest of them.

"This is getting ridiculous," I snap. "Enough with the secrets."

Conrad's gaze is steady on Amelia Laurence. "I didn't want to do this in front of everyone, but you've left me no choice. You know the contract is binding. You can see the test results for yourself. Have your people call my people first thing Monday morning, and we can get started on the equity transfers."

He turns on his heel and disappears into the party, leaving the rest of us to clean the mess he left behind. Cooper should leave, too, but he doesn't. He stands at the edge of the group, eyes heavy like he's waiting for something. Finally, his gaze meets mine, and something dark flashes there. Once again, I'm reminded this is no longer the man I used to know.

"Mom, what's going on?" I try again, but my mother is no longer hiding behind anger; it's pain that's written all over her face. The kind of pain she endured at my father's hands after we found out about the affair with her best friend. And in that moment, I know without a shadow of a doubt, that whatever is in that paperwork, it has to do with Dad.

"Later, children. We'll talk about this later. *After* the party," she instructs.

She takes a deep breath and steadies herself like she's simply ironing out wrinkles in a dress and not covering something that has shaken her to the core.

She takes her leave, following in Conrad's footsteps.

"We don't have to go out there," Ethan whispers to Arden.

My sweet baby cousin's face has turned as white as a sheet. She blinks rapidly, holding back tears. She might even be on the edge of one of her panic attacks. Ethan catches it the same time the rest of us do, and he shoots his twin brother a scathing look.

"You could've warned me," he hisses before ushering his wife out a back door.

They're going home and *not* returning to their own party.

"Let's go, too," Hayes says, taking our brother's hand. "Mom will tell us everything at home. I'll call us a car."

I can tell Chandler wants to protest, but he doesn't. Within seconds, I'm alone with Cooper.

"Shame they all left," Cooper mutters. "He wasn't supposed to hand over the test until the party was over. I do regret that part, at least."

Is he trying to make himself feel better?

"What's a shame is you not telling me what the hell is going on." I get close to him, angling my face slightly upward as I glare at the man who has the answers I need. "I have a right to know."

A long auburn curl falls across my eyes. I don't touch it; I'm too angry to even think about it for more than a millisecond, but Cooper reaches out and gently tucks it behind my ear. I slap his hand away.

"Slapping me again, Valentine? I didn't know you were so violent."

"Only for you," I sneer. "Now tell me."

"Your mother will tell you soon enough," he deadpans.

Frustration overtakes me, and I try to shove him, but he doesn't budge an inch. "Does our friendship mean nothing to you?"

He snorts. "Friendship? You ditched our friendship years ago. Gave me up like I meant nothing. We don't have a friendship, Valentine." He leans in close, and the spicy-clean scent of his cologne surrounds me. "Actually, I don't think we're *not* friends anymore... We're less than that. We mean nothing to each other. Maybe we even hate each other."

Right now? Yes. I hate him.

"I didn't mean that we have a friendship, you dipshit," I hiss. "I meant all those years of friendship we shared... You act like they never happened. Like you owe me nothing."

His jaw ticks. "I learned from the best."

I shift, putting space between us while acceptance floods my system. "Fine," I say coolly, brushing past me to leave the room. "Don't tell me. Someone else will."

"Arden is your sister."

Four words.

Just four simple words, but they change everything.

They ricochet through the kitchen like a bullet, and I stop, turning to him, the world shifting on its axis. "What did you say?"

"You heard me. Arden is your *sister*, not your cousin. Well, technically, she's your half-sister. You share the same father."

I shake my head. "You're lying."

But I already know he's not. He can't be. Not by the way everyone reacted.

"Your father had her DNA test results altered to suit his agenda. My father knew the truth all along. When he called your father about it, he agreed to let Gregory play Arden off as a long-lost cousin to spare Amelia's feelings."

The breath leaves my body. "Why would he care to spare her feelings?"

He laughs darkly. "Hate my father all you want; he's no angel, but he's not a monster, either. Think about it, Sybil. This was *before* your mother tried to ruin our family by blaming Ethan for your father's death. Despite everything that had happened, he still cared about your mom's feelings. He knew this would destroy her. He didn't want that."

My vision blurs.

"You're stunning when you're angry," he says, his words kind but his tone cruel, "but somehow even more stunning when you're sad. That's unfortunate, Sybil. I always liked your smile most."

"That's some messed up shit to say," I whisper.

"And I'm an asshole for noticing." He shrugs, his eyes intent on mine.

I shake my head. This is a lot to process. If this is true, it means my mom's little sister, a woman who was estranged from the family and who died from drug addiction, was also a woman who had slept with my father.

They had a child together.

"The old contract still stands," Cooper says. "Our fathers made it when they went into business together, and now that Arden has been proven to be Gregory's child, the contract will be enforced."

I hold up my hand to stop him from continuing. "I get it, Cooper. You're legally taking ten percent of our company, and we're taking ten percent of yours, but since we only own fifty-four percent, you now have the power to make it so we no longer have majority equity in our own company."

The fucker smirks. "How is it my fault your father let so much ownership go over the years?" he argues. "That's not something my father would've ever allowed to happen to King Media. He would've let the whole company burn to the ground before relinquishing control."

I don't care; they're two totally different companies, and I could argue that King wouldn't have had the success he did without Laurence helping him along the way.

"So what happens next?" I ask.

"Time will tell."

What a cop out.

He brushes past me, leaving me alone in the kitchen as he walks into the party. If there was anything left in his heart for my family, then maybe he feels a little awful for what just happened. From the looks of it, though, he feels fantastic. That's a man who's been vindicated.

And I'm a woman who has to reevaluate everything I thought was true.

Six

C ooper
Past - Age 18

"The days of getting perfect grades are over, aren't they?" Sybil sighs, plopping her face into the open textbook and groaning. I'm tempted to do the same, but basking in the scent of paper and desperation isn't going to fix the hell that is finals week. I thought our prep school was hard, and studying for the SATs had been awful, but nobody warned me how difficult studying for finals would be, especially at Harvard. Guess Sybil didn't get the memo, either.

"Unfortunately, perfect grades might not be possible here," I say, offering a conspiratorial smile.

We're sitting across from each other, Perry Hargrove at my side and my brother next to her. It's a miracle we all got into the business school, but thank God I'm not doing this alone.

"Why don't we take a break?" I offer. It's the weekend, we've been at it for hours, and my brain is mush. "Let's go find a party or something. We can come back to this tomorrow."

"I'm down." Perry closes his textbook with an audible *thwack*. "Besides, I'm ready for the final."

Of course he is. Perry is a genius. He's even got the Mensa card to prove his high IQ. Right now, he's smiling like the fucking Cheshire Cat. He has the best smile, was even voted "best smile" back in school. Probably because he's so fucking smart that life seems to come easy to him. That, and he doesn't have his family demanding every move he makes. He actually gets to *choose* what he's going to do for a career. Imagine that.

"You're ready for the final?" Sybil scoffs. "I kind of want to throw my textbook at you right now."

At least Perry has the decency to look sheepish.

"Yeah, 'cause he has a photographic memory," Ethan points out. "The rest of us need to keep studying."

That's Ethan for you. He's like a drill sergeant when it comes to school. I probably wouldn't be at a school like this if it weren't for Ethan's constant pestering.

"You're right. I *know* you're right," Sybil says, all high-pitched and sounding like she's on the verge of tears. "But I think if I read through these macroeconomics notes one more time, I'm going to cry. Honestly. My soul is tired."

Well, shit. The last thing I want to see is Sybil cry.

I've shoved my romantic feelings toward her into the pits of hell where they belong, but that doesn't mean I want her to suffer. Perry is ready to go, but Ethan is staring at us like we're being dramatic. We're not. We need a fucking break.

"Listen, this semester has been like preparing for a long-distance marathon, and next week is the big race. We know it's important—that's why we've been training for it for months—but even marathon runners take breaks, don't they?"

Ethan rolls his eyes. "This is academics we're talking about here."

"Yeah, and we're also young and in college. It can't be *study, study, study* all the time. We need balance."

Sybil turns on him with the sweetest grin, and I'm sure she's going to get him to see our side. "Please? Let's have a few hours of fun, go to bed early, and then study all day tomorrow. That's what Sundays are for."

The fucker has the audacity to shake his head.

My fingers curl into fists under the table. Doesn't he see that she needs this? Doesn't she see he's controlling her? They're already so fucking codependent they might as well get surgically attached at the hip.

"Don't look at me like that." Ethan turns on me with narrowed eyes. "I'm not going to apologize for being responsible. We've had our fun this semester, but it's time to buckle down. There are different ways to approach education here. We've talked about this, Cooper. You know what Dad said."

Off at college and our father still controls our lives.

The lectures have been endless, so I can see exactly where Ethan is getting this from. Truth is, like us, a lot of our peers know they are going to be set for life either way. Most of those kids don't worry about their grades so long as they pass their classes.

And then there are the kids who need Harvard as a stepping-stone. They don't have connections, and they're not necessarily going to find them easily, not like they probably thought they would. They have to do everything right to leverage this education into something great. Honestly, more power to them. I'd do the same thing if I was in their shoes.

But as for us? Our father expects perfection. He expects the Dean's list. He expects high honors. He *especially* expects us to make it into the master's program at the business school, a feat that won't be easy whatsoever. It doesn't matter that we are required to work for King Media or forgo our trust funds; we must impress our father.

And our father has a way of getting exactly what he wants.

But Sybil? Her father babies her. She doesn't have to get perfect grades or anything even close to them. She's going to work for the family company when it's all over, same as us, but she's not required to graduate. But Sybil has a type-A personality with high standards for herself. She wants to succeed, make her family proud, and *earn* her place with Laurence International. She's got something to prove, and she will.

It's obvious her family members aren't the only ones she wants to make proud. Now that she has Ethan, she's not willing to lose him, even if it means disagreeing about how much studying is an appropriate amount. It's infuriating how quickly she's needed his approval. This is not the girl I knew for eighteen years.

I can't sit here and watch this.

I get up, packing my things. "Last chance. Are you guys coming?" I look at Sybil. "You don't have to do everything Ethan does just because you're a couple now."

"Oh, fuck off. It's not like that," Ethan says, putting his arm around his girl, proving my damn point.

She hesitates before she says what I know she's going to. "I'm staying with Ethan. You guys have fun."

Doesn't matter if I call her out. Doesn't matter if I try to talk to him about it. They're *together* and won't listen to anybody when it comes to their relationship, which—in my opinion—has quickly become unhealthy.

But nobody asked for my opinion.

"Let's go," I say to Perry, and after dropping our bags at the dorm, we spend the next few hours getting shitfaced at the bar with our fake IDs and hitting on pretty girls who aren't obsessed with my brother.

I wouldn't mind finding one to sleep with. It's the only thing that helps get the thought of Ethan and Sybil out of my head. They've been doing it since August when she gave him her virginity after a few months of dating. I didn't know she was still a virgin, but Ethan told me all about it. He tells me everything. Even the things that keep me up at night, sick to my stomach.

"Ready to go?" Perry asks after finishing his beer. The girls we were flirting with went to the bathroom, and he's obviously not feeling it anymore. "Everyone's too fucking stressed tonight."

He's right. I'm not into it tonight, either. I'm so ready for this semester to be over. So I agree to leave, but when I stand, I wobble, and Perry has to catch me. Shit. I'm way more inebriated than I thought.

"I got you," Perry says, practically holding me up as we make our way to our dorm building. "Damn, I didn't realize you had so much. You really need to lay off the alcohol."

I nod, but I'm not listening. I'm thinking about *them*.

"It sucks now that Ethan and I are sharing a dorm room," I say, slurring my words.

"And why is that?"

"He's constantly fucking Sybil in there," I say angrily. At least, that's how I mean to sound, but it comes out all slurred and sad, like I'm on the verge of tears. I'm not. "And then I have to find somewhere else to crash, and it's annoying."

"He does the same for you when you bring a girl over," Perry points out.

"Not the same."

"Right, because Sybil is the girl you've secretly been in love with for years?" Perry asks.

"Yeah," I choke out, immediately regretting my confession. "Wait. No. Wait. Don't say anything."

"I wouldn't dream of it," Perry assures me with a light chuckle. "You can trust me, don't worry. But it's not like you're inconspicuous. I've suspected your crush for years, man."

I grimace, my head starting to pound.

"Next year will be better," he continues. "We're getting that off-campus house, remember? Separate bedrooms."

"Thank Jesus," I slur out, not sure if I mean it.

Next year's housing arrangements *were* supposed to be better, but then Ethan and Sybil made plans to share the primary suite like a fucking married couple. So, it might actually be worse. I'll have to live with them playing house.

We round the corner, only to find the pair of lovebirds in a passionate embrace. My stomach curdles, but I let out a low whistle to fake how I'm really feeling inside. God, I'm pathetic.

"Get a room," Perry yells, and the couple breaks apart.

I drop my head low, letting the hair fall to shadow my face.

"Are you drunk, Cooper?" Ethan asks, the judgment thick. "I know it's not abnormal for college freshmen to drink a lot, but you've been getting blackout drunk every weekend like it's your second job."

"Shut up," I grumble, but I'm already half asleep, leaning against the wall of a man that is Perry.

Sybil puts her hand on my shoulder. "Are you okay?"

I gaze at her, admiring the way her hair looks vibrant red under the streetlight. She's so fucking pretty. "Valentine, did you get your studying done?"

I duck from under Perry's arm and practically fall into Sybil, but Ethan catches me. "Hey brother, why don't we go find you some water and a bed?"

I keep my gaze on the girl of my dreams. "Well? Are you ready for the final?"

She nods, and I smile, pointing between her and my brother, trying to pretend all is fucking right with the world. "You two? You're good for each other. Everybody says so. Everybody knows so." Shit, my words are slurring again.

Her eyebrows furrow together and those pretty lips pout. "Really, are you okay?"

"Never better."

Ethan and Perry help me to the dorm, and while part of me feels bad that my brother has to babysit a drunk tonight, most of me is pretty damn happy with how this night is ending. Me in my bed. Ethan in his. And Sybil in the next building over.

But my joy doesn't last long. I fall asleep quickly, my heart aching in my chest. It shouldn't ache so badly when I've never given it to anyone. I shouldn't care this much. Why do I fucking care this much?

I need to get over her, and it's killing me that I can't.

SEVEN

C ooper
    Past - Age 19

I'm half asleep when Sybil's hand runs down my chest, feather-light fingers drawing goosebumps across my bare skin.

I must be dreaming. I've been having a lot of dreams about her lately—a byproduct of forced proximity. Maybe. Or maybe it's because I always dream of that woman.

Open your eyes. Wake up.

But I don't want to. It's too good. I want to stay in this dream forever, with her hands on me, her intoxicating honey and sunshine scent everywhere.

She writhes against me in only a bra and panties, breathing softly into my neck, then hitches her long slender leg over my hips. My cock instantly thickens in my briefs.

The dream intensifies as I slide my hands under the cotton of her panties, greedy fingers gripping her bare ass. She's so round, so warm and perfect, and groping her ass sends a shock-wave of desire through us both. She slides up on me, and her knees fall open as she rides my cock through our flimsy nightclothes.

She's a goddess. In a few seconds, I'll be slipping our underwear out of the way so she can mount me for real. In a few seconds, I'll find her hungry mouth and kiss her with everything I've got, swallowing her breath like it's a special kind of oxygen made just for me.

In one long deft motion, she rubs her heat up and down my erection, and even with the fabric between us, the feeling explodes into pure fire, jolting me awake.

"Ethan," she moans softly, pressing harder against me, ready for more.

Oh.

Oh no.

No...

She's not supposed to be real—a figment of my imagination and nothing more.

But she's very, very real and very much on top of me in the darkness, practically seconds away from fucking me. Hers is the kind of warmth that burrows into my soul and heats a man from the inside out. A heat that is somehow both electric and calming. A heat that shouldn't be here. That I can't have. Ever.

My entire body stills.

She murmurs Ethan's name again, her mouth searching for mine.

No, not mine. My brother's.

I jerk my head to the side and search the room, vision adjusting. It crashes down on me as I realize what the hell is going on.

We all went out to celebrate the end of our first year, and everyone had too much to drink. Sybil crawled into the extralong twin with my brother, and the three of us passed out hours ago.

Sybil must have gotten up to go to the bathroom, and in her haze, found herself in my bed instead of my brother's.

Through a thin layer of panties, I can feel how wet and ready she is. She's rubbing herself on me in tantalizing circles, half drunk and mostly asleep, but her body is wanting and ready...

For him.

The alcohol lingers on her breath.

This cannot happen.

Gently, I lift her off me, scooting so I'm against the wall and she's next to me. There are only a few inches of space between us, but that's enough for her body to settle and her breathing to relax. A few minutes later, I'm sure she's asleep. She can't stay here. If I fall asleep with her in my bed, this exact scenario might repeat itself. It can't.

I inch the blankets away and maneuver over her without touching her. It's a good thing I've been in the gym a lot this year; a weaker version of myself would've definitely woken her. The bed barely sleeps one grown man comfortably, let alone a grown woman as well.

I land on the floor with a soft thud and freeze, making sure the noise didn't wake anyone. Ethan is totally out of it. Sybil stirs for a moment, then falls still. My body buzzes from the shock. My cock is still hard as a rock, and I have half a mind to text one of my friends-with-benefits.

Instead, I count to sixty, then I ease Sybil into my arms.

"Cooper? Is that you?" she asks, her voice sweet and sleepy as she curls into me. She feels so good, and for the millionth time, I hate myself for wanting the woman who belongs to my brother.

"Just putting you to bed, Valentine," I whisper, gently laying her next to Ethan and hating how good they look together.

She rolls toward him, and they tangle limbs automatically, like they've been doing this for years. A few seconds later, they're asleep. Their bodies know each other. They're comfortable. Happy together.

I'm the intruder.

"Fuck my life," I whisper, regret thick and cock still pulsing. Having her on top of me like that, her body ready? It might have been the most alive I've ever felt. I'm wracked with so many emotions—jealousy and guilt and longing, but most of all, self-loathing.

This is too hard. I don't know how to not want her.

The only things that have helped are sleeping around and booze. I know that's hardly healthy, but it's my only reprieve, even if it's a temporary one. Because wherever I go, there she is, corroding my walls, finding a way to make herself known.

I even talked to my dad about transferring during the holiday break, but I couldn't give him the real reason. Told him I thought it would be good for me to switch to a different Ivy and gain some independence. He didn't go for it. Dad's crimson through and through. In his mind, it's Harvard or bust.

I return to bed and try to sleep, but eventually morning comes. The couple next to me wake up, unaware of what happened. I eye Sybil, but she seems to have no recollection of crawling into my bed and grinding on me.

"Do you know what you did last night?" I ask over breakfast, my tone teasing as I'm inwardly chastising myself for being an idiot.

But I must know if she remembers.

She plops a purple grape into her mouth, lips scrunching around it as she contemplates and swallows. "I mean, we drank too much, but I don't remember a lot after we left the party. I assume we all crashed?"

Ethan rubs at his temples, clearing a hangover. I'm nursing one, too—a Sybil hangover.

"Just tell us," Ethan says.

Sybil gazes between us curiously, her eyes rounding as she drums a restless rhythm against the cafeteria table. "Yeah, what happened?"

"Whelp, you got up in the night to use the bathroom, but when you came back, you climbed into bed with me." I waggle my eyebrows. Like this is all hilarious.

They both stare, Sybil with her mouth open and heat blooming across her cheeks and into her hairline. A muscle ticks in Ethan's jaw.

Trying to make this lighter, I wink. "I always knew you wanted me."

The silence about kills me, but Ethan finally rolls his eyes, and Sybil shakes her head, an expression of genuine confusion marking her face. "I'm so sorry. Shit, did I?" Her voice trails off as she wracks her brain.

"Didn't know you thought of me like that, Valentine. Not that I blame you. Sorry to say, Ethan and I don't share." I lean back, folding my arms across my chest. "Isn't that right, brother?"

Stupid. Stupid. What is wrong with me?

Ethan's posture is ridged, and I know I've gone too far now. My brother values loyalty above all else. He's a lot like our father in that way, and I'm pissing him off.

I'm laughing and putting on a show, even though my insides have been filleted wide open. Of course Ethan's mad, and of course Sybil doesn't remember. She was a lot more inebriated than she usually gets, and I was wide awake. She clearly thought I was Ethan when she crawled on top of me.

I'm the one making this awkward, not them.

"Don't worry. Nothing happened," I assure her, though

something kind of did. "I moved you to Ethan's bed, though your subconscious clearly wanted to be in mine."

Why am I still joking about this?

I need to stop, but I feel like I'm losing control, like I'm a runaway train and can't stop myself from destroying everything in my path.

"Shut the fuck up," Ethan growls, and I go still, letting his anger snap me out of it.

That's fair. I would be a bull if she was my girl, and someone talked to her like this.

"God, I can't believe I did that. I'm so sorry." She's apologizing to the both of us, and still that pretty shade of pink, which only makes her green eyes that much more beautiful.

I give my brother a cheeky smile, needing nothing more than to make light of this before I dig a hole I can't get out of. "Need to keep your girl more satisfied, so she doesn't crawl into my bed again, alright Ethan? Don't blame me."

Ridiculous. She moaned *his* name, not mine.

He finally relaxes, throwing his napkin in my face. "Get your own girl, Cooper. This one's mine."

Don't I know it.

"Speaking of which..." I open my text messages, scrolling through the girls I've met this year who are up for noncommittal hookups. After this disastrous conversation, I definitely need to bury myself in another woman and fast.

Ten minutes later, we're walking Sybil to her dorm, I've got a date lined up for tonight before we head home tomorrow, and they're acting like the conversation at the dining hall didn't even happen. Maybe it doesn't matter. Maybe to them, Sybil choosing my bed last night means nothing. But I can't help but wish that none of it had been an accident and that maybe, somewhere deep down, Sybil wants me as much as I want her.

EIGHT

S ybil
  Present - Age 27

It's bright and early the Sunday after the reception, and somehow that feels wrong, as if it should be raining. Storming. Flooding. The outside world should reflect the turmoil our family feels inside.

Father had an affair with mother's sister. Arden is our half-sibling. The betrayal runs deeper than anything I could've imagined.

How do we deal with something like this when the person to blame is dead?

Grief and anger tangle into one unbearable ball of emotion. This must've been how Ethan and Cooper felt after their mom died. It's hard being mad at someone you miss, hating someone you love, wishing more than anything to talk to them, to hug them, but also wanting to demand answers from them, to cry to them and let them know how much they've hurt you.

But you can't.

I know I'm not the only one who's feeling this way. I can see it in the eyes of my siblings as we sit on Mom's couch. We're in the NYC penthouse. It's not the main family home, but Mom brought the boys up for the week. We started out with so much excitement about the wedding reception, and now we're ending it with a conversation none of us ever thought we'd be having.

I blame Conrad King. He could've found a better time; I don't care what his excuses are. And I blame Cooper. He sat back and watched as the pieces fell into place, creating a disaster of a scene instead of the one my cousin and Ethan deserved.

No. Not cousin. My *sister*.

Mom is the first to speak. "I want you to know I love you, and none of this is your fault," she says, taking the time to look us each in the eye. She often does this, like she read some parenting book years ago that told her eye contact was the key to communicating with children.

"It's Dad's fault," Chandler replies, his voice breaking. "I hate him."

That nearly kills me. Chandler idolized our father. He's been in the dark for too long. I hate that he knows the truth, but I'm glad I won't have to lie to him anymore.

Mom's lower lip trembles. "Don't say that." She wraps her arm around Chandler. "Your father made a lot of mistakes, but he was *not* a bad person. He loved you very much. You do not need to hate him. It is okay to be angry. It is also okay to love your father and not like the choices he made."

I have to look away. I can't sit here without my face revealing exactly how pissed off I am. I turn to Arden, but she's staring into nowhere, like her mind is somewhere else.

"How can you even say that?" Hayes asks, interrupting the moment between Chandler and our mother. "He was a cheater. He had a child with your *sister* and lied about it. He let her grow up in foster care. I'm not sorry to say it, but I hate Dad, too. The person I knew? That person was a fake. He never existed."

What would my therapist say about this? Doctor Miranda has been with me for years, but she's been especially helpful since Dad's death. I wonder what she's going to say when I see her next week and tell her the update. Probably something about how two things can be true. A person can make good and bad choices, can have good and bad parts to them, can be real and fake—it all depends on the situation. What matters isn't what they did, it's what I do. How am I going to internalize this? What do I want to do? Can I forgive him?

As messed up as it might be to my brothers, I already know I have to forgive Dad. Not for him, but for myself and my own sanity. I can't live the rest of my life hating him.

Mom doesn't seem to know what to say, and Arden seems to have returned to herself, shifting in her seat. Ethan dropped her off this morning and went for a walk. This is a Laurence family discussion, but knowing him, he's not walking. He's in the lobby, waiting for Arden close by, just in case. I love that for her, I really do, but part of me wishes it was me. I miss having somebody like that in my life.

The only one who takes care of me is me. That's how it goes. Even with Ethan, that's how it went.

Maybe that's how Mom feels. Maybe Dad never took care of her the way she needed. And maybe, once she works through the pain of his cheating and death, she will be able to move on and be happier than she's ever been. God knows she deserves it.

"There's something you children don't know about your father and me," she says, taking Chandler's hand and squeezing. The two of them are on the loveseat. The other three of us are on the couch. I feel like she'd take all our hands if she could. She's being so strong, and I hate she's the one who should be breaking down, but she can't.

"We told you we met in college, fell in love, got married, and had you all. While most of that is true, it's not entirely how it happened."

Her voice is shaking. That unmistakable tingle of warning runs down my spine. More secrets?

"Your father and I had an arranged marriage."

The air whooshes from my lungs, shock hollowing me to nothing. Of all the things she could've said, this wasn't what I expected. I look at my siblings and each of us are as blindsided as the next. Chandler's eyes are filling with tears and Hayes's face is beet-red. An arranged marriage is for daytime soap operas and people in other countries, not our family.

Not our parents.

"We knew of each other from the time we were very young, but we didn't officially meet until we were in college. The start of our relationship was rocky at best, and so was the beginning of our marriage." She looks at the ceiling and releases a long-suffering sigh.

"He wasn't a bad guy. He was really kind to me. He was funny and smart and handsome, but there was a big problem." Her face is pink, which is not a color I see often on my demure, sophisticated mother. "He wasn't *interested* in me romantically. He saw me as a friend, and then he met my little sister." Her eyes flash to Arden. "It was love at first sight. He would've chosen her if he'd had the option, but she had a longtime drug problem and was the black sheep of the family. Even though I loved her dearly, not everyone saw the potential in her I did." She clears her throat. "That your father did."

I can't imagine being with someone who only sees you as a friend but your sister as someone to love. It must have been so painful.

Ethan and Arden flash through my mind, and I realize I could've been exactly like my parents. Had history repeated itself, Ethan would've cheated on me with Arden, and I'd be in Mom's shoes now, making excuses for the people I love who love each other more than they love me.

Both relief that it wasn't me and regret that it was my mother slide through my veins.

She didn't deserve this.

"By the time I found out they cared for each other, he and I were already married. It was doomed from the start."

Arden is the first to speak. "I don't have any memories of my mom," she says. "I imagined her to be tortured, but kind. I can't believe she betrayed you like that, Aunt Amelia. I'm so sorry."

Mom shakes her head. "I don't blame her. You shouldn't, either. Your mom was a wonderful person, but you have to understand what the drugs did to her brain. I really believe if she'd been sober, none of this would've happened... at least not without lots of conversation first."

Is that true? I don't know, but fragments of a sinful kiss I shared with the wrong person come to mind. I quickly bury them, refusing to go back there.

"She didn't try to steal him from me. In fact, she kept her distance. And I didn't blame either of them all that much, considering our marriage was arranged. It was a sad situation. They swore they'd never act on their feelings."

Obviously, that's where the lies started—the real betrayals.

The look in Mom's eyes is nothing short of haunted. "Her drug problem got worse, and she became estranged from the family. Your father and I tried to help her, but she didn't want it, and she disappeared onto the streets. It was hard; you can't help people who don't want to be helped. So we did what we had to, and we moved on with our lives. At least, I thought we moved on."

They had two children before Arden was born. The timeline is rife with betrayal.

"It's not your fault, Mom," I interrupt. "You don't have to tell us more. We get what happened next."

Mom shakes her head. "I want to tell the whole story. It's important you understand." She clears her throat, straightening the wrinkles in her skirt. "Once we started having children, your father and my partnership grew into more than an arrangement. We fell in love. We really did. We were happy for many years." She swallows hard. "I believe your father was in love with both of us. There's no other explanation."

He was torn between the sisters, a tale as old as time. God, what a mess.

"I realize Arden came in the middle of me having my children. I didn't know Greg had seen my little sister and gotten her pregnant." She gives my half-sister a pointed look. "But I swear to you, honey, I don't blame any of this on you. You are a gift and a blessing. I'm so glad you're here. If anything, I blame myself for not realizing the truth sooner, for not finding you. I'm truly sorry you had to grow up the way you did. You never should've been without a family. We were here all along."

Arden's eyes spill over with tears, little streaks of painful truth splashing down her cheeks. This story is the kind of bombshell none of us could've seen coming. It's confusing and horrible, but it's the reality of our situation, and at least we got Arden out of it. Mom's right. Arden really is a gift.

However, there's one thing I don't quite understand. "Why did you guys agree to an arranged marriage in the first place?" I ask.

Mother grew up in a wealthy family, and father did, too. There were plenty of prospects for both of them. They could've married anyone they wanted.

"My parents were extremely controlling. That's why we didn't visit very often while they were still alive."

It's true. We hardly ever saw our grandparents.

"They were hard on us girls, and honestly, I blame them for contributing to my sister's addiction. They had no mercy for her, no matter how life threatening it became and how much she needed us." A ghost of a smile lifts her mouth, but her eyes stay heavy. "You have to understand, people who value money and power above all else will sacrifice their own children if necessary. Ours did it to both of us." She's quiet for a long moment, and I can practically see the highlight-reel of childhood memories running through her mind.

"I had to please my parents. There was no other option for me. It was a similar story for your father. Laurence International needed an influx of funds, and my wealthy father was willing to give them what they needed if they brought my family into their sphere of influence. These kinds of deals happen more than you'll ever know."

She shrugs. "Even today, many prominent people arrange their children's marriages. This marriage contract your father signed with Conrad? It's similar. I guess he never learned the lesson."

I wonder what that would be like to be forced to marry a man who was in love with my sibling. That could've happened if Ethan and I were still together. In another life, had circumstances been different, I could be the one sitting across from my future children, trying to explain away my husband's indiscretions.

As horrible as this situation is, at least I'm not my mother. Arden is not her mother. Ethan isn't Dad.

It's Cooper I can't place. I really thought he was good at heart, but his behavior recently says otherwise. He's become his father's son, through and through, and I wonder if the old Cooper is still in there somewhere, or if we've lost him forever.

NINE

C ooper
  Past - Age 19

Two weeks. That's all we get on Nantucket this year. It's been this first week over Memorial Day weekend and another over July Fourth. Besides that, my brother and I are expected to work at King all summer. We'll be stuck in the hot city, but in mostly air-conditioned high-rises, so it's not all bad. Still, I wish we could be on this island, having fun all summer instead.

Nantucket is our sanctuary. However, given the week I had watching Ethan and Sybil act like a blissful married couple, I'm more than ready to get to Manhattan.

All I care about is getting them out of my mind and being able to breathe again. In Manhattan, the Laurences have their own place, and Sybil will be busy with her internship over at Laurence International. Sure, I'll see her around, but it won't be all the damn time.

Not like it is here.

I pad to the kitchen in my gym shorts, the smell of sleep and sex still on my skin. When I woke up this morning, my friend from last night had already gone home. That's fine by me. We're here to have fun.

The only thing killing me besides my brother's relationship is the raging hangovers. I've drunk my ass off every night we've been here.

I want to crawl in a hole by the time I get myself a large glass of water, a piece of toast, and ibuprofen, but I take care of myself instead of texting our chef Camilla. I refuse to be *that* pathetic.

"Good morning, sunshine," Sybil says when I enter the dining room. I sink into the chair across from my brother and his girlfriend, wishing the stairs didn't feel so damn far away. "Don't you look chipper."

"Shut up," I grumble.

"Did you have fun last night?" Ethan asks, taking a sip of his green juice. They look like they've returned from a workout and are ready to conquer the day. Lord, help me.

"I did." At least that's the truth.

"Looked like it." Sybil lifts her eyebrows. "You probably have a horrible hangover, though, huh?"

I tip my head in her direction and get to munching on my toast, wanting more than anything for the lovebirds to leave me alone.

They're so compatible, so perfect, so wonderful, but damn it if my pathetic heart still swoops low every time I see them kiss.

"We're going to the botanical gardens today. Do you want to join us?" Sybil asks.

I glance at my brother. The botanical gardens aren't really his style, but he's busy playing with his phone, so I guess he doesn't care.

"No thanks," I say dryly. I'd rather poke my eyeballs out

with a fork than watch them stroll hand in hand, looking at flowers and taking selfies together.

"Suit yourself," Sybil says, getting up and pulling Ethan with her. They leave, and I'm left at the table with my sad piece of half-eaten toast and my pounding headache and my jealous heart. Pushing the plate away, I drop my head onto the table and slow my breathing, forcing my thoughts to mellow.

It's fine. I'm going to get over her. It's only a matter of time. I'll meet the right person for me eventually, and my crush on Sybil will be a distant memory. One day, most likely, she'll be my sister-in-law. I have to move on.

I can see her like a sister. I can.

Even as I'm telling myself this blatant lie, my mind betrays me. All I see are the things I love about her. The way she cares for the ones she loves. The openness of her laugh. How smart her mind is. Her perfect body, tall and strong. Her expressive green eyes. The arch of her pale neck when her hair is up. God, that hair. It's like a sunrise, fiery and soft at the same time. She's beautiful inside and out, and she understands me in a way nobody else does.

I am fucked. Why do I keep thinking like this? Torturing myself?

"You okay, son?" Mom's voice pulls me to the present as she places a hand on my shoulder. I didn't even realize she came in.

"I'm fine." That's the standard answer I give to my parents and has been for years. *"How was school?" "Fine." "How are you doing?" "Fine." "Are you okay that the woman you're secretly in love with is openly in love with your twin brother?" "I'm fine."* Okay, so they haven't asked that last question, but it's only a matter of time before Mom figures it out.

"Let's go sit outside. I want to talk to you."

Well, shit.

I blink, chest constricting, but I do as she asks. The back

porch has several places to lounge, and she thankfully leads me to the one with the most shade. My headache thanks her.

"What's going on?" I ask.

She sits and smiles. "Have a seat, Cooper."

I have a feeling I'm about to get lectured, but at least it's coming from her. Dad's lectures are the absolute worst. They're full of expectation and disappointment and long-suffering sighs accompanied by hard stares. At least Mom knows how to come from a space of understanding.

"Just say what you need to say." I sigh, plopping onto the chair beside her. She takes my hand, squeezing, and we both watch the horizon instead of each other.

"I'm worried about you, and before you say anything, please hear me out."

I nod. I've always respected my mom. She's been the parent who's really there for us—the one who actually cares about our emotional well-being and not just our social status. She's the glue in our dysfunctional family.

"You've been drinking a lot, and you've had a lot of girls sleeping over. Every night this week. Don't get mad, but I talked to your brother, and he says this behavior was standard for you at school last year, too."

I pull my hand away. "I'm an adult."

"You're nineteen, Cooper. You shouldn't be drinking *at all* at nineteen, let alone in excess."

"It's college. It's normal. I have good grades, don't I?"

"You do, and I'm grateful for that, but that's not the point. I want you to be safe and healthy and happy. Frankly, you're not taking care of yourself, and you need to cut it out before you end up hurting yourself or someone else."

Do I get where she's coming from? Yes. Do I have any intention of changing my ways? No. At least not while Ethan and

Sybil are together. Booze and women are the only coping mechanisms I've got.

"I'll do better," I say. Not a blatant lie.

It'll be easier to focus when we're busy with our internships and Sybil is busy with hers. As for college next year, I don't anticipate things getting any better.

"Cooper, is there something you want to tell me?"

It would be so easy to confess, but I can't. What can she do about it? All our parents are thrilled about Sybil and Ethan, and they're not going to break up. So why reveal my secret? It would be mortifying.

"Nope."

She studies my face, and I look right at her. She's aged more in the last two years than she had in the previous decade. She looks so tired. Suddenly, I feel like an ass for just now noticing.

"Is there anything you want to tell me?" I try.

She smiles. "I'm good. I'm only being a mom, checking on my boys. It's my job."

"Yeah. Yeah."

She sighs, as if she's done, but then she stops herself. "You know, it's okay to be sad when we don't get the things we want. But you need to understand what is truly meant for us will never pass us by."

"Okay…" I swear she can see right into my brain.

She pats my knee. "One day you're going to meet your person, honey. I know it. Be patient and take care of yourself in the meantime, okay?"

My cheeks flame, and I nod.

She leaves me with those thoughts, and I stare at the sea as my headache slowly lifts away. Maybe she's right, and I should be more careful, lay off the drinks, stop sleeping with women who I have no future interest in, but then what would I replace the distractions with? How would I numb myself?

Maybe that's the point. Maybe I'm supposed to feel it all. I don't know if I can put myself through that, to feel all the shit in my life and just be patient and hopeful that one day things will be different. The fact remains, I don't know how to be the person everyone wants me to be. I can't change my circumstances, so how am I supposed to change me?

TEN

S ybil
Present - Age 27

I've never liked lawyers, and right now, in this stale conference room, I *really* don't like lawyers.

"This contract is ironclad," King's head lawyer practically booms across the oak table. He reminds me of an angry pit bull with a bone. "Due to the marriage between Ethan and Arden, of which we have copies of the certified marriage certificate, ten percent of the Laurence family ownership will go to the King family, and vice versa."

Our legal team is top-notch, but they have found no room for us. Their red faces are boarding on purple, and it's painfully obvious there's no getting out of this. Doesn't help that I'm avoiding eye-contact with Cooper. The man has a smirk glued to his face, like he couldn't be happier to intermingle our company shares.

At least Ethan appears pissed off. His chest is puffed out, and his eyes are narrowed.

Our head lawyer speaks up. "Gregory Laurence never intended Arden Laurence to be included in this contract. He didn't acknowledge his parentage while he was alive, nor did he leave her anything in his last will and testament. As far as we're concerned, it's egregious she be considered a child for this contract only—a clear violation of the spirit of the contract in the first place."

A tug-of-war of emotions battle inside me. Arden is family, but Dad didn't put her in the will. He was an ass not to, but it was also his wish. I don't know how to feel about this.

"The spirit of the contract?" Cooper mocks, rolling his eyes. "I believe the term you were looking for was spirit of the *law*. Enforcing a contract is upholding the law, and if Gregory didn't want Arden to be included in his family, he should've amended the contract."

Ethan stiffens.

"He would have if he'd known this was going to happen," our lawyer argues. "He didn't *know* Arden and Ethan were together until the day of his death."

Unable to look at anyone, my gaze falls to my lap, and prickles of discomfort crawl up my body.

"Sounds to me like there's more we should subpoena for our discovery if you want to take this to trial," the King pit bull challenges. "What else was Gregory hiding that not only involves King, but that would be of interest to Arden herself? It's clear Gregory Laurence was playing a different game than the rest of us."

Oh hell, they want to dig up more dirt? My heart aches, imagining what other surprises could be out there. Tears threaten to come, but I turn them into a glare instead, gazing at Kings and putting on an air of righteous indignation.

"My husband is dead," my mother snaps, her eyes jumping from person to person across the table. She's so poised, even in this, but I know her—she's dying inside.

At least Arden isn't here. None of us are angry at her for what's happened, but she doesn't need to hear this.

"I'd appreciate it if you'd show a little compassion for our situation," Mom finishes, and I'm not lost in the irony. We weren't the most compassionate last summer when the police came for Ethan... or when Cooper lost his leg.

I meet Cooper's gaze, and a quiet intensity builds between us. I'd do anything to undo the past. I think he would, too, but we're stuck on opposite sides of what's becoming a war.

Conrad King speaks up, taking control of the room like he always does. "It doesn't matter what Gregory intended or didn't intend; the law is on our side, so we can drag this out, speak to the media, see what happens to your stock prices, and wait for a judge, or we can hash it out right now. What will it be, Millie?"

Millie. The nickname only my dad and my mom's closest friends use for her. Nobody has used that name since last summer, and hearing it now is a twisting knife of history. Millie isn't here anymore; it's Amelia now.

She frowns at Conrad King like she doesn't recognize him.

We all know why he's changed—why he's bitter and vindictive. He loved his wife, and when Victoria died, he buried not only the woman he shared a life with, but the future he planned for them. Then he buried the idea of her. She wasn't who he thought she was. She was a cheater and liar who had an affair with his best friend and business partner.

It destroyed Conrad King, and he rebuilt himself to be someone who is cold, calculated, and hell-bent on revenge.

When my mother didn't stand up for Ethan when our father died, that's when Conrad turned his revenge directly on her. The media went after the King family, and now Conrad is going after us. Does it matter Mom did the right thing, eventually? No. The damage to King Media's reputation was done, and if there's one thing that was drilled into me during my marketing classes in college, it's that perception is everything. It's going to take a lot of time and effort to return the King family to their pedestals.

But it doesn't explain one very important thing.

"Why do you want to do this?" I ask, attempting to sound calm and collected. "I know why you'd want ten percent of our ownership, but why would you want us to have ten of yours?"

Conrad gazes at me like I'm clueless, and I'm struck by how much has changed. He used to see me as a daughter.

"Even if you have the majority stake in King," I continue, "you've never been the type to let go of control so easily. It's why you never went public. Is giving up ten percent of your company really worth it?"

While I'm talking directly to Conrad, Cooper is sitting next to him, and his eyes narrow.

"Control is *exactly* why I'm doing this," Conrad clips.

Ethan's mouth is a thin, angry line. Does he hate my father even more for what he's done to Arden? I get it, I do, but Dad is *dead*. Haven't they already won?

"It's not enough that my father died," I growl, my eyes jumping from King to King to King. All three of them. "You have to take this, too?"

"I do," Conrad confirms without hesitation. "Your family will no longer have majority ownership of Laurence. When you want things done, you may have to run them by Ethan and Cooper, and I think that's fair, given everything your family has put my family through."

The only consolation in this is that the shares go to the children, so Conrad won't have his hands on them. But if there's one thing I know about this man and his sons, it's that Cooper and Ethan will bend over backward to please their father. They're terrified of him, and he's used that to shape them into his perfect yes-men. In the end, Conrad will be pulling the strings, and we all know it.

"Ethan and Cooper will each get a five percent stake in Laurence," Conrad brags. "And Gregory's four children will each get two-point-five in King."

And Arden is one of the four. It still feels so surreal she's my *sister*.

"We're going to fight this," our lawyer starts, but our interim-CEO, Lance Vale, gently raises his hand to speak, and the room goes quiet.

Vale has been silently observing this entire interaction, barely showing an ounce of emotion. That's Lance—unflappable and unreadable, the kind of person who could make a killing at poker.

I know him fairly well; he's been around the family a lot. He was our dad's right-hand man for decades as the chief operating officer and has since stepped up to CEO while the board deliberates on who will be the next for that job. It's not common to take this long to fill the job, but it's not unusual, either. CEO of a multi-billion-dollar conglomerate is one in a million.

Honestly, they'll probably elect Vale soon, especially if he can figure out a way to navigate this new mess.

"Are you sure you want to do this, Conrad?" Lance asks. "You separated from Laurence for a reason. You wanted *out* of these relationships, and now you're intermingling them, and to what end?"

The two men exchange an unreadable glance, and I wonder how much bad blood is between them.

"It's done, Lance," Conrad says with finality. "Let's move forward, shall we?"

Lance shakes his head, not breaking eye contact, but doesn't say more.

"What's your *plan* here, Conrad?" Mom asks, drawing the word *plan* out like it's a lifeline.

Conrad smiles. "You'll have to ask my sons. This is all part of *their* legacy, after all. Let the children show us what they're made of."

Ethan shifts, his expression grim, but Cooper doesn't move a muscle. He's a statue. Unreadable. Unmovable.

"I'm giving my ownership to Arden," Ethan says, and his father and brother turn on him with dark gazes. "I don't want it. She should have it. She *was* Gregory's daughter, after all, and she didn't get shit in his will, but she will get this. She can do whatever she wants with her shares."

Ethan makes a great point, and knowing Arden, she'll probably sell them off. I'm sure we could get her to sell them to us at market value if we asked. She's been pretty clear she's moved on with her life and doesn't plan to work for Laurence again.

Annoyance chips at Cooper's steely-gaze, and I have to stop myself from doing a happy dance. I know it's small, but Ethan's decision couldn't have been in Conrad's plans.

Way to go, Ethan. Way to stand up for your wife. Way to stick it to your father.

"Is that really a wise choice?" Conrad gives Ethan a hard look—the kind that normally produces the exact response he's after—but Ethan shrugs.

"Sorry, Father, but I'm not going to war with my wife or her family. This is your game. I'm not playing." With that, he stands and walks from the room.

Relief bubbles in my chest, and I don't think I've ever prouder of the guy.

Then a smug smile tugs at Cooper's lips. "I'm not giving my shares away," he states. "And last I checked, your family has fifty-four percent ownership, which means now you'll have forty-nine. It'll still take my five percent to get the sway you'll want if things come into question. I heard a rumor your board doesn't often agree on things."

"The board is fine," I snap. "We vote on important matters together."

He chuckles. "Does that mean I get a vote now?"

"No. My family gets *one* vote."

Conrad shrugs. "Great. So, tell whoever casts the Laurence votes they need to run things by Cooper first."

"It doesn't work that way."

"It works that way now," Conrad says, steepling his fingers together and smiling as brightly as blinding headlights on a dark highway. Cooper may be doing his dirty work, but no doubt this is all about Conrad and his suffocating ego.

"Alright, that's enough," Lance Vale interrupts. "We see what's done is done. Let's move on from this. We've got work to do."

Everyone gets up, and it kills me that we are leaving this conference room defeated.

"You're welcome, by the way," Conrad says to Mom over the noise of people preparing to leave. "Your stock is down. With Cooper's influence, I'm sure we can turn that around."

They're gloating yet again, and I hate them for it. Why did it have to get so messy between our families? If someone would've told me ten years ago this would be my life right now, I never would've believed them.

On his way out the door, Cooper leans close, his warmth flittering across my ear and sending frustrating shivers down my spine. "I have some ideas for Laurence you and I need to discuss. How about dinner?"

I steel myself. "No thanks."

As if I'd have dinner with this asshole.

He chuckles like we're sharing a private joke when really, he's being slow to remove himself from my personal space. "I'll be in touch."

ELEVEN

Cooper
Past - Age 22

I stare at the sea of black caps, paying more attention to them than the boring commencement speaker. Going through the motions, we get to the part where we all throw our caps in the air, crimson tassels swinging and cheers erupting. I do the same, putting on my smile like I always do. But inside? I'm a robot.

This has been four years in the making. I should be excited. I've done what was expected of me, and I'm proud of my degree, but celebrating feels forced.

I fasten my cap onto my head and follow the others as we leave the auditorium, Sybil next to me and Ethan on her other side, their hands entwined. We're graduating with our undergraduate business degrees. My emphasis was in strategy, Ethan's was management, and Sybil's was public relations. We make a great team, had most of our classes together, studied together, and even *lived* together.

Ethan and I are returning in the fall for graduate school. Sybil's staying in Manhattan to start her career with Laurence International, and I can't imagine what it will be like without her.

Missing her is going to kill me, but I can't tell her just how much. Not having my best friend is one thing, but knowing Ethan is going to propose to her soon? That's something else entirely. It's the most bitter-sweet pill I've ever had to swallow.

Their plan is to get engaged at the end of the summer and get married two more summers after graduate school. They're going to tie the knot at the Nantucket house. I can picture it all so clearly, and it's like a train wreck I can't stop, but one that only hurts me and makes everybody else happy, so why would I stop it?

Our trio makes our way through the hordes of students, congratulating friends and classmates on the way out the doors. It's too crowded, like the walls are closing in. I do my best to ignore the claustrophobia and be the fun-loving guy everyone expects, smiling and laughing and even throwing out a few high-fives until we finally make it onto the front lawn where we're instructed to meet our parents.

Sybil looks like she's going to be sick. Her face is paler than normal, even her lips are void of color, and she's staring at her feet with haunted eyes.

I cup her elbow and lean in. "Are you okay?"

"Everything is great." She's lying, but I know better than to press the issue. I study her, looking for cracks in her armor. My own feelings drift away. All I'm worried about is making sure Syb is okay.

"She's great," Ethan parrots. "We've got our whole lives ahead of us, don't we?" He kisses her on the cheek, and she nods numbly.

"Right..." I say, unease curdling in my gut. This is our graduation—she should be thrilled, but she looks terrified. Maybe this is about Ethan. She doesn't want to have to do the long-distance thing at the end of the summer. I don't blame her for that, but we don't have a choice about graduate school. We *have* to have a Harvard MBA before we can eventually take over King Media. Our lives have been planned out, no chance of changing them now.

"Everything is perfect," Sybil says to me as we search the crowded lawn for our families. "I've got the Ivy League degree, the best boyfriend, awesome best friends, a great family, and I'm stepping into the career I've dreamed of. I'm fine, Cooper. Don't read into things that aren't there."

Right. She's fine. Sure.

I know her, and she's definitely lying; she can't even look me in the eye, and her voice is doing this wobbly thing it does some-times when she's trying to hide her emotions. Maybe her perfect life *is* the problem. She's followed all the plans that have been laid out for her since she was a child—plans she didn't actually make for herself. If anyone can relate to her, it's me, but she clearly doesn't want to talk about it.

"Whatever you say," I deadpan.

"I just... I loved school. I'm going to miss it. That's all."

Ethan leans in, finally waking the fuck up that his girl is upset. "You're okay in there, right?"

"I'm *fine*. Like I said, I'm sad about leaving Harvard. It was really special, wasn't it? I will forever remember this time of our lives."

"It's not too late to apply to graduate school," Ethan tries. We both have been encouraging Sybil to go for the MBA with us, but she's been adamant it's not something she wants to do. She's ready to work.

Shaking her head, her perfect auburn curls bounce and shine in the sunlight. "Yes, it is. Deadline was weeks ago."

"Maybe, maybe not," I reply. "There are ways to get what we want."

As messed up as it is, that's the truth of our status. We're the children of billionaires. We've got extensive connections and access to the kind of fortunes most people will only ever dream about. Doors open for us that are locked for everyone else. Sybil might be able to walk into the Harvard-MBA program without applying on time.

She shakes her head. "I don't have interest in that."

We've talked about this at length. We know how she feels. She's going to be at Laurence International's foundation, doing nonprofit work. Eventually, the plan is for her to become the president of the foundation, but it will take years of earning that spot before she can successfully call it hers. Laurence is publicly traded, so unlike King Media, her parents can't give her whatever job they want. They're beholden to the board and the investors. Everyone agreed to give her this opportunity, but she must prove herself.

It's unseasonably hot today, and the warmth is wrapping around me like a wet glove, especially with my suit and the graduation robe. I'm ready to get to Nantucket for a weekend. That pool is calling my name.

"It's too hot for this shit," I mutter. "When is our flight again?"

"Not until tomorrow morning," Ethan answers. "We've got the graduation party tonight, remember?"

Yes, I do, but it's not the kind of event I consider a party. Organized by our parents, this is solely an opportunity for them to parade us around. We're grown-ass adults, but we're still accessories—something to show off to their rich friends.

I run a hand through my wavy hair, trying to get it off my sticky forehead. "Thank God we get to leave tomorrow. I can't wait for a long weekend with friends."

They nod, and excitement sweeps through me. Our best friends from Harvard have all been invited to join us at the Nantucket house. I can picture it now, the real partying, the house on the bluff overlooking the Atlantic, the crystalline pool, and the fun we're going to have together. A true slice of heaven —a real celebration.

"I can't believe I convinced my parents to sell the Hamptons place and build in Nantucket," Sybil sighs wistfully, rubbing her hands together, the light returning to her eyes.

Sybil has been trying to get her parents to agree to a Nantucket house for years. The Hamptons are her parents' speed, but they finally agreed after realizing they didn't spend enough time there. Now that Ethan and Sybil have gotten so serious, it makes sense to have two houses on Nantucket instead of one. The families will be more united than ever.

"There you are!" Mom's happy voice cuts through the crowd as she waves us down. "We've been looking for you."

"It's a zoo out here," Dad adds, sounding annoyed. "I forget how big these undergraduate ceremonies can be."

Mom pulls us into a hug. "It was wonderful. Congratulations, kids."

Everyone is here. Our mom and dad as well as Sybil's parents and her two little brothers, Chandler and Hayes. We're one big happy family, and someday Ethan and Sybil will get married, making that sentiment true.

"Line up," Amelia Laurence directs. "We need pictures."

She motions to the photographer my mom hired for this very moment. Mom is beautiful and sophisticated, with my brown wavy hair and Ethan's bright blue eyes. Today they twinkle in the sunlight.

"Can you believe they're graduating college?" Gregory adds, elbowing my mother playfully. "It was just yesterday they were starting preschool."

God, parents can be so sappy. If I'm ever a parent, I'm not going to be so idiotic. I'll be more like my father.

Scratch that. I don't want to be like him.

I line up with Ethan and Sybil, and after those photos are snapped, the photographer has us take single shots.

"We need one of Ethan and Sybil, too," my father instructs the photographer, sounding all business-like. "They're together."

Immediately, I step out of the frame. I'm used to this, but it still stings. It's like saltwater to a wound, the way the golden couple lights up for the camera without me. It's a good thing those two clearly love each other. I don't know what the future holds, but at least Sybil will be in it. Even if it's with my brother, it's better than not having her at all.

They'll build a life together, and I'll build my life adjacent to theirs, eventually finding someone to love, even if it's not perfect. Somehow, someway, it will work out. I have to believe that.

I study Sybil as the photographer does her thing. I know I shouldn't stare, but this is a great opportunity to do it without getting caught. She's stunning today, her auburn curls perfectly smooth and shiny, her green eyes bright as emeralds, her makeup light and pretty, and a smile that never leaves her face.

There's still something behind those eyes—that same upset that's been there all day. There's more she's keeping from us. I'm certain of it.

TWELVE

S ybil
Present - Age 27

We need to talk asap. Where can we meet and when?

Cooper finally texts a week after he left me in that boardroom with his cryptic whisper in my ear. This last week has been a shit-show, but the ownership shares have been exchanged. It's done. Leave it to him to get his five percent stake before bothering to contact me.

The board is outraged, several members upset about a contract they knew nothing about. I'm surprised Lance Vale is holding it together so well. It's a clear indication he's gunning for the official CEO position, and I think he'll get it in the near future. Hayes is earmarked for the role down the road, but it's going to be a long time before my little brother will be ready.

My goals haven't changed. Soon, I'll become president of the Laurence Foundation. Despite my age, I've proven myself capable of the role, and it's what my father wanted for me. His legacy still matters.

Through all this, it's been him I can't stop thinking about. Dad is constantly on my mind.

Staring at my phone, reading over Cooper's text again and again, I debate what to type back. Part of me never wants to see Cooper again, but I know that's not realistic.

Frustration swirls in my stomach. I have to see him face to face, even if reason says I should turn this conversation into a phone call. I can't bring myself to do that.

I open the thread to reply, thumb hesitating over the screen. The old me would've told Cooper to come over, but he's never been to my new apartment, and there's no way I'm letting him into my safe space.

We're not friends anymore.

Meet for drinks in an hour? I reply.

His response is instant. **Yes. Where?**

I send him the location of a nearby hotel lobby bar, hoping for a discreet and neutral public place.

An hour later, I've put myself together, brushing out my hair and slipping on my favorite jeans and a simple black sweater with matching boots. I look stylish, casual, professional, confident, and not like I'm trying too hard. *Perfect.* Forget the fact that on the inside, I'm a nervous wreck.

When I arrive, Cooper is at the bar, talking with Perry Hargrove. I smile immediately. Perry has been able to keep all his friendships alive after the split between the Laurences and the Kings, which is saying something, considering most everyone else chose sides. But that's Perry, always keeping it real and doing his own thing despite what everyone else says.

"Hi guys," I say, sliding onto the barstool beside Cooper. "What's going on?"

The men turn on me, Perry with that dazzling smile on his

broad lips and Cooper with a wicked glint in his eyes. *Oh boy, they're up to something.*

"Sorry I had to crash your... uh... meeting," Perry says. "There's something I wanted to talk to you both about."

Cooper waves him off. "Let's order the lady a drink first." He motions the bartender over. "Do you still prefer cosmopolitans?"

I do, but I'm not about to let him think he knows my drink order.

"I'll have your house Pinot Grigio, please," I tell the bartender.

"I'll have a whiskey sour," Perry says, and Cooper opts for a Coke.

The bartender gets us our drinks, and I eye Cooper. I've never known him to go alcohol free at a bar.

"You're not drinking?" I ask.

"Not tonight."

There's something more, his tone guarded. Maybe he took what I said to him at New Year to heart, and he's laying off the alcohol. He was drinking too much—a problem he's had since college. If he's sober now, I'd be surprised. More likely he's realized his limits, and he's not drinking before business meetings.

I raise a brow. "That's not like you."

His eyes snap to my face, his mouth hardening. "I've changed a lot over the last year."

My stupid eyes flit to his pant leg and back up again, shame immediately burning across my cheeks when he catches me. I shouldn't be looking for his prosthetic. I don't know how to act about it, what to say or do.

"Alright, let's talk business." Cooper shifts the subject, leaning so I can get a better view of Perry on his other side.

Perry is a dazzlingly handsome African American man. He's

got beautiful dark skin and onyx bedroom eyes and the kind of open smile that's framed by deep dimples, drawing people in.

But it's Cooper I can't stop looking at. His face is hard and closed off. His hair has been recently cut into a shorter, harsher style than when I last saw him, as if to match his mood. He's as devastatingly handsome as ever, but he's different.

He's unreachable.

"You ready to have your mind blown, Laurence?" Perry turns his charm in my direction, and I prepare for a pitch. "I have an incredible idea for a television show I want to co-produce with King Media and Laurence International as my backers."

I blink rapidly. *Uhhh... what?*

Maybe I shouldn't be shocked, considering he's building a career in television production and has had success already launching and selling a hit show. Why would he want Laurence to have anything to do with his next project? Laurence got completely out of the media business when we cut ties with King. We're in almost every other sector—especially technology—but our media holdings were so tied up with King that when the relationship imploded, Dad convinced the board to take our money and run.

"Why would you be pitching this to me?" I ask. "No offense, but I'm with the Laurence Foundation. I work in phil-anthropy. We have nothing to do with television production, let alone reality television. Cooper, I understand, what with all of King's media holdings, but me?"

The men stare me down, completely unflappable.

"Hear him out," Cooper instructs, unable to fully mask his annoyance.

Perry nods. "The show is a modern, younger, and fresher take on popular reality shows, similar to Real Housewives."

"Okay, I know those are popular, but I hate those kinds of shows. I'm not the right person for this. I'm sorry, Perry."

Perry smiles like I'd be a fool not to hear him out.

"Will you let the man talk?" Cooper snaps, and I shoot him a scathing look and take a long drink of my wine.

"You may hate those kinds of shows..." Perry laughs. "Hell, I don't love them myself, but most Americans eat that shit up. Do you remember that old MTV show, *The Real World*?"

"Vaguely. I think it got canceled when we were little."

"Doesn't matter. It was incredibly popular. That cancellation was an MTV-issue, not a Real World-issue."

Perry leans forward, his eyes not just bright with passion, but burning with it. I'm not surprised. This is how he's always been. Perry double majored in business and film studies. We were twenty when he decided he was going to carve his own path with his career in television production instead of walking the one his parents had ready-made for him in plastics manufacturing. He's stronger than most of my friends, considering he actually followed through on his dreams.

"All those people lived together in a house and moved to a new city for a set amount of time. That was the premise of the show. Simple, but it worked."

"Your new show is going to be like that?"

"Kind of. We're going to pick people who already live here in New York City, but we're going to move them in together and follow their lives for a three-month span."

"What makes that special?" I don't say it, but this sounds like everything else out there already. I don't see it landing with audiences. Been there, done that.

"It's all in the casting." His eyes sparkle with determination and his large hands steeple together. "With enough funding, we can get the kind of people on the show everyone in America will tune in for. Young, attractive people who are already famous. I'm talking about athletes, supermodels, and movie stars. People like *that* will have everyone watching my show."

Cooper turns to me, his gaze holding mine. "You know the kind of people he wants to cast, Valentine. They're the ones everyone wants to be or wants to be with."

For a second, I imagine Cooper on the show. At least half of Americans would tune in for this man. A gorgeous billionaire and heir to a media empire? Absolutely.

"You honestly believe those people will agree to go on a reality television show?" I lean across the bar toward Perry, suddenly very aware I'm in Cooper's personal space, the scent of coke and expensive cologne mixing with his maleness. "Look, I'm not one to nay say on my friends' dreams. If this were possible, you're right, people would tune in. But the high-profile cast you're looking for won't live together with cameras in their face all day and night."

"How do you know?" Coop asks.

I turn on him. "Would you? We've lived in these types of circles our entire lives. We're trained to avoid negative media attention."

Perry's grin catches my attention, his enthusiasm like that of a little kid at Christmas. "What would you say if I told you I already have agreements with several cast members?"

My spine straightens. "I'd say you're more serious about this than I thought."

"I'm dead serious. I want to be filthy rich and successful in my *own* right, and this show is how I'm going to make that happen." He's more certain of himself than ever. I'll be honest, it's pretty impressive, and he must agree, given the cocky grin on his face. "I've been shopping this idea for months, and King would like to partner with me, but..."

"But my father doesn't want to invest the amount of capital that is needed to land the high-caliber cast," Coop cuts in. "We need more money—a lot more—and that's where Laurence comes in."

I try to relax in my chair, the weight of this heavier than I thought. I don't want to let Perry down, but I can't get his hopes up. "I'm sorry, but the board won't agree to something like this, and I don't have the kind of money you're talking about. No offense, but Laurence is trying to distance ourselves from King, not enter into more agreements."

A hush falls between us. For a second, we're at a standstill. Whose move?

"Perry, why don't you excuse yourself? There's something Sybil and I need to discuss in private," Cooper says, and my stomach drops.

His move, apparently.

"I actually need to head out, but I'll be in touch. Sybil, you don't want to miss this." Perry finishes his drink and disappears out the front door, his hand raised to hail a cab.

I glower at Cooper. "If you think you're going to use your little five percent to blackmail me into going to the board for you, you're crazy. I love Perry, but our two companies working together is not a good idea, and I'm not going to be the one to pitch the idea that has a snowball's chance in hell."

Cooper is slow to answer, as if methodically thinking every word through. I wish I could be like that. I'm hot-tempered, the words often rolling off my tongue as soon as I think them.

"He's trying to build his career. Do you blame him for asking?" Coop asks.

"I'm trying to build my career, too."

He lets out a small laugh. "I thought your career was already made for you."

Anger burns hot. I *know* I'm a nepotism hire, that I come

from immense privilege, but I fight tooth and nail to prove myself every day. Cooper should understand what that is like, considering we're in the same position.

"As if you have room to talk." I take a long sip of my remaining wine, trying to hide my frustration behind the glass.

He raises his Coke in a touché gesture and takes a long drink.

"If you agree to do this—really do this—get the board to give you the money to fund the first season successfully. Then I'll give you that five percent stake I took."

The world has been upside down for the past two weeks and suddenly it flips right side up. I set my glass down, trying not to gape at him or get my hopes up. "Are you serious?"

"We'll put it in writing, but there's a caveat."

"Of course, there is," I sigh, the hope gone as quickly as it came.

"The show has to be good. It *has* to succeed, for Perry's sake, or it's all a waste." He pauses, and a faraway regretful look overtakes his features. "I'm doing this for my best friend. I've had a lot of friends over the years, and Perry is the *only* one who stayed with me when it mattered most."

Ouch.

Everything I was about to say falls flat on my tongue. He's talking about me. I know he is. And while I had my reasons, I still don't blame him for hating me. I ruined our friendship. I gave it away.

Because I had to.

"I don't need stake in your company," he continues. "As much as it delights me to have your panties in a twist, it's not what's driving me forward."

"As if you have any effect on my panties." Once again, my words tumble out without going through my brain first.

He smirks, his eyes dropping down my body and slowly

back up again. Traitorous heat floods every inch of my skin. This cannot keep happening. It's been years. Cooper shouldn't be able to rattle me like this with a suggestive look.

"Sure," he drawls. "No effect at all."

Damn him.

THIRTEEN

S ybil
    Present - Age 27

"I knew you'd do anything for your family," Cooper says to me when I slide into the booth across from him and Perry a week later. I bite my tongue from snarking back.

"Don't worry," Perry adds. "You won't regret this."

Somehow, I doubt that.

It only took one meeting with Mom and another with the board and Vale to convince them to agree to Cooper's proposition. One week for both teams of lawyers to draw up the contracts Cooper and I signed.

Mom didn't like the idea at first. She wanted to find another way, but I didn't see another opportunity like this coming along, and she agreed to let me try.

I'll make sure Perry's show is successful. While I don't necessarily trust Cooper, I know he won't do anything to sabotage one of his best friends.

Deep breaths. It's going to be okay.

Perry hands me a menu, but I don't feel even the slightest bit hungry. I've been too nervous about this lunch since we put it on the calendar. "In the end, this will be a win for me, a win for King Media, and a win for Laurence."

I nod, perusing the offerings but not really seeing them.

There's more on the line I'm not telling Cooper or Perry. If I'm successful in getting that five percent, then the board has agreed to promote me to president of the Laurence Foundation. This is my dream, and I'm so close I can taste it.

"By the way, I know about Arden's shares," Cooper says, and I peek over the menu to level him with a hard stare. "She let you guys buy out her inheritance? Typical. Love the girl, but she needs to grow a spine."

"She didn't want ownership," I bite.

He shrugs. "Maybe, but she should've kept it, anyway."

"Not everybody is out to play the games your father taught you."

Perry holds up his hands. "That's enough. We have to work together, and I can't deal with constant bickering. Let's talk about the show, shall we?"

I sigh but nod. We need to make this show *the* breakout success of the year. It needs to go viral on social media, and to do that, the drama needs to be hot enough to spark debate online without being so hot that famous people end up suing us for defamation.

According to the contract, both Laurence and King contribute three hundred million to the project. If the show makes enough to earn out more than what was put into it—and if it hits a high benchmark of viewership—then the show will be green-lit for a second season by King's television network, and we'll get Cooper's five percent back.

If we fail? Coop gets to keep his stake in Laurence, and we

can never negotiate it away from him again. He'll get to be included in our board meetings and tied to Laurence for as long as he'd like. And really, that means *Conrad* will be tied to us.

"Tell us where we're starting from." Cooper turns on Perry, and for the next hour, Perry explains in meticulous detail everything he's accomplished so far. He's got a penthouse rented for filming, most of the crew lined up, and has been recruiting an impressive cast. It's almost like the royal family agreed to let cameras inside their homes and film everything—that would take a great deal of convincing and loads of money.

"We'll call it *Top of the World*," Perry says with a devilish grin. That sounds perfect. I'm not someone who watches this kind of stuff and even I'm intrigued. "I've got the cast lined up, except for one key person... if we're going to pull this off."

"And who's that?" I question.

"We lost our star athlete. He checked himself into drug rehab two days ago and wants nothing to do with the show. That means we've got a gap in casting. Any ideas?"

I look up to the ceiling, thinking through the professional athletes in Manhattan. One name immediately pops into mind. He's *perfect*.

"It needs to be a local who won't be traded within the year and isn't prone to injuries," I say, leveling the guys with a grin. "A man. Someone popular. Someone with influence in this city. Single and attractive. And with a playboy reputation."

Perry and Cooper look at each other with blank expressions, clearly at a loss, and I want to kick my legs gleefully.

"Benton Beal."

Cooper narrows his eyes, skepticism flashing across his face. "Doesn't he have a horrible reputation? He gets into fights and sleeps around."

"He's a hockey player; fighting is part of the appeal. And who cares if he sleeps around? You do the same thing."

Cooper shakes his head. "He sounds like a liability."

Or Cooper doesn't want me to have a win. "I see it as a positive. He's incredibly popular with his fans and has about a zillion fan-edits on social media. People are obsessed with Benton." I hold up my phone. "And lucky for you guys, I have his phone number."

"Do I even want to know?" Perry laughs.

Coop glares, and I have to stop myself from calling him out. He's clearly being judgmental, especially given what he said to me at that New Year's Eve party about needing higher standards.

I give him my steeliest glare. "Don't slut shame me for having sex with Benton Beal." I say it like it is. "It's not a big deal when two consenting adults who want to get together and safely have fun. Besides, don't you have a phone full of women who casually sleep with you? Are you judging them for doing the same thing?"

Coop shifts but doesn't say a word.

"Benton Beal is a fantastic idea," Perry cuts in. "Call him. Convince him. Whatever you've got to do, Sybil. Make it happen. He's *perfect*."

"Not *whatever* she has to do," Cooper growls. "We're not prostituting Sybil out for your show."

I bite my tongue, a million thoughts eager to spill over.

Perry holds up his hands. "Chill. That's not what I meant."

"To hell it wasn't." Coop turns his sour expression on his friend. "I love you Perry, but sometimes you can be so singularly focused on your goals you forget to check yourself."

I roll my eyes. "Hate to break it to you, Cooper, but Benton Beal can get any woman he wants. He doesn't need me to convince him by offering sexual favors. Besides, he's already slept with me on multiple occasions. He can get me into his bed because I *like* him."

Cooper's jaw tightens, nostrils flaring. I've clearly struck a nerve and have to bite back a grin to keep myself from seeing just how deep that nerve goes. Truthfully, I haven't slept with Benton in a while. We're friends more than we're friends with benefits.

"I don't care who you sleep with, Valentine," Cooper cuts in.

That name again. He keeps using it, and I would keep correcting him, but an expected realization stops me. "Seems like you do care."

"Don't mistake this for something it's not."

"And what am I mistaking it for?" Because to me, it seems like jealousy and possessiveness, and as strange as that is coming from Cooper, at least it's not cold indifference or hatred.

He takes a deep breath and pinches the bridge of his nose. "Listen, we don't do unethical shit like that at King Media." Dropping his hand, he pins an accusatory gaze on me. "In fact, if Benton decides to do the show, you'll need to keep your legs closed around him from now on. We can't have any conflicts of interest."

Logically, I get where he's coming from, but emotionally, my veins are burning with righteous indignation. "You're already accusing me of being unprofessional?"

Cooper chuckles, and Perry intervenes. "Okay, I'm going to stop you two *again*. We can't start fighting before we've even done anything. You're going to have to learn how to get along. You used to be friends, remember? I'm not saying you have to be friends again, but for the love of God, figure out a way to work together without fighting all the time. If you want to talk about being professional, how about you start with *that*?"

"Fine." I extend my hand across the table to Coop. "Truce? We can be professionals and *not* friends."

He holds my gaze, but when he shakes my hand, I don't feel as vindicated as I thought I would. A hollowness has opened in my chest, aching to be filled. "Besides securing an athlete, are we ready for the dinner party tonight?" I ask Perry, dropping Cooper's hand.

While we want the cast to meet each other for the first time on camera, there are a few Cooper and I are unsure about. Perry had the idea to bring them round to dinner first. They're a brother and sister pair, children of a political dynasty who are now coming into their own, and I'm not sure they're famous enough or interesting enough for *Top of the World*. No offense to them, but politics is divisive, and a lot of people try to avoid it when they're watching television. But Perry is adamant they're a perfect fit for what he's looking for.

"I've got my private chef lined up," Cooper says. "Tonight's a go."

Wait. What?

I frown. "We're going out to dinner, aren't we?"

Perry shakes his head. "Cooper thought it would be more discreet to have them to his place, and I agree. How about you see if you can get Benton there tonight, too, so we can talk to him about the opportunity?"

Going to Cooper's place is the last thing I want to do, but he makes a good point, so I don't push it. But Benton? Tonight? Already? "Shouldn't Benton meet his potential new cast mates on camera? Maybe we should wait on him."

Perry waves off my concern. "It'll be fine. We might not cast all three people, and if we do, it's not a big deal if they've met in advance."

I sigh. "I'll see what I can do."

As nervous as I am to contact Benton, I'm more nervous about going to Cooper's apartment. I've been to his building a bunch of times. Ethan and Arden live there. But Cooper's place feels like crossing into enemy territory.

We finish lunch, and on our way out, Cooper holds the

door for me. As I pass under his arm, his familiar scent nearly stops me in my tracks. He's not covered up by the new pricy cologne he wears these days. Instead, for just a second, I'm back with the boy I grew up with, the one I considered one of my best friends. A weight presses down on my heart that I can't acknowledge. I won't.

We step onto the sidewalk, and his phone rings. A flash of a smile crosses his lips, and his eyes dance when the name pops up on the screen. *Roxanna*.

The weight on my heart presses harder.

For years, Cooper had a roster of beautiful women ready and willing to hook up with him. Could Roxanna be one of those? Or maybe he's dating someone. Finally gotten serious about a relationship.

How much do people really change? I wonder.

He doesn't bother with goodbye as he strides away to take the call. I can't help but notice the way his right pant leg looks a little different than the left or how his gait has changed. I don't know if I'll ever be able to see Cooper the way I used to. It's as if he's become someone else entirely, someone who's been forever changed by a summer evening that cost us both so much.

FOURTEEN

S ybil
    Present - Age 27

"So, what did you want to talk to me about?"

Benton slides into the backseat of the town car and buckles in. I have a full-time driver to get me around Manhattan; my father insisted on it for all of his children. Dad was above public transport—said it was dangerous and dirty. But I like it. It makes me feel more like a normal New Yorker. If Dad knew how often I ride the Subway, he'd probably find a way to haunt me.

"Hey, you," I reply, giving Benton my best smile. "It's been a minute. Sounds like you had a great season. It ended a few weeks ago, right?"

Don't think I didn't invite Benton out tonight without first doing my research.

He's been busy with the New York Storm and honestly, I'm

a little amazed I was able to get him to agree to hang out on such short notice. The man is busy.

Nerves race through my belly. I don't want to spring the show on him, but I also can't beat around the bush.

"It was an okay season," Benton says, shaking his head. "At least we ended with a decent winning record, but we could've done so much better." His handsome face drops all professionalism, his grin lifting and eyes following the curve of my neck. "Anyway, yeah, it's good to see you too, Syb."

His frown turns to a smile, and I take it in. He's got two dimples framing his mouth, making his otherwise devilish appearance fucking adorable. He leans in to kiss my cheek.

"What's the plan for tonight? Your place or mine?"

I elbow him in the ribcage, and he laughs.

If I could blow off this dinner, I would. It's been a few months since I've had anyone in my bed. And while I have a few situationships I could call on, I haven't been feeling it lately.

I'm pretty sure I'm broken when it comes to loving someone romantically. I haven't done it since Ethan, and that was years ago.

"What are you up to now that the season has ended?" I ask.

If Benton is committed to something great, I won't bring up the show. I'll have the driver make a left at the next light and take Benton to my place, rescheduling a time to meet with the politician's kids.

Benton sighs, the bridge of his nose scrunching. "The playoffs sucked. We barely made it, and we got eliminated in the first game. The fans were assholes about it."

"I'm sorry to hear that."

He nods. "And the paps were fucking vultures, too, but you know what that's like."

I only *kind of* know. We had a lot of press right after Dad's passing. Benton and I had quite a few heart-to-hearts when all that was going on. He had really good advice on how to avoid the paparazzi, which was helpful, but eventually the news cycle moved on, and so did everybody else.

"Are you still enjoying hockey?" I question, eyeing him carefully.

Might be too intrusive to ask that of a starting NHL center, but Benton is my friend, and I care about him.

His smile is guarded. "I'll always love hockey, and I'll play as long as my body will let me and a team wants to pay me."

"But...?"

He sinks into his seat, staring into nothing for a long second. "Listen, I know how lucky I am to be doing what I love most for a career and getting paid a shit ton to do it. Hockey isn't the issue. It's everything else that comes alone with it that's been hard lately."

Whelp.

We need to cast perfection if we're going to get *Top of the World* green-lit for a second season. Only the best will get our show the kind of viewership and ad revenue needed to hit our goals.

I remind myself why I'm doing this.

For my family. My name. My chance to be director of the Foundation and all the good I can create with that position. For Perry's future and even for Cooper. As messed up as it is, I'm also doing this for Dad.

Even though he's gone, I *still* want him to be proud of me.

"Tell me what's hard about it being a professional athlete, besides the obvious?"

He shrugs. "When you're the biggest star on the ice, the manager is going to be up your ass about being perfect. You'd think they'd be happy about the wins, but they care a lot about public image and the brand. Not just one player."

"Hmm." I nod. "Sounds like you need to do some PR."

He rolls his eyes. "Don't even start."

"Let me ask you this. Do you have plans for the summer?" I really hope Benton is open to what I have to offer. *Top of the World* will catapult his stardom to the kind of fame that could take him far beyond hockey.

He turns on me. "Why do I get the feeling you're about to pitch me something?" He catches the look on my face, and his playful expression falls. "Oh shit, not you, too."

Guilt—instant guilt.

"Hear me out," I try as the car turns onto Cooper's street. "You can say no, and I'll respect your decision and never bring it up again. I'm a producer on a new reality television show I think you'd be very interested in hearing more about."

He immediately shakes his head. "Fuck no."

I sigh. "Okay, that's fine, no hard feelings. We'll find another athlete who wants guaranteed millions and fame and extra years added on to his career."

He laughs, clearly annoyed, and I hope I didn't just lose his friendship. "Extra years on my career? Be real, Sybil. Like a fucking *tv show* could do that."

We stop at the red light, and I give him an incredulous look. "Do we not live in the same century?"

He arches a skeptical eyebrow, but I'm being serious.

"You think teams don't care about fame? They do. Athletes who bring in more money through merchandising and name recognition get better and *longer* contracts. Why do you think so many athletes try to date popular actresses and pop-stars? The added attention is mutually beneficial to both parties involved." I give him a pointed look. "Try to deny it, but what you do off the ice does matter."

"You sound like my manager," he deadpans.

"Your manager must be a smart woman."

He rakes a palm through his thick brown hair. "She is... and she'd probably tell me to hear you out."

"See? What do you have to lose? If it's a no, that's fine. We'll find another athlete."

He slumps back, a weary sigh escaping his lips. "Fine, give me the elevator pitch."

I laugh. "Oh, no. We're going to go meet some people tonight who are much better at pitching than I am." Namely, Perry Hargrove, the pitch-master.

"We're *what*?" Benton snaps. "What the hell is going on, Laurence?"

The streetlight switches to green, and we accelerate again. "Relax. It's at a private residence. No cameras. Nobody there to post your private business online. And we don't have to stay long."

"Will there be food?" he asks, and I bite back a grin.

"Yes, as well as a couple of other people who are interested in the show. You can talk to our show creator and see what this is about. No pressure."

"I don't know," he mumbles, and I feel bad for springing this on him.

"Listen, the payment will be great. It might even be more than your NHL contract."

He snorts. "Bullshit."

"Tell your manager we are working with seven and even eight figure payments for three months of filming." I give him a wink. "I'm sure she'll be happy to negotiate a payout for you both."

His mouth drops open. "That's better than most of my endorsements."

Money always talks. My Dad taught me that.

Benton is wealthy from his hockey success and the endorsements that followed, but he doesn't have the kind of wealth that comes from generations of success. I obviously don't regret my upbringing, but I'm aware of the privileges I've been afforded. It's my duty to give back. It's part of why I'm so passionate about the Laurence Foundation.

"Well, you will have to do more. We'll be filming for three months of your life over the summer. It won't mess with your off-season too much, so I think it's perfect for you, which is why I asked you before anyone else."

"Fine, I'll hear you guys out, but if this bites me in the ass, I'm going to blame you for it."

I'll blame myself, too.

"It won't," I assure him. "It'll make America fall in love with you more than they already have. At least the woman will." I give him a sly smirk, and his dimples pop again.

I've got him.

Ten minutes later, we roll up to Cooper and Ethan's building. I refuse to be nervous, pressing my palms to my thighs and ignoring my rising heart rate.

Benton and I ride the elevator together to the penthouse floor.

The building is newer, with the largest apartments at the top. There are only two penthouses, and Ethan and Cooper purchased them both.

Ethan's was impressive before, but now that Arden is living with him, it's even better. Mostly because I helped them design it. Neither of them has an eye for that stuff and asked me for help.

The elevator opens, and we step out into a long, luxurious hallway, a door on either end.

"It's this one," I say, pointing toward the door I've yet to use.

Benton whistles low, his eyes roaming the decor. "Who are

we meeting, Syb? Nobody on my team can afford a place like this. Not in this city."

Cooper and Ethan inherited billion-dollar trusts a few years ago. I don't talk about how much I inherited when my dad died. It's not a billion, but it's millions, plus the stocks. It's more money than I'll ever know what to do with, and I'll always be more than comfortable, but I'm trying to focus on my career goals regardless of what's in my bank accounts.

"This is Cooper King's place. He and Perry Hargrove are the other producers on the show, but Perry is also the creator. Cooper is offering his place for these dinners since it's discreet. Nobody will ever know what you talked about here unless you decide to do the show."

"King?" Benton shakes his head. "Is that the family you hate?"

I wince. "Hate is a strong word."

His eyes widen. "Come on. You hate them."

"I know what I'm doing."

"Do you?"

I elbow him in the ribcage for the second time tonight. "Shush, you. Just think about the money, will you? There's new money and old money coming to the table for this show. My family is the old, but King Media? They're the new money, and they have a lot of it. The Hargrove's money runs deep, too, but Perry is doing his own thing. He gave up the family ready-made career in plastics manufacturing and is following his talents instead. It's admirable. Have you heard of a tv show called *The Verb*?"

Benton nods. "I watched some of it. That show is insane."

Yes. It's a social experiment show where contestants have to live together, competing under a different "verb" in each episode. One might be "compete" and the next might be "compromise" but the way it's built creates tons of drama. It's a fun and interesting concept and has gone on to do well.

"It's popular," I say. "That was Perry's first show. He sold it, and this new show is his baby now. He needed capital, and we came together because we believe in him."

He raises a big brown eyebrow. "That's pretty weird, considering your companies hate each other, but okay. Whatever you say. Let's go talk to these guys."

"Great! We've already got three people who have signed contracts. We're looking for six cast members in all. You and two other people will be in there tonight to talk about the possibility of joining the show."

He scratches the stubble on his jawline. "Who's already in?"

This is what I've been waiting for.

"Oh, no big deal, only a pop star, an international supermodel, and a movie star."

He blinks. "Names?"

I shake my head. "Gotta save that for cameras."

"What about the two who are already in there?"

"Members of the Maguire family."

He thinks on that for a second. "Aren't they a political dynasty?"

"And their father plans to run in the next presidential election."

He shakes his head. "That's... intense."

"Indeed."

He lets out a deep breath, and I realize he's probably as nervous as I am right now. Maybe it's contagious.

I knock, and a few seconds later, Perry greets us with his megawatt smile, immediately extending his hand toward Benton. "Benton, we're so glad you could make it. I'm a huge fan. I'm Perry Hargrove, creator and executive producer of my new show, *Top of the World*. Please, come in."

"Uh—hi," Benton stumbles over his hello, which is unusual for him. The guy is typically as smooth as the ice he plays on. "Thanks for having me. You know, my manager has been wanting me to find something like this. She wanted me to do *Dancing with the Stars,* but I turned it down. I need something more on brand for me, and I don't want to leave the city. I've got my systems here, and it's important that I keep on top of training."

"Of course, that makes perfect sense. *Top of the World* will showcase your lifestyle and let your fans behind the curtain and into your world," Perry says. "Does that sound like something you'd like to do? For the right price, of course."

Benton pretends to think about it, but I'm certain he's in. When he nods, walking into the apartment, I chuckle to myself, my nerves instantly unraveling.

Convincing men to agree with my ideas is one of my specialties. No doubt that by the end of tonight, we'll have secured our guy.

At least, that's what I think until I actually step into the apartment and see the icy glare on Cooper's face... directed right at Benton.

FIFTEEN

C ooper
      Past - Age 22

Something is wrong. After a wild party-weekend in Nantucket with our friends, we're officially on a small, chartered jet in route to Manhattan. It only fits eight people, so tell me why Ethan and Sybil aren't sitting together? They're not even looking at each other. I've been watching them the entire flight, waiting for their usual selves to return, for a shared smile or familiar look, but it never happens.

Ethan is in the back, and Sybil is up front. His hood is tugged around his head, and he stares out the window all through takeoff. Meanwhile, Sybil is busy chatting with our friends, putting on a persona of sunshine and rainbows. I see right through that bullshit. Her eyes are weary, and her mouth is tight. Even her voice is strained.

Something is definitely wrong.

We land at the private airport, and everyone says their goodbyes, climbing into their hired cars. Ethan gets into ours without carrying Sybil's luggage over or even opening the door for her. *What the fuck?* She frowns in his direction, then wheels her bag toward the little terminal building instead of the car. Is she calling herself a cab? The thought makes me want to strangle my brother. I don't care what is going on between them. He still needs to treat her with respect.

I leave Ethan with a scathing look and catch up to her. "Where are you going?"

"My parents' place." Her voice is clipped.

She's got her hair piled on top of her head. I love when she wears it like this. Her neck and jawline are some of her most feminine features. She's too pretty for her own good. God, it kills me that she'll never be mine. Every damn time I think I've made peace with it, she'll do something as simple as putting her hair in a messy bun, and I'm suddenly sixteen again, obsessing over the idea of tracing her creamy neck with my mouth.

I shake the thought away. "Why aren't you getting a ride with us?"

"I don't want to ride with you," she snaps.

"But we always take you home." Our parents' apartments are only five blocks apart, both on the north side of Central Park. It's not much distance; there's no reason for her to get her own car. Not unless something happened.

"What did Ethan do?"

She turns, lifting her sunglasses to rest against her hairline. Her eyes are almost as red as her hair, shimmering with unshed tears. My stomach swoops, and I itch to wipe away the proof of her pain.

"Ethan broke up with me last night," she says.

Shock ricochets through me like a fucking pinball. "Ethan broke up with you?"

"Yes."

Her voice is soft and defeated, a wisp of her normal self.

I shake my head, pressing my lips together.

It doesn't make sense. He's obsessed with her. He loves her. He's already picked out a ring. I should know; I helped him choose it last month. As much as I hated every minute of that experience, I want my brother to be happy, same as I want Sybil to be happy. That's exactly why I've supported their relationship from day one. Why I've kept my feelings buried.

"I don't want to talk about it." She drops the sunglasses on her nose, freckles scrunching around the frames as she fights tears. "I'll talk to you later. Go be with your brother."

She turns, head held high as if she isn't breaking on the inside.

White-hot anger torches through me. This wasn't supposed to happen. Sybil and Ethan are the best people I know. They're supposed to be together. Ethan can't just break up with her—that will ruin not only their relationship, but the balance of friendship between the three of us. Not to mention our parents are going to lose their shit.

I storm to the car, practically ripping the door off its hinges as I open it and barrel inside. "What the fuck did you do?"

"So she told you." His mouth is set in a grim line, but his eyes are heavy with pain.

My hands flex into fists involuntarily, and I force them to strap on the seatbelt instead. "She said you broke up with her."

He nods.

"Un-fucking-believable."

"Stop, Cooper."

"You have this once-in-a-lifetime girl, and you're going to throw her away?"

He shakes his head as if I wouldn't understand, and that movement alone kills me. If I had her, I'd never break it off. But I don't have her. He does.

Or he did.

"Tell me why," I demand. My voice has gone dark, rage simmering on the other side.

He bristles. "It's none of your business."

Those five words spear me right through me, carving out my soul.

I don't want them to be true. We're all best friends. Sure, it's not my relationship, but what they do directly affects my life. That makes it my business, even though deep down, I know it's not.

The driver starts the ignition, and we're off. Ethan doesn't talk. He *won't* talk. All through the silent drive, I keep my gaze pinned on him. I'm trying to read him, to understand what could've possibly caused him to break up with Sybil days after our college graduation.

Is he angry about it? Heartbroken over her? Relieved to be done with her?

The guy is an unreadable fortress when he wants to be. That's the thing about Ethan. He knows how to shut down his emotions like a pro, a skill modeled by our parents. I'm not so talented.

A half hour of silence later, and I can't take it anymore. We're almost home, and I'm not getting out of this car without answers, but maybe I need to have some compassion for the guy. He's obviously sad.

"Ethan, you can talk to me. I know you love Sybil, so if you ended things, you must have a good reason. I'm just trying to understand what that reason is."

If I was in his shoes, if I had the love of a girl like Sybil Laurence, there is no fucking way would I break it off. Sure, I might be the one to fuck it up, but I wouldn't be the one to end things.

"For once in your life, can you leave me alone?" Ethan chides.

"No."

He pinches the bridge of his nose. "Cooper, I know we share our secrets, but this one isn't about you. It's about her. It's not something you can fix—it's something she has to take care of, so why don't you butt the fuck out for once?"

Ouch.

But I see through his hurtful words.

This is what Ethan does when he's upset. He pushes people away. He hates to let anyone in on his vulnerability, but that doesn't give him an excuse to treat me poorly, nor is it my fault he's going through this.

"Fine, get angry, be a dick about it, push me away. Be like Dad."

"I'm not Dad," he snaps.

"Whatever you say. If I need to be your punching bag right now, then so be it, but just so we're clear, I know what you're doing."

We don't speak after that, both too pissed off. My hands are tight fists, and I wish we could fight this out like we did when we were kids and our punches didn't hold the same impact they would today.

I shake my head, still in disbelief. If Ethan is this broken up about it, I can only imagine how shattered Sybil is right now.

I need to see her and make this better somehow. Ethan might demand to be alone, but I don't want her to be by herself when she's hurting. Maybe if I talk to her, I can help them mend whatever is going on. Ethan is an introvert, but she's more extroverted, more like me. She needs to be surrounded by people she cares about when she's hurting, and I'm pretty sure her family isn't in the city, so she's probably alone.

There's got to be a way to fix this, and if Ethan won't tell me what the problem is between them, maybe Sybil will.

Sixteen

C ooper
Past - Age 22

Sybil lets me into her parents' place, and I immediately gather her into a hug. I'm six-foot-two, and she's five-foot-ten, which makes her a lot taller than most of the girls I'm used to holding, but her height is one of my favorite things. It suits her take-charge personality, even though right now she feels smaller, sinking into me like she needs my protection.

Like she needs *me*.

I should let her go, should step away and put distance between us, but I can't. For a few seconds, I let myself hang on tight, imagining holding Ethan's girl isn't total asshole behavior. I imagine, just for a moment, I'm my brother—the one she needs to hold her and tell her everything is going to be alright.

I breathe her in, inhaling her intoxicating perfume and the soapy-clean scent of her freshly shampooed hair. I shouldn't close my eyes, but I find them shutting anyway, savoring this moment. I hate to see her so broken and sad; she doesn't deserve it. She should know how special she is and how much she's wanted.

God, if I could tell her how much I want her, have *always* wanted her, maybe she wouldn't look so broken-hearted.

The only consolation is she's obviously showered and gotten herself ready after returning from the airport. I half expected to find her in bed with puffy eyes and a pint of her favorite Ben and Jerry's, Cherry Garcia.

Does getting ready mean she's okay?

Wallowing in bed was never Sybil's thing. She's not the type to feel sorry for herself or let someone else pick up the pieces for her. She's type-A with her shit together and go-on-with-life attitude, even though she's hurting on the inside. Honestly, it's a miracle she's letting me hug her instead of pretending everything is fine.

"Are you okay?" I ask in a throaty whisper, stepping back but keeping my hands on her elbows.

She nods, then shakes her head, and then nods again, and my heart aches for her.

"I'm not crying anymore, so at least there's that."

Her eyes are much greener than normal—the color of spring grass after the rain and a clear sign of her tears. My aching heart sinks.

"He won't tell me what happened," I say with a frustrated growl.

She closes the front door behind me, resignation set into every soft line of her body. "At least my family isn't here." She sighs. "I'm not ready to tell them. I keep thinking Ethan will change his mind, so why create drama? I... I might be in denial. I never thought he'd break up with me." Her mouth trembles, and I want to deck my brother.

If the man had two brain-cells, he'd be here instead of me.

The girl deserves the world, and Ethan was going to give it to her. This shit doesn't make sense.

I swallow hard. "You don't have to tell me why, but if you know..." My voice trails off. This isn't my place, but she leads me into the living room.

The Laurences own property all over, but their Manhattan penthouse is by far my favorite. It's the top two stories and rooftop of a historic building. Massive and ornate, this is the kind of real estate that is only found passed down for generations. You can't really find available places like this in New York City anymore, at least not this close to Central Park. It's large enough for the family of five and then some, has two kitchens, two offices, two family rooms, and of course, it's expertly renovated and decorated.

It's not their main residence, but they use it all the time, so they keep it staffed. But right now? Right now, it's only me and Sybil, and I'm painfully aware of that fact. We're rarely alone together... and never like this.

"Come on," she says, "can we just hang out?"

I nod and follow her to the tv room where she tucks into the corner of the sofa and flips on the television to a home improvement show. She's really into home design, so I'm not surprised. She pats the spot next to her, and instead of continuing to stand around, I let myself sit. We're a foot apart, but it feels like we're closer, the space between us buzzing. Eventually, she shifts her weight and leans into me, curling up like a kitten. My body betrays me, cock thickening and muscles tensing at how much I want this woman.

Fuck. I should leave.

But I can't seem to bring myself to do the honorable thing.

"Are you going to tell me what happened?" I finally ask, no longer able to pretend I'm here to watch television and cuddle.

She mutes the show and lets out a long-suffering sigh. "He thinks I'm not sure about him."

She doesn't look me in the eye; she's still curled next to me, and I stare at the outline of her face, blinking in shock. Is my brother a complete idiot? I've never seen a girl look at a boy the way this girl looks at Ethan. It's so clear the two are obsessed with each other, and he's questioning her?

"Why would he think that?" My tone is too raw, and I cringe internally. I can't let her know what this conversation is doing to me, how it's tearing me up inside.

"Because I pretty much told him I wasn't sure about him." The world tilts off its axis. "I didn't mean it the way he took it, but still, I was trying to be honest about my feelings."

Every nerve ending in my body fires with warning. If she's not sure about him, then what the fuck have they been doing for four years?

She turns to gaze up at me, those bright green eyes making me forget my own name, and I know I'm in trouble. Her hair is a red halo around her pale face, making her my damning angel in this moment.

I didn't know there was a world in which Sybil wasn't madly in love with Ethan. What is she even saying? Does she mean it?

"You're... not sure about Ethan?"

Her eyebrows furrow with regret, and it tells me everything I need to know.

"Last night he ended things, and I was so mad at first, but now I'm starting to think he was right. I need to figure out what I really want, and maybe it's not actually our relationship."

My gaze flicks toward her lips, and I'm such a fucking asshole for it. Those lips are like candy, cherry-colored and shiny and full and kissable. I often fantasized about their taste. I've dreamed of them in so many ways, of feeling them over every inch of my body.

Don't go there.

This is so fucked up. Ethan is my *twin* brother and best friend. He didn't break up with her because he didn't want her; he did it because she's confused. He's probably still planning to propose once she realizes how much she loves him and is sure about their future. But what if that doesn't happen? If she doesn't want to marry him, if loving him doesn't reach all the way to her core, then she shouldn't do it, and having second thoughts before they're even engaged is a red flag.

"Ethan thinks being single for a while is going to help you figure it out how you feel about him?" I ask hoarsely.

I'm still looking at her lips. I can't seem to stop myself. I'm a dying man in the desert who's been searching for water for years, and it's finally right in front of me.

Fuck. What is wrong with me?

She shrugs. "Maybe he's right."

Maybe, but he's also an idiot. There's no way I would ever let this girl go if she were mine. Being single means she can do whatever the hell she wants, and he can't have a say in it. She can kiss other people. Sleep with other people. She can move on.

He could lose her forever, and the fact that he's willing to take that risk makes me want to scream.

Her eyes flicker to my lips and hold, and my entire sense of the world and of what's good and what's right flips upside down, and I forget even my own fucking name.

"Cooper?" her voice trails off as she shifts closer, her body turning so that her chest is brushing against my bicep.

My cock is painfully hard at this point, and I can't stop staring at her lips. Every nerve ending has turned into a live-wire and every breath feels like an eternity perched on the edge of a cliff.

This woman, the one person I've wanted for years, is staring at me like she's about to kiss me. I can't let that happen. I can't *not* let it happen. I'm completely fucked.

"What?" I'm on the verge of losing control.

"What are we doing?" she breathes softly.

That's a damn good question. I'm thinking about throwing my morals out the window and taking what I want. While I can't put words in her mouth, I know what it means when a woman looks at me the way Sybil is, and I know she's thinking of doing the exact same thing.

"What we shouldn't be doing," I answer, hating every word, but knowing it's the truth.

It's as simple as that. Just because they're broken up doesn't mean shit. It's fresh, and it would be a huge betrayal. Ethan *loves* her. He'll hate me if I cross the line I'm currently sprinting toward. And Sybil? She'll hate me, too, once she has a chance to clear her head.

But she's a gorgeous flame, and I'm a pathetic moth, and even though I'll burn if I get too close, I can't stop from throwing myself into her fire.

"You've never looked at me like this before," she whispers with a husky vulnerability that's like a riptide about to pull us under.

But I have, Valentine. You've just never looked back.

She shifts her weight even closer, her warmth so intoxicating I could live in it forever. Her eyes dance over my face, indecision in her gaze quickly replaced with resolve.

And hunger.

"Please," she whispers, and the frail string of my resolve snaps.

"I've never been able to say no to you, Valentine."

Her mouth is on mine first, and I'm quick to respond, pressing hard against her soft lips. She's sweetness personified, but our kiss is bruising—a delicious punishment for mutual sins. I expect her to retreat quickly, but she doesn't, and I can't. She groans into my lips, and I deepen the kiss, our tongues fighting for dominance as I lose all rational thought and lift her onto my lap.

Her knees widen automatically to straddle me, and my cock presses against my jeans, searching for her warmth under her buttery-smooth leggings. I slip my hands under her shirt, greedily running up her back and then down to her ass.

Her hands are everywhere—first my biceps, then fingers raking through my hair, down to cup my jaw, my neck, my chest. For a moment, I wonder if this is what it's like for Ethan. Does she touch him like this? Is she wild for him?

The thought almost ends this for me, but she releases a long moan and rolls her hips against my erection, setting us both aflame. I thought we'd be a slow burn, but we're a fucking wildfire. We can't get enough. I bite down on her lip, and she bucks against me, her frantic hands quickly dropping to the button of my jeans. All we can do is burn and burn and burn.

Nothing has ever felt so right. So inevitable. This woman is a goddess, and if she needs me to kneel at the altar of her body for her to understand that, then watch me worship.

My pants are undone. She did that. I still can't believe she did that. She's about to slide her fingers under the band of my underwear, about to stroke my cock and send me to another dimension, when she cries out against my mouth. She sounds so vulnerable, like she's about to cry for real, and ice-cold reality washes over me.

I go completely still, every muscle in my body tight, and force myself to stop kissing her. She whimpers and presses her lips to mine again, but this time I don't let myself kiss her back. Instead, I lift her from my lap and gently set her on the couch beside me.

Reality is a bitch that slaps us both hard.

I stand, wiping my lips and adjusting my pants. "I'm so sorry," I plead, hating myself for what I've done. This isn't her fault. She kissed me, but only because she's hurting. I never should've let this happen.

From the horrified look in her eyes, she knows it, too.

"It wasn't your fault," she tries. "I kissed you first."

I shake my head. "The kiss was both of us, but it was my fault, Sybil. You're vulnerable, and I took advantage."

"But I kissed you first," she repeats, insistent this time.

Doesn't matter. She was in emotional pain, not in her right mind, and as soon as she gave me the go-ahead, I was on her like my brother didn't exist, and that was my decision. It's my mistake. My failure.

We're silent for a long moment, staring at each other. Is she comparing me to Ethan? Is she hating me right now? Her eyes are brimming with tears, and I hate myself for what I've done.

The last five minutes may have been the best of my life, but they were the worst of hers. She loves Ethan. Not me. We've made a huge mistake. I'm about to ask her how much she regrets this and how much she hates me when she says three words that shatter me.

"Don't tell Ethan."

It's the confirmation I need, as much as it kills me. Ethan is the one she loves most. My stomach roils with shame. I'm going to be sick. Ethan and I tell each other everything, and here's this horrible secret I'll have to take to my grave.

I'm a traitor, and I've made her a traitor, too.

Sybil is the best person I know, but if I were to step away from this situation and see it for what it is, even I can admit my brother deserves better.

"I won't say anything, but maybe Ethan was right. You don't know what you want," I admit.

Her face falls, and the guilt eats me up even more.

"I'll go now," I add. "I promise not to do that again. You— You didn't deserve that." I clear my throat and take one last look at the girl, committing everything about the way she looks tonight to memory. "I'm sorry. For all of it."

I turn and stride away, making it to the door and barreling into the hallway, then down the elevator and out to the city street below. She's haunted me for years, and this day is going to absolutely wreck me, like a poltergeist of my own making.

We have to leave this in the past, to let it go, to wish it had never happened, even if it's a lie. Even if regretting a kiss like that feels like a sin.

But I know what's coming next.

She's going to get back together with Ethan. Those two? They're already on a path not even I can derail them from. It doesn't matter that Ethan ended it with her. I know it won't last long. Sybil loves him, and she loves her family—and Ethan and her family want them to be together. It's a done deal.

As it turns out, I'm right. Less than twenty-four hours later, Ethan and Sybil reconcile.

And even though it spears me right through the heart, I tell myself I deserve to feel like shit, and I remind myself everyone wants them to be together. So I keep my dirty secret buried deep and try my best to be happy for them.

Seventeen

S ybil
    Present - Age 27

"Nice place you've got here. It's really something else," Benton compliments Cooper, who, thank goodness, has the decency to wipe his glare away the second Benton makes eye contact with him. Not that he replaces it with a pleasant expression. It's more like he smells something a little less potent than a skunk.

"Yeah, I like it." Cooper's voice is clipped, and I bite my tongue from saying something snarky. I swear, if Cooper sours this deal with Benton, I'm going to kill him.

"Can I speak to you privately?" I grab Cooper by the arm.

Perry steps in with Benton and the two other cast members we have here tonight, making introductions I'll have to catch later. I march Cooper away from the group, knowing exactly where the home office is, since it's the same floor plan as Ethan's.

I can't help but take in Cooper's design as I go, noting it's more high-end than I expected. When I helped Ethan and

Arden with their place, it was pretty sterile and needed a woman's touch. But Cooper's home is the perfect blend of modern-masculine meets cozy-artist. He either hired an interior designer or there's more to Cooper than I know. I'd compliment him if I wasn't so pissed.

"What's your problem?" I hiss the second we close ourselves inside his office.

His jaw ticks. "I don't have a problem."

"If you weren't looking like you hoped Benton would spontaneously combust, maybe I'd believe you," I say.

"Are you done embarrassing yourself, yet? We have guests to attend to."

We have guests to attend to? I've never heard him talk to me so formally, and it unnerves me even more.

"Getting Benton here was no easy feat, and if things go well tonight, I'm certain he'll take this to his manager, and we can work out a deal."

His eyes darken. "We don't need Benton. We can find someone better."

"What's your problem with Benton? He's perfect."

"He's your lover," Cooper growls, inching forward until I'm pressed against the door. He sounds jealous, but I know better than to think that. Years ago, maybe. But now he hates me.

"My sex life is none of your business."

"Put one of your fuck-buddies on national television, and your sex life will be *everyone's* business, Valentine. I'm doing this to protect you."

I study his face, my gaze dancing across his features. An intense longing surfaces deep in my belly, and how much I've desperately missed his friendship comes bubbling up. "If you're trying to protect me, does that mean you don't hate me anymore?"

"I never hated you, Sybil." An unreadable expression crosses his face. "You were my best friend, and you dropped me like I was nothing."

"I had to," I whisper. "You know why I had to…" A torrent of emotions swirls through my body, mingling with flashes of long-ago memories that nearly killed me.

He sighs. "I don't hate you, but don't hate me for building a wall between us. I can't take that wall down just because you want me to."

I may not like it, but I understand, and I don't want to argue anymore. I close my eyes briefly, shoulders slumping as the weight of our broken friendship presses down. "Okay," I say, opening my eyes again to see him unmoved. "I hear your concerns about Benton. If he gets on the show, I promise to keep it professional between the two of us. A sexual relationship between a cast-member and a producer is not okay."

He nods slowly. "Fine. Great. You're good at cutting people off. Do it to him, and I'll agree to him being on the show."

His words send a pang of regret right through me. He thinks I'm cold and unfeeling, that it didn't hurt me when I ended our friendship. He should know it killed me. Why doesn't he see it the way I see it?

"Maybe we can be friends again?" I try, sounding unaffected but wanting it so bad I could cry.

He stares at me for a long moment. "You mean that?"

"I do."

"Maybe."

It's not a yes, but I'll take it.

"But it's probably for the best if we focus on our work and nothing else."

Ouch.

A knock sounds on the door, and I step aside to let Cooper open it, expecting it to be Perry asking us to return to the group. It's not Perry.

It's not anybody I know.

A gorgeous young woman stands in the doorway. She's not one of the cast members, and my hackles rise as she gives Cooper an alluring smile.

"Hey, Cooper. Sorry to show up unannounced, but I think I accidentally left my phone here earlier." She grins. "When we were... hanging out."

I immediately know 'hanging out' is synonymous with fucking, and a pit grows in my stomach.

"Roxanna." Cooper's clipped voice softens for her. "Always good to see you."

"Likewise." Her gaze slides from him to me. "Hi, I'm Roxanna. I'm Cooper's friend."

Cooper turns between us. "Uh, yes, Roxi, this is Sybil Laurence. She's a co-producer on the show I was telling you about."

I don't know why I expect a catty smile instead of the genuinely kind one I get, but it unnerves me. I want to hate this woman, but I can't. She radiates kindness underneath her natural sultriness, and she didn't do anything wrong by being here.

She begins small talk, and it's obvious she's got something romantic going on with Cooper. I'm happy for him, I am. She's gorgeous and kind, and she's the face behind the name I saw on his phone at lunch earlier. They must have met up here after that and left her phone behind.

The familiarity between them makes my chest ache. I wish I could be a little more familiar with Cooper, that things didn't have to be so broken between us. If we were still friends, I'd already know who Roxi was, and my stomach wouldn't be hollow right now.

"Anyway, my phone?" She turns to Cooper. "I think it's in your bedroom. Probably got knocked under the bed when I was kneeling."

My mouth pops open, and I gape at them as Coop chuckles. Roxanna turns bright red, and she looks at me with wide, embarrassed eyes.

"Shit. Sorry, TMI," she gushes. "Sometimes things come out of my mouth without going through my brain first."

I hold up my hands and smile, though I'll be the first to admit it's a little forced. "I'm not here to judge. It was nice to meet you, Roxanna. I hope you find your phone."

I hurry past her, heading to the dinner party and hoping my face isn't beet-red. Why do I even care? I don't normally blush over this stuff. I'm a sex-positive modern woman. And besides, Cooper used to have half a dozen of willing women on rotation, especially during our college years. He was, *by far*, the biggest playboy I knew. I'm not sure if he's still that way, but I'd like for him to have a committed relationship with someone who loves him.

Don't I?

I shake away the doubts creeping in and find I'm half-listening as I'm being introduced to the politician kids. I shouldn't say kids—they're grown adults, and Sloan and Dane McGuire are exactly the kind of people who are going to make our show more interesting. Their family is beloved by many, but like anyone in politics, they're controversial. Perry says a little politics will help make our show a hit. I hope he's right.

"It's nice to meet you," I say, shaking Sloan and Dane's hands. "I'm happy to have you guys on board."

Sloan nods, and I immediately clock her as the politician's daughter that she is—groomed in media literacy and primped to perfection. I understand her well. Being the daughter of a billionaire meant a constant awareness of my surroundings and occasional bodyguards. Luckily for me, I've been able to stay out of the spotlight.

"You know why we're doing this, right?" she says over dinner, her eyes flashing to Perry. "This isn't for your benefit. It's for ours. We have goals that are bigger than a tv show. Top of the World is a stepping stone for us."

"Sloan," her brother Dane chastises. "Can you lay off for one night, please? Mr. Hargrove already knows all about your lofty ambitions."

Perry nods, and I catch Benton's rapt expression across the table—he's staring at the brother and sister pair like they're the most entertaining people he's met in a very long time. Hell, they probably are, and I think that we probably should've waited to introduce them all on camera.

"So, tell us about the other cast members," Benton turns to Perry. "Before I can take this to my manager, I need to know what I'm getting myself into. She'll never let me sign anything without the cast list completed." He turns to the McGuire siblings. "No offense."

"None taken," Dane deadpans. "But just so you know, I'm a New York City prosecuting attorney, so I'm not dumb enough to sign something without being sure about it first. Assuming you get the same contract I did, it's fair. Though, I can't be sure how much money they offered an NHL hockey player. Should be a lot, but not like you're a Yankee."

Benton's jaw tenses. "Whatever it is, I'll make sure it's double what they're giving you, being that you're a city prosecutor and not the attorney general."

Dane's grin is somehow smug and charming all at once. Total politician. "Not yet."

"Okay," I intervene. "Save this drama for the cameras, will ya, boys?"

"Yes, please do." Perry laughs. "We're still working on a final location, but we'll start filming within the month, so prepare yourselves. Tie up any loose ends so you can focus. Yes, you will still be working, but you'll need to stay in the city and make time for the show. We'll have cameras in your living space, which will make it easier for everyone."

"How much of our living space?" Benton asks wearily.

"Kitchen, dining, family room, outdoor space. Don't worry, you'll have privacy in your bedrooms and bathrooms, and you'll each get your own bedroom. That's part of what's holding us up on filming. We need a space large to fit all of you."

"And all of us are... who, exactly?" Sloan asks.

Is he going to disclose?

Perry pauses, considering his options, then lists names. Benton's rigid demeanor softens, and his eyes grow large. These aren't b-list celebrities who are being cast for *Top of the World*. This show is the big time, and Benton knows it. We all do.

Eighteen

I arrive early to the office on Monday morning since my workload has essentially doubled. *Top of the World* needs loads of my attention, but I refuse to put the brakes on projects with the foundation. They're too important to me, especially the fundraiser we have coming up in the fall to help raise money for disabled children.

We're partnered with *Able to Rise*, an organization that teaches kids like my brother essential life skills, partners families with the resources they need, and they even have an incredible summer camp program Chandler adored while growing up. Mom met them through Chandler and quickly fell in love with their mission, helped them get partnered with The Laurence Foundation, and now, years later, we've become their main donor.

So this fundraiser? It has to go off without a hitch. There's too much riding on the line for it to fail. Not only does Laurence donate, but so do many of the generous patrons who attend the event.

Only a few minutes after settling in for the day, Lance Vale knocks on my glass door and lets himself into my office. "I thought I'd find you here bright and early," he says, eyeing the stack of papers on my desk. "You always were a hard worker."

My hands still on the keyboard as I offer him a bright smile. "Good morning, Mr. Vale. How are you? Anything I can help you with?"

"I'm doing well, Sybil," he says. "I want to see how *you* are doing?"

I don't know him well enough to tell him the truth, and it's not as if I can be completely honest with my boss. He's not my father, someone I told almost everything to. Dad and I were close. Sure, Vale has been around the company for years since he was the chief operations officer before stepping into this interim role, but he was Dad's business associate. He wasn't really a family friend.

Frankly, Vale lacks charisma, but he makes up for it with ambition. He'll do whatever it takes to get that CEO position, even if that cost includes buttering me up.

"I'm doing well," I answer carefully. "It's been busy, but I've got Laurence at the forefront of my mind."

Vale nods, silvery eyes assessing me. He's in his fifties, with graying hair to match those gray eyes. I've always found him a little unsettling. He's not a warm person, but he's done a good job since Dad died. The shareholders are happy, and the pressure for the board to promote him officially has been growing.

But with Conrad King's newest bombshell, our stocks are precarious again, and *Top of the World* needs to be flawless. Not only so Laurence can make our investment worth it, but that five percent Cooper owns is making people nervous.

"I'm glad to hear it's going well." Vale drums his fingertips on the top of my desk. "But I want you to report directly to me for the time being."

I swallow hard. I'm fully aware a lot of eyes in the company are currently turned in my direction, so I'm not surprised Vale wants to keep close tabs.

"We have a lot riding on your success," he confirms. "I so wish your father were here to see it. I know you'll succeed. He knew it, too."

Something about the compliment rings false.

I sit up taller. "Am I right to assume you don't just want reports on the foundation work, but you want me to share what's going on with Top of the World?"

His eyes flash with approval. "That's correct. Everything you're working on is important. You have a lot to juggle, my girl."

He says "my girl" like my father used to, like he thinks of me as a child looking for his guidance. It makes me instantly miss Dad and puts a sour taste in my mouth about Vale.

"I won't fail," I reply.

"Don't worry, I won't let you. Talk to HR about hiring an assistant. You're going to need help, and I expect you'll do whatever it takes. Do you understand?"

I run my hands across imaginary wrinkles in my skirt. "Yes, sir."

"Good." He knocks once on my desk as if to seal the deal. "Every Friday, I want a full report. Contact my admin to set up a standing fifteen-minute one-on-one meeting."

With that, he exits the office, closing the glass door behind him. It's not until he's completely removed from my eye-line that my muscles relax. Vale never made me nervous before. He wasn't someone I needed to worry about. My dad had my back, and I knew no matter what, I had a place at Laurence International.

Now? I'm not so sure.

Just because I don't need this job for money doesn't mean I don't want this career.

I love this job. This is my company, too.

My legacy.

As a massive conglomerate with holdings in many sectors, there are a lot of things I could do here, but the foundation work holds my heart. I don't see myself doing anything besides nonprofit work. Sure, I love interior design, but that's a hobby, and it doesn't fulfill me like this fulfills me. There are other ways to do it, of course, but The Laurence Foundation is mine.

Just then, Miriam Katz, my real boss and the current president of the foundation, barrels into my office like an angry Karen, ready to ask for the manager.

"What was *Lance Vale* doing in here?" she demands, spitting his name out like it's a curse word.

I sigh and lean into my chair. "He wants me to report to him now."

Which means he wants me to go above her.

She presses her hand to her heart in outrage, eyes going wide underneath her round spectacles. "That man! I *knew* he never liked me." She mutters a few Yiddish curse words and paces the length of my small office. Miriam isn't the type to sit down for long, even at her age. Not that I know her exact age. She treats it like a state secret, but she's got to be pushing seventy.

I shake my head. "He likes you fine, Miriam. He wants me to report to him because of the show I'm co-producing and the issue with the five percent stake in the company."

She knows all the drama, but she still turns on me with her hands on her hips and incredulous lines around her mouth. "As if you'd ever fail. You're the most capable employee I've managed in decades. That greedy little bastard is trying to get me to retire faster. Mark my words, he wants me out. He's never liked me, not since I told him off in 2003 for wearing too much cheap cologne and giving me a migraine."

I snort. I can't help it. Miriam Katz has been with the company for ages and has been talking about retiring for the better part of ten years. She's the type who will move somewhere glamorous, like Europe, instead of the typical Florida or Arizona like most retirees flock off to after leaving Manhattan.

"You've already told everyone you're leaving in the fall. I think he can wait a few months, Miriam."

Her white bob bounces as she shakes her head. "He better give you my job when I leave or I'm not going anywhere. I'll die in this office if I have to."

I stifle a laugh. As much as I'm gunning for her job, I love the woman and wouldn't mind working for her for many more years. But that's not what *she* wants. She's ready to retire.

"I don't think it works that way," I say. "You can't demand I get your job when you leave. You're not on the hiring board for higher-level positions."

"Well, it *should* work that way. Nobody can fill my shoes like you can."

She gives me a wink, and I return it with a smile.

This woman is incredible and has worked tirelessly to build The Laurence Foundation to what it is today. We provide millions of dollars to charity every year, providing a great tax write-off for Laurence International. This job is highly sought after since it pays like a regular corporate job, but the work is more rewarding. I'm not the only person in New York City who knows this work like the back of my hand. There are many qualified people who would kill for this chance.

But this is *Laurence* International. My last name. My legacy.

And I want it so badly I can taste it.

"We're both gunning for me to get the job," I assure her. "But either way, you will be able to retire in October as soon as our Able to Rise event wraps up. You have nothing to worry about."

She tuts to herself. "We'll have to make sure we do excellent work for the next five months, right? They'll have to hire you in my stead. We won't give them any excuse not to."

"They will."

She shakes her head. "I don't know. I don't like that Mr. Vale. I don't have a good feeling about this."

"Shh." I look at the door, grateful it's closed, but this is a busy office, and there are listening ears everywhere. "Keep your voice down, would you? He's your boss, too."

"No, *your father* was my boss. Vale is the interloper here by default."

"He's done a pretty good job, though. Most of the board has recommended him to be the next CEO hire. Mom is on the fence, but I think she's almost convinced."

"Your mom said it's better the devil you know than the devil you don't. I told her he's still the devil."

I bark out a laugh, then cover my mouth. "Don't say that."

She points at me. "He's missing a lot of the qualities your father had."

My heart sinks. As if my father was an angel? "My dad..."

My voice trails off, and my eyes burn. I don't know what to say, nor do I want to cry at work. Doesn't matter if I see Miriam as more than a mentor; it would be embarrassing and unprofessional to cry here. My office is like a fishbowl sometimes.

Miriam doesn't care. She comes around my desk and tugs me into her arms, hugging me tight. She feels small but strong in my arms, and yet she's the one who's holding me upright.

Grief is a sleeper-cell sometimes. I was good this morning. I've been busy and distracted. Maybe it's because the one-year anniversary of his death is coming up. That and having to talk to Vale about work when I should've been talking to my dad.

"Gregory was a good man," she insists. "He did some bad things and made mistakes. He had secrets. But he was still good, and don't you ever forget that, okay, honey?"

I nod and let go. She steps away with a tight smile. "And don't ask me to suck up to Vale. I've never done it before, and I'm not about to start now. As far as I'm concerned, when I retire in October, he can kiss my crusty-old ass on my way out the door."

I can't help but giggle-snort for the third time during our conversation. Her humor has a way of lessening the sting of sadness. God, I love this woman. I want to be just like Miriam Katz when I grow up.

NINETEEN

C ooper
        Past - Age 22

"As you know, we leave for grad school next week," Ethan remarks to me over lunch. "A lot is about to change." It's the end of the summer, and we're almost done with our last internship before returning to school to start the MBA program.

"Thank God. I can't stand to be around Dad for much longer." The man is the tyrant king of King Media, taking our company name way too literally. He's spent the last eight weeks "molding us" as he does every summer, treating us like we're incompetent minions instead of capable adults. Everyone who works for him experiences this to a degree, but it's so much worse for me and Ethan. We're our father's retirement plan, the future of his company, the ones who will continue his legacy—so we have to be perfect.

"Yeah, Dad's tough, but that's not what I wanted to talk about," Ethan says.

I take a huge bite out of my pastrami sandwich to keep my mouth full. I am pretty sure I know what Ethan is going to say next. I'm also pretty sure this sandwich is going to become as heavy as a fucking rock the second he does.

Ethan leans across the table, his lunch forgotten and an excited glint in his eyes. "Before we leave the city, I want to propose to Sybil."

Like I expected, my stomach hardens, and my mouth goes as dry as sandpaper. I wipe at my mouth with the napkin to cover my expression. My brother can't know what I'm really feeling, can't know my emotions this summer have been eating me alive.

"Okay." I feign enthusiasm. "That sounds great."

An engagement means a marriage. It means lifelong commitment. Before we know it, it will also mean a family.

Ethan and Sybil are going to have a whole life together. Their plans will finally come true, and I'm not the least bit surprised. But I am bothered... I kissed that girl in May, and we haven't talked about it since. Sybil made her choice, but that doesn't mean I haven't been going crazy for the last three months.

I set my remaining sandwich on my plate, lean back in my chair, and try to appear relaxed. Ethan literally looks like a kid in a candy store right now, and I don't blame him.

I don't know how I'm going to live like this. If anything, I'll have to remove myself from their lives, but how can I do that when I'm being forced to work for King Media or forgo my trust fund? I'd be crazy to walk away. As annoying as Dad is, I actually do like the work.

"So, I need your help." Ethan rubs his hands together.

I take a long draw from my water to buy time to think.

If I refuse to help him, he'll want to know why. If he suspects anything, I'll crack and tell him the truth. I can't do that to him. Sybil is madly in love with Ethan, not with me. Our kiss may have destroyed me, but it meant nothing to her.

Obviously, it's Ethan she wants, since she got back with him the very next day. I was her mistake that became her secret and her regret. Thank God we only kissed and didn't take it further, but it's enough of a slip up I can't tell Ethan about it. I have to protect him.

I give my brother the best grin I've got, like the expert faker I've become. "What do you need?"

"I want to throw a surprise going away party and use it as a front to ask her to marry me in front of our families. Can you help?"

It's easy to get the families to agree to come to Manhattan for a "surprise," because even though it comes from me, they all can guess what this is really about.

Ethan and I are living in our parents' Manhattan apartment since our father says we cannot buy our own places until we've earned it. That's fine with us. My brother and I have gotten a lot handed to us over the years, and we know how lucky we are. Besides, living in our family apartment overlooking Central Park isn't a hardship.

Except it has been for me lately when the Laurence home is only four blocks away. Having Sybil that close when I know what her lips taste like has made my life so much more miserable.

I've already decided what I'm going to do about it. When Ethan and I graduate from business school and sign our contracts with King Media, two things will finally happen. We'll give our lives to the company, and we'll get our trust funds. First thing I plan to do with my money is find a space far away from Ethan and Sybil.

Ethan's not going to like that, since we've already been eyeing a new construction building in midtown and planned to get penthouses next door to each other, but he'll just have to deal. He'll have a new wife to worry about, so it won't matter if I decide to live in another part of town.

It'll be for the best.

"I love what you've done with the remodel," Amelia Laurence remarks to my mother, the wineglass in her hand sweeping in an arc as she surveys the kitchen. "You've outdone yourself yet again, Victoria. You know, I really should get you and Sybil together sometime to work on a project. Maybe our new Manhattan house? You both have such an eye for interior design, and it would be fun to see what you could create together."

I turn to my mom and frown. "You redid the kitchen?"

It literally looks the exact same as it did last summer.

"The counters are different," Mom remarks, like it's obvious. "And the cabinets. Flooring is the same, though."

"Wasn't this all white before?"

Mom rolls her eyes playfully, and the women exchange amused glances. "Yes, it was white, but it wasn't a marble countertop. It was granite. I also refaced the cabinets and added new knobs."

Okay then...

"It's a good thing Ethan is marrying Sybil and not you, Cooper." Amelia laughs, her voice airy and warm, reminding me so much of her daughter that my chest aches. "Ethan notices these things, and they're so important to my girl."

I gulp down my wine. I highly doubt Ethan notices shit about interior design besides "looks good" and "looks bad", but she's right that Ethan and Sybil are meant to be together. He's the better choice.

He's about to prove it when he proposes to her in front of

the people she loves most. I can't think of a better way to propose to her. Sybil has always been and will always be a family-first girl.

"They're here!" Dad booms, practically sprinting into the kitchen with Gregory on his tail. I've never seen these men look so young and enthusiastic as they do right now. I imagine this is how they were in college when they met. "The doorman called to let us know they're in the building. They'll be up any second."

We hurry to the living room where Sybil's two little brothers wait and turn the lights off. A minute later, the sound of the front door unlocks, making this moment all too real.

Voices murmur in the hallway, and Sybil laughs freely at something Ethan says. Hearing her relaxed laugh is the confirmation I need that she's in the right place with the right person...

But I don't know if I can be here.

All summer I've been trying to talk myself out of my feelings, but there's no denying the truth. I'm head over heels for Sybil Laurence—so far gone I don't even recognize myself.

And there's nothing I'll ever be able to do about it.

Ethan flips on the lights as the happy couple enters the room.

"Surprise!" everyone yells in unison, and shock flits across Sybil's pretty face.

Dressed up from dinner, Ethan wears a crisp suit and tie, and Sybil's body is perfectly fitted into a velvety red dress. It complements her striking hair and hugs her curves in all the right places. She's breathtaking in a way that digs into my soul.

She turns to Ethan, and he's grinning openly. "But it's not my birthday..."

That's when Ethan drops to one knee.

And I watch, my smile fake, my stomach hard, and my

world turned upside down, as Ethan asks Sybil to be his wife. Her pretty cheeks flush, and her eyes fill with loving tears.

She looks so happy.

Her eyes dart away from my brother to all of us, sweeping across the people she cares about and brushing right past me— I'm insignificant in her decision—and they land on my brother. He tells her he will be the luckiest man alive if she'd become his wife, and it's the truth.

"I will," she whispers. "Yes."

He beams as he slips the diamond onto her left ring finger, then stands to pull her into an embrace. It's a three-carat solitaire on a gold band. Not too big and not too small. Perfect for our girl—*his* girl.

They kiss, and everyone cheers, especially her little brother Chandler, who whoops like his favorite baseball team won The World Series. I'm happy for them, I really am, but I'm miserable for myself. I need to get over her like I need oxygen, but somehow, I've forgotten how to breathe.

TWENTY

S ybil
     Present - Age 27

"Filming in NYC gives us a lot of opportunities, but it's also a city with limited square footage," Perry says. "Money talks, but there's only so much we can do with our budget."

Cooper and I exchange a skeptical glance. Sorry, but our companies have invested an insane amount of money in this venture. Budget shouldn't be an issue. Perry catches our shared look and backtracks. "It's enough money, don't get me wrong, but you've seen what we had to offer to get the talent on board. We're using most of our budget on them."

"Don't ask for more money," Cooper starts.

Perry holds up his hands. "I wouldn't dream of it."

Somehow, I doubt that.

We're in Cooper's office for a producers meeting, and I have to admit, being here feels odd, like walking onto hostile ground that once was home.

When Ethan and I dated, I came here often. Boy, have things changed. While the building is the same, Cooper and Ethan have moved to the highest floor. Soon Ethan will be the CEO and Cooper the COO, so it makes sense. But such proximity to their father and the other leaders of King Media makes everything feel much more real. Even though Ethan has softened over the years, Cooper has hardened. I can't help but wonder what their father thinks of them.

"We have enough money," Perry continues. "But we have to be smart about our next moves. Keep in mind that money in Hollywood goes fast."

"This isn't Hollywood," Cooper deadpans, and Perry shoots him an incredulous look.

"You know what I mean."

"Just tell us what you want," I say, and Perry offers me a cheeky smile that reminds me of his younger years, when he could catch girls with nothing more than a grin in their direction.

"Well, we need to find the perfect place to film *Top of the World*, and I'm asking for your help to make that happen."

"What do you have in mind?" I prod.

Perry straightens his spine, filling out his suit-jacket, as his gaze bounces between me and Cooper. "We need six bedrooms. We can get away with some of the contestants sharing bathrooms, but it's non-negotiable in their contracts that they get their own bedrooms. We have to film in the city, since that's also in the contract, besides a week-long trip we're going to take in July. The location is as important as the cast. It needs to be luxurious—the kind of place people only dream about."

Both men look at me, and I can actually feel the blood draining from my face.

"No," I state.

"The Laurence New York apartment would be perfect,"

Perry tries. "I don't know of anywhere bigger or nicer or more old-money New York than your family's place."

"*No* is a complete sentence."

"Could you at least talk to Amelia and see if she'd be open to it? It's only for three months."

Season *one* is only three months.

I shake my head.

Perry doesn't give up. "We'll move all the valuables and furniture into storage, dress it up for filming, do our thing and take really good care of it, and be out before you know it."

The problem?

Our home will be immortalized in film forever.

Not only that, but the thought of strangers infiltrating it makes me want to vomit. Sure, it's the perfect size, and it's beautiful. And sure, Mom and my brothers plan to spend most of the summer on Nantucket. I have my own SoHo loft apartment now, but that doesn't negate the fact that I don't want *Top of the World* filmed there.

Dad would've never agreed.

He's not here to say no, so I'll do it for him.

"I don't have a good reason to say no," I say firmly, annoyed that my voice cracks. "But if you must know, my father would've hated that, and I can't imagine doing this, even though he's gone."

Perry pats my knee, his eyes going soft. "I get it. Forget I asked, okay?" He continues to both Cooper and me. "We need to think of something. Do you have any connections for a similar filming location? We're already up against short notice if we want to film soon."

Considering we're contracted to film through the summer, he's right. We're running out of time.

"I don't know of anything, but I'll see what I can come up with." Am I being selfish? Maybe I should talk to my mom about using the house. Maybe I'm being overly protective of it. It's not like we spend a lot of time there like we used to.

Even thinking about it makes my eyes burn.

"We can use my place," Cooper interjects, and Perry and I both turn on him. He's sitting behind his desk while Perry and I are in the chairs across from him, looking the perfect picture of a Manhattan businessman, the midtown skyline silhouetted behind him.

"Your place is big enough?" Perry asks dubiously. "You have six bedrooms?"

"If we clear out the office, then yes, that would make six."

"How many bathrooms?"

"Three and a half."

It would work. Cooper's place is gorgeous. New, modern, and worth millions.

"Are you sure?" I can't imagine Cooper wanting to give up his space like that, especially when we all know I'm not willing to give up my family's place despite it sitting empty.

He gives me a steady look—one I can't dream of reading. "It's fine. I can find somewhere else for the summer. Besides, my place is more modern and fresher and will do well with the younger demographic we're after."

"Where will you stay?" Perry asks. "Next door with Ethan?"

Cooper barks out a laugh. "Fuck no. I'm not crashing with the newlyweds. Those two are like rabbits."

He runs a hand through his tousled hair, messing it up, and I can't help but wonder who he's been sleeping with lately. Just Roxanna? Anyone else? Maybe they're exclusive. But thinking of him having sex makes my nerves fire, and I hate myself for it. Since when did I care who Cooper sleeps with?

"I'll rent another apartment somewhere else in the building. There are some available. That will make it easy to move my stuff."

Perry's eyes light up. "Perfect! If you rent a place in the same building, we can use it as our crew headquarters."

"Now you're just being a dick," Coop growls.

"I'm being a show creator. Trust me, saving money now will come in handy when we need it later."

Cooper thinks it through. "Fine, whatever I've got to do for the show, I'm in. It's only three months, right? How bad can it be?"

I have a feeling he's going to live to regret those words, but I keep my mouth shut. Cooper's selflessness in this matter has not only solved a problem for *Top of the World*, but it's lifted an enormous weight off my shoulders. I sneak a thankful smile at my old friend, but he's too busy discussing the next steps with Perry.

"You know, you're going to have to run this by your building's board. Some buildings won't let us film. Of course, we'll have to pay a fee for this, and we have the budget. Do you think you can make it happen?"

Cooper smirks. "My brother and I own the largest units in the building and are quite chummy with the other residents. Just leave it to me."

I hope he can pull this off, so they don't end up asking for filming rights in my family home again. I don't know if I can take the pressure.

After we finish, Cooper walks us to the elevators to see us off. King Media has the top seventeen floors of one of midtown's nicest high-rises, and I won't be surprised if in a decade from now they're able to take over the entire fifty-story building. They've become an American media giant and the people who work here take their jobs very seriously. Of course they do. They work for Conrad King.

Cooper and Ethan are no different.

My opinion? Like your boss, and you'll work hard for them.

Conrad's style? Scare the shit out of your employees, and they'll be too afraid to make a mistake.

Despite my father's personal mishaps, *he* had respect from his employees because he led with kindness and enthusiasm. He was a true leader, and sometimes I have a hard time seeing what he saw in Conrad King. Those two got along for decades before their relationship imploded.

But that was Dad's fault.

The elevator dings, and I shake myself from my thoughts.

The doors slide open, and Conrad King steps out. My mood instantly sours.

"Perry. Sybil," he says in greeting. "It's good to see you with my son again. Reminds me of old times." His words are kind, but his tone is cold.

"Hello, Mr. King," I say. "If you'll excuse us, we are actually leaving now."

I make to step toward the elevator, but Conrad blocks my path.

"Nonsense. I want to hear how things are going."

My lips twitch. "Mr. Vale is seeing to my progress, and I work for him, not you. You're welcome to call him and ask about my progress, but it would probably be best if you asked Cooper, seeing as he's standing right here."

Cooper's mouth is a thin line, and his expression is unreadable.

Conrad laughs. "You're right. Lance will make sure everything goes exactly as it should. Pardon me for intruding, Sybil. I forget my place sometimes when it comes to your family, given all our *history*." He gives us a wink, pats Perry on the shoulder, and strides away.

I release a frustrated sigh. Every damn time I see that man, I can't help but feel completely unsettled. I can't trust him to be anything but self-serving.

"Goodbye," is all Cooper says before swinging around on his heels and heading to his office.

"Well, that was weird," Perry remarks, hitting the button for the elevator again, since that first one is long gone.

"Tell me about it," I gripe. King Media belongs in another time, a past life, and being back there feels like opening an old wound.

The elevator opens again, and this time it's blissfully empty, but it isn't until I've completely left the building that I can finally relax.

Twenty-One

C ooper
    Past - Age 22

"What about Christmas?" Amelia beams at the happy couple. "New York City is so beautiful during the holidays."

All of five minutes after they get engaged, and our mothers are already planning the wedding. That's just great. A long engagement would've been nice, but I guess we're ripping the Band-Aid off now.

"*This* Christmas?" Sybil releases an uncomfortable laugh. "That's a little fast, isn't it?"

"When you know, you know," her father booms. "In our day, people didn't need years to plan a wedding."

"This isn't your day; it's ours," Ethan says, squeezing his fiancée's hand, and I thank God Ethan is a logical man.

My brother and I are about to be at Harvard, and graduate school will take two years. That's the perfect length of time for their engagement. Sybil will have time to plan exactly what she wants.

"We're getting married after I finish grad school," Ethan confirms. "Sybil wants to have the wedding on Nantucket the summer after graduation."

Sybil as a bride comes to mind, her auburn hair down in loose waves white a white veil covering her face. My brother, removing that veil to kiss her. Our favorite place in the world becomes the backdrop to their new life together.

It's perfect, but it fucking hurts.

"At the new house?" Her mother frowns. "That could be a ways out."

Sybil shakes her head. "No, of course we want it at the King's place. That's how I've always imagined it."

The nostalgia alone will have everyone in tears.

"I'm thinking on the lawn at the edge of the bluff overlooking the ocean," she continues. "We'll get married at sunset and have a nighttime reception outside with big white tents and flowers everywhere."

"Hydrangeas, of course," Ethan says. "Your favorite."

She looks at him, her smile faltering. She loves hydrangeas as they remind her of her favorite place, but they're not her favorite flower.

"Yes, hydrangeas," she says. "And other flowers—"

"Magnolias," I can't stop myself from adding.

Everyone turns toward me, but I stare at Sybil, waiting for her to respond.

Her cheeks flush. "Uh, yes, magnolias." Then she clears her throat. "With graduate school, we want to wait for the wedding so we can plan every last detail."

She leans over to press a small kiss to Ethan's cheek, and her eyes flit to me again. It's only the second time she's looked my way since he slid that ring on her finger. I have a feeling she'll be looking at me less and less.

"Maybe we could do the wedding early next summer?" Amelia presses. "Why wait two years?"

"I don't want to be long distance with my husband. It's like you guys forget Ethan and I won't be in the same city."

The room falls silent, and I get the sense that we're missing something big here. I gaze around, looking for clues. The boys and I are on the couch, the parents spread throughout the armchairs, the newly engaged couple on the loveseat. We're supposed to be celebrating, not bickering over wedding dates.

Why are the parents rushing this?

"Long distance is nothing when you're in love," her father says. "And we have the resources to make sure you can get every weekend together. A Christmas wedding sounds delightful."

I gape at the man, honestly stunned he wants them to get married so quickly. Sybil looks my way again, and I swear this is a woman who wants to be rescued.

"Are you fucking kidding me?" I deadpan.

"What's wrong with Christmas?" Gregory shoots me an annoyed glance. He obviously thinks I should butt out. "There are so many venues we can choose from right here, and even if they're booked, we can pick a weekday."

I can't help it—I fucking laugh. Meanwhile, Sybil looks horrified, Ethan's jaw is set in an angry line, her little brothers are wide-eyed, and the parents are all chummy with the idea. It's fucking ridiculous.

"Why are you pushing for a shotgun wedding?" I demand.

No answer.

Why the hell isn't my brother speaking up?

"Cooper," my mother says, exasperated. "Please, let us handle this."

"This wedding isn't about you," my father adds.

I laugh again. "This wedding isn't about you, either. Don't push them to get married before they're ready. Two years isn't too long to be engaged, and this *isn't* a shotgun wedding. There's no need to rush, so leave them alone."

Mom looks at the rug as if it's the most fascinating thing she's ever seen. The three other parents exchange frustrated glances, and a sudden shock of fear jolts down my spine.

"There's something you're not telling us," I accuse. "What's going on?"

"We'll talk about this later," Mom says, her voice cracking as she waves her hand dismissively.

"Mom?" Ethan questions. "What's going on? What's wrong?"

It's about time he spoke up.

"Maybe we should tell them." Dad's eyes are pained as he takes Mom's hand. I don't think I've ever seen him wear this kind of broken expression before. It's as if his walls have shattered.

"Not today. Not now," Mom says.

Fuck this. If she doesn't want to make anyone uncomfortable, it's too late for that.

Next to me, Chandler groans. "Please tell us, Tori." He uses her nickname, which normally makes her heart melt, but she stiffens.

I grab Chandler's fisted hand and hold on tight. "You might as well spit it out, Mom. We're not leaving here with questions."

Her eyes bounce from person to person. She looks like a cornered animal. Her expression crumbles, and my heart crumbles with it. Fear claws up my throat, my mouth tasting of pennies.

"I'm so sorry, kids. I don't know how to tell you this…" She wipes a tear with shaky fingers. She shakes her head, like she can't say it, and looks to Dad for help.

He shifts in his seat, reaching across the armchair to take her hand, eyes turning to me and Ethan. "Your mother has stage four pancreatic cancer."

What?

No.

No. No. No. No.

My stomach churns violently as cold sweat breaks out on my forehead. The world turns as the denial echoes through my head.

This can't be happening.

Chandler is the first to speak. "What does that mean?"

It means the cancer is advanced, spreading, and in at least one vital organ. It means it's deadly. It means she probably won't survive this, and probably has limited time left. But I don't say those words, because I can't... not with this invisible thousand-pound rock on my chest.

I release Chandler's hand and sink into myself. "You'll fight it," I demand. "You'll beat it."

Mom shakes her head, and Dad cuts in. "We're looking into clinical trials. Anything we can do, we're going to do. We'll spare no expense."

"It's too advanced." Mom lets out a bitter laugh. "Money can't save me."

What the fuck?

She's already giving up?

Her eyes lock on mine. "I'm angry about this, too, but I can't change it."

She's right; it's not like this is her fault, and I can't be mad at her. It's the cancer I hate. How could this happen to her? Her lifestyle is so healthy. She doesn't even eat sugar, and she attends Pilates classes religiously.

"We'll have the wedding at Christmas," Ethan blurts. "Sooner, if you want. Thanksgiving, even. Or fall break." He turns on Sybil, panicked. "Fall break is in October, and we get an entire week off. We can make that work, can't we?"

Two months to put together a wedding is utterly ridiculous, and I expect her to say as much, but she forces a smile. "Of course. I've love autumn weddings. We'll do it here in the city."

The world is spinning. It wasn't supposed to happen this way. There was supposed to be time. Time for the wedding.

Time for Mom.

Ethan hugs Syb, and everyone smiles through their tears, as if the rushed wedding is going to make this okay, as if this is a streak of sunlight on a dark night. It's not. Mom will be gone soon. I understand why Ethan and Sybil want her at the wedding, but it's not going to save her, and saving her is what we should be focusing on.

"You said something about clinical trials?" I turn to Dad. "Can we please talk about that?"

Mom frowns, but Dad nods. How I wish she were nodding along with him.

"Mom, please."

She sighs. "I'll do one if I can get in one, but can we please talk about the wedding? I want to focus on some happy news today."

"Of course we can," Ethan chimes in, shooting me a glowering look, as if I'm somehow making this day worse for Mom.

Sorry, but I'm not putting my head in the sand and ignoring the shit littered around me.

Sybil's verdant gaze catches mine, and we stare at each other for a heartbeat. Can she see the heartbreak in my eyes? Does she know it's for more than just my mother? That I think about her all the time? That her kiss has stayed with me all summer? Has haunted my dreams?

She tears her gaze from mine, and I'm not even surprised. She's always the first to look away. That's okay—we're friends, and that's all we'll ever be. As much as the engagement hurts my heart, Mom's diagnosis hurts my soul. She's who I need to be concerned with right now. I get up and go to my mother, wrapping her tight in my arms and silently begging for her life to be spared.

TWENTY-TWO

S ybil
   Present - Age 27

Cooper hurriedly opens the door to his penthouse apartment, which got approved for filming as soon as Cooper shared how much money this would bring to the building.

"I need your help in here," he begs, ushering me inside. "I'm about two seconds away from losing it on this woman."

I take in the movers carrying furniture and the petite middle-aged blonde woman with a Karen-haircut bossing them around. She reminds me of an orchestra director with the way her hands fly as she speaks.

"Did they get all your stuff out first?" I whisper to Cooper.

"Thankfully, yes. Half of it's in storage and the other half one floor down in my temporary apartment. It's a mess and needs to get organized, so there's space for crew, but I'll deal with that later."

One of the movers turns in what is apparently the wrong

direction, considering the woman shrieks. "That piece is for the *upstairs* bedroom. You know there are two floors in this penthouse, right? Or do I need to give you a tour again?"

The burly man sets the nightstand on the hardwood with such a loud thud that I wince on impact. He makes eye contact with Cooper and stomps over to us. "I can't work with this woman. Either you get rid of her, or my crew is out of here."

"What did you say to them?" The woman strides over, hands in the air like she's a referee calling a play. "I'm the set-designer, and you're the mover. *I'm* your boss. You talk to me, not them."

The burly guy bugs his eyes out.

Cooper turns on the woman. "You know we're the producers on this show, right? So, he may work for you, but you work for us."

She tuts. "I work for Perry. Where is he? He should be here. I'm sure you're wonderful, but you don't have the experience Perry does."

"Perry had a conflict," Cooper growls. "As I've already told you, this is *my* home you're standing in."

"Right now, this is *my* set."

"It's only a set because I'm generously allowing it to be a set. And as my home, I say who gets to be here. You're no longer welcome, so leave."

I blink, shocked at how quickly this escalated.

She steps back, her manicured hand flying to her mouth. "Do you know who I am?"

"Do I *care* who you are?" Cooper snorts. "The fuck not."

She shakes her head, holding up a single finger. "I have more experience on set in this finger than you do in your entire body."

Okay, this has gone on long enough. "I think what Cooper was trying to say is you need to work with the movers instead of being cruel. We're all professionals, and if we're willing to act like it, then—"

She holds her hand to my face, her manicured finger practically on my lips, and I jerk away from pure shock.

"Hush. Nobody was talking to you," she says, and I blink at her.

Coop's shoulders stiffen, and he steps in front of me, knocking her hand from my face with his body. "Clearly you don't know who the fuck *I* am." His voice is so low it's almost criminal. "I'm Cooper *King,* the next COO of King Media, and this is *my* house you're disrespecting me and Sybil *Laurence* in, as in *Laurence International* and the other company funding this project."

As he speaks, her eyes go round, and her face turns red. Today is not her day. I'd feel bad if she hadn't just shushed me like I'm a toddler.

Cooper continues, pointing to the door. "I don't care how many years you've been in this business. You're unprofessional and rude... and you're fired."

Her mouth pops open. "I-I'm sorry... I didn't know."

"Get. Out."

She practically sprints from the apartment, muttering angry nonsense under her breath as she goes.

Cooper's shoulders relax as he turns to me. "You okay, Valentine?"

I don't have it in me to correct him. "I'm fine, but now we don't have a set-dresser, and we're running out of time to hire a new one."

"We don't need a new set-dresser. You can do it."

I scoff. "I don't know anything about set design."

He studies me with furrowed brows, and for just a moment, I feel like he's letting me back in, like we're mending something between us I thought would be broken forever. "How hard can it be? This isn't a sci-fi film—this is a reality television show. Make it look nice, and Perry can tell us if something needs to change."

I fold my arms over my chest, noticing the way his gaze intensely tracks my movements. It sends a wave of heat through my body, but I don't let myself think about that for too long. "I'm pretty sure you have offended an entire profession."

"You're good with design. Help these guys place all the rugs and furniture where you think they should go. Plus, there's Google." He gives me a wink, and I get a glimpse of the old Cooper, the one who had a knack for bringing levity to a tense situation. My heart twists with longing for our old friendship.

"Yeah, I guess there's always Google." I elbow him playfully, and he smiles.

"Are we good?" the large burly man interrupts, raising a brow. His hands rest on his hips, and the back brace fastened around his stomach tells me he means business.

"Can your crew take ten?" I ask. "I need to walk through the space and look at what I'm working with."

He nods. "Sure thing, boss. I'm just relieved the other lady is gone."

The crew waits in Cooper's kitchen, raiding the last contents of his fridge and pantry that haven't been cleared at Cooper's insistence.

I stride from room to room and up the stairs, taking frantic notes as I go. There are two bedrooms upstairs with a shared bath, and then downstairs there's the primary bedroom with its own bath, the guest room with its own bath, and the office. The tricky part is the office-bedroom doesn't have a bathroom. There's a half-bath in the nearby hallway, but whoever gets that room will have to use the shower upstairs or share with someone else on the main floor. It's not ideal, but it works, and it fulfills our contractual obligations.

I turn to Cooper. "What rooms are going to whom? That's going to help me design this thing."

"Your hockey player gets the shitty office-bedroom, if that's what you're asking."

"He's not *my* hockey player."

"Not anymore." His eyes smolder, and I'm suddenly aware we're alone. I clear my throat and walk away, heading to the main living room where all the rugs and furniture are waiting to be placed.

I can do this.

An hour later, we've successfully placed all the furniture and rugs in what I hope are the correct spots. There are odds and ends to sort through in the boxes, things like wall art and lamps, dishes and toiletries, but the movers don't need to be here for that. The sunset is fading into frothy swaths of pink over the Manhattan skyline, and it's obvious they're ready to head out.

"Thanks for everything, guys," I gush to the four of them as they wipe sweat from their foreheads.

"Of course. Thanks for not treating us like shit."

Cooper gives them generous cash tips, and then it's the two of us in this quiet space.

It's large in here, modern and beautiful, but I turn to the boxes of *stuff* and cringe. What a long day this is turning into.

"Where is Perry?" I ask Cooper. "I thought he was coming today."

"I didn't want to freak you out, but he's actually at the hospital. One of his sisters is having an issue. I don't really know what. He didn't say."

My heart drops. "Did he say which sister?" I don't know them super well. They're a lot younger than us. Last summer when they came to our home for dinner, they were in high school, glued to their phones or each other.

Cooper shrugs. "He didn't."

We fall silent, the space between us a wide chasm made even wider by reminders of hospitals. When his mom died, we lost so much. Then he lost his leg... Well, there's no returning from that. Sometimes I wonder if he blames me. I was there. It was my dad's fault. He probably hates to even look at me.

"How about we take a break?" He strides to the living room with its new leather couches and sits. "I'm going to turn on the TV, but you pick whatever you want, and I'll order us some food."

My stomach growls at the mention of food. I've been so busy today I haven't eaten since lunch. I peer over at the clock. It's 8:00 pm. I need to eat.

"Yes, to the food, but we don't have time for a break. Perry needs the set dressed by the end of the night."

"We both need a break." He points to his right pant leg. "At least I do. I've been standing for too long."

My cheeks burn, guilt instantly rising. "Shit, sorry."

He lets out a groan. "Don't feel sorry for me. That's not why I said something. I just think we should take a break, okay? Rest for thirty minutes to an hour, and then we can tackle these boxes."

He doesn't look at me when he sets the remote on the coach next to him and pulls out his phone, opening a delivery app.

I awkwardly sit next to him, grabbing the remote, careful to keep plenty of space between us. "I'll find us something to watch if you promise not to veto all of my choices."

He gives me a sidelong look. "Are you hangry? You seem hangry."

Immediately, I'm annoyed, and then realize my emotions have proved his point, so I laugh. "Guess I am."

"What sounds good?" He taps away on his phone. "Is Mexican still your favorite? I know you like Indian, and there's a good one nearby."

"Either sound amazing."

He looks at me for a long moment. "We need tacos."

He's right. An hour later, I'm totally re-energized thanks to crispy chips, homemade salsa, and the best greasy tacos I've had in a long time. I barely even paid attention to the comedy I turned on since I was too enamored by the food. God bless this city.

We clean up, and I start going through the boxes, immediately growing overwhelmed. It's going to be a long night.

"I can help, you know." Cooper stands over me. "Kneeling might be a little tricky, but I can take things where you tell me to."

I peer up at him. "Of course, Cooper." I don't know what to say to make him feel better. This is all so fresh. It hasn't even been a year since everything happened.

"Three weeks until the one-year anniversary of the boating accident," he says. "How do you feel about that?"

The grief comes at me like a rolling wave, and I turn away, busying myself with the box. "I feel... I don't know. Sad. Angry. Numb. Part of me has come to peace with it and part of me never will."

"Same," he mutters. I hand him a stack of towels and tell him to take them to the upstairs bathroom.

Maybe this is a truce. Maybe we're becoming friends again. I don't know, and I'm too scared to ask. I'm afraid the answer isn't going to be something I can numb out like I do all my other feelings.

Twenty-Three

C ooper
      Past - Age 22

I thought watching Sybil marry Ethan would be the hardest thing I'd witness in my lifetime.

I was wrong.

There's no way anything could be more painful than witnessing my mother wither away to skin and bones in a matter of weeks, my father scramble and fail to find a treatment, and my brother fixate on his studies to avoid reality.

Hardest of all, is staring at Mom's casket minutes before it lowers into the cold, hard earth, knowing her body is inside, but *she's* gone. She didn't believe in an afterlife, and I don't know if I believe in one, either, but I know this sinking feeling in my chest will live with me forever. There's nothing I can do or say or will into existence to reverse what has happened.

Instead of a wedding, we got a funeral, and instead of life, Mom got death.

It's not fair.

My gaze locks on the white roses as family and friends place them on top of the casket—a stark contrast of white against a black day. Dad has finished his goodbye. Now it's our turn. It feels like everyone's eyes are on us as Ethan and I place the final two roses.

Ethan whispers something under his breath. I only catch the word "sorry" before he steps away.

"I love you, Mom," I say, my voice hoarse.

Those four words are all I can manage. I took so much for granted, living a life without loss or hardship. Mom created magic for me and Ethan. Now, there's nobody here to make magic for us. We've been adults for four years now, but nothing could've prepared me for losing Mom.

A final prayer is offered. Dad insisted on having a Catholic priest here, even though we never went to church. Maybe he finds comfort in it, but I don't. We're told we can stay to watch the casket lower into the ground, but most families choose to leave before that happens.

Dad says we're leaving, and he's right; I can't do this anymore. The hourlong drive to the luncheon is brutally silent and lacking in tears. I rub my forehead, a dull headache pulsing behind my temples, as though every ounce of energy has been stolen from me. I know I'm not the only one---we're all emotionally spent at this point. The luncheon is being held at the Laurence's Manhattan apartment, which feels wrong somehow. Mom loved to entertain, and being Mom, she planned the whole thing.

I want the hell out of this city, but where would I go? The Nantucket house is tainted with her death, too.

Just get through today, get back to school, and finish the semester.

Not that I give a shit about school right now, but when I

asked Dad if I could take a leave of absence, he wouldn't hear it. He said life must go on, and quitting school would only disappoint Mom.

But Mom isn't here, and that's the fucking point.

"I want you to be extra cordial today," our father says to us like we're at work, about to give a presentation. His posture is rigid as he looks me and my brother over. "No hiding. I mean it. You're grown men, and you'll need to act like it. Do it for your mother's sake."

"I don't think she cares how we act anymore," I mutter.

Ethan's mouth thins as he glares at our father. "Why wouldn't I be cordial?"

They share a charged look—one I can't read. That's not like them. There's something going on they're not telling me about, a secret context growing underneath the moment, but I'm too exhausted to root it out.

"Don't start with me, Ethan." Conrad sighs. "We've already discussed it, and now is not the time. I'll deal with it when I'm ready."

"What are you two on about?" Do I even care? My grief certainly doesn't, but my curiosity says otherwise.

"None of your business," Dad replies, and Ethan laughs bitterly but doesn't say anything.

It pisses me off.

Maybe I shouldn't be angry at the only family I have on the day of my mother's funeral, but this is bullshit. I'm sick of being the third wheel.

"Tell me," I demand, looking at Ethan this time. We don't keep secrets; he knows that.

"Except for when we do," a little voice in my mind whispers.

"I'll tell you later," Ethan mutters.

"Ethan," our father says sternly, "we talked about this. Let *me* handle it."

The car stops in front of the Laurence's historic building, and Ethan tears out of it, leaving the door wide open as he stomps away. I jump out after him, and my father is quick on my heels. He grabs my bicep, stopping me.

"Let it go, Cooper," he demands. "This is not the time for drama."

I turn on him, anger rushing through my veins. "Last I checked, I was part of this family."

"I'm telling you to let this one go."

"Or what?" I growl.

He pauses, taking me in, then finally nods. "Later." He suddenly looks so old and defeated, I almost don't recognize him. "Trust me on this, Coop. Not today. Okay? Not. This. Day."

He drops my arm and heads inside.

I want to be angry, his words taking me right back to the day we got Mom's cancer diagnosis that they were clearly trying to keep from us, but then I take a breath and remember Mom. She wouldn't want us fighting at her wake.

The next hour goes exactly as expected. The caterers serve a light buffet lunch and drinks, and the people closest to Mom mingle and mourn. It's a sea of black dresses and suits. Sybil is glued to Ethan's side, so I leave them be, though I can't help but notice the far-off angry sheen in his eyes.

I end up in my usual spot between Sybil's brothers. They're good kids. Talking to them helps keep my mind busy. Hayes is fifteen and going into high school, and the kid is athletic as hell, so he's got big plans for varsity sports.

Chandler is eighteen and got admitted into a collegiate professional development program for kids with cognitive disabilities. His excitement is as endearing as it is infectious. I love this kid—I wish I could be that excited about anything in my life.

A raised voice catches my attention, and I'm shaken from my haze.

This is not a voice I'm used to hearing in any other way but calm and collected. It's not my father's voice. It's not Ethan.

It's Gregory Laurence. My gaze shoots across the room to where Sybil and Ethan stand next to Sybil's father. She drops Ethan's hand and recoils, her face going white.

Hayes and I clock the incident at the same time.

Something is very, very wrong.

Twenty-Four

C ooper
  Past - Age 22

"Hey, I could play some video games right about now," I say to Hayes. "Can you guys get it started? Maybe GTA? I'll be up in a minute."

Hayes twists his mouth in frustration before agreeing, leading Chandler away. I set my plate of unfinished appetizers on the coffee table and stride from the living room.

"You don't know what you're talking about," Sybil says to my brother. She turns to her father. "Say it isn't true."

If horrified and heartbroken at the same time had a look, it would be the expression on Sybil's face. This is worse than when Ethan broke up with her. This is worse than I've ever seen.

The silence she's met with is damning.

My father appears behind them, his anger palpable. "This is not the time nor the place to have this conversation."

"What's going on?" I ask, and they all turn on me, then look away. Damn it, I'm tired of feeling an inch tall around them.

"Daddy, tell them it's not true," Sybil presses, her pretty eyes filling with tears.

Gregory Laurence, a man I have viewed as a second father, looks like he's a rat caught in a trap. His mouth is grim, and his eyes shift. Then he leans on his heels and lets out a resolved breath. "I'm sorry. It's true. I... I loved her, and she—"

"Don't," Ethan growls at Gregory, pure venom in his gaze.

"And she loved me," he finishes.

He loved who? Who loves him? What is he—?

Realization hits like a slap to the face.

He loved her, and she loved him.

"How dare you." My father's voice is low and guttural. I've never heard this tone directed at his best friend. The two face off like they're about to start throwing punches, their shoulders tense and faces purple.

Sybil turns away, catching my expression.

"Is this about my mother?" I ask, pleading with her to confirm.

Her voice is soft and shattering. "They were having an affair."

My stomach curdles, and I don't want to believe it. "They... as in my mom and your dad?"

Nobody answers, and the world stops turning. I turn to Gregory. He's the one with the answers now. "Were you having an affair with my mother?"

He finally gives me the time of day, looking at me like he's never looked at me before—like I'm some idiot kid bothering him and not someone who grew up with him as a second father figure. This is not the man I know. This is an adulterer, and one who doesn't even regret his actions.

"Like I said, I loved her, and she loved me. Is that what you want to hear, Cooper? Then hear it. It's true. Your mother and I had something special."

Acid builds on the back of my tongue, my stomach roiling with upset. I whip toward Ethan. "You knew and didn't tell me?"

"I barely found out myself. I overhead him talking to Vale about it at the viewing last night. I didn't want to believe it, but Dad told me to drop it, that we needed to honor Mom's memory and deal with this later."

I look over at my father, who is standing there, his mind who knows where. *Shit.*

"You need to leave." Ethan turns on Gregory.

He laughs. "This is my house."

"I don't fucking care. Be somewhere else."

I glance at Dad, and that far-away mask disappears. Fury twists his features, reddens his neck, and sharpens his jaw. He loved Mom more than anything. It's unbelievable she'd ever do this, but why would Gregory lie? He doesn't gain anything by admitting this *at her wake.*

I close my eyes, picturing Mom over the last few months. She left this earth with such courage, and the whole time she was a lying coward, having an affair with her husband's best friend—a man married to *her* best friend.

It's sick. Imagining them together makes me gag. I step back from the group, pointing at the only person left alive I can blame. "You heard Ethan," I seethe. "Leave."

Gregory shakes his head. "I have as much a right to grieve her as anyone else. Our relationship wasn't some torrid affair. I don't conduct myself like you do with women."

My vision goes fucking red, and I swing without thinking, punching the asshole right in his smug face. His nose cracks, and he stumbles away, glaring at me but not fighting back like I wish he would. Blood pours from his nose, staining his white shirt.

I don't regret it...

Until I see the tears staining Sybil's cheeks. Ethan holds her as she gives me a sorrowful look, the trust in her eyes now gone.

So much innocence lost.

Gregory-fucking-Laurence took that innocence, and I want to beat him to a bloody pulp. But I can't, so I turn away.

I make it a single step before I freeze. Amelia Laurence stands behind me, her eyes huge. She's staring at her husband like she doesn't know him.

Then Amelia Laurence, always the cool, calm, and collected leader of the Laurence family, turns on her heel and runs from the room. Her daughter rips away from Ethan and rushes after her.

Guilt creeps in when I think of the torch I've been carrying for my bother's girl and the kiss we shared. Would I have been willing to start an affair with Sybil? I want to say I would never do that to my brother, but the truth is... I might not be a good person. I might take the chance if it presented itself. At some point, my resolve to hold myself back from Sybil might snap.

It's a cold, hard, bitter truth.

Crack!

Gregory goes down hard, and my father stands over him, rubbing his fist. The entire party has gone silent, literally *everyone* a witness to Gregory on the ground with blood all over his face and clothes. My hit may not have laid the man flat out, but my father's punch sure as hell did.

Dad's voice is frighteningly calm when he leans over his best friend of over thirty years. "You and I are done."

TWENTY-FIVE

S ybil
     Present - Age 27

I leave my office after lunch to see how things are going on set. The doorman recognizes me by now, which is oddly relieving. I used to visit Ethan and Cooper without having to check in with their doorman. I was practically a member of the family. Now they're in a new building, separate apartments, and everything has changed.

When I head up, Coop's apartment is busy again. Perry is there with a camera crew and assistants, and Cooper intercepts me out the door.

"Fair warning, if you get in the shot, they'll castrate you."

I chuckle. "Don't think they're getting anywhere near my vagina."

He raises a brow. "You know what I mean."

"Yeah, yeah."

We shuffle inside, and as the camera pans our way, Cooper

grabs my hand and tugs me into the nearby office turned bedroom. "We're safer in here," he says, closing us inside.

I stand by the window, looking at the city streets and imagining what's happening with all the tiny specs below. People watching is one of my favorite things about living in this city. Up close or far away, there's always somebody doing something interesting.

I turn to find Cooper staring. I expect him to break eye contact, but he doesn't. He studies me like he can't figure me out.

I clear my throat. "What are they doing today, exactly?"

"They're setting up the camera angles and lighting. Everything needs to be ready before the talent arrives."

"Well, I'm exhausted already," I joke, but he doesn't play along.

"You want this to be a success so you can get the five percent, don't you?"

Why did he have to bring that up? Our friendly moment bursts like a bubble in the wind.

"Yes," I say, voice clipped. "I have a lot riding on Top of the World, but I still don't understand why you're so on board. I'd think you'd want us to fail, so you'd get to keep your little percentage of power."

Cooper continues to stare, and I wish I could read the hell that's going on inside that pretty head of his. To know what he's *really* thinking, not what he believes I want to hear.

"Helping Perry is important to me."

"Really? As I recall, you guys got into a fight last summer when we were all at that dance club in Nantucket."

I remember it as if it were yesterday. Perry got drunk and hit on Arden, getting handsy while they were dancing. Ethan lost his shit, and Cooper got in the middle of it. I thought that fight might have been the end of their friendship, but apparently, I was wrong.

"Perry was an asshat, but he apologized to Arden. Ethan, too."

"Ethan forgave him? Just like that?"

I find that hard to believe. Ethan is insanely protective of Arden.

Cooper shrugs. "I don't know. Not my problem. Ethan's friendship with Perry is not the same as my friendship with Perry. Perry has never betrayed me."

Knife? Meet my heart. And twist.

"Yeah," I whisper. "He's... been great to you."

Even if he can be a jerk. Nobody here is perfect. Me, least of all.

"Anyway," Cooper continues, "our deal wasn't only about funding; it was about making sure the show is successful. A flop this expensive will ruin Perry's career. We figured having more money and more people gunning for success would be a good thing."

He says this with utter conviction, but I feel like there's something more he's not saying. My gut is screaming to dig for more, to ask questions and demand answers. But I have no right to push him, not when I haven't been there for him. I'm probably the shittiest friend he's ever had.

And being around him this much lately? It's killing me to know how badly I hurt someone I once considered my best friend.

"I want our friendship back," I blurt, and instantly regret it when his brows furrow.

Too soon.

And finally—painfully—he breaks eye contact.

"Maybe we should get back out there," he mutters.

I deflate, and tears burn my eyes. "Sure."

I move to walk past him, and he catches my arm, pulling me against his chest and wrapping me in a tight hug. It's familiar and wonderful and immediately makes me sob. I shake against his hard body as he holds me tight, the tears pouring out of my eyes a firehose. I'm not normally such a baby, but I can't help it. I need this hug so fucking bad.

"I'm so sorry for leaving you," I blabber into his broad chest, comforted by the warmth of his hard muscles and the beating of his steady heart. "I didn't know what else to do. I didn't know how else to cope. I fucked up. I'm so sorry."

Cooper holds me, letting me cry. It's not fair he's the one consoling me when he's the one who got hurt.

We've both been through so much. We're collateral damage—the wreck left behind in the wake of our family's life-altering mistakes. And yet, that doesn't excuse how I treated him when he needed me most. I added to that damage, but I only did it because I didn't know how to heal. I'm still healing, but I realize what a terrible person I've been.

I want to be better. For myself. For him. For everyone.

Cooper doesn't forgive me—he doesn't say it's okay or offer any words at all. But he does hold me, and I really need to be held right now, so I can't be anything other than grateful. At least there's something left between us that isn't completely broken.

Twenty-Six

C ooper
      Past - Age 22

I stare at my phone, dead-eyed while trying to read the message from my professor about my midterm. I fucked it up, and he's going to let me retake it. I should be happy, but I don't feel anything other than numb indifference. This year has been the worst of my life, and this semester has been hell on earth.

We took a week off in October when Mom died, and then immediately returned to Boston. It was fucked up, but Dad was adamant we do not wallow. That was the term he used. Mom made us promise to stick by our father before she passed. Apparently, we're only allowed to grieve when it's not interfering with family plans.

The phone lights with a call from Sybil, and I'm momentarily taken aback. We're all products of our generation, texting more often than not, so I rarely get calls without a text first. That said, since things with Ethan went long distance, she's been video-calling more and more. Sometimes she calls me because Ethan sucks at answering.

"Sybil. Hi. How are you? Are you okay?" I clock this is a voice call. "Do you want to video?"

"Not today." She sighs, sounding so defeated I want to reach through the phone and give her a big hug.

Her well-being is front and center in my mind lately. With the drama between our parents over the last month, things have been awful for everybody.

"Are you with Ethan?" she asks, and I hate that her voice sounds so guarded. My hackles instantly rise.

"He's at the library with our study group. What's going on?"

I don't blame Ethan for being at the library every waking moment we're not in class. That's how he copes. When he's upset, he works. It's a trait he got from our father and one I don't think anyone will ever break him of, not even Sybil.

Sybil sighs. "I feel so alone."

Yeah. I know exactly how she feels. "You're not alone. He's grieving. And... you have me."

We've talked about this extensively since the funeral. We don't want everything going on with our parents to ruin our friendship or their engagement.

"He's too busy with his MBA, yet you're talking to me and you're in the same program. How is that okay?"

"Well, he does get better grades than I do," I joke. She doesn't take the bait, and I let out a sigh. "He's stuck in denial. We can't put a timeline on his grief. You need to keep being patient."

"I know," she whispers. "But that doesn't negate the fact that my fiancé hasn't been available to me on any level, not physically and not emotionally. I've got nothing. I was prepared for a long-distance relationship, but I wasn't prepared to be iced out."

I swallow hard. Sybil deserves better—that's what I should say. But this is Ethan. My twin and built-in best friend for life. His heart is shut off right now, but it's a result of our mom's death and the affair, not because of Sybil.

"I'll talk to him," I try. "He'll come around soon."

She's quiet on the other end for a long minute, and I lie back in my bed, staring at my ceiling and not wanting her to end the call. I wish we could talk about normal things again. Every time we talk, it's about our parents or my brother. It's never about us, and it's never fun. Every time I ask her how she's doing, she tells me she's okay, which means she's lying. I should know, considering I do the same thing.

I'm never okay these days.

"I guess if I'm being completely honest with myself, I know it won't matter. I already know the truth about what I want," she says.

My heartbeat speeds. "What are you saying?"

"I'm saying you should plan to be there for your brother. He's going to need you."

Panic slides up my throat, rendering me breathless. I cried the day Mom died, and I haven't cried since. I think those floodgates are threatening to open up. I wish I could see Sybil's face. She can't really mean this. She loves Ethan more than anyone. And Ethan? He's in pain. He can't lose her, too.

I pull the phone away from my ear and immediately click the video-call button.

"I don't want to see you right now," she complains. "I'm all blotchy."

"Too bad. I need to see your face for what you're about to say, or I swear to God, I won't believe it."

Her beautiful face fills my screen. She smiles softly, but there's deep sadness behind her soulful gaze.

"What are you doing?" I ask slowly. "Please don't tell me

you're doing what I think you're doing. The timing couldn't be worse."

She peers into the distance, unable to meet my eyes. "I'm a shitty person; I know that." Her voice cracks and tears spring, slipping down the sides of her pale cheeks.

"You're not a shitty person, no matter what decision you make." She needs to know I'll *never* think that of her. "You've been through a lot. We all have. But we don't need to go through any more big changes right now. I don't think you want to do what you're going to do."

She finally looks at me. "I've been going to therapy," she says. "It's really helping. Mom got us all going. It was one of the conditions she set for Dad. He wants to stay together, and she's giving their marriage another shot."

My stomach clenches, and I sit on the edge of the bed, suddenly filled with the desire to move. Run. Get out of my own damn skin. "Of course he does." My voice sounds bitter. Angry. "His mistress is dead, so it makes it easy for him to choose his wife. How very convenient."

"Don't do that," she pleads, and I stop myself from saying more. "But... I think you guys should go to therapy, too. Grief is so hard to handle, and it's been really nice to have an unbiased professional to talk to about everything."

"My father doesn't believe in therapists," I reply bitterly. "He says they mess with your head and get into your business."

When we returned to school, the college tried to set us up with grief counselors, but Dad forbade it. We could've gone anyway, but neither Ethan nor I had any desire to anger our father.

"That's kind of the point." She rolls her eyes. "Your head is already messed up, so why not let someone else in there to see if they can help?"

"Sign me up," I deadpan.

She smiles and for a moment it feels like everything is going to be okay, but I know *okay* is a very unlikely end to this situation.

"So what are you going to do, Syb?" I question, staring her dead in the eyes through this puny little screen.

"I've already made my decision. I know it's the right thing, as hard as it is to let go sometimes." She pauses, but only briefly. "I'm breaking up with Ethan."

I have no words.

Part of me is elated she'll be single, but that's the fucked-up, shit-for-brains side to myself I won't entertain. Most of me is heartbroken for my brother. This is going to wreck him.

"I really think you should hold off. It's too soon to make a rash decision. Wait until Christmas break, after you've had time together again, and Ethan isn't so focused on classes."

We're almost to the holidays. A few more weeks, and she can be with him in person. Mend things. Or end things. At least there will be more time for Ethan to get himself together. I'll talk to him. Tell him he has to change or else she's going to leave him. Make sure he does right by her.

She shakes her head. "Christmas is not going to change my mind. If anything, the holidays will make it more painful. I know this is heartbreaking. My heart is shattered too even though I'm the one doing the breaking, but I really feel this is the right decision for both me and Ethan. It's necessary."

"Why?" I demand. "Why the fuck would it be necessary?"

"Sometimes you have to break things before you can put them back together."

I shake my head. "That sounds like some bullshit line your therapist fed you."

She goes pink, but she also glares at me, and I know I'm right.

"If Ethan and I were strong enough to get through this, do you really believe you and I would've kissed—"

"Stop," I cut her off. "That was one mistake during your breakup, and we both moved on from it. You can't count that against your many years of loving Ethan."

She's silent, and I wonder what she's thinking. Did that kiss mean more than she let on? Does she think about it like I think about it?

"But it happened. It meant something. It didn't mean you and I are meant to be together, but it meant that me and Ethan aren't. I can't keep pretending like Ethan and I are some perfect couple anymore."

"It was one kiss," I insist. "One time. One mistake. One stupid moment when you were at your lowest, and I was trying to make you feel better. It clearly didn't mean *something,* since you went back to Ethan the next fucking day. So don't blame that and don't blame me for your relationship not being perfect, because guess what? From the outside, it looks pretty fucking amazing to me."

"I'm not blaming you. I'm blaming me. And I'm blaming Ethan for not showing up for me or even answering my calls."

"He lost our mother," I grind out. This one—this is the one that will finally get through to her. "He can't lose you, too."

She goes quiet for a long moment, hopefully considering my words, and I can't help but wonder if Ethan would fight for his relationship the way I'm fighting for it.

"I get where you're coming from, but Ethan's already lost me. The longer I wait, the harder it'll be. Ultimately, I need to choose my family right now. They don't want me with Ethan anymore, but they're willing to support me if he's willing to love me." She chokes on a sob, her anger transforming to deep sadness so fast it's like whiplash. "I'm sorry, but I don't think he does. I think it may have happened a long time ago, but it's taken the last three months of hell for me to admit it to myself. Did he care when we canceled the October wedding? No. He only wanted that wedding early for his mom, not for me, not for us. And now that everything has happened—"

"You've decided you can't be attached to someone with the last name King." It was the wrong thing to say, and I immediately want to take it back. "*I* can't lose you," I add, voice cracking into a great chasm.

Her tears fall freely, and pain racks my chest. I want to scream. But I can't. I have to sit here and wait and know that losing her is exactly what's about to happen. We're going to have to pick sides. She's going to choose her family, and I'm going to choose mine.

She wipes the tears, and a calm sense of finality falls over her. "I'm only telling you because Ethan will need you. This conversation was meant to warn you, nothing else. You won't change my mind."

"It's like that, then?" My voice is as cold as ice. It has to be. The pain is too thick otherwise.

"I'm sorry, but it's time to move on."

"From Ethan? Or from me?"

She stares at me for a long second, her features hardening.

"From both of you. I'm sorry, Cooper. I really am."

She doesn't sound sorry. She doesn't even sound broken anymore.

How can she be so sure about something like this?

"Yeah, I'm sorry, too," I finish coldly.

"Goodbye, Cooper."

I stare at her for a second longer, and then she hangs up. There's no goodbye from me—there can't be when it comes to this girl. I love her too much to treat her the way she has treated me. There's only silence, a blank phone screen, and the cruel realization that I've lost her.

PART TWO

"The evil that men do lives after them;
The good is oft interred with their bones."

William Shakespeare's Julius Caesar

Twenty-Seven

S ybil
    Present - Age 27

Time flies, and before I know it, it's the first day of filming, and I'm a nervous wreck. Benton calls me early, asking if he's doing the right thing.

"Think of your games," I say, knowing I have to pep-talk the shit out of him so we can both get through this day unscathed. "Do you get nervous for those?"

"Sometimes."

"How do you get past that?"

"I don't let it get to me. I know how to handle myself. I've trained. I know I'm one of the best. I'm prepared. Am I prepared for reality television? Hell no."

"Were you always great at hockey, though?"

He's quiet on the other line for a long moment. "No. I had to work at it."

"I bet you had setbacks, same as everyone else. It's not how you win that makes you a winner; it's how you lose."

He snorts. "You sound like a coach."

"Why'd you call me, then?" I laugh. "Come on, let's get our butts out of bed and get ready. We have a big day ahead, but I promise I have your back. Think of me as your teammate. We're all in this together. We all want the show to be great."

"No offense, but it's pretty obvious you don't have experience working in reality television. I've seen these shows. Drama pays the bills, and somebody's got to be the villain, and usually that somebody doesn't know they're the villain until it's over and keyboard warriors are sending them death threats." He sighs, but I hear him getting out of bed, so at least there's that. "How do I know if I'm the villain?"

I snort. "That's easy, Benton. Don't do villain shit."

He draws in a long breath, as if thinking it through. "Fine. Let's do the damn thing."

After we hang up, I'm motivated to push past my nerves and go in there like a boss. Benton needs me, and so do the other cast members. But I can't help but think about what Benton said as I shower and get ready. *Do* we need a villain for the show to be successful? If so, how are we going to handle that? Who's going to fit that role? Perry will know what to do, but I wonder how far he's willing to go to make sure *Top of the World* is successful.

I have a sinking feeling someone isn't going to leave this show unscathed.

I arrive at set an hour before my call time, dressed in a cute black jumpsuit. We're calling the penthouse the "set" and Cooper's new apartment a level down "basecamp." The new apartment is three bedrooms, and Cooper has relegated himself to the primary suite, leaving the other two bedrooms, two bathrooms, kitchen and dining area to the show. It's selfless of him, but I can't help but wonder why he doesn't get a third apartment. The man is practically made of money, so why live at basecamp?

An overwhelming flurry of activity greets me as I enter the penthouse. I find Cooper first. "How are things going?"

"Perry's nervous," he says, peering at me with a grim expression. "Not that he'll show it, but look at the guy."

Perry has gone into full-director mode, and a thin sheen of sweat lines his face.

"Yeah," I say, "but that means he cares. He's going to do great."

"I agree." Cooper leans in. "Fake it till you make it and all that. How are *you* feeling?"

"I'm nervous, too. Excited, though. All the feelings."

Cooper bounces on his feet, a familiar move he used to do all growing up, and I wonder what that's like for him now with a prosthetic. Does it hurt? Does he notice the difference?

"Same," he says. "Only one hour until the first cast member arrives."

And we'll be rolling.

A middle-aged woman with a clipboard strides over to us, an earpiece visible under her short haircut and a take-charge gleam in her eyes.

"Hi there. I don't believe we've met yet. I'm Perry's production manager, Ricki."

I smile and shake her hand. "Hi Ricki, I'm Sybil Laurence. I'm one of the producers."

She nods. "Yes, I know. And you're Cooper, right?"

Cooper shakes her hand, and something about Ricki makes me relax. She seems like she knows how to make a set run smoothly, and she's not afraid to make a few people cry to make that happen.

"What do you need from us?" I ask.

"That's up to Perry. I won't tell you to do something unless

Perry wants it or has delegated it to me to delegate to you. Sound good?"

Coop and I nod like schoolchildren.

She points between us. "You should act like omnipresent gods around here. You know, watch the shit happen, but don't get in the way. Let the little humans figure it out, and only intervene if it's life or death."

I frown. "Perry told us we were going to produce the talent. Doesn't that mean we have to talk to them, at least?"

She gives me a polite smile. "Here's how it works. You talk to Perry if he's not busy or you talk to me. We'll tell you *how* we want you to produce your people. If we say you need to make them cry on camera, then you bring up their dead grandma. Got it?"

"Fuck," Cooper groans. "Are you for real?"

"I'm for real, for real. Say it with me, *'drama is conflict, and conflict is drama.'*"

Cooper rubs his hand over his mouth to hide his chuckle. I know that move, too. It's also one he's been doing since we were kids. "Drama is conflict, and conflict is drama."

She points to me. "Your turn."

Oh, she's serious. "Drama is conflict, and conflict is drama."

She pats me on the shoulder even though she's a good six inches shorter than me. "Good. That's what's going to pay my bills."

Coop and I exchange a look. What the hell have we gotten ourselves into?

Ricki claps her hands. "Alright. The talent each have different call times. They're entering the penthouse in the order Perry thinks will create the best content. We'll have plenty of reactions for episode one the editors can play around with. The cast are all superstars, so try not to be starstruck."

This time Cooper doesn't try to hide his chuckle. "Not sure

I can do that. Have you heard Audra Mason's newest album? Pretty cool."

I don't know everything about Cooper, but I know for a fact there's no way he's listened to Audra Mason's newest album.

Ricki's eyes widen. "You can't fawn over these people. They need to respect you."

"He's kidding," I say, and she shakes her head like she gets the joke but doesn't find it funny. "What about the three cast-mates who have already met?" I challenge. "How are you going to play it off like they're meeting for the first time?"

Ricki immediately hushes me and looks around. "Don't speak of that, okay? Just let the magic happen."

Besides Perry, there are several camera operators, two sound technicians, a woman I think might be Ricki's assistant, a lighting technician, and a couple of people for hair, makeup, and wardrobe. That's for production, and Perry says it's a small crew. Post-production will have editors, marketers, and more.

All with iron-clad NDAs, of course.

But Cooper and I still have to thrive in our day jobs. I'll be producing Benton, as well as the international pop-star Audra and the supermodel Gloria. Cooper is assigned to the politicians Sloane and Dane Maguire, as well as the movie star hunk Justin Crawford.

"Don't sleep with anyone," Perry emphasized when we were assigned. "Ever. Ever. Ever. Got that?"

We both agreed, though I couldn't help but wonder if Cooper would end up sleeping with one of the women, anyway. Coop's kind of hard to resist. The man has swagger, and he may not think so, but his prosthetic leg gives him even more appeal. I've seen the way women look at him; it's impossible not to notice, and the level of attention the man gets has only increased since his accident. What can I say? Women love a tortured soul.

Ricki struts off to her assistant, and Cooper turns on me. "How well do you think your boy will do pretending to meet Sloane and Dane for the first time?"

I kind of hate we're starting the show off with a lie, but I guess that's show-biz. "Benton is good. What about the siblings? I mean, they're in politics, so I'm sure that makes them excellent liars already."

He snorts. "Nothing like starting a reality show off with some good old-fashioned acting."

I smile. It feels like we're edging toward being friends again.

"We're starting with the siblings," Perry announces at the front of the room, gaining everyone's attention. "We already filmed intro packages and interviews, but we need interaction of when they first meet. This is key material for our pilot, and as you know, that first episode is everything. There's a screening room set up downstairs, so anyone who doesn't absolutely have to be on set needs to head there now."

"Guess that's us," Cooper says.

I elbow him playfully. "Let's go."

We take the stairs instead of waiting for the elevator. The apartment is smaller than the penthouse, but it's incredibly beautiful, with killer views.

"The only quiet place in here is my bedroom, but that's because I put a lock on it from the outside."

I raise my eyebrows at him. "So you're saying I can't go in there?"

His dark eyes hold mine for a moment too long, and my stomach flips. "You can go in there anytime you'd like, Valentine. All you have to do is ask."

The words are friendly on the surface but dripping in sexual innuendo.

It's the kind of thing the old Cooper used to say all the time, and I know it's a joke, but it still makes my cheeks warm. I need to cut it out. While Cooper might be okay with me using his bedroom if I need to step away, he's not inviting me to join him in there for anything else.

Does it matter we once shared a toe-curling kiss? Nope. That was two young people making a mistake, and we aren't those people anymore.

The rest of the unnecessary crew follow behind us, and that's all I expect, but what I don't expect is his father and my mother to come in shortly after, bickering already.

"Oh fuck," Cooper mutters, bee-lining toward our parents. I'm right on his heels. Oh fuck is right. If there's anyone who can throw a wrench into what needs to be a perfect day, it's these two. *Drama is conflict, and conflict is drama*, that's for damn sure.

TWENTY-EIGHT

S ybil
    Present - Age 27

Cooper makes it to them first. "Dad, Amelia, what are you doing here?" Even though his voice is calm and collected, I can tell by his ridged posture he's pissed.

Conrad gives a condescending smile. "Glad to see you two on set today. This is an important day for you both."

"You didn't answer my question," Cooper says, crossing his arms.

"We're here to make sure our money is being well invested," Conrad says coolly.

Mom steps forward, her eyes narrowed. I didn't even know she was in Manhattan. She's normally at the family residence in Greenwich. Hayes is finishing his senior year, and then she and the boys will be in Nantucket for the summer.

"*I'm* here to make sure that *nobody* sabotages this project." She shoots Conrad a pointed glare. I know exactly what she's thinking; I've worried about their intentions as well. Despite everything Conrad and Cooper have said, this show's failure would still give the Kings a win.

Cooper's spine straightens. "I assure you, Amelia, you have nothing to worry about. This is *our* project, and my father has already agreed to be hands off."

Mom raises a perfectly groomed brow at Conrad. "Then tell me why I walked into the lobby to find this one already waiting for the elevator?"

Cooper and his father stare at each other for a long moment, something unspoken passing between them that makes me uneasy.

"Fine," Conrad says, his eyes bouncing between me and his son. "You two have got it handled, and Perry knows what he's doing. I'll be off, but I trust if things start to fail, you will let me know immediately."

"Of course," Cooper and I say in unison.

Mom pats me on the shoulder. "Is there anything I can do to help?"

I shake my head. "No, go home. I'll see you at Hayes's graduation in a few weeks, and then you should go to Nantucket like you planned."

Her face pales, but she agrees.

Nobody says what we're all thinking—none of us have been on that island since the accident. I can't say for sure about Cooper and Conrad, but I'd bet my life on it.

"I'm off," Conrad says, quickly turning on his heel and striding out of the apartment.

"I'd better get going, too." Mom gives me a quick hug. "You're right, I need to get home, but can I stick in town for a few days?"

I know she wants to spend time with her daughter, so I can't say no. As busy as I am, I love spending time with her as well, and I know that makes me a lucky daughter.

I turn on Cooper. "Do you think your dad actually went upstairs?"

Cooper winces, and I quickly pull out the walkie-talkie Ricki gave me earlier.

"Ricki," I say into the comm, the whole thing feeling a little surreal. "Do you copy?"

"What's wrong?" Her voice comes through quickly.

"Nothing, but watch out for Conrad King. He's an older version of Cooper. He said he was leaving, but you may have to intercept him."

"Got it," she says with an annoyed clip, signing off immediately.

Okay, that was way faster than using a phone, so I get why they use walkies on set now.

"Have you seen the screening room?" Mom says, giving me a bright smile. "It's amazing what technology can do."

I follow her into one of the two guest bedrooms that's now been transformed into our screening room. There's a sense of excitement in the air, and the person in charge enthusiastically introduces himself by the name of Roland. We shuffle to the back of the room to let the professionals do their work, and everyone gives us a wide birth.

I can't help but wonder if word got around about the set dresser. I'm sure. If there's one thing people love, it's good gossip.

We're standing against the windows, which are currently covered by curtains. The other side of the room has been turned into a wall of televisions mounted to the wall to show the different camera feeds upstairs. Not only are there three camera people up there, but there are several permanently mounted cameras all over the shared living spaces.

Some of the show's content will be staged interactions we

get to watch play out, like putting people around a dinner table together and seeing what they talk about. But a lot of the content is going to come from the cameras set to catch everyday interactions.

Conrad strides into the room with his arms over his chest and a little line between his eyebrows.

"I thought you were leaving," Cooper says.

"I was," he clips. "But I wanted to go upstairs first, and some tiny woman with purple hair yelled at me."

I snort, and Conrad frowns. This man is *never* chastised. I make a mental note to give Ricki a high-five next time I see her. She's such a badass. If I were gay, I think I'd already be in love.

"Alright people, it's go time," Roland announces, and everyone quiets down.

Our attention turns to the television with the camera feed facing the front door of the penthouse. Anticipation vibrates through my veins and doesn't let up until Sloane and Dane McGuire step through.

They're beautiful, wholesome-looking blonds with giant blue eyes and huge, enchanting smiles. America's sweethearts or America's demons, depending on which side of the political spectrum you fall under.

Their family has deep roots both in democratic politics and in the state of New York. As children, they grew up in the governor's mansion, constantly in the spotlight, and now *Top of the World* is introducing them to the world.

"Wow," Sloan gushes, turning to her brother and pulling him into a side-hug. "Isn't this place incredible? Oh, and that view! Reminds me why I love this city so much."

Dane strides toward the floor to ceiling windows. He smiles, dimples popping in his clean-shaven cheeks. Dane is an out and proud gay man, and definitely gorgeous enough to have women all over the country crying that life isn't fair. Once again, the gays won this one.

"You're right Sloany-bologna," he says. "This is going to be fun."

Cooper snorts. "Sloany-bologna? That's cheesy as fuck."

"It's cute," I counter.

Sloan turns on her brother and points at him. "Don't you dare use that nickname around the others. Last thing I need is those hot men thinking of me and bologna in the same sentence."

I laugh to myself, already loving this girl, and Mom elbows me.

"This might work," she whispers, giving me a wink.

I sure hope she's right.

What we just witnessed was something enduring and sweet, and I loved it, but we need more. Enduring and sweet is not going to make good reality television. It's important to balance the softer moments with juicy drama, at least that's what Perry told us.

I have to trust this is all going to work out.

"Let's go find our rooms," Sloan says, and the two head off to explore the apartment, finding their bedrooms on separate floors. Hers upstairs and his on the main floor.

Explore is an operative word, considering they've already been here. The camera follows the siblings, getting their reactions, but I'm sure most of this will be cut from the episode. This is the boring part. The fun stuff comes next.

Five minutes later, someone else walks through the door.

"Let's see if your guy was worth all that money," Cooper says under his breath, nodding to Benton's ruggedly handsome face filling up the screen.

Mom whistles low, and I suppress a grin. Benton is gorgeous. He's got that I-will-beat-up-my-enemies and steal-their-girlfriends swagger, and he strides into the apartment like he owns the place just like I told him to... not that he needed me to tell him how to look good.

I catch Cooper glaring daggers at the screen. He's like a big dog who marked his territory, and another big dog has come to play.

"Relax, will ya?" I place my hand on Cooper's upper arm. "Benton called me this morning super nervous. He's putting on a front like he usually does. I *told* him to exude confidence. Doesn't mean he's feeling confident right now."

Cooper tenses even more, and I can't help but notice how nice and large his bicep feels under his dress shirt. I bet it would feel even better without the shirt.

Wait, what? I immediately rip my hand away. *Don't even go there, Sybil. You know better.*

We're right that Benton and the McGuire siblings fake it for the cameras, acting like they're meeting for the first time. They compliment Benton on his hockey accolades, and he compliments them on their father and asks them about their own interests and accomplishments.

Things are practically normal until the front door opens for a third time, and the Italian supermodel walks in.

"Now we're talking," Cooper remarks, and a streak of jealously burns through me.

Dumb. What do I care?

This woman is hot, and everybody knows it.

Especially Benton.

Benton also knows his way around a woman's body, and right now he's looking at Gloria Ricci like he's about to know his way around her body, too.

The attraction between them is instant and electric, and the cameras pick up on it immediately.

This is exactly what we were hoping would happen.

Introductions are made, small talk continues, rooms are explored, and then it's Justin Crawford's time to shine. He walks in, and it's obvious why he's a movie star. The man sparkles on camera. I don't know how else to put it.

He's a stunning, mixed African American man with an athletic body, endearing smile, and the kind of sultry bedroom eyes that have captivated an entire generation of women. The light caramel color of them pop on camera.

"Woah," Mom remarks. "Can't wait to meet *him* in person."

Make that two generations.

Conrad throws her a scathing look. "Way to act your age, Amelia. He's what, twenty-five?"

She sticks up her nose, not even bothering to look at him when she replies. "Last I checked, *you're* the one who married a woman half your age. Twice."

I snort. That's true. After Victoria passed away, Conrad married a younger woman a few years later, divorced her not long after that, and has remarried yet again. I don't even know their names. I lost track.

"She's got a point," Cooper whispers to his dad playfully, and I think I might die of shock. I've *never* seen him tease his dad, and I gotta say, seeing this looser side of Cooper gives me hope for his future. I have to bite back a smile to keep from giving myself away.

"I have more important places to be," Conrad says, exasperated.

I can't help but notice his red cheeks. He leaves without another glance, pulling out his phone to check his calendar on his way out of the room. He's CEO and founder of a media empire. He probably *does* have more important places to be, but I still find his exit hilarious.

"It's okay," Cooper whispers in my ear. "I know you want to."

We turn to each other and bust up laughing.

Mom heads out a few minutes later, but Cooper and I stay at the back of the room, watching the film come in.

I make a mental note to add seating here, so I don't have to stand. If the last hour is any indication of how this is going to go, I'll be in this screening room as often as I can. It's fascinating to watch this unfold, especially knowing these people are only a floor above us.

These are some of the most influential twenty-somethings of our generation, and they're going to be living together for three months. It's going to be the ultimate form of people watching.

What do famous people do behind closed doors? How do they act? What are they really like? I didn't think I cared that much, but now I'm dying to know. They're putting on a show for the cameras now, but nobody can put on a show for three months straight. We're going to see the real them soon enough.

Just when I think it can't get any better, Audra Mason, the world's newest and hottest pop star sensation and the Grammy's latest best new artist award winner, struts into the penthouse with more confidence in her pinky finger than most people have in their entire bodies.

She's got *diva* written all over her, from her head-to-toe black leather outfit to her long sleek raven hair. This is a woman who is hungry for her star to shine even brighter, no matter what it takes.

Bring on the drama.

TWENTY-NINE

C ooper
Past - Age 23

The booze is flowing, the music is thumping, the atmosphere is electric, and the women are eager. So can someone please explain to me why the fuck I'm not interested?

"Are you depressed or something?"

Count on Perry to say it like it is.

Um, yes. Exactly that.

Considering Perry has been one of my only friends who has stuck by my side after college, it makes sense he would be able to tell how messed up I am.

"We're at our favorite club on Nantucket, and you're moping," he adds.

I don't know how long grief is supposed to last, but I'm starting to think it will be with me forever. It's my new normal. I can't even remember what it felt like to not be sad.

"Yeah, guess I'm depressed." I offer a defeated shrug.

He offers a sympathetic tilt of his glass. We've talked about my year from hell to death. There's nothing he or anyone else can do.

"You know what you need?" Perry's voice is a little slurred, and he talks as if he's had the most brilliant idea on the planet. "You need a hot woman to suck your cock."

I slow-blink at him. "Don't be a dick."

"Shit. Sorry," he says sheepishly. "But you know I'm right."

While I'd normally agree with the guy, I can't cope in the way I used to.

At least, I don't think I can.

We're on Nantucket for the summer after finishing our first year of graduate school, and Perry came to join us for the weekend. He knows how to have a good time and dragged me and Ethan out to this club, declaring we were going to *have fun, damn it.*

"Do what your brother is doing." Perry points to Ethan. "Don't let him show you up."

Yeah, Ethan doesn't seem to have a care in the world. My twin is on the dance floor, surrounded by women, looking like he's ready to take one of them to the bathroom for a quickie.

Honestly, it makes me a little uncomfortable.

It's not that he shouldn't be with a woman, but it's weird he's not with Sybil. It throws me off to see him grinding on some random girl like he's a player and not someone who was engaged recently.

But who am I to judge? It's the first time he's shown an ounce of interest since Sybil broke up with him last fall.

The man desperately needs to get laid.

And I need to stay by the bar and nurse this whiskey.

Only good thing that came out of all this pain and suffering? Dad is letting us spend this summer and next on Nantucket. No work. No internships. No responsibilities. No adult shit. None of it. Just fun and sun and women and booze.

The whole thing is kind of ridiculous, but who am I to complain?

Dad says he doesn't want us to burn out, and he feels bad about rushing us to school after the funeral. I haven't told Ethan this, but I suspect Dad wants us gone this summer because he's dating. For all we know, he's got a revolving door of women coming to the apartment at all hours, and he doesn't want us there.

Manhattan is a big city, but it feels like we're on top of each other when we're all there in the same space. It was one thing when Mom was alive, but it's different with her gone.

Ethan and I can't wait until we can buy our own apartments. That's on the top of our list when we secure our Harvard MBAs and our trust funds.

"What about her?" Perry points to a familiar face out on the dance floor. A friend of a friend of a friend type of girl who I consider sexy, but she's a little too wild for me.

"Bree?" I scoff. "No way." I've heard all kinds of stories about how territorial she is. No thanks. I like my women commitment-phobic, same as me.

"Bree's cool," Perry assures me. "And she's a freak in bed."

"You slept with Bree?" I grimace. "I'm *definitely* not interested."

"It was years ago and only one time, but it was memorable." He waggles his thick eyebrows. "She'll make you feel better, I promise."

I eye her wearily, my gaze slipping over the curve of her hips and the press of her breasts against her tight dress as she sways to the music. Maybe he's right. I have a rotation of willing partners in Boston and New York, but there's not as many on Nantucket, and I've barely called anyone up lately.

"Think about it, but if you don't want Bree, let me know." Perry broke up with his college girlfriend four months ago. The man is hurting, too.

"Go talk to her."

Perry takes another drink, then leaves me standing at the bar to flirt with a group of girls who just walked through the door instead of going to talk to Bree.

What a guy.

He doesn't know what to do with me—none of my friends do. They're so used to me being the fun one, the positive one, the easy-going life of the party. I haven't been any of those things lately. They've all noticed, even Ethan, who's been living in his own world of denial. He's decided to gun for top of our class. Good for him, but he's already been hand-selected to be the next CEO of King, so what's the point? If he got a C in a class, would it hurt his future? Nope.

Maybe Perry is right. I need a distraction, and Bree looks like the perfect one for the job.

Swallowing the last bit of my whiskey, I leave the glass on the bar top and watch Bree. Let's see how long it takes for her to notice me. Less than a minute later, our eyes lock. When she moistens her lips and smirks suggestively, my cock jerks in response.

Fuck it. I'll do anything to feel better at this point. At least it's not drugs.

I stride to the dance floor, and she greets me with a breathy, "Hey there." Her arms wrap around my neck instantly as we start moving together. Up close, her tanned-skin glistens with a light sheen of sweat, and I have the sudden urge to lick her up and down to see if she's more sweet or more salt.

This is who I am. I'm the playboy.

Good for a fun night.

Not boyfriend material.

It's time to suck it up and embrace my true self.

THIRTY

C ooper
      Past - Age 23

I wake up in Bree's bed the next morning, my head pounding and mouth as dry as sandpaper. I let her take me to her place. There was no way I was getting behind the wheel, and she swore she wasn't drinking. As a personal rule, I don't fuck drunk women, especially not drunk strangers.

I'm half in and half out of Bree's yellow comforter. She's gorgeous and leggy, with her hair fanned across the pillowcase like a raven's wing.

I feel nothing for her. I barely even know the girl, and I'm not staying for breakfast. I shouldn't have come home with her at all. I know better than to hook up with a clingy woman when I have zero intentions of making her my girlfriend.

Sliding from her warmth, the woman's eyes pop open, and she sits up as I get myself dressed.

"Where are you going, baby?"

"This was fun." I give her a smile. "But I need to get home."

She holds up a hand. "Let me stop you right there."

Well, shit.

"You probably think I want to date you, but I don't. I'm only here for the summer, and I want to have fun and be with whoever I want to be with." She gives me a coy smile. "I've heard you're the same way. As long as everyone uses protection, I shouldn't be shamed for that, and neither should you. We can have fun together and have fun with other people. What do you think?"

I chuckle, wondering if I'm a complete asshole for agreeing. "I would never shame you or any woman. Are you sure this is what you want?"

She tilts her head, eyes sparkling. "We've been friendly for years, Cooper, but we've never gotten to know each other." She bites her lip, and what memories I have of last night rage through my body. "I think it's time you and I get to be really good friends."

I climb into her bed and kiss her. It's not until a good half hour later I'm leaving her bedroom for real, a cocky grin plastered on my face.

I feel a million times better than I did last night.

Perry was right.

I hurry onto the street, heading toward the closest main road to call a car with my app. We don't use a driver when we're on Nantucket, and I didn't drive last night, knowing my plans to get plastered.

I'm a few blocks away from Bree's place when a streak of familiar red hair catches my eye. I stop, heart slamming and anxiety rippling.

Turning to take in an empty lot is none other than Sybil Laurence. She's wearing a yellow hard hat and directing the crew around like a boss.

"What the fuck?" I mutter.

This is not wishful thinking. It's really her.

My Valentine.

I stand frozen, staring at her as she talks to the crew, knowing I should turn and walk away, but I can't.

Suddenly, all I want in the whole fucking world is to talk to her. It's an itch I can't scratch, and it kills me. I ball my hands into fists to keep myself from pulling her into a hug. My teeth dig into my tongue to keep from yelling out her name.

As much as I want to see her, to talk to her, I also want to scream at her for doing what she did.

A brawny man with at least ten years on us struts over to Sybil, his thumbs hitched into the pockets of his jeans. He sports a hard hat and a plaid shirt, a total walking cliché, but I bet women love his blue-collar look. The two begin talking, heads tilted toward one another, and a streak of jealousy darts through me.

Her family must be building their Nantucket house.

It shouldn't surprise me, but it does. To see it happening despite all the bad blood makes my chest ache. Everything I'd numbed last night crashes into me all at once—pain, anger, sadness, hope, longing...

Do I want Sybil on Nantucket? Yes.

Can I have Sybil on Nantucket? Absolutely not.

Nantucket isn't that big, not even with their house being on the other side of the island from ours. There's no way this ends well.

Sybil laughs, her chin lifting high with her neck exposed as she releases the carefree sound. I used to take that laugh for granted, and now another man is making her happy.

Fuck. I'm still not over her.

How fucked up is that, considering we were never even

together? This is unrequited love, and it's bullshit I need to work through.

Like an idiot, I stride across the dirt lot, weaving through construction workers, standing a foot away from Sybil, her back turned to me. My eyes roam her body, taking in her black tank top against her pale skin and the sexy curve of her ass in her jeans. She turns to me with her adorable smile lighting her face and then goes still. Her smile drops, and so does my heart.

"Cooper."

There are so many ways I could play this.

I pick the worst one.

I smirk, trying to appear unaffected. "Don't look so surprised to see me on Nantucket." I inch closer and nod to the construction site. Her sweet yet somehow spicy citrus scent is so familiar I nearly sink to my knees. "Is this what I think it is?"

Her green eyes flash with a million unsaid things. God, I want to hear them all.

She turns to plaid-shirt guy. "Rake, if you'll excuse me. Cooper is an old friend, and we need to catch up."

An old friend, huh?

I don't know how to feel about her using that term for me.

We walk away, and I mutter to her under my breath, "What the hell kind of name is Rake? Is his brother named Shovel, and his sister named Backhoe?"

The Sybil I knew would laugh and elbow me in the ribs, but this Sybil does neither. Instead, she grabs my arm and marches me to the sidewalk, her nails digging into my bicep like cat claws.

"I never knew you liked to scratch," I tease when we stop, smirking at where she's left little indents on my skin.

"Don't do that."

"Do what?"

"Don't treat me like some girl you met at a bar. You wanted to talk to me, so tell me what's on your mind."

"I don't think you want me to do that."

"Whatever. You guys don't own Nantucket, so don't act like we can't be here. Yes, we're building our house. So what?"

I lean in, eyes narrowing. "I haven't heard from you in seven months, and this is how I find out your family is building here? Don't you think you could've at least given us a heads up? Not even a text?"

"I don't owe you an explanation."

I laugh. "You guys could have built your fucking beach house on some other island. You know how much Nantucket means to my family."

Our beach house was my mother's favorite place in the world. She even made sure one day it'd be mine and Ethan's. It's trusted to us.

Despite all the shit that has happened in our lives, Ethan and I agree; we'll never get rid of the Nantucket house.

I expect Sybil's face to soften, but it doesn't.

She points behind her. "This is our property, and your property is your property. They're on opposite sides of the island, and we don't have to associate with each other. How about this for an idea? If you see me, walk the other way, and I'll do the same."

I wince. "Where did my best friend go?"

Hurt passes through her eyes, but it's gone as quickly as it appeared. "This is the way it has to be."

"Is it?"

She nods. "Don't tell Ethan about any of this. He doesn't need to know about the house until it's done. And for fuck's sake, don't tell your dad unless you want more drama between our parents."

"*Your* parents," I snap. "I only have one parent left, remember?"

She shakes her head, but her face is draining of color. "You know what I mean."

Damn it.

She's dead serious right now. She wants *nothing to do with me.*

"Wow," I deadpan. "So that's it, huh? We're not friends anymore?"

So many things flash in her eyes at once—heat and hurt, and maybe even regret, but she pushes them all aside.

"Yup. That's it. Please leave."

I let out a dark chuckle to hide the pain. She drew the line in the sand and there's no crossing it, but I don't know if I can accept it.

"What happened to the girl I knew and loved?" I ask coldly.

Tears spring to her eyes, and that just pissed me off. This is her doing, not mine. Never in a million years would I push her away like she's done to me.

"That girl had to make an impossible choice, and so she did." With that, she turns and walks away.

I do the same, all the while thinking that Sybil chose her family. The thing she doesn't understand, the reason I'm so hurt, is I truly thought Sybil considered me to be part of her family, too.

THIRTY-ONE

S ybil
     Present - Age 27

"I have good news," I tell Lance Vale at our next Friday morning meeting.

Sitting in my dad's old office hurts, but I try not to think about the time I spent here over the years and the many meaningful conversations that happened when I started working for him.

At least Vale has changed the furniture and switched the artwork. A photo of a much younger him while with his wife on a vacation sits on his large oak desk.

"I take it filming went well this week?"

"More than well." I smile from ear to ear. King Media's primetime tv network has already slotted *Top of the World* in for the fall. I have a feeling it's going to be a massive hit, especially since they've agreed to run with Perry's idea of having the episodes air alongside live social media reactions.

I can already imagine the funny, unhinged things people are going to say.

"I couldn't be present for all of filming," I say, "but I pop in as often as I can. Perry sends out nightly emails to keep everyone up to speed."

He's also been pretty good at the group text between him, me, and Cooper. We all want this to work—are all gunning for the same juicy footage that's going to make our show a big hit.

"Tell me more about that," Vale prods. "What was the best thing you filmed this week?"

My cheeks flush, but I instantly think of the scene that's going to have women at home screaming at their television sets.

"Well, the film crews are following the stars around their daily lives, but we also have stationary cameras filming twenty-four-seven. One of those picked up a steamy kiss in a hot tub." It was between Gloria and Benton, to nobody's surprise.

He raises a bushy eyebrow. "There's a hot tub at Cooper King's penthouse, is there?"

I shrug. "It's on the rooftop, yes."

Cooper and I were in the screening room when the kiss happened. He'd given me a charged look, the kind that made my panties melt, but he quickly ruined the moment by asking if I was jealous my booty-call had moved on.

"I've been with Laurence for most of my career, so I can't say I know a whole lot about reality tv," Vale says. "The few holdings we with had with King weren't in the entertainment media space. I'll admit, I don't watch trashy tv at home."

I can't imagine he would.

"That's fair, but you know how they say sex sells? Show-mances are a big deal."

"Showmance?"

I wave my hand. "Trust me, this will help the show tremendously. People are going to lose their minds."

"Hmm." Vale leans in his chair, the age-lines in his face more prominent as he considers. "I can't help but wonder if Laurence has gotten into something untoward here. Is there a chance this will reflect poorly on us?"

My stomach sinks. "Not at all. There's going to be a lot of variety on the show besides romance. The point is to make money, and it's going to make us a ton when advertisers are lining up to work with Top of the World."

He seems skeptical. "I hope you're right. As I recall, Top of the World cost us over a hundred million."

I swallow hard. King and Laurence each invested three hundred million—Laurence in pure capital, and King in a mix of money and resources. It's one of the highest investments *ever* in this space.

"I believe in Perry and Top of the World," I assure him. "As far as company reputation, you really don't have to worry. Nobody thinks of Laurence when they think of media—they think of King. This will be no different. If scandal does break up, it's King's liability, not ours."

Besides that, they're the ones airing the show.

His lips press together briefly as he tilts his head. "As we both know, King is rebuilding their reputations after the events of last summer. I'm sure they're invested in making sure Top of the World doesn't embarrass them further."

My mood instantly sours. "Which means we'll make sure everything is done well."

I hate that my boss is grilling me, but I'm not scared of him. This show is going to be huge. I can feel it in my bones.

"Okay, good. How are things moving along with the foundation work?"

Just thinking about the foundation excites me and I sit up taller. "We're on track with the planning for our gala scheduled the first Saturday in October, and I've got four meetings set up next month to fundraise for our causes."

I slide a printout of my donor meeting schedule, pretty damned pleased with myself. I've landed huge prospects and am thrilled to tell them all about our partners. We work with some incredible nonprofits and are passionate about helping them grow. I can get my nonprofits in front of people they'd never get in front of otherwise.

"Looks to me like this disability nonprofit gets a lot of your attention," he says, peering through his glasses at the sheet of paper. "That's great, but Laurence International raises for a number of charities which appeases the interests of various shareholders."

"Yes, you're right, but—"

"It can't be all about you and your passions. I understand Chandler has inspired your disability work, but don't forget about the Foundation as a whole."

His words are like a slap to the face. I take a deep breath and carefully word my reply. "You're right that I'm most passionate about the disability advocacy, but that doesn't mean I'm not also passionate about our other nonprofit partners. We provide a great deal of funds and resources to our environmental protection organization, the local nonprofit for feeding the hungry and housing the homeless here in our city, and then we have the international organization that uplifts women and children in developing nations."

And they're all wonderful. Just because I'm not just as passionate about them as I am about disability advocacy doesn't mean they're not all near and dear to my heart, nor does it mean The Laurence Foundation neglects anybody.

He gives me a long, steady look, and I swear he's disappointed. My entire body tenses. Honestly? It pisses me off.

"I already know who we support. I'm telling you to make

sure you're following through on all fronts. I want to see a schedule that reflects that."

My cheeks burn. "Oh, of course, let me explain what you're looking at there." I motion to the paper in his hands. "While the foundation supports all four charities year-round, we take quarters to direct focus on one of our nonprofit partners one at a time. Quarter three is for the disabled children. Quarter one is environmental protections." He should know, that's the one Laurence pours the most money into. "Quarter two is for uplifting women and children across the globe. And quarter four is about feeding the hungry and housing the homeless right here in our city, which goes over great around the holidays."

Take that!

"Hmm...very well, but we may want to rethink that down the road. Did you hire an assistant like I told you to?"

I can't seem to win one today. "I thought that was more of a suggestion."

He shakes his head, a line forming between his graying eyebrows. "Consider it a mandate. You have a lot on your plate. I only want to see you succeed. I'm sorry if I sound like I'm being rough on you, but it's my job to push you to your fullest potential."

Vale is looking at me like he expects no argument. Hiring someone sounds like tedious work, let alone training them, but I might not have a choice.

"I'll get on that. Anything else?"

He studies at me for a beat. "Are you going to Nantucket this summer?"

My emotions immediately spiral. I haven't been to Nantucket since Dad died.

I shake my head. "As you've said, it's a busy summer for me. I don't have time."

His face softens. "The anniversary of your father's death is coming up. Do you have someone to talk to? Mental health counseling? We can get you set up if you need help. Or you can always talk to me."

My spine turns to steel, and I can't move, can hardly even breathe. Vale is not someone I want to be talking to about my father's horrible death. I don't care if I've known Vale for years or that he was close to my dad. It's not like he's close to me. We're not friends; we were coworkers, and now he's my boss. That's all.

"I've got it handled."

"It was a terrible tragedy. We're all sad he's gone. If I could bring him back, I would. Sometimes I hate that I'm sitting here instead of him."

Does he, though?

The words fall flat, but that's probably because I can't handle this conversation.

"I do plan to take next Friday off of work," I say. "I hope you understand why I won't be in a state to work that day or have our weekly meeting."

"Of course. I wouldn't expect anything less. We'll touch base in two weeks."

"Is there anything else?" I scoot my chair away from the desk, readying myself to leave.

"There is one last thing."

My legs shake as I sit back down. I want to get the hell out of this office. This conversation is taking way too long, and I'm practically crawling out of my skin.

"The hiring committee has officially recommended me for Laurence's open CEO position. They'll be taking this recommendation to the board early next week. I would appreciate it if you put in a good word with your siblings and mother. I know your family's vote is very important to the board in this matter."

As it should be; it's our name on the doors of this building.

"Of course," I assure him, but as I head to my office, I'm not sure how I feel about Vale being CEO. Do I really want to sit through more micromanaging conversations with him?

As much as I can see him taking on the position permanently, I have to admit... I don't want it to be him.

Maybe that's not his fault. Maybe it's grief talking, and *anyone* in that role would rub me the wrong way. It's so damn hard to accept that my dad will never be in this office again.

THIRTY-TWO

S ybil
     Present - Age 27

People have told me all sorts of things about grief over the years. They've said helpful things and not-so helpful things, beautiful lines about loving and hearts, and bullshit antidotes about fate and better places. Everyone is entitled to their own definition of grief, but here is mine.

Grief is a shadow.

It's always there. In the darkness, it's everything. In the light, it's still there, but it's sometimes small and sometimes large. The brightest things in life can make that shadow more pronounced, like when I'm having the best day, and it suddenly hits me I'll never get to experience a day like this again with the people I've lost. How dare I be happy and laugh when Dad will never do that again?

Then the shadow recedes, and I almost forget it's there.

It's not only the people who are dead that I've had to grieve, but also some of the living.

And it's the soft landing I naïvely thought would be there, but instead a hard foundation full of cracks, and when I crashed, I also crumbled.

I grieve the innocent, carefree girl I once was, but I've picked myself up and I'm okay with the woman I am now. I'm finally someone who leads her own life, even if that means accepting that I can't control everything, especially death.

I went to therapy yesterday, and it helped a little. One more baby step toward healing. One more layer off the never-ending proverbial onion, so to speak.

I still woke up crying this morning.

Today is the one-year anniversary of my dad's death, so it's no surprise I'm hurting. Since I'm not working, I'm going to do whatever I feel like doing.

By lunch I'm ready to escape the loft, so I get out, sinking into myself while I eat a hummus plate alone at my favorite neighborhood lunch spot.

After that, I head toward The Paris Theatre, another one of my favorite New York City spots. It's an old landmark that plays foreign and independent films, with the occasional classic thrown in. It's small and dark and quiet, with a nice anonymous atmosphere for a Friday afternoon.

I'll watch whatever the next film is. I don't even care what's playing.

I buy my ticket and head in for a screening of the 1991 queer film *My Own Private Idaho* starring River Phoenix and Keanu Reeves. I've never seen it before, and as I watch the story unfold, I'm not so sure this was the best decision.

The movie is incredibly sad, and tears stream down my face before the credits even roll.

This is a story about a gay sex worker searching for

belonging and home. Spoiler alert, he doesn't find it. Spoiler alert, the last scene is him unconscious in the street, being picked up by a faceless driver.

Holy shit, what was I thinking?

At least I can cry for someone else instead of my sorry ass, especially because the actor, River Phoenix, died young of a drug overdose.

Now I'm crying for the actor as well as the character.

The few patrons in the theatre get up to leave, but I stay burrowed in the padded seat, silently crying like a damn has burst. It's cathartic, letting myself feel this deeply. As much as it hurts, I know I need it.

A man sits next to me, and without even looking at him, I immediately know it's Cooper. My Cooper. God, what did I do to him? How could I have been so cruel? I ruined such a beautiful friendship, and it's my fault.

My aching heart doesn't know what to do with itself.

He takes my hand, squeezing once before setting it on the armrest and folding his own hands over his lap. I keep my eyes trained on his body, avoiding his face. But I know him so well, even in the darkness of the theatre as the credits roll. From his tan arm next to mine and the way his veins run to his hands in his hands, to his long-outstretched legs so comfortable in his jeans, even with the prosthetic on his right side.

More than knowing what he looks like, I know what he *feels* like. I know his comforting sandalwood and soap scent, his magnetic energy, and his kind soul. I could have had my eyes closed for this interaction, and I'd still have known it was him.

Cooper is as familiar to me as my own reflection.

"You had the same idea as me, huh?" I ask. "You did love coming to this theatre as much as I did."

"We both love going to lots of places in Manhattan," Cooper says. "This city is huge."

"Are you saying it's fate you're here at the same time as me?"

"I'm not sure I believe in fate. I do believe it was a lucky coincidence, and this was definitely luck I found you here to today of all days."

That makes my heart swell a little, and the tears slow. "Seeing me is lucky?"

He's quiet for a moment. "It is for me. I was already sitting in the back row when you came in. I thought I'd leave you in peace to enjoy the film."

"*Enjoy* is not the word I would use for what I just saw. More like *experience*."

"Same." His voice trails off, and I wonder where his mind took him.

Is he hurting like I'm hurting? This isn't the anniversary of the day he lost his father, but it is the anniversary of the day he lost his leg. He's been through a hell of a lot, more than most people.

The screen goes dark. Without saying a word, we get up and walk into the bright June day.

It's beautiful weather, the kind that's unfair when you're sad. Maybe that's exactly what I need, even if I don't want it.

Cooper and I don't make polite conversation; we walk together in comfortable silence. The theatre is only a couple blocks from the south side of Central Park, so naturally, we end up walking around the iconic duck pond until we're standing in front of the ticket booth for the zoo.

"Do you want to go in?" Cooper asks, and I accept the offer. I'm not ready to go home yet. Being outside feels good to my soul, especially being among the trees. The birds chirping are music to a broken heart, and maybe more animals will help me feel better.

I'm not a big fan of zoos, but this one has a lot of wonderful memories with my family attached to it, so I try to let that slide.

Cooper pays and once inside, I take in the lush landscape juxtaposed to the towering skyscrapers on the horizon. It's such a familiar scene that it soothes me. I have happy memories of coming here with Dad as a kid, but also memories of coming here with Ethan and Cooper, and many with our moms.

It's still so hard to think my dad and Victoria had an affair, and even worse to accept that they're both dead now. Thanks to therapy, I've embraced the truth that it's okay to focus on the good times instead of the bad.

When we're watching an adorable red panda eating bamboo, I burst into tears.

Again.

Cooper pulls me into a hug, and I hide my face in his black cotton shirt. I should be embarrassed by the people staring at me, but I don't care.

"I don't know why you're here with me, today of all days," I choke out.

He smiles softly and wipes the tears away from my cheeks, shaking his head slowly, a worry line forming between his eyebrows.

"I don't hate you, Valentine. I never did. It's important that you understand that. I was *angry* with you, but there's a difference between anger and hate."

I hiccup. "Really?"

"Yes, really. And for the record, I'm not angry at you anymore, either."

I'm a complete mess, and he's comforting me when I don't deserve him. "I'm sorry, Cooper. I'm sorry for everything. For hurting you when I left. For your leg. For all of it."

"I know," he whispers. "That's in the past now."

This is the part where I want to ask for forgiveness, but I can't. Even though I can offer my apology, I don't deserve his forgiveness. I was a heinous bitch; I threw him away, because I didn't know how to handle myself. I didn't know what to do. I was immature and hurt. *I am still hurting*, but maybe I am mature now.

"I don't blame you, Sybil." He peers directly into my eyes. "And I've been thinking about it a lot, thinking about what you said, and I'm ready for us to be friends again. Actually, I think we already *are* friends again, but I'm ready to embrace it fully. I want you back."

My heart swells and the weight of years carrying around shame at the loss of him lifts away.

I smile, hug him tight, then step away and mop up my tears with my sleeves. "Thank you. You have no idea how much I needed that."

He shrugs. "No need to thank me. Let's move past it, okay? I think we should start with finding you a bathroom, so you can wash off your raccoon eyes."

Oh, shit. "I knew I shouldn't have worn mascara today," I grumble. "How bad is it?"

He gives me a mocking-horrified face. "Bad, Valentine. You've been walking around with black rings around your eyes ever since we left that depressing-as-fuck movie."

I laugh, and it feels amazing. "Thanks for telling me earlier." I elbow him, and he laughs too, and that feels even better.

"I don't have a problem with your cute raccoon eyes. I think you're beautiful no matter what, but I also know you well enough to know you'll want to clean yourself up."

Has Cooper ever called me beautiful before? Maybe when we were young, but I don't think so, at least not that I remember. I tuck the compliment away to analyze later.

We head to the bathroom, and yes, I do look a mess, but I *feel* so much better. I wash my face, staring into the mirror for a minute and noticing the way my eyes are brighter and greener from the tears. I look a little younger without any makeup on and frizzy hair, but I feel more me than I've felt in forever. Years, maybe.

This was a horrible day that has become a good one. I only have Cooper to thank for that.

Funny how life works sometimes.

I return to Cooper, and we finish walking the zoo, making small talk about *Top of the World* and Arden and Ethan's wild affair that led to an elopement. There's a lot I know about their relationship that Cooper doesn't and vice versa, and it's fun having friendly gossip about his brother and my half-sister. We never mention my dad or his leg. We don't have to. We both know we lost too much, but at least we're friends again.

Friends is enough for me.

Friends is everything, actually.

Now that I have Cooper, there's no way I'm going to let anything jeopardize our friendship again. I want to keep him, keep *us*, like this, forever.

THIRTY-THREE

Cooper
Past - Age 23

Ethan and I are at our favorite little hole-in-the-wall bar on Nantucket when the text comes in. We read it, then stare at each other before busting up.

Chandler: Your boy is 21!!!!!! If you want to watch me get lit for the first time, come to this address and let's party!

It's paired with a screenshot from the maps app of a popular nightclub in town. He's here. He's on Nantucket. They must be renting a place.

"God, I miss that kid." Ethan sighs.

"Me too. Should we go?" I set the phone on the table. He's the one who got dumped, so I'm letting this one be his call, but I'll be pretty devastated if I miss Chandler's twenty-first birthday. The kid talked about it insensately, arguing with his parents that people with down syndrome can drink, same as anybody else.

Ethan's eyes take on a devilish glimmer. "I think we have to."

Thank God.

If Chandler asks us to do something, we're doing it.

"Let's go." I jump to my feet.

Chandler is the only Laurence still in touch with us. We try to keep things short with him, but we never ignore him even though we haven't seen him since the day of Mom's funeral.

"You remember when we promised we'd take him out when he turned twenty-one?" Ethan asks, and I have no memory of any such thing.

"Nope," I say.

Ethan frowns. "Maybe it was a conversation with me and Sybil. I don't know." He rubs his jaw, worry darkening his eyes to storm clouds. "Do you think she'll be there?"

We climb into the car, and I grimace at my brother. He doesn't know I ran into her last month. "I do, but we should make an appearance for Chandler's sake. If Sybil makes you uncomfortable, we'll keep our distance or leave."

Ethan puts the car into gear. "I didn't even realize they were on the island."

Guilt eats me up. I should have warned him.

"You're the designated driver later," Ethan states. "As soon as I see Sybil, I'm going to drink. Heavily."

Well, shit. It's going to be hard as fuck to stay sober with her around. How else am I going to drown out the pain? If I can't handle myself, we'll call a cab and pick up the car in the morning.

Twenty minutes later, we're walking into the club, right past the doorman—we handed the bouncer a wad of crisp hundred-dollar bills to skip the line.

We work our way through the crowd until we spot Chandler alone with an empty beer glass and a dazed smile. He's watching the dance floor, and I'm sure he's thinking about getting up there and showing everyone how it's done. The kid *loves* to dance. Nothing technical or classical, just wild and free like an inflatable wind air dancer in front of a tire shop.

"Hey buddy, happy birthday," I say, and he jumps up, his grin growing as wide as ever.

"Cooper!" He's got a small build, but his vice-like hug is world famous. It nearly knocks the wind out of me, but he quickly moves to my brother. "And Ethan, my favorite person."

I bark out a laugh. Ethan is his favorite, and he's shameless about letting everyone know. The only person he idolizes more is his own father. I wonder if that's changed since everything happened, but I have a suspicion nobody told him about the affair. We certainly haven't said anything.

"How's it going?" Ethan asks, and the two get straight to talking as we sit.

My gaze zeroes in on the bar area, searching for Sybil. She's got to be here. She would *never* let Chandler come alone.

I sure hope it's her and not Gregory. I wouldn't mind seeing Amelia, but there's no way I can be cordial with that prick.

"You're not alone, are you?" I interrupt the guys.

"Sybil brought me," he confirms. "She's buying me another beer. Says I can't mix it with tequila or other stuff. Just beers tonight."

"Your sister is smart. Listen to her," Ethan says, but his tone has dropped considerably, and his restless eyes dart to mine. I know he's nervous about seeing his ex.

Quite frankly, so am I.

When she gets her pretty ass back here, I'm going to pretend I don't have a care in the fucking world, like she didn't rip Ethan's heart out and stomp on it with her designer heels. Like she didn't destroy my heart in the process.

The hardest part? I don't feel like I have a right to miss her like Ethan does.

"So, your parents are okay with you drinking?" Ethan asks.

Chandler rolls his eyes. "It's legal. I can do what I want."

Ethan holds up his hands. "I'm not judging. I was only checking."

"I know the risks," he says, gripping the edge of the table and raising his voice. "My parents made me go to a doctor a few months ago to make sure it would be okay for me, and the doctor said it was fine as long as I don't drink too much."

I hate to see him agitated, so I pat his round shoulder and give him a wink. "Don't worry, we're not here to stop you. We just want you safe. That's all."

Maybe I'm ignorant, but I would rather Chandler not drink at all. I know firsthand how addicting it can be—how easy it is to fall into bad habits with something that numbs the emotions.

At least he's got Syb here to take care of him.

And us.

Helpful for him, but not for me, considering I can't stop looking toward the bar, searching for her in the crowd, simultaneously dying to see her and not wanting to see her.

Then there she is, her brother's beer in one hand and an ice water in the other. She falters when she sees us, mixed emotions rippling across her face like deep ocean currents. She straightens her shoulders as she approaches with a murderous expression.

God, she's beautiful when she's mad. She's stunning in a way that makes my chest ache. Dressed in a little black dress, she's got the attention of every male in here, but she acts like she couldn't care less as she marches toward us.

"Cooper and Ethan," she says coolly, her eyes flashing emerald as they jump from me to my brother. "Crossing boundaries, I see. What are you doing here?"

"I invited them," Chandler announces, giving her a death-glare of his own.

Atta-boy.

"Yup, we were invited," I supply nonchalantly. "We wouldn't miss Chandler's twenty-first birthday for anything, not even your *boundaries*. Isn't that right, Ethan?"

Ethan sits up taller, but his voice is strained. "That's right."

Sybil is still standing, towering over us, when Chandler reaches out to grab the beer in her hand. After weighing her options, she passes him the drink and sits next to him with a pout.

I return Sybil's charged look with a completely unaffected one of my own, even though I'm equally pissed off. Ethan, however, isn't so good at hiding his feelings. My boy looks completely shattered.

Fuck.

Thank God Chandler cracks a joke. "Tastes so bad but feels so good," he says after taking a long swallow of the beer and following it with an exaggerated sigh.

"The world is your oyster now, kid," I confirm, and Ethan and Sybil both shoot me annoyed glares.

I hold up my hands. "What? You heard the man. He's going to be responsible. That's more than any of us can say. Do you remember what we did for our twenty-firsts?"

"Still putting your foot in your mouth, aren't you?" Sybil hisses.

Yeah, maybe. "I need a drink." I step away. "Do you want anything, Ethan?"

Ethan holds my gaze for a long moment. "I take it we're calling a car tonight?"

I nod like the functioning-alcoholic I've become lately.

"That's fine with me," Ethan confirms. "I'll get whatever you get, but please make sure it's strong."

Amen to that.

Making my way to the bar, I can't help but wonder about Chandler's intentions tonight. Does he think getting Ethan and Sybil in the same room will get them back together? It's not the worst plan.

The thought of having to endure them as a couple again makes me want to vomit. Then again, I want her in my life. I want things to be how they were compared to how they are now. Truth is, I'm just as fucked up about this girl as my brother is, and I'd rather lose her to him than lose her entirely.

The bar is crowded, and it takes forever to get drinks. This isn't one of those clubs that has good waitstaff and tables like in Manhattan. It's definitely a wait-in-line kind of establishment, but I'm grateful for that. I don't want to sit and listen to whatever conversation is happening at that table, or more likely, the long awkward silences stretching out between Chandler's attempts to make things better.

Things are never going to be better.

I end up with two double whiskeys and return to the table, trying not to glower at the way Ethan and Sybil have their heads leaned close while they talk. I set his drink down a little too forcefully, and the pair jump apart.

"Here you go," I seethe.

"Thanks." Ethan doesn't seem to give a shit that I'm pissed off.

Whiskey is one that's best drunk slow and steady, but my brother treats it like a cheap shot, downing it remarkably quickly. Then he stands as I'm sitting.

"Where are you going?" Sybil asks Ethan, her tone borderline angry.

Ethan doesn't answer, his shoulders rigid as he strolls to the dance floor. It takes less than a minute for him to find an attractive girl to dance with.

Chandler's staring after them like Ethan just took his birthday cake and threw it against the wall. I reach for his hand, giving it a squeeze. "Hey, don't worry about it. They broke up, but that doesn't mean we can't be friends. Right, Sybil?"

"Right," she says, lying straight through her teeth.

"You ready to get out there?" I ask Chandler with a wink, and he perks right up.

We finish our drinks, Sybil sticking to her water, and the whiskey numbs me enough to get through this evening without causing a scene. Are we going to be friends with Sybil after tonight? Nope, but her decision to ice us out doesn't mean I can't make sure Chandler has the best fucking birthday of his life.

THIRTY-FOUR

C ooper
Past - Age 23

I'm having a good time with Chandler. It helps that women keep wanting to dance with us. Chandler is eating it up. He loves attention even more than I do, especially from the female persuasion. But I'm keenly aware Sybil is *not* having a good time. She's watching us like we're taking a piss on her baby blanket. I guess, in a way, Chandler has always been her comfort person.

Ethan notices it too, and he returns to Sybil. They're talking again, and I'm dying to know what they're saying. After a minute, Ethan stalks to the dance floor.

"What was that about?" I ask him.

"I asked her to dance, *as friends*, and she refused. She says we're *not* friends and told me I need to move on."

Luckily Chandler doesn't hear this part. It would break his happy-birthday heart. Ethan finds a new dance partner, and the bright neon lights mixed with the thumping music juxtapose the awful anxiety in my chest.

This isn't fun, but it's not about me. It's about Chandler, so I continue to do what I do. I make sure the guy is surrounded by beautiful woman and encourage him to show us what he's made of, unable to hold in my laugh when he does his signature "raise the roof" move. I sure love this kid, and I hate we can't have more than the occasional text. Soon, I'll fade from Chandler's life forever.

Despite the fun he's having, that I'm pretending to have, I keep my eyes on anyone who gets near him. Most people are kind, but not everyone. I swear to God, I will hurt anyone who dares to make fun of him or treat him less than anyone else.

When my eyes aren't on Chandler, they're on Sybil. She's at the table, watching us, being a sourpuss. And she *still* draws me in. Flashes of our one shared kiss return to my mind... and my body. My muscles tighten, and my cock twitches just thinking about that moment. I'll never forget the heat of her, the way I so quickly threw away my morals to get one taste of my fantasy. I shouldn't be thinking about that kiss, not after everything.

I'm sure she doesn't think of it, either.

Then her eyes connect with mine, and I question everything.

Her gaze is wanting. Needy. Angsty as hell. But also sad. Everything I'm feeling. Have all the things that have plagued me also plagued her? Dropping me doesn't undo what we did. It happened, and it was one of the most real moments of my life.

"Stop that," I mutter to myself, shaking the thoughts away. This is a betrayal of my mind and body and especially of my brother, and it needs to end.

The song changes from an upbeat pop number to one with a low, sultry base. The tone of the dancers changes with it, people coupling up to dance close, many of them grinding their bodies together. A woman immediately zeroes in on me, which is typical, and I'm tempted to give in to someone else's body instead of the one on my mind, but this isn't the time or place. I take Chandler back to the table.

"Next round's on me. What do you guys want?" I ask.

Sybil shakes her head, that gorgeous hair of hers catching the lights and mesmerizing me for a moment. "Nothing for me."

"I'll come with you," Chandler says, following me to the bar and leaving his sister again.

"Are you having fun?" I ask him.

He nods happily, clearly buzzed from the two beers he's had and excited for the next one. I don't know how much it's going to take to get him drunk, but I'm guessing the third will do it. Everyone's a lightweight at first, and Chandler is small.

Maybe it'll be good for him to wake up with a hangover and rethink the whole alcohol thing. If we're lucky, he'll never want to touch the stuff again.

Not that I have room to talk. I was fifteen when I had my first drink. It's been a source of both pain and pleasure ever since.

"Why is Ethan dancing with that girl? Is she his girlfriend?"

The questions catch me off guard.

Oh man.

I wish I could make this easy for him.

"No, they're not together," I say carefully. "But if they were, it would be okay. Ethan deserves to find a new girlfriend, you know? He deserves to be happy."

Chandler's expression crumbles, and I feel like a total asshole. Sometimes being the messenger of bad news is the absolute worst.

"He doesn't love Sybil anymore?"

I give his shoulder a little squeeze. "They'll *always* love each other, but not the kind of love that's needed to be boyfriend and girlfriend."

"They were gonna get married."

I nod because I get it. "Not anymore."

Chandler's face turns red and splotchy. "Why won't anyone tell me what happened?"

I wish I could answer his question, but it's not my place. Still, I can't leave him hanging. He deserves some kind of explanation.

"They've changed as people and don't want to do marriage together anymore."

"That's stupid."

"Well, Ethan is focusing on school right now, and your sister is focusing on her career, and that's okay."

"If Ethan wants to focus on school, then why is Ethan dancing with other girls?"

We edge closer to the bar. "It's fun. You had fun dancing with girls too, didn't you? That doesn't mean you're dating them. Boys and girls can have fun without romance."

He nods, and then it's our turn to get drinks. We bring them to the table where Sybil has turned her glare in Ethan's direction. I've got to hand it to my brother. He is giving zero shits tonight. In fact, he's currently gyrating on some girl so fucking hard that it looks like he's about to come right there on the dance floor. Good hell. Most people don't act like this in clubs anymore, and Ethan rarely does, but apparently he's channeling his inner 2000s.

Chandler is visibly upset again, his face beet-red and his eyes watering.

"Hey, you stay here, okay?" Sybil says to her brother. "I'm going to go talk to Ethan."

He forces a smile as she marches off. I don't think for one second she's jealous about Ethan dancing with a woman. This is about Ethan being seconds away from taking a woman home when we're supposed to be celebrating Chandler.

That said, Sybil doesn't get a say in what Ethan does anymore. She can't break up with him and then get mad when he wants to hook up with someone else. Ethan's cheeks redden after she spends a minute with her hands flying around her, clearly upset as she yells at him. He returns to the table with his tail between his legs like a disobedient puppy getting chastised.

Sybil follows, but the woman Ethan was dancing with grabs hold of her arm and yanks her back, yelling something I can't hear over the music. I'm out of my seat in less than a second.

"Go sit with Chandler," I instruct to my brother, not sticking around as I make it to Sybil.

"You're a real bitch," the girl spits at Sybil.

"Back up," I growl, and the woman throws her hands in the air and storms away.

"You didn't have to do that." Sybil turns on me, and anger bangs through me like a thunderclap. I think of the pain she's caused and all the shit she's put us through.

Grabbing hold of her wrist, I march her to the other side of the dance floor. I lead her right up to the far wall with the darkest shadows. She shakes her wrist from my hand and presses herself against the exposed brick. I tower over her, staring down at this woman who drives me crazy in every way.

"What do you want?" she snaps, her familiar perfume enveloping me in the small space, reminding me of how many times I've been reeled in by her sweet scent.

What I really want becomes very clear by the way my cock thickens in my pants. *Fuck.*

Despite my better judgment, I let out a dark chuckle. "Don't ask questions you won't like the answers to, Valentine."

Her mouth pops open, those pretty lips doing ungodly

things to me without even being on my body. *Double fuck.* I need to back this up real quick before I get myself into trouble.

"Don't call me that," she says, but I ignore the comment and continue.

"This isn't about what I want. It's about doing the right thing by Ethan."

She shakes her head. "I don't know what you're talking about."

"You're not being fair to him," I say, a little annoyed I have to spell it out for her. "It's been hard for him to get over you, but he's finally putting himself out there again."

She glowers. "So? There's a time and a place for everything."

"And a nightclub is a pretty good place to find a woman to dance with, don't you think?"

"It was hurting Chandler's feelings."

"Chandler can handle it. He deserves the truth, and that's what I told him. Guess what? He is okay. He's an adult, old enough to drink alcohol, right? So, unless you're planning to get back together with Ethan, you have no right to tell my brother what to do."

Her eyes narrow, sparking with fire.

"So you're mad I told Ethan to go to the table and not for any other reason?"

I don't know what she's talking about. "You're not his girlfriend anymore," I say slowly.

"Fiancée. I was his fiancée," she says.

"You're not his anything anymore, and that was your choice."

Our gazes are locked in, sparks dancing between us.

"Why do you care so much?" The challenge in her voice is unmistakable.

"He's my brother."

I'm such a liar.

"That's the only reason you care?" Her eyes drop to my lips, and I realize what she means. She's calling me out. She knows. She knows I get jealous anytime she so much as looks at Ethan, that I'm turned on right now being alone with her, and even though she's not explicitly saying it, it's not a secret I'm hiding well.

Why do I care so much? I care because it's her, because I don't want them getting back together, can't stomach the idea of them working it out, not when I've dreamed about burying myself in her body too many times to count. I'm haunted by this woman.

"That's all," I lie. But I'm inching closer, closer, closer.

"I don't believe you," she whispers.

We're too close for comfort, but I can't seem to pull away. I've got her against the wall, and I raise my arms to cage her in, my head bending toward her. It would be so easy to erase the space between us. A few measly inches are all that stands between me and this woman who could decimate my life. Forget about the fear of rejection; I would be sick if Ethan saw me kiss her.

I step away so I can breathe again, but I can't say I like oxygen more than I like Sybil Laurence.

"You don't have to believe me," I say, "but our brothers are waiting for us. Let's finish out the night, and tomorrow you can pretend like none of this ever happened. You're good at that."

"Fine by me." Her eyes sparkle, the green flashing in challenge. She steps away from the wall and marches to where Ethan and Chandler are waiting.

I can't help but watch her from behind, following her like I always do.

THIRTY-FIVE

C ooper
      Past - Age 23

Chandler is sitting at the table with a row of shot glasses. People I don't recognize surround him, chanting for him to, *"Drink! Drink! Drink!"* I feel like I've walked into an unsanctioned frathouse basement party seconds before the cops are going to bust it up.

"What are you doing?" Sybil practically pounces on the group, pushing past drunk girls tottering on heels to get to her brother. I'm right behind her. "Where the hell is Ethan?" she practically screams.

Good fucking point.

"He went to the bathroom," Chandler says, slurring his words. He's clearly had too much, and my heart jumps to my throat when he starts to sway.

"We're leaving," Sybil says, trying to help her brother from his seat, but as soon as he stands, his knees buckle.

"I'm drunk!" he cheers, pumping his fists in the air. Most of the crowd cheer along with him. From the empty shot glasses littering the table, it's safe to say Chandler is more than drunk. He's plastered.

"Shit," I mutter. He might get alcohol poisoning from this. "How much can someone like Chandler drink?" I ask Sybil, feeling like an ignorant ass for not knowing.

"Unless there's an underlying liver issue, people with Downs can metabolize it the same as you and me," she says, while on the verge of tears. "But... but..."

But she's not sure how much he'll be able to handle emotionally.

I help Chandler to his feet, patting him on the back. "You okay?"

"He's having fun," some random girl says with a shrill laugh.

"That's enough," I yell at the crowd, unable to hold down my anger. They don't know Chandler except that he's visibly disabled. He's a human being, not some joke for their entertainment.

"Hey, give the kid a break. He asked for shots, so we ordered him shots." The same girl snorts, sounding like a smug bitch. "It's his birthday." She pats Chandler on the head as if he were a puppy. "Happy birthday, little guy."

Sybil shoves the girl's hand away, and I see red.

"He's not your fucking little guy," I hiss.

The girl's face pales, and her eyes widen. "I mean, we didn't pay for the shots. They did." She points to two older men hanging on the outskirts of the crowd. They look like the kind of creepy leaches that come to places like these with a fat wallet, hoping to pick up drunk women.

I stalk right up to them, getting in their faces. "You ordered a flight of shots for a Downs kid and cheered him on to binge drink?"

The men smirk, and the fucker with a bald spot and a red face responds. "What's it to you?"

"That's my little brother, you fucker."

Not *technically*, but close enough.

Baldy chuckles, and his loser of a friend steps in closer. Two against one, but I'm not afraid in the slightest.

"You want to fight us for getting the retard drinks?" He laughs, the scent of alcohol heavy on his breath. "The kid *asked* for them. I'm not a bad guy; I'm a Good Samaritan."

Rage bursts inside me like an inferno, exploding through my fist, connecting with his face. He falls to the ground, and I'm on him in seconds. "I'll fucking kill you for calling him that, you motherfucker!"

I beat the shit out of this guy, barely aware of my surroundings. Sybil is crying. Chandler is in his chair. The guy's pudgy friend is unsuccessfully trying to haul me off him. And this mother fucker deserves to have his face rearranged.

They land a few punches on me, but it's nothing I can't handle. The pain doesn't even register. It's only when the bouncer hauls me off his ass that the fighting actually stops, and the two men scurry away like rats. Ethan's returned, and he's got Chandler, practically holding him up since he's so wasted. Tears stream down Sybil's red face, and the entire scene goes from loud and hot to cold and quiet.

The crowd disperses.

"You're out of here," the bouncer says, hauling my ass out of the club and depositing me on the curb. "You're lucky I don't call the police, but I heard what that guy said. I let you get in a few good punches, but I still have to do my job."

"Yeah, no problem." I salute him, spitting out a mouthful of blood onto the pavement as I stand. The bouncer leaves, and Ethan and Sybil find me, Chandler slumped between them.

"What did the bouncer say?" Sybil asks.

I shake my head and keep my mouth shut. Even though Chandler won't remember this in the morning, I don't want him to know.

"Where were you?" I turn on my brother instead, fighting the rage churning in my chest. "We leave you alone with Chandler for five minutes, and suddenly he's downing shots?"

Ethan's face is pale, and I already feel bad for putting this on him.

"I had to pee," Ethan says in a strained whisper, sounding absolutely gutted. "me,I should've taken him with me, but we didn't want to lose our table. I'm an idiot." He turns to Chandler. "I'm so sorry."

Chandler can't even answer; he's *that* drunk.

Sybil's tears have stopped, but the tracks of mascara across her face make me want to punch someone all over again.

"I want to know what that guy said," she tries again. She's really not the type to let this go.

I sigh. "Let's get Chandler to the car first."

Chandler's head is lolling. Five minutes and he'll be asleep, but if he has alcohol poisoning, he needs to get to a hospital. The thing is, we don't know how much he had to drink. Three beers and who knows how many shots...

Shots someone else supplied and could have been tampered with.

"We should take him to the hospital," I say.

Sybil stiffens. "I'll handle it. Let's get him in the backseat."

A few minutes later, he's buckled in Sybil's car. Ethan slides into the backseat with him, trying to keep him awake.

Sybil and I step away from the vehicle so I can quickly relay what happened. Maybe I'm an idiot for expecting her to thank me for standing up for her brother, but she doesn't look too happy.

She pinches the bridge of her nose and growls. "I think getting into a fight only made it worse. I hope Chandler doesn't remember this tomorrow."

"Are you serious? You think I overreacted?"

She shrugs. "I don't know, but getting in a fight wasn't a good for anyone."

"And I'm supposed to let some guy call him a slur and do nothing?"

Bottom lip trembling, she frowns. "I took him out to have fun, and he didn't. *That's* what I know. Now I have to call my parents to meet us at the hospital. Sorry, but this never would've happened if you two hadn't shown up."

"You think this is our fault?" I glare, utterly shocked she's blaming us. Sure, Ethan fucked up by going to the bathroom, but we were *all* there to watch Chandler.

"It certainly never would've happened if you and I didn't leave the table to go off and argue about stupid shit." She runs a hand through her hair. "I don't have time for this. I've got to go."

"Fine, but don't blame any of this on me, Ethan, or yourself."

She circles her index finger between us. "I absolutely blame this. Us. You and me. Me and Ethan. You and Ethan. We're all toxic together."

That word feels worse than any punch those guys landed on me. "Toxic?"

"Yes." She sounds so worn out. Defeated. Heartbroken. "We can't be friends anymore, Cooper. We can't be anything. There's too much bad blood between our families, and quite frankly, you're not a good influence on me."

I step away as if she slapped me. "You really mean this, don't you?"

"I'm sorry, Cooper. Tonight can't happen again. We can't pretend to be friends when we're not friends anymore. We're not anything."

I stare, letting her words sink in deep. Maybe I can accept them.

Her eyes water. "Goodbye, Cooper. Take care of yourself."

She turns her back on me, but I can't let her walk away. I catch her wrist and twist her around to face me, gathering her against my chest in a tight hug. She lets out a squeak but doesn't pull away. The heat between us is an electrical storm, making me feel alive in the worst way.

Alive and terrified.

"You're going to pretend we're nothing?"

She shakes her head, hissing between her teeth and keeping her voice low. We're both well aware Ethan and Chandler are in the car a few paces away. "Don't you see? This a problem. I was engaged to your twin brother. Our parents had an affair. Our families broke apart. It's over, Cooper. Please, let me go."

I can't believe I'm really losing her.

I lost her months ago, but I couldn't *believe* it then, and I told myself she would come to her senses, and that no matter what, I would never let something ruin our friendship for good.

But here she is, practically *pleading* with me to leave her alone.

She's done. It's over.

I release her from my arms and my mind and my heart. For the first time in our lives, I'm the one to turn my back and walk away.

THIRTY-SIX

S ybil
    Present - Age 27

"Nothing like trial by fire, huh?" Arden says with a cheeky grin, and I give her an exasperated nod. "Well, if anyone can do this, it's you. You're *great* with people."

We're in her living room, our feet kicked up under us as we lounge on their couch. I'm hiding from the responsibilities waiting for me in the penthouse next door and told her as much.

They say learning by doing is best, but learning the ins and outs of producing a reality show *while* we're doing it has been exhausting. Luckily, Perry hired a great team.

"The biggest thing is gathering enough content," I say. "The editors will pick apart and piece the puzzle together in post, making sure what actually gets aired is interesting to enough to keep the viewers hooked."

"From what you've told me so far, I think you guys are going to be fine."

Arden's good about bringing levity to a stressful situation. She's one of the most logical and levelheaded people I know. Now that she's with Ethan, I can see why they work so well. I used to think people needed their opposite to balance them out, but I feel differently these days. They can better support and accept each other since they *understand* each other so well. It works.

"So tell me about school?" I ask. "How's the computer science degree coming along?"

If you ask me, that sounds like the most boring and complicated degree out there, but I'm not her. Arden loves this stuff. She has a number's brain and insists that coding is fun.

She smiles, her amber eyes lighting up and the spattering of freckles on her face crinkling. "It's so good." She sighs. "I love the program. It's hard, but I'm up for the challenge."

She's at Columbia, finishing out her bachelors. Initially, she was going to work for Laurence, but she's decided to forge her own path. She plans to find a normal coding job after graduating. I wish I could see her in our offices every day, but I admire her for sticking to her convictions.

She waves me off. "Enough about school. I want to hear more about the show. What's drama? I'm dying to know what's going on over there."

I snort. "I thought you and Ethan wanted to stay out of it."

That was one thing they were adamant about when Cooper told them about the plan.

"I never said I didn't want the tea. These are famous people, right? They've got to be interesting."

I sink further into the couch. "I don't even know where to start, and I am supposed to keep this a secret."

"From who? The general public?"

I nod.

"Well, I'm not going to say a word to anyone about anything." She tosses a pillow at my face. "Spill it!"

"Fine, fine." I giggle, hugging the pillow to my chest. "No need for violence here, *sister*."

"Oh, God," she shakes her head. "I'm still not used to that."

"You and me both. Okay, well, first of all, the hockey player and the supermodel hit it off." I snort. "They were making out in the hot tub by day two, and they're already sleeping together. Which would be fine, except the movie star is also super into Gloria. Oh, and Gloria loves the attention, so of course she's entertaining the flirtations with a new man."

Benton doesn't seem phased, but I'm pretty sure he's putting on a front.

"And the pop star and the politician's kids don't get along. They agree politically, but other than that, they're so different. Audra is kind of a punk and says whatever she's thinking, and the politician kids have media training and keep everything above board."

Arden grins. "Sounds juicy."

"And then Dane, the politician's kid, got dumped on camera by his longtime boyfriend last night."

She frowns. "Poor guy."

"There's more, but those are the highlights."

"You guys have a lot to work with."

"We do. We haven't had to do much to produce drama; they're doing it for us."

It's made my job easier than I expected. I check in on my cast often, but they don't need a lot of advice or direction.

She stares at me deadpanned. "I never would've guessed putting six super famous, super hot, and super opinionated celebrities in a house together would create drama."

I snort. "Who'd have thought?"

She gives me a wicked grin. "But this hockey guy... He's the one you were sleeping with, right?"

"Yes." I smirk, remembering the fun times Benton and I have had together.

"You're not bothered he's with the supermodel now?"

"Not at all," I say, surprising myself. I chew my bottom lip for a second. "Actually, I haven't slept with anyone in months. My sex-life has been nonexistent lately."

Of course, that is the moment Ethan pops his head into the room, having gotten home from work. "Didn't need to hear that."

"Then don't eavesdrop, you creep." I chuck the pillow at his head. It grazes his perfectly styled dark hair and his blue eyes spark. "It's not like *you* need to worry about getting laid, Mr. Newlywed."

Ethan shrugs. "What can I say? We're supposed to be naked as often as we can be, and actually, it's good you didn't come over after I got home or else you'd probably would've interrupted."

Arden is beet-red and jumps from her position on the couch, waving her hands around in surrender. "I don't care if you guys have known each other forever. We're not talking about what I do in my bed."

"Yeah, it is a little weird," I relent.

"Fair point, baby." He grabs her round the middle and lays one on her. "Our sex life is *all* yours."

She giggles, and that's my queue to leave.

"I'm out of here. Text me later and let's get lunch?"

She nods before turning to make out with her new husband.

I head across the hall to check in on filming. We're doing one-on-one interviews today, so I'm able to slip inside without causing an issue. Those interviews are filmed in the individual bedrooms and not a confessional room like what is done on most reality shows. Perry says the bedrooms add personality to the characters, letting the audience see them in their private environments. We don't normally have cameras in the bedrooms, for obvious reasons, so these confessional interviews are some of the only times we get access. Obviously, the set was not designed by the cast, but they've all made their spaces their own.

Once in the penthouse, I zero in on Ricki arguing quietly with someone in the kitchen.

My hackles immediately rise.

It's Lance Vale.

What the heck is he doing on set? He hasn't been here once, and every time we have our Friday morning meetings, he's more interested in lobbying for CEO with me than what *I'm* actually doing. That board meeting he was worried about? Didn't go his way when the board agreed to interview more candidates and reconvene in August. To say he's not happy about it would be an understatement.

"Everything okay?" I question, sliding between Lance and Ricki.

She turns on me. "Your boss thinks we're going to cause bad press for Laurence International," she says hastily. "He threatened to pull funding."

My stomach drops.

"Is this true?" I turn on Vale.

"We need to talk," he says gruffly. "Is there somewhere we can go, or should we head to the office?"

He's looking at me like I'm still the child he met years ago and not the capable adult I've become.

I'm immediately annoyed as my lips press into a thin line.

I give Ricki a "don't worry" look and lead Vale downstairs.

"This is our crew headquarters," I tell him.

Craft services has just finished preparing lunch, and it's busier down here than it was upstairs.

Maybe we need to find another place.

I'm tempted to take him into Cooper's bedroom, but the last thing I need is a rumor that I was seen going into a bedroom with the boss.

"Are you hungry?" I ask. "Looks like it's a deli spread today. We could grab some food and find some place to talk."

"No." He gives me a pointed look, and I sigh.

The third bedroom has been set up for hair and makeup, but since the stars mostly use their own people, this room isn't in play as often as the others. Sure enough, it's empty when we go inside.

I still leave the door partially cracked.

"What's this about pulling funding?" I ask, folding my arms across my chest and standing up to the man who might one day be able to fire me.

"We're not in the business of skeezy reality television," he states. "Leave that to King. If they want this show, then by all means, they can have it, but I still don't think it's good for us."

"We're weeks into filming and have a contractual obligation."

"I looked at the contract and think there's a way out of it, but I came here today just to be sure of my decision, and after meeting the cast, I'm certain we need to distance ourselves from this asinine project."

My mouth pops open. "Are you forgetting why you and everyone else agreed to do this show in the first place?"

"That five percent is not going to make or break us. We should be putting the company first."

"We *are* putting the company first."

"That five percent is your family's problem; you've made it the entire company's problem. What happens when this thing airs, and an embarrassing scandal breaks out? What happens when our shareholders demand answers? I'm the one who has to answer to them, not you and not your family. Not anymore. It's going to be on me."

The reality of his words sinks in. He doesn't view my family as important to Laurence anymore.

"But like you said, you're not the CEO," I remind him, trying to sound as calm as possible even though I'm seething. "So it *won't* fall on you. And anyway, the show is going to be a huge hit and make us a lot of money."

His eyes narrow. "I'm not the CEO *yet*, but I will be."

I can't believe this guy.

"Listen, I told my mom you had my full support, so you're welcome. You should be talking to her about it, not me."

Suspicion dances behind his eyes. "Do I have your support? Because she, in fact, did *not* recommend me for the position."

My entire body prickles. I thought for sure she would, but I didn't get confirmation. I'm the only Laurence currently working at the company; it's my butt on the line with Lance fucking Vale.

"Wait..." My eyes narrow. "Do you *want* my projects to fail?"

Is pulling funding some sort of sick revenge?

He releases a long breath, pinching the bridge of his nose. The guy looks like he's aged ten years since my father's death. He didn't ask to be burdened by the company fallout, but that still doesn't mean I'm okay with him screwing me over.

"I apologize, Sybil. Of course I don't want your projects to fail. I'm worried what this show is going to do for Laurence, I truly am. For *both* of our not just mine." He straightens his suit and takes a deep breath. "This has been a hard year for Laurence, and not only because your father passed away. Fiscally, it's been tough. There's a lot on the line. If this show is a failure, I can't say what will happen. I know it may not sound like it, but I'm honestly looking out for us both."

I nod. I get his fears even if I disagree with his approach.

"Please understand the more drama this show has, the more money we're all going to make. As much as the shareholders love their reputation, they love money more. Everything is going to be okay. You've got to trust me on that."

"I hope so. And what about your work with the foundation? That's not slipping, is it?"

He clocks my hesitation immediately.

"A little behind," I admit, "but I plan to make it up. I care deeply about my job."

"Which one?" He looks pointedly around the room.

It throws me off, as if I don't care about the foundation because I'm here instead of at the office. "You know how important the charity work is to me, even more important than this show, but I'm only one person and—"

"I've been asking you to hire an assistant, and you still haven't done it," he interrupts. "Have you even posted a job or taken interviews?"

I wince. He's got me there.

It's been busy and nothing I'm currently doing is something I want to give to an assistant. It's one thing to have help hosting an event, but it's something else entirely to have someone else doing my job for me. They'd have to talk to our donors and charities, and I don't like that. I've never been good at sharing control.

"I thought as much. Well, lucky for you, my brilliant nephew has finished at Vanderbilt and needs a job. I'm giving him the assistant job on your behalf. Make sure you're in the office on Monday to go over his duties with him."

I blink rapidly, lost for words. Lance Vale leaves, brushing past me and out the door.

That's when Cooper walks into the room. "What was that about?" His question is sharp and defensive.

The truth spills out of my still shocked lips. "Vale is worried about the show and about me doing my job well. He doesn't think I can hack it."

Furry lights those dark eyes. "Vale's an idiot. Don't worry about that guy."

How can I not? Because at least for now, Vale is my boss.

THIRTY-SEVEN

S ybil

Present - Age 27

We've finished the interviews, so Cooper and I are in the screening room.

Perry ran to the hospital to check on his little sister, Madeline. Poor girl has officially been diagnosed with breast cancer—a rare diagnosis at her age—but her prognosis is good, and she's handling treatment well.

After a long day of filming, he asked us to watch everything and make notes of the most interesting sound bites for him to review later. The crew has gone home for the evening, so it's extra quiet.

I would say the exhaustion is starting to weigh on me, but I'm keenly aware I'm alone with Cooper, and something about him charges me like nothing else can.

"Why are you acting so weird?" He eyes me, leaning back in his chair, his hands behind his head. His biceps flex under the soft edge of his cotton t-shirt, and he looks completely comfortable with his prosthetic underneath his gray sweatpants.

And those sweatpants? They send me into a tailspin. Why are they so attractive?

"Am I acting weird?" I respond, wincing slightly at the crack in my voice.

He presses his lips together, fighting a grin. "Uh huh."

Well, I'm attracted to you, and I shouldn't be.

"I'm fine."

It took five years to restore my friendship with Cooper. *Five years.* I'm not going to screw it up in the matter of five seconds.

His gaze locks on mine, so piercing it's as if he can read my mind. "Okay, just checking."

He hits play on the footage and picks up his pen.

Back to work.

I do the same, but I'm distracted. I can't stop eyeing Cooper, my mind wandering to places it shouldn't go.

The smallest things about him have suddenly become all-encompassing, like the way he scratches his thick eyebrow when he's thinking, or the tiny scar just below his bottom lip that he got in a baseball game when we were twelve. It stretches when he smiles, emphasizing the fullness of his beautiful lips.

My gaze drops to his chest, and I'm reminded of how he felt under my fingertips. There's no doubt his muscles have broadened over the years. I used to see him as a boy but he's all man now.

Then down to those damn sweatpants again and my entire body hums with want. How can a simple article of clothing make me want to do naughty things to his body? Is it because I like seeing a man comfortable or is it because Coop's the one wearing them around his hip bones and I'm curious about what's underneath?

This is bad.

We're friends.

But that doesn't mean things between us are what they used to be. I've changed since giving up monogamy when Ethan and I broke up. I prefer open relationships with men like Cooper, and he's *everything* that's my type.

If our friendship was new for the first time, I'd proposition him right here and now, but I can't risk something so reckless. I finally have my best friend back after a five-year break, and I can't mess us up again.

He smirks in my direction, and the dark suggestive glint that transforms his gaze is unmistakable—the man knows I'm checking him out.

I jump up. "I'm going to the bathroom." Hurrying to the half-bath of the living room, I lock myself inside and stare into the mirror, hands hooked over the porcelain sink. "What are you doing?" I whisper. "Get it together. This is *Cooper.*"

The kiss we shared five years ago comes spiraling to the forefront of my mind. I don't know if I'm playing it up in my mind or if it really was as good as I remember it.

Five years is a long time to make something a bigger deal than it actually was.

After a few deep breaths, I splash some water on my face and get back out there. Cooper is waiting for me in the kitchen, a glass of red wine in his hand.

"I think you might need this," he says.

I march over there and take it, the liquid touching my lips before I can blurt out a thank you. He chuckles at my enthusiasm.

"Aren't you going to have any?" I ask when my mouth is free.

He shrugs. "I'm not drinking right now."

My breath catches in my throat, and I blink rapidly. "Since when?"

He waits a beat. "Since New Year's."

Silence falls between us.

New Year's Eve was not a good night for either of us, but six months of sobriety is kind of a shock.

"I want to apologize about that night," he continues. "I was out of line."

"I wasn't exactly kind to you, either."

He shrugs. "Yeah, well, I woke up ashamed of what I could remember. Some of it's black, and I didn't like the person I was anymore. Drinking only made that worse." He taps his fingers on the countertop. "I've used it as a coping mechanism. I knew I had a problem, but I wasn't motivated to change. After that party, I realized I couldn't handle alcohol responsibly anymore."

"I'm proud of you."

He lets out a self-deprecating snort.

"It's true. It takes a lot to admit you have a problem and actually fix it. Are you going to try to stay sober forever, or what's the plan?"

He shrugs. "For now, I'm not going to drink at all. Maybe I'll be able to handle it someday, but I'm okay if I never go back."

He shifts, drawing attention to his prosthetic. "I have a lot of buried anger about my leg. Drinking only makes that anger come out where I don't want it to. It's like this molten lava that's burning underneath the surface, but when I drink, every-thing erupts. I can't allow that anymore; people will get hurt."

I set the glass on the counter and erase the space between us, wrapping him into a tight hug. He immediately embraces me, and it feels amazing, like returning home after years away.

"I'm sorry about your leg, Cooper," I whisper into his shirt. "I'm truly so proud of you for how you're handling things. You're doing better than most people would."

"I'm not so sure about that." His breath tickles my scalp, voice rumbling in his chest as he holds me tight.

We hang on until the hug lingers, the energy shifting from comforting to something more primal. My body buzzes, like electricity traveling under my skin.

He's still holding me, but his thumb slides up and down my elbow, the feel of it erupting shivers across my skin. His masculine scent envelopes me, signaling safety and anticipation at the same time.

"Is this okay?" Cooper asks, and I nod into the soft fabric of his shirt.

God help me... I want this.

I want *him*.

His hands slide downward, cupping my ass. We both hold our breath as he presses me against the hard erection under his sweatpants, and God, I want to slip my hands below the hem and feel what's ready for me.

He leans back ever so slightly, his brown eyes locking on mine. Questions battle behind his expression, knocking over each other and none making it through his parted lips. I answer them just as silently.

With a sexy half-smile, he leans close, his nose tickling my jaw.

He's going to kiss me.

And I'm going to let him.

The lock rattles, slicing through the moment. We jump apart as if shocked by an electric current. Perry shuffles in, looking worse for wear, and Cooper casually slips behind the counter to hide the bulge in his pants. My cheeks are on fire.

"Hey, guys," Perry says on a sigh, seemingly unaware of what he walked in on. "How's it going?"

Cooper clears his throat, and I find the hardwood floors suddenly fascinating.

"Going well," Cooper answers, his voice masking our moment better than I trust mine to do. "How's your sister?"

Perry drops his bag on the couch and plops down, rubbing his forehead. Cooper and I exchange a worried glance and my chest tightens. We went through Victoria King's cancer experience, so this is triggering for us, but especially for Cooper.

"Is it bad news?" Cooper rasps.

Perry looks up at us with a small smile. "No. No, sorry. She's doing okay, actually, but it's so hard to see her going through this. She's only seventeen. She's so *positive* about it all, so optimistic, and the rest of us have to show that same optimism when we're with her. We don't want to be the assholes who bring her down, you know?"

Cooper nods. "Unfortunately, I do know."

"Fuck cancer." Perry lets out a long breath. "She's decided to do a double mastectomy. No seventeen-year-old girl should have to make the decision to lose her chest."

My heart drops, and the three of us sit in silence for several minutes. Given the situation, I wouldn't call it a comfortable silence, but it's the kind of silence that can only happen between friends when times are tough, and you just need someone to sit with and hold the space without trying to solve things.

"So anyway, you know how we have that trip coming up for filming?"

We're taking the cast to Cabo for a week next month. One of the typical things with reality shows like this is to get the cast out of their element, into bathing suits, and hand them unlimited drinks. Drama is sure to ensue. I'm looking forward to this trip, though I'm not sure I should go after my conversation with Lance.

"What about it?" Cooper asks.

Perry sits up strait and leans forward, his fingertips pressing together, and I instantly know we're about to be pitched an idea.

"Cabo is far," he says. "And it's so hot this time of year. I'm not sure if it's the best call. I don't want to be that far away from my sister, and you guys probably don't want to be that far from work, and the cast definitely won't want to be sweating on camera."

"What's the alternative?" I ask.

"What if we filmed it at one of the Nantucket houses?"

It's like an anvil drops on my shoulders. I'm *not* ready to return to Nantucket, and I highly doubt Cooper is.

"Hear me out," Perry continues. "We can film it at my family house, or one of yours if they're available. We have three great options. All big houses, all on the beach, and all amazing properties. It's only a two-hour flight between the island and the city. We can still get them in their bathing suits and film a bunch of content. What do you think?"

Cooper runs a hand over the back of his neck. "I don't know, man. Sybil and I haven't been there since..."

Perry's eyes widen with mortification. "Shit. You're right. I wasn't thinking. Don't worry, we'll come up with something else. Maybe The Hamptons?"

"We sold our Hamptons house," I say, "and it's not easy to get a property that big there this time of year, let alone accommodations for the crew."

Perry adjusts in his seat and lets out a long sigh, accepting his fate. "You're right. I'm sorry. We'll stick with Cabo." But he sounds defeated, and that kills me.

"What do you think, Sybil?" Cooper turns on me, his expression matching exactly what I'm feeling. "Do we go back? We can do it together."

A painful ache pierces my chest, but I force myself to think this through. I miss my favorite place, and I don't want to avoid it forever. Mom and the boys are already there, and she's been hoping I'd join her.

"Okay..." I say slowly, softly, unsure. "But I don't want any cast or crew at my house. My family is there for the summer, and I won't displace them."

"My family is here, obviously," Perry says. "We can use mine."

"We can use mine, too," Cooper offers. "Ethan and I own it now, anyway. He won't care if we use it for this."

There's hope in Perry's eyes. "Are you guys sure? You really don't have to do this for me. I shouldn't have even suggested it."

But he did, because he loves his family. And honestly, it's a good idea. Nantucket is luxurious, and our homes are top of the line. Whatever home gets featured in the show is only going to boost the ratings. Part of the reason *Top of the World* works is because it gives everyday people a look into the lives of the rich and famous. Nantucket feeds right into that narrative.

I'm not going to stay here. I can't let Cooper face this alone, but I really hope I don't regret going back to the place full of so many shattered memories.

THIRTY-EIGHT

C ooper
     Past - Age 24

The first time I saw Arden, it was like being punched in the chest.

Auburn hair flashing in the firelight. Freckles scattered across the bridge of her nose like constellations. Big, haunting eyes, and a heart-shaped mouth that could ruin a man. For a second, I forgot how to breathe.

She looked like *her*. The resemblance was so uncanny; it was honestly painful.

I hadn't seen Sybil in almost a year, and here she was again, only it wasn't her. Not even close. Seeing Arden was like looking into a distorted mirror. Almost the real thing, but not quite right.

The commonalities stopped at appearances. Their backgrounds, personalities, and energy couldn't be more different.

Sybil is summer's golden hour—warm and radiant, but only in your life for a moment before leaving you in darkness.

Arden is moonlight on a quiet winter's night. Wounded. Guarded in a way that makes me wonder how bad her childhood really was. She's more fantasy than girl—out of reach and not quite real, haunting me with who she isn't.

It's been a little over a month since Arden arrived at our beach house, introducing herself as our live-in housekeeper for the summer. In that time, she's become a sort of mirage to me. She's this vision of false promises and a constant reminder of what I can't have.

It hurts me to look at her, but Ethan?

Ethan is unraveling.

I've never seen him so *bothered* by anyone before, not even our father. He claims to hate Arden, but despite this claim, he's more possessive than I've ever seen him.

Sometimes I think he's far more obsessed with Arden than he ever was with Sybil.

My interest is shallow. I only want to sleep with her because she reminds me of the one girl I'll never get to take to bed.

But she told me she's a virgin, and her innocence makes this whole thing way too complicated.

So... tell me why I'm currently kissing her?

I found her on the beach watching the sunset, and I couldn't help myself. I convinced her to get in the water with me, and now I've got my hands in her hair and my mouth on her wet lips.

It's wrong, but it doesn't matter. I never claimed to be a good person.

Before I know it, I've got her in my bedroom, and I tangle in her like gravity pulled me here instead of my own selfish greed. She's small, and her trembling hands speak to her lack of experience as she runs them over my body.

I shouldn't, but I strip her down to her panties, anyway.

I'm completely naked two seconds later.

Rational thoughts disappear; all that matters is our bodies and what I want them to do. I take her breast into my mouth, savoring her nipple until she moans. I know how to bring a woman to orgasm, and that's all I focus on.

I'm a shitty person for using her, but at least I can make her feel good in the process.

"You like that?" I pull away with a smug grin, and when she nods, I grip my erection, loving the way she looks down at it with complete awe and need. It feels amazing, knowing she is looking at *me* like this, that I'm the one she wants. That I'm the one being chosen for once. That my brother isn't the man she picked...

Fuck. What am I even thinking? This shouldn't be about Ethan at all, but Arden looking the way she looks makes this about a lot more than just me and her.

Taking her hand, I wrap it around my cock, savoring the sensation of her needy fingers and the sense of urgency building between us. We kiss again, and I grow feral, practically fucking her hand as we explore each other's bodies. It's not enough, not even close, so I lead her to the bed and kiss my way down her torso, readying to yank her panties off her hips and plunge my cock inside her wet virgin cunt.

The door flies open.

"What the *fuck*?" Ethan's voice slices through the haze. He's storming toward us, wild-eyed and furious, like he has a right to this woman, and I don't. It's utter bullshit. *Arden is not Sybil.*

He yanks me from Arden, and she scrambles away, covering herself like she's been caught doing something wrong. Her eyes fill with confusion, guilt, and shame, knocking the air out of me.

Wait... did she not want this?

"What are you doing?" he spits at me.

"What does it look like?" I'm fucking pissed, and I don't even care that I'm naked.

Sybil chose him. That was my burden.

Arden? She chose me. That's *his* fucking burden for once.

"You agreed not to fuck her," he snarls, pushing me against the wall. I can't believe he's bringing up a conversation we had when we *very* first met Arden, when we'd *both* agreed to keep things with our young housekeeper professional. That went out the window when we got to know her. He knows things have changed. He's been hot and cold with her for a month.

Arden yells at Ethan to get out, and he yells back at her that our conversation is none of her business. She sits up, covering herself while she and my brother continue to argue, and the truth hits me hard, opening a wound I thought had been healed.

She doesn't want me. She wants him.

I can't be here for a moment longer. I snatch up my clothes, my mind spinning numbly as I walk across the hall to Ethan's room and turn his shower to a scalding temperature. I'm freezing from the ocean water, my erection is gone, and more than anything, I need to wash away everything that just happened.

What the fuck is wrong with me? I almost took that girl's virginity because of my selfish fucking ego.

It's one thing to sleep around with willing participants, but it's another to fixate on an eighteen-year-old virgin with gaping emotional wounds. Whoever she gives her virginity to needs to take it with care and respect, and they also need to take her heart and cherish it. I wasn't doing any of those things. I don't think I'm capable of them.

I wanted to fuck her like an animal, pretend she was Sybil, and get her out of my system.

I'm such a prick.

I step out of the shower, towel off, then find Ethan waiting for me. He's standing by the door, his arms folded over his chest as if he's playing bodyguard.

"Are we going to talk about what the hell that was?" he asks, his eyes narrowed into angry slits. "What is *wrong* with you, Cooper? Arden is a virgin."

Yup. The man is *livid*. "What's there to talk about?" I sigh. "You're right. I shouldn't have done that."

The mask of anger cracks, relief smoothing his features. "*So...* you're not going to sleep with Arden?"

"She's not worth the trouble."

The anger returns, and in an instant, he's on me, shoving me against the wall. That's twice in ten minutes.

"She's worth the trouble, you asshole, but she's not like one of your hookups. If you want to be with her, you have to actually date her and treat her with the respect she deserves."

I crack a smile and push him off, my index finger in his face. "I *knew* it. You like her."

He shakes his head. "I'm looking out for her."

I snort. "Pretty sure she didn't appreciate you ripping me off her when she wanted to fuck me."

"Don't call it fucking when you're talking about her."

His face is a thundercloud, but I laugh it off and walk past him, slipping into my bedroom. Thankfully, it's empty. I don't know what the hell I'm going to say to her when I see her again, but I know Ethan well enough to know he has real feelings for the girl, even if he won't admit it. He won't act on anything until he's ready to be that guy she needs. Or maybe he won't act on anything at all. Either way, I'm staying out of it from now on.

An hour later, he knocks on my door and asks me to go to the bar with him.

I'm not sure I'm up for it, but he sounds pathetic. "Please. I need to get out of this house. It's too goddamn small tonight."

Interesting word choice, considering our house is a fortress.

What's my brother going to do next? Will he find a random girl to hook up with? He's been uncharacteristically celibate this summer. If he finds a woman, I can't help but wonder who he's trying to chase from his mind.

Sybil or Arden?

But Ethan doesn't hook up with anyone.

Me, on the other hand? I never claimed to be perfect.

THIRTY-NINE

Sybil
      Present - Age 27

Gloria Ricci storms into the crew headquarters like a cyclone. Her black hair is in rollers and her eyes are sharp with anger. She looks around with utter determination, and when her gaze locks on mine, my stomach drops.

"You. You're Sybil, right?" she hisses in her thick Italian accent.

What has Benton done now?

"Yes, I'm Sybil. How can I help you?"

"You're producing Benton, right?"

"That I am."

Her face rushes with red. "Tell him he can't break up with me on national television."

Umm, what?

Behind her, Perry slashes his neck with his hand. If shit is about to hit the fan with Benton and Gloria's relationship, it needs to happen *on* camera and not down here.

My eyes widen. Easy for him to call. Perry's not the one with a hot-headed Italian supermodel in his face.

"I will talk to him," I say with a friendly smile. "But Gloria, he really likes you."

I mean, that's true to a degree.

Benton *does* like her.

He also doesn't want her to be his girlfriend. I thought she knew that, considering she was also flirting with Justin until a few days ago. It sounds like Gloria and Benton have different interpretations of what's going on between them, and I'm pretty sure if things go down the way I think they're about to go down, Benton is going to further his playboy reputation, and that might not be good.

I promised I wasn't going to let him walk out of this show with America angry at him, but maybe he shouldn't be sleeping with his costar.

Gloria huffs, anger making way for vulnerability. Again, this is something Perry would love to see *on* camera, but I'm not completely heartless. This is a tale as old as time: girl likes boy more than boy likes girl.

I pat her on the back. "What happened?"

Perry steps into the conversation. "Let's go upstairs and set up a confessional in your room. You can tell us all about it."

Gloria shoots him a hateful glare. "You would love that, wouldn't you?"

I mean, that *is* his job.

Perry gives her a sympathetic smile. "It's not what you think. This is about a narrative. If we don't talk about how you feel and what's going on with your relationship, then the editors will only be able to cut what's on film. The *narrative* might not go the way you want it to go."

She glares. "Are you threatening me?"

He shakes his head, the picture of professional charm. "Of course not. I want to help you. You're my girl." He lowers his voice. "Between you and me, I want you to get the better edit if it comes down to Team Gloria versus Team Benton."

My mouth pops open. *What the hell?*

Benton is going to kill me if that happens.

Gloria nods, and the two of them head out the door. I move to follow, but Perry stops me. "Go handle Benton," he whispers.

Does that mean he wants me to make Benton look like an asshole for ratings, or does that mean he wants Benton to pretend to date Gloria seriously?

As much as I want our show to succeed, I care about my friend.

As Gloria and Perry leave, Perry motions Cooper to join them. I have to admit I hate the damsel in distress doe-eyes Gloria flashes at Cooper. I'm sure he's attracted to her, same as any hot-blooded straight male.

I head out to find Benton, debating what to say to him, and sending him a quick text to ask where he's at and if we can talk privately.

Benton: I'm training. Talk later.

Whelp, I won't be hearing from him for hours.

Sybil: Call me before you leave?

He adds a thumbs up to the text, and I wait for the elevator to take me downstairs. I need to get to the office.

My new assistant, Jarod, started yesterday. I'm having him take care of menial admin tasks, but I should check in and see how well he's fairing. Plus, I need to take care of some phone calls with a few vendors.

My phone buzzes, and I almost expect it to be a text from Cooper or Perry, or maybe even another one from Benton, but it's from Mom.

Mom: Call me as soon as you get this. It's important.

My stomach flips, and I immediately press the call button.

"Sybil," Mom answers, her voice strained and far away. I can hear the faint crashing of waves in the background of our Nantucket beachfront home.

"Hey, Mom. What's going on?"

The pause is long, the kind of long that makes my heart hammer uncontrollably.

The elevator arrives, but I ignore it. It opens and shuts without me.

When Mom speaks again, her voice is husky with grief. "Are you sitting down? Are you alone?"

"I'm on set right now."

"Okay, honey, find somewhere private."

"One second." My legs move before my mind can even think.

Returning to crew basecamp, I head to the spare bedroom that's been set aside for makeup and hair, but people are in there. The second spare bedroom is the screening room, so it's guaranteed to be busy. Without hesitation, I stride across the living room for Cooper's bedroom door.

He normally keeps it locked, but thankfully it opens. I stumble inside and close myself in. My legs shake, and I have to lean against the door. Maybe this is PTSD kicking in or something else, but my body feels like it has a mind of its own.

"Okay, you can tell me now. What's wrong?"

"It's about Dad." Mom chokes on a sob, and a million emotions burst to the surface, including delusions that he somehow survived the boating accident. It's my secret hope that I know will never come true.

"Honey, they found some of his remains. His skull washed up near Great Point Beach. The authorities ran forensics and were able to match Dad's dental records. It's him."

My legs give out as I sink to the ground.

We found him.

We can finally lay him to rest—or at least, part of him. This is that final confirmation he's really gone, and my heart cracks all over again. My body battles between relief and heartbreak, neither winning nor surrendering to the other.

I know I wasn't the only one. Chandler has said multiple times he thought Dad had amnesia and would return to us. Mom sometimes tells me how she can't believe he's gone. And Hayes hasn't been the same since it happened.

None of us have.

"How are the boys taking it?" I ask. "Have you told them already?"

"I wanted to have you come out so we could tell them together, but they saw me crying and got it out of me. They're... not well."

"I'm supposed to fly out next week," I say. "I'll come early."

"That's up to you. Nobody will judge you either way. You have a lot on your plate."

"I need a break. I have an assistant now. It will be okay. I'll come out tomorrow, okay Mom? First thing."

"I'll have your bedroom ready, sweetheart."

I pause for a minute. "Are we going to bury the remains?"

"Of course. We'll do it soon. I can't think about that right now, though."

We hang up, and I stay on the floor for ages, eventually finding my way onto Cooper's bed. The blue comforter is cooling, and I find myself crying into it while I stare out the window, the cityscape outside blurring.

It feels like he died twice. I'm sure Mom will want to lay what we have of him to rest in the family plot. That will be hard. This is *all* so hard.

Eventually, I fall asleep, dreaming of his funeral last summer.

I wake up sometime later, and the sky outside has turned to ink. For a brief second, I don't know where I am.

Panicked, I sit up, searching for my phone.

"Hey," Cooper's calm voice breaks the darkness. "It's okay. I'm here."

The memories of the day rush back. I have no tears left to give. I'm completely drained. Before that phone call, I was worried about Gloria and Benton having drama on the show—that feels so trivial now.

"Do you have my phone?" I croak.

Cooper reaches through the darkness, handing it over. "Lie down."

My body instantly obeys. Cooper joins me, pulling me against him while I open my phone.

Benton called me hours ago, but I slept right through it. I hope he didn't walk into drama.

"Sorry I broke into your bedroom," I mumble. "It was unlocked."

"I talked to Ethan," he says, his breath warm on my neck. "Your mom called Arden to tell her about your dad."

My chest tightens. "So you know."

"Do you want to talk about it?"

"No."

"That's fine." He shifts slightly, but his hold stays strong and firm. "Do you want to go home?"

I don't want to do that either. "Can I sleep here tonight? I don't want to move."

"Of course. I can sleep on the couch or go up to Ethan's place and sleep in one of their guest rooms."

I shake my head. "Stay here. It's nice... not being alone."

We lie in silence for a while, and I focus on the way his breathing settles my nerves, the consistent rise and fall of his chest against my back like ocean waves.

"I'm going to Nantucket early," I tell him. "Tomorrow. I'll be ready to work on the show again when you guys come out next week."

Cooper mumbles his approval and continues to hold me until my emotions settle. He kisses the back of my neck, laying a careful press of his lips on the nob at the top of my spine. It's possibly the most comforting gesture I've ever felt, and it's the last thing I think about as I finally drift away.

The next morning, I wake up, and he's gone—another thing to widen the chasm in my chest. It's not like we had sex, but somehow sleeping in the same bed felt more intimate than most of the sex I've had. I don't think I can take any more heartache, so I refuse to let myself be bothered.

I pad to the open living and dining room, and the scent of bacon stops me.

"You're cooking?" I practically squawk.

"Don't look so alarmed." He peers at me with an adorable grin. "I can cook, especially breakfast."

Then he winks, and I melt.

"Oh, that makes sense. Gotta feed the women," I joke, though it's hard to feel happy when I'm so damn spent from crying all night. I'm not bothered by him feeding women, but it stings a little to know I'm one of many, and we didn't even have sex. "What else is on the menu?"

"Protein pancakes sound okay?"

"No carbs for me. I don't feel like eating much, if I'm being honest."

"Eggs? Bacon?"

"Sure, but only if I can make the eggs." I'm picky as hell about my eggs, and I really need something to do.

I dig through the refrigerator, past the random items left by the crew, locating the carton of eggs. Then I get busy scrambling them so they're perfectly fluffy.

We sit together to eat when the first of the crew arrives, and if anyone notices I'm wearing yesterday's clothes, they don't say a word. Not that I'd care. I was here last night because my world fell apart, not because I was having sex with Cooper.

I *wish* I had been having sex with Cooper.

My hand stops, and the eggs tumble to the plate. Where the hell did that thought come from?

Coop gives me a sideline glance. "You okay there, Valentine?"

Flustered, I set my fork down. I can't handle all these emotions anymore. I need to get the fuck out of here. "Sorry, but I gotta get going. I'll see you on Nantucket."

Without looking at anybody, I gather my things and hurry from the apartment before anyone can question me about my choices.

FORTY

S ybil
Present - Age 27

The next week passes in a strange mix of haze and slow motion. Each moment drags painfully, yet it's also as if the days have evaporated. Nothing feels real—like I'm living someone else's story—but I'm not. This is my life now. These events are mine to live through.

Arden isn't here, and Dad is dead. Things will never ever be the same.

We try to hold on to normalcy as a family. We share meals, wander through shops, visit the beach, watch movies, and sleep in as long as we can. These are the little joys of being on the island—things we once treasured. But the absence lingers, heavy and impossible to ignore. We aren't whole anymore.

It feels surreal... being on this island, a place saturated with Dad. The new house itself is almost a stranger. We barely had time to fill it with memories of our own. It was just last summer we stayed here for the first time. Two weeks of sunshine and exploration, only to have it shattered by the boating accident.

By the end of that trip, Dad was gone.

What haunts me most are the fragmented memories from that day. They come in flashes—sharp images that cut deep and blurry gaps in time. I remember the accident. I remember Cooper on the boat, his right leg mangled beyond recognition. The blood. The screaming. The gut-wrenching panic.

I don't remember the last time I saw Dad.

I had called for him, my voice raw with desperation. I remember searching the water, scanning every ripple and shadow. He wasn't there. Then came the police, the paramedics, the search and rescue teams.

Still, no Dad.

Each time I revisit these memories, it's like dissecting a wound that refuses to heal, asking myself over and over what I could have done differently, how I could have changed the outcome. Then there's the nagging unease—the faint but persistent feeling I've forgotten something critical, something hidden beneath the bloody waters of that day.

My therapist says I might never remember everything. My brain might be protecting me, locking the trauma in some unlit corner of my mind.

I know she's right.

Maybe it's better this way.

"There's another delivery," Hayes announces.

It's mid-morning, and we've been lounging around watching television when the doorbell rings. Hayes answers it, returning with a robin egg colored cake box.

"It's food. Smells good. I'll take it to the kitchen."

I follow him as he adds it to the many vases of flowers already clogging up the kitchen counter. The flowers are all condolences from friends and family who have read the news.

The media broke the story before Mom had a chance to tell anyone besides us kids.

It sucks, but we weren't surprised, considering the frenzy his death created in the first place. Billionaire CEO dies in a freak accident? People ate that shit up. And they ate it up even more when the police tried to pin the accident on Ethan.

It was never Ethan's fault.

As much as I wish Ethan wouldn't have dated Arden in secret, but I understand why he did. He loved her then, and he loves her now. It wasn't Ethan who drove his boat like a maniac. But the police wanted to arrest someone, and Ethan was the perfect scapegoat, at least until the truth came out.

Hayes opens the box, and the milky-sweet scent of cheesecake floods the kitchen, shaking me from my tumultuous thoughts. I practically sprint around the kitchen island to get a better look at the box. Sure enough, it's from my favorite bakery in the entire world.

A smile tugs at my mouth. "It's from Ethan. He sent another cheesecake."

"Had it shipped all the way from Boston, looks like," Hayes says, pointing to the logo. "Should we put it in the fridge for later or have it for brunch now?"

"Definitely now." I give my not-so-little-anymore brother a wink and retrieve dishes and forks.

Before long, the rest of the family joins us, and we chow down on what I consider the best cheesecake out there.

I first found it when I was a freshman in college. I told Ethan I wanted a cheesecake for my birthday, so we spent our Valentine's Day and my birthday traipsing around downtown Boston to all the spots claiming to have "world famous" cheesecake. Once we found Little Blue Bakery, it was game over.

We shared a slice, fell in love with it, and took an entire cake home to my little dorm refrigerator and spent the rest of the week munching on it while simultaneously complaining about inflammation and bloating.

Totally worth it.

Every year since, Ethan has bought me cheesecake for my birthday.

Even after we broke up, the cakes were sent to me in New York.

They've been arriving anonymously, but I know it's Ethan's way of letting me know that, despite everything, he doesn't hate me. We've always wanted what's best for each other. That will never change.

I'd kinda thought he'd quit sending them after meeting Arden, but that blue box still showed up on my birthday.

And here it is again.

"This is very thoughtful of him," Mom remarks. "Especially after everything we've put him through."

She'll forever regret the choices we made.

Mom has taken what is, in my expert-cheesecake opinion, way too small of a slice. I sneak more to her plate when she's not looking, hoping she won't be able to resist. She's lost too much weight recently, and I hate to see how grief has changed her body as well as her mind.

"Hey Syb, can I meet Gloria Ricci?" Chandler asks between bites, giving me the most hopeful look I think he's ever given me.

I'm instantly amused. "You want to meet the supermodel?"

He nods, a cheesy grin on his face.

"Why does that not surprise me?"

"I think she'll love me." He's probably right; Chandler is the most lovable person I've ever met.

Hayes snorts. "Gloria is hot, but I want to meet the pop star. What's her name again? Audry?"

"Audra Mason. You don't even know her name, and you want to meet her?" Mom questions.

She hasn't touched her food. I frown but try not to let it get me down. Everyone grieves in their own way.

Hayes shrugs. "All the girls at school are obsessed with her. If I can get a selfie with her, I'm sure the girls will try to get to her through me."

Mom tuts, but I laugh.

Honestly, it's not a bad idea, except for the fact that Hayes already graduated. He's off to Harvard in the fall to follow in the family footsteps. Life is about to get a whole lot more grown-up for him. But hey, the girls at Harvard aren't so different from girls at his school, and I'm sure a lot of them will also be Audra Mason fans.

"Always thinking about girls." Mom points to her boys. "You're going to have to think about more than girls soon."

"I think about more than girls, Mom," Hayes says. "I also think about football."

That's not what she wanted him to say, of course. I intercept before the lecture on his responsibilities to the family commences.

"I'll take you to meet the cast when I head over to the Hargrove's place tomorrow," I tell my brothers. "You can come with me, but you have to promise to be on your best behavior. This is a professional working set with people's livelihoods on the line. No horsing around or pranks. Do anything to embarrass me, and you're kicked out for good."

"I'd better come, too." Mom sighs, and I don't disagree. She *needs* to get out of the house.

True to my word, I let the family tag along with me. Perry's place is on the western side of the island, where the water isn't as choppy as the Atlantic. Not as good for surfing, but much better for swimming, which suits our filming purposes. None of the cast-mates know how to surf, but Perry wants to get lots of shots of them in the pool and down at the beach.

We pull up to Perry's house, and I'm instantly glad we chose his place for filming. It's in the traditional Nantucket-style, the architecture similar to mine with shingled siding, white squared columns, and peaks in the roofline. His house is white instead of blue, but otherwise they're very similar, except his beach is a little more private.

Leading them inside, I quickly find Ricki and explain that my family wants to meet the cast. I can tell she's fighting her annoyance, but she makes the introductions, and everyone is really nice, thank goodness. It helps that Chandler has an excellent way of making everybody laugh.

Benton pulls me aside. "Hey, are you okay? I heard about your dad."

"I'm as okay as I can be," I say. "I don't really want to talk about it. How are you?"

He grimaces. "Gloria is *a lot*. If I don't give her exactly what she wants while we're filming, she's going to drag my reputation through the mud. So looks like I have a girlfriend now."

"Shit. I'm sorry. I tried to warn you, but then my mom called about my dad and—"

He grabs my hand and squeezes. "It's okay. I don't blame you. You promised this show wasn't going to screw me over. Just keep that promise."

"I will. But you have to be careful, too."

"Come here, Laurence." He pulls me into a hug, and I melt against his hard chest. He's going to hate me if I can't keep my word, and I can't bear to lose another friend.

Someone clears their throat. "You'd better step away from Sybil before your girlfriend loses her shit again."

We turn to find Cooper glaring in our direction.

Benton chuckles and releases me, patting me on the

shoulder and giving Cooper a devil-may-care smirk. "Are you sure you're not the one who's about to lose your shit, boss?"

He doesn't stick around for an answer, and I can't help but notice the way Cooper glares daggers at Benton's back.

"If I didn't know better, I'd say you're jealous," I tease.

Cooper's mouth thins. "We've talked about this, Sybil. You have to be careful with him. Especially now that he's dating Gloria."

My face burns. "I get it. Benton and I are just friends."

"He wasn't hugging you like you're *just friends*. He was hugging you like he wants to take you to bed."

I snort, hiding the frustration bubbling under my skin. "I thought we'd gotten past all this, Cooper. Yes, Benton and I have been together many times, but we're not anymore. So get over it."

I shove past him, fighting everything I have in me not to turn around and see what's written across his face. Jealousy? Indifference? Frustration? Whatever it is, I shouldn't care.

But I do.

FORTY-ONE

C ooper
　　　Past - Age 26

I hate these stupid parties our father drags us to. I thought we'd have to go to less of them once we finished graduate school and got busy with work. Nope. We have to go to even more of them, even on our short vacations.

We're on Nantucket for a break, and Dad insisted we appear at a yacht club party. The man doesn't even like yachts, but his new wife does, so he bought her one. This is his third wife, by the way. The second one since Mom died.

His first one, Malory, only lasted a few years. She was a control freak who made the mistake of trying to control our father. At least this new one, Kayla, keeps to herself, though I won't be surprised if this marriage ends in divorce as well. She's only a few years older than us, but dumb as a doornail. She's arm candy for Dad, nothing more, and he'll grow tired of her.

I go for the bar, and then Ethan and I start to mingle. Right when I'm getting comfortable, bright auburn hair catches the corner of my eye, and I turn to find Sybil and her cousin Arden.

They're standing together, heads bent together conspiratorially. They're smiling, probably because they haven't seen us yet.

I watch as Gregory Laurence takes Arden away to introduce her to people and show her off, but it's Sybil I can't stop staring at. Eventually, she sees us. Her eyes bounce between us like she doesn't know which brother to look at, her face paling.

Looking is too painful, so I turn and stride away.

There's going to be arguing soon. Drama. Our dads won't be able to stop themselves from jabbing at each other. I don't want any part. Fuck that.

I end up by the water, staring at the rows of docked boats and finishing my whiskey. I wish I didn't care so much or want to go home as badly as I do.

Someone approaches, but they don't seem to notice me. I don't care. Then I turn to find Sybil, and I very much do care.

"I bet you're loving this, aren't you?" I ask, stepping from the shadows.

She stops in her tracks, her expressive eyes seeing right through me. "Loving what?"

I laugh bitterly, looking her up and down and stepping forward until we're only inches apart. I take a strand of her hair and twist it between my fingers. "You got your way, Sybil. You cut us out of your life. Is it fun to come to a party and show off your new cousin and pretend we're not even here?"

She doesn't look like she got her way. She looks shattered by my words. Then angry. Walls fly up, shutting her off from me entirely.

And me? I'm *affected*. Why does seeing Sybil again feel so angry? I expected sadness, and I hoped for nonchalance, but instead I'm so fucking mad.

I loved her. And she walked away so easily.

"You act like I wanted to cut you out, Cooper," she whispers. "I didn't want to. I *had* to. There's a difference."

I shake my head. "Your lack of accountability is truly astonishing."

The energy between us shifts.

"Don't you dare judge me." Her green eyes narrow, going dark. "You have no idea what I gave up."

I shift closer. "Don't I?" My voice is hoarse with frustration.

Why the fuck does she have to be so beautiful? Everything about this woman draws me to her. I used to love her for it, but now I hate her for it. Yeah, I've grown bitter over the years, but I'm smarter, too. I have her to thank for that.

"What are you saying?" She swallows hard, her slender throat bobbing.

"You threw away something special and refuse to admit it."

"Ethan and I never would've worked out. I see that now."

"I'm not talking about Ethan."

Her breath catches. "What do you mean?"

"I mean you and me, Sybil. There was something between us. Friendship, yes... or maybe something more. I don't know, but you broke it. You broke us. And you did it on purpose."

I don't think I've ever been so bold with her, but I've had years to think about this conversation. All the things I've wanted to say have been building and building. Meeting Arden only made it worse.

"There was never anything between us besides friendship, Cooper."

Lies. And they hurt like a knife to the back. "Don't be fake with me, Valentine. I know you better than that."

"Don't call me that. I'm not that anymore."

My eyes narrow. "But you were."

Does she need me to spell it out for her?

"It was one kiss, Cooper. A long time ago. You need to get over yourself."

I wince, hating myself immediately for the reaction. There *was* something in that kiss. I'm not crazy.

A cascade of soft auburn curls spills down around her bare shoulders and back. Her breasts heave up and down with her breath—breasts that look a size larger than the last time I saw her. Fuck me for noticing, but I can't help myself. I have the sudden urge to wrap her hair around my fist, twist it until she gasps, then silence that gasp with my tongue.

Instead, I step away.

"How is Arden doing?" I ask, forcing myself to calm down by changing the subject. "Is she happy?"

I need to get a hold of myself before I do something truly stupid. I'm spiraling out of control, and I hate that. I've worked hard to suppress wild emotions for the last few years and need to fucking act on those emotions before I lose it.

Her eyebrows draw together. "Why do you care? I know how your family treated her."

"Oh, do you now?" I highly doubt she knows everything about that summer, but maybe I'm wrong. Arden was a closed book to me, so it's hard to imagine her opening up to Sybil, but maybe she did. Things change. Maybe Arden did, too.

"Yup. I know all about it," she quips.

"So you know about the time we almost fucked but didn't because Ethan pulled my naked ass off of her?" I say, hoping to get a rise out of her.

Her cheeks flame. "W–what?"

I shrug. "Don't worry. We didn't do anything, but we wanted to."

"You're a dick."

I shrug. "Why do you care so much? You jealous?"

"You wish." Her cheeks are flaming, and her eyes are focused on my mouth. It sends a jolt through me, right down to my cock.

"Want to know what I liked most about Arden?" I prod. "She reminded me of you." My eyes flick down to her lips. "But without the prissy attitude."

Her glare is lethal. "What the hell is wrong with you? Are you high or drunk or something?"

"Right now, I'm too sober. Want to get drunk together and make some bad decisions?"

She's speechless for once, which is exactly what I wanted. I'm being an asshole, but I need to know if she's missed me like I've missed her.

"What? Nothing to say?" I smirk. "Maybe we should have hate-sex. I've never tried it. Sounds fun."

"You know what? Do whatever you want, Cooper. Drink or get high or whatever. Honestly, I don't care."

Ouch. "It's okay," I retaliate, my voice dangerously low. "You don't have to keep tabs on me, but I do keep tabs on you. Your sex life has become as infamous as your last name."

Her face falls, and I immediately want to take it back, but I'm too angry to do the right thing. Too proud. Too broken. Too much of a fucking asshole.

"You're judging my sex life? That's rich, coming from you."

I laugh bitterly. "You must've realized that sex with no attachment is the best sex, huh? Better than my brother, is it?"

"It's none of your fucking business," she hisses, her eyes filling with anger and unshed tears.

It should feel nice to get some honest emotion out of her, but it doesn't. It just leaves me gutted.

Arden appears in my peripheral. "Are you okay?" she asks, concern laced in her tone.

Sybil and I answer with a quick, simultaneous, "Fine."

Arden steps next to her cousin, folding her arms over her chest and glowering at me. Seeing her dressed up makes the family resemblance even more striking. I have to catch myself from gaping at them. They look more like twins than Ethan and I do.

"This is a new look," I say to her, trying to sound positive, but it comes out mocking.

"What's that supposed to mean?" Sybil's immediately on guard.

I lighten my tone. "Only that you're different. I didn't say it was bad. Maybe it's a good thing."

It's not entirely a good thing.

Seeing the confidence in her that wasn't there before is a *great* thing. She has a family she didn't have before. But knowing whatever friendship we have is decimated? That she hates me? That part sucks.

There's so much I want to say to her, but Sybil quickly grabs her cousin's hand and drags her away. I don't know if I should go after them, don't know my place in this situation anymore. Maybe I have none at all. I'm conflicted as hell when Arden looks over her shoulder at me, and I catch a glimpse of the girl I used to know. I make up my mind, going after them.

As soon as I catch up, Sybil shoots me a scathing glare, but what I have to say isn't for Sybil. I need to get this off my chest.

"I should've realized you were related to the Laurences the first time I saw you, Arden. I can't believe I chalked it up to coincidence. You two look even more alike in person."

"Like I said, it's none of your business," Sybil answers for Arden, and I have to stop myself from telling her off for it. I swear, this woman is going to be the death of me.

"You should've called me," I try with them both. "At least

when you met her and learned the truth, you could have picked up the phone. We don't have to hate each other just because our parents are idiots."

I'm expecting to be put in my place by Sybil, but Arden is the one to do it. "Are you kidding?" She laughs. "Am I forgetting the part where you gave me your number? Oh, that's right, you didn't. You pulled that frost cold-shoulder bullshit on me for weeks before you left. Even if I could have called you, I wouldn't have."

Sybil was trying to get Arden to walk away a minute ago, but now she drops her hand and turns on me, pressing her hands against my chest to push me away. I don't move. I'm frozen to the spot, staring at her. There's so much hurt in her eyes, and it makes my heart shatter. But that's the thing about shattered hearts—they're repaired best by building thicker walls.

"And *you* should have called *me*," Sybil hisses. "The second Arden walked into your house and you saw the family resemblance, you should have picked up your phone. But you didn't, did you? I had to find out from my parents months after you guys met her."

Is she for real?

I'm so fucking frustrated I could scream.

Yes, I should've called her, but she's acting like she wasn't the one to cut me from her life. I'm not the only one who messed up.

"I guess we're even," I growl, searching her face for something I can use to make this right. Regret? Forgiveness? Or even some goddamn understanding would be nice.

She shakes her head slowly and inches back, her face an unreadable mask. "We're not even. We're not anything."

Those words are like salt sucking me dry. The worst part? She means them. She's not so unreadable after all.

"Let's go." Arden leads her away, and I don't follow and or say anything more. Sybil got the last word, and all I can do is accept she's right about one thing.

Sybil Laurence and me?

We're not anything.

FORTY-TWO

S ybil
Present - Age 27

Another week to look forward to on Nantucket, except this time I'm going to be busy every day on set, filming late into the night, crashing at home in the small hours of the morning, and dragging myself out of bed the next day to do it all over again.

I can't think of a better distraction.

"You've talked to your people, and they're ready?" Ricki asks through the walkie-talkie on our private channel.

"They're on their way to the pool now."

After a pep-talk about having fun and showing off for the cameras, I follow the cast to the pool area, careful to keep away from the cameras. They're dressed to impress and ready to film the first group scene of the trip, which is an outdoor dinner on Perry's gorgeous pool deck. A glittering blue Nantucket sound is the backdrop.

Considering the drama brewing between pretty much everyone, this should be interesting. Gloria is definitely getting the most camera time, but I don't think she means to be. She's a huge personality, trying to get along with other big personalities... and failing miserably. Case and point: last week she got into a screaming match with Audra Mason for reading Audra's songwriting notebook to the camera without permission.

I slink to the side, finding shade under a willow tree as I watch the scene unfold from a distance.

Perry's family home is one of the larger ones on the island, so it's working out perfectly for our needs. We've set up the cast in the bedrooms on the main floor and crew headquarters upstairs. Ricki and Perry are also staying upstairs, and everyone else is staying at Cooper and Ethan's place.

We've rented cars to bring people in and out when we're not working, and because our crew is relatively small, we didn't have to scramble to find extra accommodations. Money can only go so far on Nantucket when the entire island is booked during the busiest tourism week of the year.

We'll be filming the Fourth of July episode here, and I can't wait. The cast and crew are going to love the Nantucket Independence Day experience. It's my favorite holiday for a reason—fireworks and barbecues and patriotic parades in the most cozy and gorgeous place in America.

A high-pitched voice catches my attention, and I frown. Benton is in trouble.

"Wait, you *slept* with her?" Gloria points at him accusingly.

He looks like a deer in the headlights but doesn't deny anything.

Gloria flies up from the outdoor dining table, throwing her napkin on her untouched meal, and storms away from everyone like they've betrayed her in the worst way possible. She's still managed to keep a full wineglass in her hand as she goes.

All eyes go to Benton as he chases after her. "Not for

months, not since the show even started," he says. "She's just my friend."

"She's your producer!"

The blood drains from my face, and my skin prickles with the horror of what's unfolding *on camera*, especially when Gloria catches sight of me and stomps in my direction. The cameras follow her until I'm in the shot.

I'm frozen in place, completely blindsided.

"Gloria," I manage shakily. "It's not what you think. We're not like that. We haven't been together in ages."

Her eyes are pure rage. "I don't know what's worse... that you didn't tell me you'd slept with him, or that you knew how much of a player he was, and you didn't think to warn me."

Ouch.

Gloria Ricci flings her wine toward me, the arc of red moving too fast for me to get out of the way. Wine drenches my vintage Gucci sundress from top to bottom.

Fuck!

She doesn't even wait to see my reaction. She swivels to Benton and starts crying. "I trusted you, Benny. I thought I was the only girl."

With a final dramatic wail, she runs inside, and the cameras pan to Benton.

He's standing there, horrified and out of his depth. He's used to sleeping around and not committing to one woman. With the way the romance with Gloria has unfolded for the cameras, he's basically trapped in a relationship with a possessive woman.

He'd be an ass to lead her on, and yet he's here for his reputation, for brand recognition, to make his manager and team happy, and further his career. I'm not about to let Gloria ruin that. He swears they talked off camera, and she knew they weren't exclusive, and I promised to help him.

Right now? He's got to help himself.

"Go to her," I mouth, eyebrows shooting up, and thankfully, he takes off after her.

"Sorry about that." Perry jogs over, his eyes sparkling with excitement. "Go up to my room and find a change of clothes, but I gotta get in there."

I bury the hurt prickling at the backs of my eyes. I get it; he needs to be where the action is, even if that action is them going into a room and closing the door while Benton tries to figure out how the hell to handle this woman.

I hurry to Perry's room, take a quick shower, and slip into one of his long dress shirts, all the while my hands shake, and my breath comes in short little gasps. I need to calm down, determined that my personal life isn't going to be televised. The network doesn't have the right.

I find a belt to tie around the dress shirt, hoping it doesn't look too bad. I don't want to run all the way home to get changed and miss out on everything that's happening downstairs, but I will be sending one of the set assistants off to dry cleaning, that's for damn sure.

I'm pretty sure the Gucci is ruined.

I know it's shallow to care so much about something as trivial as a dress, but I loved it, and vintage is irreplaceable.

Someone knocks on the door, and I open it while still toweling off my hair. Cooper greets me with that boyish grin.

"If you came here to say you told me so," I grumble, wringing out my hair, "don't bother. *I already know.*"

His smile twitches. "I would never say I told you so."

"Liar."

"I'm actually here to see if you're okay. Anything I can do to help?"

I let him in, twisting my wet hair to the top of my head. I retrieve a hair tie from my bag and secure the messy bun, turning to find Cooper staring at me. There's heat in his gaze I haven't seen in a while. A shiver ripples up my spine.

"What?" I prod.

He clears his throat, brushing the tips of his fingers over the collar of the dress shirt. "This shirt looks good on you, Valentine. I just wish it wasn't Perry's shirt."

"Why do you care?"

We're standing too close, but not close enough. The shirt must have ridden up while I was putting my hair back. Did he get a look at my panties? Do I *want* him to see my panties?

"Because I wish it was *my* shirt."

His voice I pure gravel.

Yes, I very much want him to see my panties.

"I wish it was your shirt, too," I whisper, and his gaze darkens with desire.

"There are a few ways I can comfort you right now," he offers. "I can give you a hug. That's option one."

"And option two?" I ask with a coy smile, suddenly feeling much better.

He turns around and closes the door, locking it, then turning back to face me. His hair has fallen across his forehead, looking like a tortured soul who needs me to save him from his misery. "Option two is whatever you want it to be."

I pretend to think about it, but I already know my choice. "Option two."

Before I can rationalize why this is a bad idea, I close the distance between us, pressing my lips to his. He's quick to respond, immediately returning the kiss with so much heat he might set me on fire. Our mouths open to each other, tongues exploring, hands everywhere. I moan, and his approving growl weakens my knees.

As if sensing I can hardly hold myself up, he grips the backs of my thighs and lifts me. His erection is hard against my core as I wrap my legs around him.

"Fuck," he hisses.

Fuck is right——my pussy weeps for how long it's been untouched by a man. And now to have this? To have him so close?

Glorious.

He pushes me against the door, and I faintly register the click of the lock.

My body rocks as he explores my mouth with his own, and when I think I can't take anymore, and we need to move to the bed, he sets me down and kisses along my jaw, my neck, my collarbone.

A large steady hand grips my ass as he moves lower and lower, unbuttoning the shirt on his way down. Hungry kisses pattern my sternum, the smooth flesh beneath my bra, my soft belly, and farther until he's on his knees. That can't be easy with his prosthetic.

"Does that hurt?" I ask gently.

"No," he growls. I'm not sure if I believe him, but then he breathes me in with a low rumble in the back of his throat, and I could choke with how needy I am for his mouth to keep going.

"Cooper," I plead, voice husky and wanting. "Please."

He peers up at me, those darks are bright with desire. "This is what you want?"

"Yes."

"Say it. Tell me you want me to eat you out."

"Please," I beg, "eat me out."

"Say my name." That boyish smirk returns, and if I wasn't so heated, I'd smack it off him. "Ask nicely."

"Cooper, for the love of God, will you please eat my pussy?"

With a wicked grin, he pushes my panties to the side and presses his mouth to my clit. The sweep of pleasure is so instant that I cry out, arching against his tongue. He slides it up and down, putting exactly the right amount of force into his movements, and my knees nearly give out.

I sink into him, and he must sense my needs because he sits back long enough to shuck my panties, and then he's there again. He takes my leg and places it over his shoulder. I can't help but sink even farther.

"Ride me," he commands before returning his expert tongue to my core.

He wraps one hand around my lower body to help me stay upright and the other slides to my ass, fingers digging into my flesh.

Then he moves two fingers into my pussy, hooking them perfectly, and I die on the spot. A primal need to be fucked by his mouth and his fingers and *by him* washes over me, and I buck against his face, the door rattling behind me.

He groans in pleasure, tongue lapping expertly against my bundle of nerves. A third finger pumps inside me, stretching me out, and I could cry at the perfect pain of it all.

No part of me wants to hold myself back or think too hard about this, so I don't. I let myself have this one thing I've secretly coveted for years—I let myself have Cooper.

My best friend.

The one man I was never supposed to want.

And it's fucking incredible.

It's so good that I have to bite my fist to keep from moaning too loud.

Men have gone down on me before but never like this— never with so much animalistic need, never while I stand above them riding their face like a damn chair.

I love it.

Cooper loves it.

He's a man unleashed, a mirror to my own need, grunting his approval and gaining satisfaction from my pleasure.

I could ride him forever, but my body has other ideas, the orgasm hitting me like a quick and powerful tidal wave.

Unstoppable.

Inevitable.

Perfect ecstasy crashes over my entire body, and I cry out, whimpering his name as I come. He doesn't stop, drawing out the orgasm until there's nothing left, until I'm a completely spent.

I fall to my knees, and he wraps me in his arms.

His erection is hard and ready underneath me, and I'm prepared to return the favor, but when I reach for him, he stops me, kissing me on the temple.

"Later," he promises, and I don't know how he can have such self-control right now. It truly defies reason. "We have to get back to work."

Sure enough, someone knocks on the door, and Ricki's annoyed voice calls out, "Get your asses down here. We've got a situation."

FORTY-THREE

S ybil
  Present - Age 27

"What situation?" I ask through the door, straightening Perry's shirt and giving Cooper a pleading look. He's still holding me, and he's still hard, but the rush from my orgasm is fading, and nerves tingle through my chest.

"Just hurry up," Ricki commands. I'm certain she knows we were doing something naughty behind this locked door. How loud was I?

Her footsteps retreat.

Cooper and I share a conspiratorial look, then we both burst out laughing.

"Oh man, I don't want anyone to know what we were doing in here," I say.

His laughter falters. "Are you ashamed?"

Ashamed? No. Embarrassed. Yes. This isn't either of our bedrooms, and we shouldn't have done that *at work*.

I shake my head, but my response comes too late. Cooper stiffens, and the moment of levity evaporates. "Don't worry. Nobody will say anything, and it doesn't have to happen again."

He carefully extracts me from his lap and helps me stand. Dread slinks through me. We both agreed we wanted to be friends again, and this has complicated that. But... it felt so good. Right.

"Cooper, we should talk about it," I whisper.

He shakes his head. "You don't have to say anything. I get it. You don't want to ruin the friendship, and I don't, either. We can chalk that up to me helping you out, and let it be a onetime thing."

He doesn't wait for me to reply as he slips out the door and closes me inside Perry's room.

Confusion sweeps through my body, and I don't know what to do with these feelings. We're going to have to have a heart-to-heart about this soon. The way he left will eat me alive. Since when did I care so much about my relationship status with a man?

Since Cooper, I guess.

I freshen up and hurry downstairs. Perry and Cooper's low voices carry from the mudroom off the garage. They're clearly in a heated discussion, and when I hear my name, I know I have to intercept.

"You will *not* ask her to do that," Cooper says.

"It's good for the show," Perry argues. "At least let me ask her."

"Ask me what?" I step into the room, arms folded over my chest. "Well...?"

"Benton and Gloria are having it out right now, and your name is coming up a lot. I let her know you and Benton weren't anything serious and aren't sleeping together anymore."

"I already told her that."

"But you weren't mic'd up, and we didn't get it."

My body prickles, as if a million eyes are watching me at once, but I can't see them. I like my privacy; it's been drilled into me since birth. A million eyes on me is exactly how it will feel if my personal life airs on *Top of the World*.

"You can't cut around my name?"

"We can, but it's better if we don't," he says. "People will want to know."

Logically, I get what he's saying. This is juicy drama—the kind needed to make the show a success. But I'm also not a cast member for a reason. And yes, the cast have guests they bring into episodes, but I never signed up for that.

I'm a producer.

A Laurence.

I have a reputation to uphold.

I'm trying to get a promotion at work, for fuck's sake. My family has been in the media eye this past year when we never asked to be.

This isn't something I want to do.

"She's not doing it," Cooper says.

Perry frowns. "But it's my job to—"

"Your job is to make the show great, not exploit Sybil any more than you already have. Find another way."

Perry gives me a pleading look, but Cooper is firm, and honestly, I'm grateful for it. My heart flutters for him in this moment but also for the one we shared upstairs, my feelings for him growing.

"I'm sorry, Perry. You'll have to find a way to edit me out of this."

"But—"

Cooper grabs my hand and pulls me from the mudroom, back upstairs, and for a second, I think he's taking me to finish what we started, but instead, he takes me into the screening room.

Pointing at the editor, he practically growls his instructions. "You will delete *any* footage you have of Sybil and *any* mention of her name. Do it, or you'll be out of a job."

The guy's eyes widen, and he nods. I stand there frozen in the doorway, mouth open like a dead fish. I don't think anyone has stood up for me the way Cooper just did.

"Thank you," I whisper.

"You don't have to thank me, Valentine," he says. "It never should've happened."

Then he speaks up again, loud enough for anyone nearby to hear. "If I hear of anyone talking shit about this or gossiping, they're done. Do you understand?"

They nod, and Ricki strides in, looking like she's about to blow, but she doesn't argue with Cooper.

Perry is the boss, but Cooper and I are the money. The fact is, I didn't consent to being on camera or airing my personal life.

Ricki catches the stricken look on my face and gives me a little smile. "You don't have to worry, Sybil. We'll take care of it."

Perry pouts for the rest of the evening, but nobody says a word to me. Fortunately, Benton is able to win Gloria over. Their fight will get watered down for the episode, and I know Perry is not happy about that.

Luckily for us, Gloria and Benton aren't the only ones making *Top of the World* interesting. Audra and Justin have a new flirtation going, plus Dane's cheating ex-boyfriend has been begging for forgiveness, and Sloan isn't having it.

The night wraps late, and I head to my car, exhausted but fulfilled, my body lighter and looser than it's been in ages. This was one of the most eventful evenings of my life, and I'm glad it's over. I can't wait to crawl into my bed and sleep...

after analyzing what happened upstairs with Cooper, of course.

Cooper's waiting next to my car, and I approach with hesitation, not quite sure how to handle this. If I'm honest, I loved what has evolved between us, and I want to explore more, but I'm scared. I don't want to lose him again. Not even for what will probably be the best sex of my life if that oral is anything to go by.

I'm a logical person, and logic tells me to stay friends.

My heart? It's screaming to go for it. To kiss him again. To let this thing between us become something bigger. For once, I might let my heart win out.

"Hey," he says. "Some night, huh?"

His eyes flick down my body, lingering on the hem of the dress shirt, and a flush of heat washes over me.

"Yeah." My voice sounds breathy and wanting—an outward reflection of everything inside.

He wraps me in a hug, and I melt into him, relieved to be exactly where I want to be and also totally turned on, wicked fantasies flashing through my mind. What would it be like to be held by him like this, but in a different way? Our naked bodies clinging to each other as we tease out the pleasure we both deserve?

He lays a soft kiss on the top of my head. "We're finally friends again," he whispers reverently against my hair as if in prayer. "What happened doesn't have to change us, right?"

"It doesn't. I promise."

And I promise it won't if we keep following our desires, even though I'm not sure that's a promise either of us can keep.

"Good. I'm sorry. It won't happen again."

My heart sinks.

He steps away, leaving too much space, and despite the warm July night, I'm suddenly cold. I nod numbly, wishing I wasn't so confused by this man. I hoped we were on the same page, that we wanted to take our relationship to the next level, but maybe that's not possible for us. Maybe if we did more together, we'd want more together, and someone would get hurt.

I'm pretty sure I'd want more, and that's terrifying. And risky.

He must know that, and this is his way of letting me down gently.

"Have a good night, Cooper," I say with a big, fake smile, and then I get in the car, and I drive home in disappointed silence.

FORTY-FOUR

C ooper
Past - Age 26

Nothing makes me more nostalgic than the scent of the ocean drifting on salty morning air, my feet in the water, and the sun on my shoulders. Ethan and I are on the water, straddling our boards and waiting for the next wave to come in. For the first time in weeks, I feel at peace. This place, this beach, this water... they hold so many memories. From our time spent here as a family since we were children, to picnics on the beach with Mom, to playing in the surf with our friends, and even falling for the wrong girl.

Two women have been occupying my thoughts recently: Sybil and Mom. Losing them will never stop hurting.

Admittedly, this hasn't been the best surfing trip. The waves are too mellow. Right now, we're not bothered. We're both too lost in our thoughts.

I'm sure his are similar to mine. He misses his girl. Misses our mother. Say what you will about the mess she left behind, Mom wasn't a bad person, and she was a *great* mother. She was always there for us, always pushing us to be better people. She knew how to really listen and not just talk at our problems. Not a lot of people have that skill.

Sometimes I miss her so much it physically hurts.

And Sybil? Well, the girl I used to love is long gone.

Ethan seems as troubled as I am. I can see it in his face, the swirl of frustration underneath every interaction. I don't blame him; they were good together, but it's been years. I guess that proves they really were something special. If things didn't fall apart back then, they'd be married.

"Are you okay?" I ask, breaking him from his thoughts.

I don't expect him to give me an honest answer, but I need him to know I've got his back.

He releases a long sigh, regret clear as day in his storm-cloud eyes. *Fuck*, I've never seen him this bad.

He shakes his head, but no words pass his lips.

"I won't ask you to explain," I say carefully, "but can I guess why?"

He lifts a shoulder. "Do your best."

Water laps at our legs and ignored waves push us closer to shore.

"I'd say seeing Sybil again has thrown you off your game."

He grumbles, gazing out to shore.

"I want you to know I'm here for you if you need to talk."

A quiet moment passes. We let a few good waves go by, swimming underneath the big ones and popping up on the other side, shaking our hair free.

Finally, he turns, a troubled gaze traveling my face as if looking for confirmation that I'm safe to confide in. Why is he holding back? We're twins, we're supposed to tell each other everything, but we stopped doing that years ago. We both know it. We're still close, but it's not the same as when we were kids.

Maybe it's because we learned to be hard on ourselves.

Maybe we understand the world better now.

Or maybe this is about Sybil—has she finally come between us?

I don't want this to be our fate. I want our bond to be strong again.

"You can tell me," I urge. "I would never judge you."

But if he knew my past, would he judge me? The question pops into my head, reminding me of the traitor I am. He'd probably hate me for touching Sybil, let alone loving her.

"Okay," he relents, tortured emotion pouring out like a storm splitting the sky on a hot summer's day. "It's Arden. I'm in love with her."

I blink, but I manage to keep my mouth shut. We sit on our boards, floating on the water as the sun travels across the sky, and Ethan tells me more truths than he's told me in years.

"*Arden* is the one you're hung up on." I let out a little laugh. "This actually makes so much sense, but I can't believe you didn't tell me."

He gives me an incredulous shrug. "I guess I was embarrassed. We had a secret fling, and it didn't work out."

Can't say I'm surprised. I saw the way Arden looked at Ethan that summer. She was as obsessed with him as he was with her.

"Why didn't it work out?" I ask.

He runs a hand through his hair, tossing the dark strands back. "I'm an idiot, and I didn't tell her about her resemblance to Sybil. She found a picture of her on our last day together. Freaked out. I don't blame her. She thought I was using her to get over Sybil."

That sounds familiar. "And you weren't?"

He shakes his head. "I got over Sybil before I met Arden, but I didn't want to admit it to myself. When Arden came into my life, there was no denying she was so much better suited for me than Sybil ever was."

I can see that. Arden has a grounding energy to her not many people in our lives seem to possess. She's quiet and sweet and is the type of girl who needs protection and kindness. She's nothing like Sybil, who is as stubborn as a fucking mule.

"Why didn't you tell Arden that?" I wonder aloud, and he groans.

"I almost did, but by then, Dad called me and told me the truth about her being Sybil's cousin. I couldn't believe it... but I also could. The resemblance is uncanny."

I get it. We were both stunned to meet Arden... and confused as fuck.

"There Arden was, about to have a family—something she desperately wanted and never got to have. If I told Arden how I felt, there was a chance she'd choose me over them. I wasn't going to be the one to take her dream away."

Wow. My brother is definitely in love. Here I thought he was going to check on the house during the hurricane because he was worried about losing something tied to Mom. All along, he'd been hoping to get Arden alone.

If he had worked things out with Arden back then, she'd likely never been close to her family. I can't believe Ethan never told me about any of this while it was happening, but do I really have room to judge? I've never told him about Sybil.

Maybe he wouldn't care anymore, or maybe he'd care for years. He doesn't mention it, but I know he took Arden's virginity. He wouldn't have done that without making sure he was over Sybil. Unlike me, he actually had some honor that summer.

"You're still in love with her." It's not a question.

His jaw ticks. "I bared my soul to her, man." Embarrassment laces his heartbreak. "I think she loves me, too, but she won't consider dating me. She's moved on and won't forgive me, especially after the bullshit lawsuit."

"Shit..." That lawsuit would've freaked anyone out, and Arden is a vulnerable soul. I'm sure it scared her.

Dad tried to sue her for trespassing at the Nantucket house after we'd told her to go home, but since the house had already been moved to mine and Ethan's names, we stopped the lawsuit the second we found out about it. But we didn't apologize to Arden. Didn't say a damn thing. I forgot entirely after I let it go.

Of course, she's not ready to do the same. She was eighteen when it happened, and a billionaire was suing her.

I gaze up at our beach estate now, admiring so many things about it, from the modern architecture to the sprawling lawn and gazebo filled with memories. Most of all, I love this house thanks to Mom. She's the one who made it special.

I pat my brother on the shoulder, nearly falling off my board in the process. He chuckles, and the moment of levity lightens things.

"You should let me talk to Arden for you. Plead your case. She's always liked me," I tease, and he snorts, but we both know it's true. "We were friends once. She might listen to me."

"You'd do that for me?"

He has no idea what I'd do for him. What I'd give up.

What I *did* give up.

The secret I've held buried since I was a damn preteen sits on my tongue, aching to have a voice. For a brief moment, I consider letting go of the heavy burden I've been carrying and confessing to my brother where my heart has been for all these years.

One look at his tortured face sucks that confession right

back to its hiding place deep within me. My signature mask covers my expression, tilting my lips into a smile.

"Yeah, brother, I'd do anything for you."

FORTY-FIVE

S ybil
Present - Age 27

The cast is drunk off their asses, and Perry is gleeful about it. *"Give your talent unlimited alcohol, and they'll give you good television."* His words. Not mine. I don't protest, but I keep a close eye on Benton.

Sometimes I swear the man forgets cameras and microphones are following his every move. It's like he's so acclimated to being on the show he forgets to check himself. He's not making my job easy, that's for sure.

We've been filming all day, and luckily the cast is getting along. We sent a crew to get b-roll of the island and holiday happenings, but our people are staying put. We've had lawn games and a pool party set up for them, as well as beach access, plenty of barbecue food, and endless drinks. Perry even got a private fireworks show approved by the city, so we didn't have to film in a crowd.

Right now, the six of them are all cuddled on the beach, cozy as fuck, with cameras behind them. The rest of us sit by the pool, watching the fireworks display color the blanked sky.

Cooper and I sit with our legs in the pool, and I'm painfully aware our fingers are only inches apart. Our necks are craned upward, and booming fireworks drum in tune with my booming heart.

He's all I've thought about for two days.

I'm working? *Cooper.*

I'm driving? *Cooper.*

Sleeping? Eating? Talking? *Cooper. Cooper. Cooper.*

I'm driving myself crazy. If he would just give me a signal that he wanted more than friendship, I would take it.

But it's like he's completely unaffected.

God, it doesn't help that he looks fucking amazing tonight. His silky brown hair has grown longer than usual, windswept by the breeze coming off the ocean. The planes of his chiseled face light up with each flashing firework, the reds and blues and oranges making him appear almost ethereal. But he's not ethereal; he's human and masculine and primal. The cords of muscles in his body, the veins in his sun-tanned arms, the rise and fall of his chest... They're doing unmentionable things to me. And his scent? Oh my God, his scent. It's always been pleasant, but lately it's intoxicating, as if my body has become attuned to the salty spice of his signature cologne.

Cooper's not a boy anymore.

Cooper is a man.

And I want him.

I'm forced to stare at him and hope he doesn't catch me looking, like a silly teenager with a crush.

In an ideal world—aka, my fantasy world—our pinkies would touch. He'd take my hand and lead me to bed within the hour.

But his pinky stays where it is.

The fireworks end, and we climb to our feet.

Disappointed, I follow the cast and crew to the house for the afterparty. Turns out, working on a holiday is still working on a holiday. I'm not complaining, but it's not the same.

Perry sidles up next to me, nudging me in the arm. "You okay there, friend?"

"Yeah," I lie.

"Holidays are hard when you've lost a loved one." It's a gentle confirmation he understands why I'm not enjoying myself.

"I think it would be worse if I tried to carry on traditions as normal. The distraction of work helps," I confess.

He nods. "I get it. You do you."

"How's your sister?" I ask. Madeline underwent surgery right before we left for Nantucket.

"She got discharged this morning. She's doing pretty well. Thanks for asking."

"That's a relief."

"It is." He smiles, but it doesn't reach his dark eyes. "You're right about work. It's the perfect distraction." He lifts his chin to where Benton and Gloria are making out in the hot tub. "I want to apologize about what happened. I promise your personal life won't end up on the show."

I give him a rueful smile. "I get why you asked. It's your job is to make good television."

"Not at the expense of my producer... and more importantly, my friend," he says. "I never should've asked you for that."

I nod toward Benton. "What about at *his* expense? Is he going to get a terrible edit at the end of all this?"

Perry shrugs, his face guarded. "It depends on how he behaves."

That's exactly what I'm worried about. I can't stop Benton from being a fuck-boy on national television, and even though Gloria is kind of crazy, she's going to have every woman in America on her side if this thing blows up.

By midnight, filming ends, and the cast goes to bed. Oddly enough, I'm not tired, and my body buzzes with untapped energy. Maybe there's too much on my mind, or maybe it's because this is my favorite holiday, and I'd hardly call working a celebration.

"Hey, Valentine." Cooper catches me as I head out. "I'm having a little afterparty bonfire at my place for the crew. You up for it?"

A smile spreads across my face, and twenty minutes later, I pull up to the King's residence. I haven't been here in years, and even in the darkness, the sight floods me with countless memories.

I love this house—love it so much that once upon a time I wanted to get married here.

We use our phones as flashlights as we make the trek down the steep stairs to the beach. A few people carry cases of beer, and someone has a speaker with trendy music quietly thumping. The bonfire isn't lit yet, but it doesn't take long to get going.

The tide is low, so the waves aren't too intense, not like they'll be in the morning. I have the sudden urge to go swimming. I don't act on that urge. Like a good girl, I stay next to the fire with the others and chat while listening to the songs change over.

Cooper and Perry light off a few fireworks and screech like little kids, and I end up on the sand in a full-bellied laugh. Pushing myself back up, I brush away the sand and stop myself from longing for the things I can't have anymore.

A wave of regret hits me anyway, so I wander along the dark

empty stretch of beach, the bluff on my left and the ocean on my right. I've walked this beach countless times. The crush of the waves is as familiar as my own heartbeat. Even though the sand is always moving, it hasn't changed a bit. The stars twinkle above me in a dance with the darkness that I've watched a million times. Nothing compares to the King's house and beach and seclusion. Nothing compares to this.

Nobody compares to Cooper.

This crush isn't going away, is it?

I don't know what to do. My heart aches with unrequited longing.

"There you are." His voice catches up to me, and I turn. My vision has adjusted to the night, so I can see him well enough, but I hope he can't see me too well. He'll know I'm upset.

I give him a small smile. "Just out for a walk."

"Are you okay?" He reaches out, catching my hand. I shouldn't, but I let him have it. His palm feels so warm against mine, so comforting, so right.

"I'm... I don't know... confused, I guess," I confess.

He squeezes my fingers and steps closer. "Are you... confused about me?"

I shake my head. "Not exactly."

"You know what you want?"

"Yes."

"And... are you sad about it?"

I shrug, but the closer he gets, the more my heart hopes. Every nerve ending in my body is alive, firing off brighter than all the fireworks.

"I'm sad, too," he says.

I blink. "Why?"

Cooper doesn't talk about his feelings, especially the hard ones, but this moment feels open with me in a way he's never been before.

"I screwed up. I never should've... done things with you. I'm so sorry."

My gaze drops as I try to hide my frown.

"Don't be sorry." I step closer. "I *liked* it, Cooper. Don't you get that? I liked it, and I like you." He tilts my chin up with his tender hand, and our gazes lock. This is the time to be brave. "I wanted you to do it, and I wish you'd do it again."

He shakes his head slowly, confusion clearing for something much more heated, as his hand travels to the back of my neck and holds tight. "What do you want?"

A breath hitches in my chest, and I search for the right words but come up short. All I can do is hope he can read the longing in my expression.

Wrapping an arm around my lower back, he draws me to him so fast and so hard our bodies crash into each other. His hard cock is an unmistakable confession, even before he parts his lips. "It's pretty fucking clear what I want, and I'll take anything you'll give me."

I should tell him I want to be exclusive, but I go with the safer option. "Maybe we could try the friends with benefits thing? We've both been successful with that, and I think we could be successful together."

God help me... I rub against him, and he groans with molten heat. I tremble under his touch, expecting him to kiss me, but he hesitates, those hooded eyes searching mine. The crashing waves in the background seem to go silent as I wait for his answer on bated breath. The moment stretches out as if on a tight wire, both of us waiting for the other to make the first move.

Do we steady ourselves?

Do we fall?

Or do we jump?

"Fuck it," he growls, lips crashing to mine.

FORTY-SIX

C ooper
     Past - Age 26

Waking up hungover is no surprise, considering most of last night is still a blur. Ethan and I went out, but then Arden texted him. I left them to do their own thing and headed to the bar, but not before Arden told us Sybil had gone home with Reed Havish.

Reed Havish? Really?

I've *always* hated that guy. He's the kind of self-serving holier-than-thou prick who doesn't deserve a girl like Sybil.

Reed will do anything in his power to be seen with the right people and then leach onto those people and suck them dry. I swear he's a future politician.

We met him in college, and last I've heard, he's still the same brand of asshole, so I had no problem not thinking of him anymore.

Until now.

Because he's with Sybil. They're not dating, but Arden made it obvious they're fucking, which might be worse.

The bar idea would've been fine if I didn't get wasted. I planned to find a woman and have some fun, but after Arden's bombshell, I couldn't bring myself to care. So I sat at the bar, slinging drinks until the bartender cut me off and insisted I find a ride home. I don't remember much after that, but I must've caught an Uber or something.

My stomach churns with regret.

I know I have problems with alcohol.

I want to be sober and have good bouts of sobriety here and there, but I haven't quite been able to cut it out of my life. It's my favorite crutch.

Rolling out of bed, I try not to let self-talk get too disparaging as I make my way downstairs. At least Dad and wifey number three have left the island. I don't think I could face a lecture from him with this headache.

Ethan is at the kitchen table when I amble downstairs, looking like sunshine is radiating from his ass. He's ridiculously in love. Not sure how it's all going to play out for them once they return to Manhattan, but I'm happy for him.

"Look at you," I say, shooting him a withering smile. "All lovey and shit."

He raises an eyebrow. "Look at you, all hungover and shit."

I groan and head to the medicine cabinet first and then the refrigerator. I need fast caffeine, and a diet whatever-I-can-find will have to do.

"I take it you're not up for surfing today."

"I'm not up for anything today."

Ethan nods. "How about sailing tomorrow? I want to go out with you one last time before we head to the city."

"Aww," I tease. "Brotherly love."

We only have two days before work owns us again. Our

legacy hangs on us, showing up like our father does—professional, driven, cutthroat, and willing to do anything for King.

"Tomorrow sounds good," I promise. "Today I sleep."

I balance a glass of water, a can of Coke, a bottle of medicine, and a blueberry muffin in my arms as I leave the kitchen. Ethan is hot on my trail.

"Are you okay?" he asks.

"Why wouldn't I be?"

He follows me to my bedroom and hovers in the doorway with his arms crossed. Sometimes I hate having a brother who cares about my wellbeing more than I do.

"You drank too much last night," he says. "I thought you weren't doing that anymore."

"Well, shit. Nothing like being called out first thing in the morning."

"I mean it, Coop. What gives?"

My jaw tenses, and I give myself a moment to collect my thoughts as I set everything on the dresser and down the pills first. Ethan stares at me expectantly.

"So? I drank too much last night." I sit on the edge of the bed and rub my thumbs into my temples. "What do you want me to say?"

"Look, Cooper, I'm not judging you."

I snort. "You *are* judging me."

He sits next to me. "Like I said, I'm worried about you."

I'm tired of people being worried about me. So what if I got hammered last night? I beat myself up about it enough on my own. I don't need Ethan to do it, too.

"You've worked so hard," he continues. "Your drinking habits have really improved lately. I hate to see you go back there, you know?"

He cares about me, but I'm defensive anyway, dangerous confessions sitting on the tip of my tongue.

"You don't know what you're talking about," I snap.

He stiffens, giving me a patronizing look, and I kind of want to punch him.

"I've been here through all of it, remember? You made an effort to control your drinking for the last two years. Don't pretend you haven't."

"I'm on vacation."

He doesn't take the bait. "What the hell happened last night?"

God damn. This is not my idea of a good time.

"What happened?" I shake my head. "You tell me, Ethan. Oh wait, you can't. You were busy fucking your new girl."

Well, that was the wrong thing to say.

His glare is harsh. "Don't talk about Arden like she's some girl I want to hook up with. I'm in love with her. You know that."

I swallow hard. "You... you don't know what I'm going through. You're in your own little world with her. Don't pretend like you didn't ditch me last night and now have a right to question why I got drunk."

His jaw ticks. "You told me to go with her. Don't act like a victim."

"What do you want from me, then?"

He sighs but doesn't leave. It would be a hell of a lot easier if he gave up like he used to.

"You do what you need to do, but I'm always going to watch out for you. Sure, I've been distracted the last few weeks, but I know you well enough to realize something is going on with you. You're acting like college-Cooper, not mature-adult Cooper who has his shit together."

Fuck.

Nerves race through my system, unraveling my secret shame. I've kept my feelings for Sybil to myself for so long that the idea of telling Ethan makes my stomach churn. If I don't tell him now, I might never tell him. At least this way, there doesn't have to be a secret between us anymore.

"Fine," I say. "I'll tell you why I'm so messed up."

He shifts his weight to face me better, eyes open and expectant. "I'm listening."

"I'm in love with someone I can't have."

He frowns, clearly thrown off guard. "Who is she?"

I release a slow breath, the will to keep this secret any longer deflating with my lungs. I look him straight in the eyes when I say it.

"Sybil."

The confession comes with an immediate sense of relief, and as I watch his hardened face soften, a chasm opens inside my chest, letting my brother in again.

"You're in love with Sybil Laurence?" He sounds incredulous.

I nod, and he stares at me in disbelief.

"How long has this been a thing? We've barely seen her in years."

I shrug. "Since we were kids, I guess."

He blinks rapidly. "Fuck. Why didn't you say something?"

"You were in love with her too, and she chose you. I wasn't going to get between that."

I can see his mind working, backtracking through years of memories and viewing them in a new light. "I thought you saw her as a sister, but this makes so much sense. No wonder you were such a miserable fuck-boy in college."

My nostrils flare in amusement. "Wow. Thanks."

He side-eyes me. "It's true, and you know it."

"There's more..." I grimace, wishing I didn't have to add to the confession, but this has been burning a hole in me for four years, and I can't leave it unsaid another minute. "Remember when you two broke up for a day?"

A wrinkle forms between his eyebrows. "Yeah...?"

"Well, I went over there to see how she was doing, and..."

The color drains from his face. "Did you hook up?"

"We kissed. I'm so sorry. It never should've happened. She regretted it. She didn't want to ruin things with you. She loved you, not me, and I took advantage of her heartbreak." My fingers grip the back of my head, tugging at my hair as I try to pull myself together. "I never should've gone over there."

He's quiet for a long moment, and I don't know what to expect. Rage? I know I'd be pissed as hell if the roles were reversed.

"Do you know why we broke up?"

She was getting cold feet about an engagement, and he got upset. I remember it like it was yesterday.

"I was right the first time," he says. "She didn't want to marry me."

"She did—"

"No, she didn't. She wouldn't have broken the engagement as soon as things got hard if she truly wanted to get married. Do you think that's the behavior of a woman in love? As pissed as I want to be with both of you, I'm not." He shrugs. "So much time has passed, and I'm committed to Arden. She loves me the way I want to be loved, and I love her, too. We're the real deal."

Wow. Okay, then...

I knew he was in love with Arden, but this is a side of my brother I never saw with anyone else, not even Sybil. Not even close.

"I'm still sorry."

He nods slowly. "I'm not mad about the kiss, Cooper, but I am mad you kept these secrets from me for so long. We're supposed to be brothers."

I smirk. "Like how you had a whole affair with Arden you never told me about? Like those kinds of secrets?"

He barks out a laugh. "Touché."

I rib him with my elbow, and an easy silence falls between us.

"What are you going to do, Cooper? Are you going to tell Sybil how you feel?"

"Yeah, that's not happening. She hates me. Hates all of us Kings."

He contemplates that for a moment, finally shaking his head. "I don't think she hates you."

Unfortunately, I *know* she does, and to think otherwise is delusional.

"There's nothing to be done. I have to learn to live with it until I eventually meet the right person."

Ethan pats my knee. "One day, you'll meet someone who makes your feelings for Sybil pale in comparison. If I can find my person, I know you can, too."

I nod like I agree, even though I don't. Ethan getting over Sybil is proof he never saw or valued her to her fullest. She's not a woman you simply get over by meeting someone new. She's a woman you love for the rest of your life, whether or not you're with her. She's not a girl you leave in the past willingly—she's the one that got away.

FORTY-SEVEN

S ybil
     Present - Age 27

Almost as quickly as he starts the kiss, Cooper breaks away, resting his forehead against mine while catching his breath.

"About the benefits... It's not for a lack of trying, but I haven't exactly been with a woman since my accident."

I pull away slightly and search his eyes. They're shadowed in darkness, and the moonlight isn't enough to see his expression. I understand the downcast tilt of his head, his ridged body, and the pained edge in his voice.

I trace my hands around his face first, then down his arms. The flesh prickles under my touch. "Do you want to talk about it?" I whisper, dropping a soft kiss to his warm neck. He smells so good, and I drink him in, my lips lingering. His throat bobs.

"It's obviously about my leg," he confesses.

Cooper is just as handsome with a prosthetic leg as he was before. I didn't want this fate for him, but it happened. It's a miracle he's alive. Since that time, he's moved forward with more strength than anyone I know.

That strength has only made him sexier.

"I don't know how to put everything I want to say into words." I move to his mouth, giving him gentle pecks. "But you're not broken, Cooper. You're perfect to me."

He chuckles with self-deprecation.

"Let me show you how much I want you," I beg, hoping to continue but preparing for rejection.

"You want *this*, or you want *me*?"

The question stops me cold, nearly breaking my heart. "You don't think I want you?"

"I don't know what you want, Valentine. Friends with benefits is what you said, and I like friends with benefits, but does it matter to you who it's with?"

"You're my *best* friend, Cooper." My voice catches, but I persist. "Losing you was so hard. That's why I wasn't sure we could add the benefits to our friendship before, but I'm sure of it now."

He smiles ruefully. "Why now?"

"I'm dying for *your* benefits, Cooper. Nobody else's."

"You want me, Valentine?" He chuckles. "All you've ever had to do was ask."

I playfully shove him in the chest, but he catches my hand, bringing my palm to his lips. "Okay," he says. One kiss. Two. "Show me how much you want me, baby, and I'll show you how much I want you, but under one condition."

"What's that?" I ask coyly, the desire in my belly spreading through every inch of my body.

He smirks. "You show me first."

"You're such a guy," I deadpan, and he laughs for real this time, openly and unabashedly, but it's so damn good to hear him laugh that I can't help but smile. He needs it right now.

Being vulnerable is hard for both of us. If he hasn't been with a woman since the accident, that's over a year. He needs this, and so do I.

I close the distance and kiss him on the mouth, the fire instantly sparking to life. It doesn't take long before I can feel his cock hardening.

Sliding to my knees, I get to work unfastening his belt buckle. His breathing is fast and labored, and I swear I'll do whatever it takes for him to feel good about this moment. He never should be ashamed of his leg. He's always been desirable.

He shifts his weight, grabbing onto my shoulder. Maybe it's harder to hold his balance, and I'm tempted to ask if he wants to lie down.

"You want this?" I peer up at him.

He nods, and I slide his pants off his body. His prosthetic leg is sleek and thin, attached below his knee. Made out of a shiny black metal, it looks high-tech and expensive. I don't shy away from touching it. I don't want him to think I'm judging it or turned off.

He stiffens. "You don't have to—"

I quickly stand and grab his hand, slipping it under the hem of my underwear. "Do you feel that?" I rasp. "Do you feel how wet you've made me already?"

"Fuck," he growls, fingers sliding along my sensitive seam and into my dripping pussy. I cry out, a rush of pleasure coating his skin. I could easily ride his hand and come right now.

"Don't think for a second your leg turns me off." My voice is hard and demanding, but it's exactly what Cooper needs. His mouth takes mine again as his hand does unspeakable things to me. I could let this go on, let him pleasure me to orgasm, but this isn't about me.

He wanted to go first, and I want that, too.

Removing his hand, I quickly return to my knees, slide his

underwear down until his cock springs free. I take him into my mouth, not even giving myself a moment to admire his impressive length. I take it all like the greedy bitch I am.

He arches into me, holding on to my shoulders as he hisses with pleasure. Determined to make this a memorable experience, I bob my head and swirl my tongue, simultaneously pumping one hand at the base of his shaft and using the other hand to cup his balls.

He holds onto me, one hand at my shoulder and the other fisted into my hair.

"Holy fuck," he groans, pulling at my scalp. "Where did you learn to do that? Wait, never mind. Don't tell me."

I giggle and pull away with an audible pop. "If you're thinking about your brother, don't. Our sex life was not that exciting."

I lick the underside of his shaft, barely registering the sand rubbing into my knees or the way my skirt rides up to my chest, completely exposing my panties. I hope he likes the view.

"I'm not going to last long," he hisses.

That's fine with me, but just when I think he's about to come, he nudges me away. "As much as I love your mouth, the first time I come in you, Valentine, it's going to be in that gorgeous pussy."

"Is that so?"

A predatory gleam settles in his eyes. "You have no idea how long I've imagined fucking you. I'm not going to pass up the opportunity now."

He kicks away his pants and underwear, sinking onto his knees with me. I'm immensely grateful for his prosthetic, and that he can do this with me, but even if he couldn't kneel, I'd still want him. His cock is hard and wet between us, pressing against my top.

"I haven't been with anyone in over a year, and I'm clean,"

he breathes. "I can show you the results on my phone, but I also have a condom in my wallet if you prefer."

I kiss him hard and rip off his shirt, tossing it to the side with the rest of his clothes. "You don't have to show me. I haven't been with anyone in months, and I'm clean also." I lean toward his ear, quickly nipping at the soft lobe. "I'm on birth control, so no condom is needed, if that's okay with you."

"Fuck," he whispers, almost in shock. "We get to ride raw?"

Desire tingles through me. "I knew you'd have a filthy mouth. I like it."

"I have more than a filthy mouth, Valentine. I know how to make a woman scream."

"Is that a promise?"

"That's a guarantee." Then he gets to work, stripping me bare under the moonlight. It doesn't take long until we're both naked and panting in the sand. It's going to be a mess to deal with later, but that's Future Sybil's problem. Right now, I'm so hot and needy I can't imagine doing anything but sinking onto his cock and riding him hard.

"Please, Cooper. I can't wait any longer. I'm not above begging." Not when I feel like I'm about to die without this, without him.

"All fours for me, baby," he commands, and I flip around until he's behind me. He pulls me up so my back is against his chest, one commanding hand at the nape of my neck and the other gently strumming my clit.

He enters me in one hard thrust.

I gasp, the sensation exactly what I need.

He pumps, his large cock filling me inch by inch. Taking me. Claiming me. Everything about this moment feels so good and right and primal.

We buck against each other, the sounds of our lovemaking an echo of the crashing ocean waves. I'm growing slicker with each thrust, the passion between us building. We should slow it down, make this last longer, switch positions and draw it out, but neither of us seems to want any changes to this flawless moment.

Despite the sand and the exposure, despite it being our first time and his initial hesitancy, this very well might be the hottest sex I've ever had. We're animals unleashed, and that only gets confirmed when the hand at the nape of my neck slips downward, fingers pinching at my nipples.

Every thought flees my mind. I turn my head and practically cry into his mouth as we kiss, his groans guttural in response. My blood races through my body on an electric current, centering where he's doing delicious things to my sex with this expert hand and hard, slick cock.

My vision blurs, my breath catches, and I scream as an orgasm rips through my body. I practically sink onto him, even deeper than I thought possible. He doesn't let it stop him from bucking into me over and over. The wetness between us thickens, his groan of pleasure echoing mine.

We stretch the moment out, the ecstasy lingering between us. Then, carefully, he slides from me and leans back on his knees, pulling me into his lap. I flip around, my legs spread, my exposed flesh wet and glistening with the evidence of our arousal. He takes his time looking at it, and even though it's dark out here, I can see the satisfaction in his possessive gaze.

Then he kisses me, long and slow and searching.

Perfect.

This is not friends with benefits.

I've *never* experienced something like this with a friend. I don't know what to do about that, don't know what we are, but that doesn't matter to me right now. I let my thoughts drift as I kiss him like I've never kissed anyone else before.

FORTY-EIGHT

C ooper
       Past - Age 26

We're on Ethan's boat as the water glistens in the fading sunset. One last sail around the island before we have to return to Manhattan. At least our work is interesting, but being on Nantucket always makes me want to stay for the entire summer, just like old times.

"You ready for the drama when we get back?" I ask Ethan while he adjusts the sails.

He understands sailing better than I ever did. It's been one of his hobbies for years. When we got our trust funds, this sailboat was his first big purchase. He named her *Juliet*, which I said was stupid, especially when he wouldn't tell me why. Since when did my brother give a shit about Shakespeare?

"What drama?" he huffs as he works, catching the practically nonexistent wind and getting us moving again. He says sailing is both an art and a science whenever he drags me out here, and I stand around clueless.

Some things never change.

"Oh come on... Your new girlfriend?" I prod. "Arden? And you? That's going to be drama."

He chuckles, a boyish smile on his face. "Whatever it is, I'm not worried about it. We're committed to each other." He catches my eye and winks. "She loves me."

Oh hell, he's in trouble. "Of course she does. You're a lovable guy, Ethan. She's lucky to have you."

"Nah, I'm the lucky one."

The sudden mechanical roar of a speedboat revving its engine makes us both jump. We turn to see a shiny small boat headed directly for us. My heart speeds, but logically, I know the driver will see us and move. People are idiots out here sometimes, but they don't run into each other on purpose. Probably some rich old guy, showing off his newest toy.

I squint, trying to make out the people on the boat... and the whole world slows.

"Is that...?" My voice trails off when I catch a better look at the man behind the wheel with his familiar tall build, faded Harvard ball cap, and the grimace on his face.

It's Gregory Laurence, and he's coming right for us.

"Shit," Ethan mutters, dashing for the steering wheel.

Greg's boat barrels forward, and I count the heads, my mouth drying. His entire family is on board.

Ethan has abandoned the sail, so I take over, fumbling with the rigging to finish getting it up. The speedboat doesn't waver.

Ten more seconds, and we're dead.

"He's going to hit us!" I point to the water. "Jump!"

Ethan and I lock eyes, understanding quick between us. We move... but it happens too fast. One second, we're on deck, and the next the speed boat is *on us*. Ethan dives into the water just before we're hit, but I'm not fast enough.

The impact is pure chaos.

Metal screeches against wood, violent and all-encompassing.

I'm thrown airborne so fast I barely have time to register what's happening. I don't know which direction I'm flying when I slam into the water. Pain explodes through my body. Pain and pure terror.

It's as if every inch of my skin is on fire, but my right leg burns beyond reasonable belief. It's so bad that I can't even scream.

I open my mouth and gag on ocean water. My vision blurs. Salt stings my eyes and throat. My lower body slices through what feels like a million razor blades.

Ice cold grips me immediately, pulling me downward, but the pain keeps me awake. I thrash, trying to pry my way to the surface. My lungs burn as I fight the weight of the water and the weight of my own panic.

Kick. Just kick.

My right leg's not moving the way I'm begging it to. It's sluggish. My stomach flips; I can't feel that leg anymore.

I force my eyes to focus, look down. A scream rips through my throat, and a rush of water invades my lungs.

Red water.

An unnatural cloud of crimson in the endless deep blue. It's thick with salt and blood and death and darkness.

The world around me grows quieter, as if the ocean is swallowing me whole.

There is a single thought—a stark truth and the last one I have before everything goes blank.

This is how I die.

———

All too quickly, my eyes snap open, and my throat constricts, heaving a wave of blood and salt water over my chin. The sharp pain returns tenfold, spreading throughout my entire body.

I blink wildly, my surroundings slowly coming into view. I'm laid out flat on a boat deck. Ethan is above me, mouth moving but no sound making it to my buzzing eardrums. Sybil is at his side, frantically tying something above my right knee.

I want to yell at her not to touch me; she's making it worse. But I can't speak unless it's to scream. I can barely even move. Blood pours out of my mangled right leg, my life draining with it. I'm fading fast.

I peer around. Chandler, Amelia, and Arden... Their pale faces are streaked with tears. They're looking at me like I'm already dead. Maybe I am. Why is there so much pain?

I don't want to look at my leg.

But I do... and my stomach hollows.

A mess of bone and sinew sits under my knee, blood seeping rhythmically from the rope-tourniquet. I don't recognize it; can't get my mind to tell me that it's my leg. Mine. This suddenly inhuman limb is attached to me, causing a fire so hot I've become numb. My eyes fall closed, salty acid churning in my stomach, threatening to make an appearance.

Ethan pats my cheek, his words finally having a sound. "Stay awake. Stay alive." He demands it, demands me to look at him, but I'm too tired to open my eyes again. I'm done. He doesn't really believe I'm going to survive this, does he? He can cry, he can beg, but it won't stop the bleeding.

I want to say something, but I can't speak. There's not even energy for that. There's nothing. I have nothing.

"You're not leaving me, Coop. Do you hear me? You're staying right here," my brother orders.

It's not like I want to leave him, but this overwhelming need to close my eyes is beyond my control. My brother and I may have come into this world together, but it's becoming clear that we won't leave it together, because this needy darkness is also calling to me.

I give in and the world, the pain, and everything disappears.

FORTY-NINE

S ybil
  Present - Age 27

I wake up, staring at Cooper's ceiling, a wave of ease washing over me. I turn, finding the beautiful man asleep at my side. The events of last night return like a warm ray of sunshine. I don't have a single regret. How can I when it was, without a doubt, the best sex I've ever had?

Cooper is an incredible lover, but our chemistry together was on another level, like he could enter my mind and anticipate my body's every need. Somehow, I did the same for him.

Good God, this is a man I need to talk to my girlfriends about over spicy margaritas.

Watching him sleep now, I marvel at the way his lips look fuller when he's relaxed, envy the length of his dark lashes, and linger on the gorgeous outline of his honed muscles. He really is an impressive male specimen. I always knew this, but to be naked in bed with a naked Cooper? It's a whole new level of understanding.

My mind races through the events of last night, greedy to parse apart every delectable moment. Every movement. Every moan. Every thrust and all the perfect orgasms we gave each other. Fuck, I'm getting wet just thinking about it, and I don't have time for shenanigans.

I grab my phone off the nightstand. It's almost ten. As tired as I am, I need to get moving. We're due on set at noon, and I've got to go home and get changed, and since it's a long drive to the other side of the island, I'm already running late.

If I wake him, we'll have sex again, and I'll be late. If I don't, he might think I used him last night.

I peer around the bedroom, trying not to think too hard about all the nights I've spent in this house. Now that I'm finally in *Cooper's* bed, I don't think I've ever felt more at home, but I peel myself from the sheets, hurry and change into my skirt and top, then give him a quick peck.

He wakes up with a smile and grabs me around the waist, a delighted squeal falling from my lips.

"Come to bed," he mumbles.

I wriggle away. "I've got to get home. I'll see you on set in two hours."

He grumbles. "I want to keep seeing you now."

I giggle. "Nope. Got to go."

I rush away without a backward glance, secure in the fact that I handled that like how a friends-with-benefits girl would handle it. At least, I think that's what we are? Are we more? The answer to that is still a little hazy. And the farther I drive away, the more my chest aches to turn around. God help me, I want to crawl right back into his bed.

Luckily, I make it to set on time. Cooper arrives ten minutes later, and we instantly lock eyes, my stomach fluttering. This is a crush on a level I haven't experienced since his brother, but I was a teenager then, and I'm an adult now. I shouldn't be so giddy.

We spend the following hours busy with our own tasks but also like two magnets rotating around each other, both knowing it's only a matter of time before we'll get to connect again. Honestly, we've been like this for weeks, but it's so much more fun knowing he wants me as much as I want him.

Until one of the random assistants sidles up next to him at craft services and starts flirting mercilessly. He laughs at something she says, and she puts her hand on his upper arm.

I'm so fucking jealous I could scream, which is ridiculous. I'm not a jealous type. I don't care if the guys I hook up with hook up with other women as long as we all agree to use condoms. This is different. Cooper is different. And we *didn't* use condoms last night.

Another mistake.

So what if we're clean and I'm on birth control? No condom is not something I do.

The only other man who ever got to have me bare was Ethan, and that was because we were in a committed relationship.

It's been ages since I've had raw sex, but now that we've done it, now that I've felt him bare inside me, I can't imagine doing it any other way.

Frustrated, I walk to the beach, hoping it'll clear my head.

The sun is high in the afternoon sky and warm on my face, so I step into the surf to cool off. The waves lap at my ankles as I dig my toes into the wet sand, watching the water foam up and retreat. It calms my senses enough for me to breathe.

Maybe we shouldn't have hooked up.

Or maybe we should be something more?

I'm toggling between the two ideas, knowing it needs to be one way or the other soon, because friends with benefits and nothing more is never going to work if I'm already a jealous lunatic a day in.

Cooper steps up next to me, his hands deep in the pockets of his shorts. "Hi."

"Hi."

He's got one foot bare, and the other is his metal prosthetic, visible today for all to see. This is the first day I've seen him wear shorts on set. He usually hides the leg, but maybe after last night, he doesn't feel the need to do that anymore. If we ever end this benefits thing, I hope I at least gave him a boost of confidence.

He fixes his gaze on the horizon, and I wonder if he's remembering what happened in this water. We're near the area where the accident took place. I'll never look at this water the same way again.

"I don't think you know what you did for me," he says.

I turn to look at him, but he stays staring at the sea. "And what's that?"

His smile quirks, and my stomach swoops. He's extra gorgeous when he smiles like that.

"I'm wearing shorts for the first time since last summer, and that's thanks to you."

I nudge him with my elbow. "That's great, Cooper. I'm happy to be of service."

He shoots me a devilish smirk. "Well, I do have a third leg to stand on, as you experienced last night, but I think this prosthetic is better suited for public exposure."

I bust out laughing.

Leave it to Cooper to make a joke out of a serious conversation.

We go quiet for a minute, the silence feeling heavy. I'd focus on the rhythmic waves if I could, but my thoughts are too loud. Too frustrating. Demanding.

"You're quiet," Cooper points out. His voice is soft, but it cuts through my thoughts. "What's going on?"

I bite my bottom lip. "Just thinking."

He quirks an eyebrow, his usual smirk tugging at the corner of his mouth. "Should I be worried?"

I roll my eyes. "Very funny."

"Seriously, what's on your mind?" He takes a step closer. "Are you okay about what happened last night?"

I hesitate, staring out at the water. The words are on the tip of my tongue, but saying them feels terrifying. "Are you sure friends with benefits is a good idea?"

He seems to deflate. "Only if you do. We don't have to do that again. It might kill me, but I can go back to being platonic friends if you need."

"No." The word flies out of my mouth, and my cheeks heat. I clear my throat, trying to regain some composure. "I don't want to stop what we've started."

"Then what do you want?" He sounds hopeful, and that gives me a boost of courage.

"With you, given our history together, I think we would be better suited to be one or the other. Friends or..."

He raises a brow. "Or?"

"Don't make me say it."

He smiles so brightly it rivals the summer sun. "I'm going to make you say it. Please, go on, Valentine. Friends or what?"

"Friends or lovers," I blurt. "Exclusive. Dating. In a relationship."

His eyes drop to my lips, and he inches closer. "Which would you prefer?"

"I think we both know the answer to that." My voice comes out husky, and fire burns in my cheeks, my heart racing. If this doesn't go the way I want to it go, I think I'll die, but something about being brave with him feels amazing.

"Yeah," he says, his voice low. "I know the answer."

My heart stumbles over a beat. "And?"

"And I have thought about this, too, but it's hard. I don't want to lose what we already have."

I get it. "It's okay if you don't want to be more than friends. I won't be mad at you. We can go back to things as they were before last night. I promise. I know how you are with women. I know you don't do relationships and—"

He stops my rambling with a soft, quick kiss. "Relax, Valentine," he whispers against my mouth. "I want you."

I break away even though I'd love to continue this kiss. "So... what now? We... try?"

The questions hang in the air between us. The thought of turning this into something real is exhilarating and terrifying all at once. But not trying? That feels worse.

"I think we do," he says firmly, taking my hand and squeezing it before threading our fingers together. It's a perfect fit. "I think we try, but only if we're both all in."

The vulnerable look he gives me weakens my knees to Jell-O. This isn't his usual cocky grin or his teasing smirk. This is serious. This is real.

"I'm all in, Syb."

I exhale my fear and breathe in this confident man instead. "I'm all in."

"Okay." Then, because he's Cooper, he adds, "You sure you're ready to give up all the other guys? I mean, Benton is pretty hot, even if he comes with a crazy fan-club and an Italian supermodel hellbent on marriage."

I nudge him with my shoulder. "Oh, please. You're the one with women fawning all over you."

He steps closer, the surf swirling around our ankles. "Damn right I am," he says, his voice softer now. "But I'm not sharing anymore, Syb. I'm all yours, and you're all mine."

"Good." My voice is barely audible over the lapping waves.

He leans down, his wonderful full lips brushing against mine, and for a moment I let the world narrow until it's only us —us and the decision we've made. This is different. It's real, and if we do it right, it might actually last.

FIFTY

C ooper
       Past - Age 26

Beep. Beep. Beep. Beep.

I'm woken by the sound of something familiar digging into my brain and forcing me out of the numb darkness. Then comes the sharp, sterile tang of disinfectant. I blink, but it's too bright, cutting through my vision with needle-sharp intensity. My mind tries to understand what is happening, but everything is heavy, like I'm surfacing from the deepest part of the ocean.

I realize immediately that something is off. My arms are too heavy. My throat is dry and raw, like I've been screaming for hours. That incessant beeping won't stop. It's the constant humming background to this new world I've woken up in.

I suck in a breath as everything comes into focus. White walls. White ceiling. Shiny windows. A monitor to my left attached to an IV taped to my arm, tubing winding upward to a bag filled with clear liquid. A whiteboard hangs on the wall across from me, my name written at the top.

I'm alive.

The fragmented memories of why I thought I'd died hit me. The boat. The crash. The water swallowing me whole. The panic. The blood. The noise.

My leg.

I shift and look down, expecting to see my leg there on the bed, bandaged and bruised.

It's not.

It's gone, and in its place is an empty space under the sheet below my right knee. But that doesn't make sense; I can still *feel* it there. It hurts, aches, but it's healing. My mind must be playing tricks on me.

Cruel, awful tricks.

I throw off the blanket, expecting to prove to myself that my leg is okay, and my world splinters apart. There's a bruised knee and bandages on a stump.

It's gone. My leg is gone.

Phantom tingles run through the empty space. A cruel lie. Suddenly, I'm drowning all over again, being dragged under by the cold, hard truth.

Door creaking open, a young nurse slips in, clipboard in hand and a furrow between her brows. She stops short when she sees me, expression changing to one of pity. It instantly makes this moment worse. I don't want her fucking pity; I want my life back. *I want my leg.*

"You're awake," she says in a sweet voice. "Let me get the doctor."

I could ask her what happened, but I already know. The chaos. The water. The fucking boat crash.

"Wait." I stop her.

She hesitates in the doorway. "Yes?"

"I remember what happened. I don't need anyone to explain that part to me. I was in a boating accident."

She nods once.

"Did anyone else get hurt?" I hesitate. "Did anyone... die?"

She pales, and my heart races, the monitor next to me beeping faster.

"Who?" I demand.

"I'm not sure if I'm allowed to say—"

"Please tell me." I have to stop myself from yelling at her. I'll try begging instead. "I can't sit here in any more agony. I need to know."

She checks over her shoulder, then closes the door to the hallway. "The driver of the boat passed away."

I blink at her, heart jumping to my throat. "Which boat?"

She can't mean Ethan. He was there. He was with me before I passed out. I think he might have been the one to pull me from the water, but I'm not sure. What if something happened to Ethan after that? What if he's gone? I can't live without Ethan.

"The, umm... the older guy? Mr. Laurence." She clears her throat. "You were in surgery for a while, and then you were sedated, so things may have changed. You were life-flighted here from Nantucket. They... they can't find Mr. Laurence's body."

The emotions that hit me are complicated and numerous. Relief. Grief. Anger. Frustration. Sadness. Everything. All at once.

Every. Fucking. Thing.

"Okay," I whisper. "Anyone else?"

She shakes her head. "I don't believe so. *You* almost died, Cooper. You're lucky to be alive."

I huff and turn away. I don't feel so lucky. "You're probably going to tell me they did everything they could to save my leg?"

"I'll leave that to the doctor," she says, and then she's gone.

I can guess how this is going to go. The doctor is going to

come in here and tell me the same things she did about how lucky I am to be alive. Then he or she will explain the surgery I underwent. Ask if I have questions. Tell me about a care plan I'm going to have to follow whether I like it or not. Rehabilitation. A prosthetic leg. Medicine. Maybe more surgeries.

I'm too exhausted to hear it, so I lay my head on the pillow and let myself cry. I don't want anyone to see me like this, but I can't help it. I'm so fucking angry and so fucking sad—this never should've happened.

I give myself five minutes.

Shortly after that, the doctor comes in, saying the exact things I expected him to say. This is going to be a long process. Lifelong, unfortunately. He leaves, and the nurse gives me more medicine, and I'm left alone.

Not for long.

Someone knocks on the door.

"I'm sorry I wasn't here when you woke up," Ethan says, rushing inside. "They told me you wouldn't be awake for another hour. I went home to shower. Fuck, I'm so sorry, Cooper."

I hold up my hand. "Don't. It's fine, probably better I faced waking to this alone."

Ethan's frown deepens, and he sits on the edge of the bed. He picks the side where my leg should be, and I kind of want to kick him in the kidney for the reminder. Not that I could forget.

"Where's Dad?" I ask.

"On his way. He'll be here soon."

Sure. Guess we'll see.

"Why did Gregory do that?" I ask, anger boiling over instantly. "Why *the fuck* did that guy drive his boat into us?"

Ethan is quiet for a long moment. "He found out about me and Arden and lost his temper... and apparently, his mind. Then he lost control of the boat."

Every nerve in my body zings with either fire or ice, waging war within me. My thoughts spiral, trying to grasp onto this reality I no longer recognize as my own. So I'm supposed to live without a leg because Gregory lost his temper?

What. The. Fuck?

"I'm so sorry," Ethan says. "This is my fault. I shouldn't have hidden my relationship with Arden."

I give my brother a long, withering look. As easy as it would be to blame him for this, I can't.

"But you told our dad about her, and you had plans to tell everyone else. This isn't your fault. How did Gregory find out, anyway?"

I can't imagine Arden told him, but then again, that girl is a goodie. Heaven forbid she tell a lie.

His lips thin. "They were on the boat when Sybil let it slip. Gregory lost his shit, and when he saw us, I think he thought he was going to scare us, but he lost control of his boat and..."

And I already know the rest.

"Gregory is dead?" I ask.

"They haven't been able to find his body, but there was so much blood in the water. It got dark. There are sharks in those waters, too. Drowned or not, they would've come for him."

Yeah. Gregory is dead. I have no doubt about that. And I have nobody alive to blame, and as fucked up as it is, my psyche can't handle it. I *need* to place blame as much as I need my fucking leg back.

"Sybil knew about you and Arden?"

Ethan nods. "Arden tried to tell her about us, and Sybil demanded we break up. We didn't, obviously, so Arden had to lie to Sybil. The truth came out on the boat."

It's been years since that girl left our lives, but I still haven't gotten over it. Now I know I never will, but not for the ways I used to think. Every time I take a step or even look at my leg, I'll be reminded of how I lost it, of the girl who couldn't keep her mouth shut, and I'll be reminded of how much I hate her.

"Why can't Sybil let us have anything good in our lives?" I spit.

"Sybil puts her family above all else," Ethan says. "I'm not defending her, but I'm not surprised."

Yeah. Well, fuck that, and fuck her.

The next six months are some of the hardest in my life, but I let my hatred for Sybil drive me through it. Like a fucked up beacon of hope, it's leading me to a better place.

Turns out losing a leg below the knee is one of the easier limbs to lose, but it's still hard as hell. I go through months of rehab and two different prosthetics before I can walk without horrible pain. There are so many times when I want to give up, but there's one driving force, one thing I cling to like a lifeline.

A promise to myself.

A promise of revenge.

One day, Sybil Laurence will pay for the pain she's caused me and my family. I don't know how and I don't know when, but it will happen.

Until then, I'll be patient, take my time, do whatever I need to do. I'll gain her trust, get in her good graces, and make her feel safe with me. She'll think I don't blame her for all the horrible shit she's done. I'll make her feel like the most important person in the world.

I swear... I swear on my dead mother, on my lost leg, on my brother's broken engagement, on her asshole father's decisions, and on everything that has ever happened between me and Sybil, I'm going to make Sybil Laurence wish she'd never met me.

I will break that girl just like she's broken me.

Part Three

*"Men at some time are masters of their fates.
The fault, dear Brutus, is not in our stars,
but in ourselves."*

William Shakespeare's Julius Caesar

FIFTY-ONE

S ybil
    Present - Age 27

I don't know if I've ever been happier... or more terrified.

With one hand in mine and the other on the heavy glass door to the restaurant, Cooper pushes it open and leads me inside. The warm wave of chatter and the savory aroma greeting us aren't enough to soothe my nerves. This is really happening —we're going to introduce ourselves as a couple to our families.

"Hey, we've got this." Cooper squeezes my hand. His voice is steady, so confident this is going to work out in our favor. I'm not so sure, but I nod along.

We walk through the restaurant as a united front. Mom and the boys are in Manhattan for the weekend to do some college shopping for Hayes, and Cooper's father is home from a business trip. The timing felt fated.

The hostess directs us to a large table where familiar faces are awkwardly conversing. They all turn to look at us, and it only takes a second for me to gage everyone's reactions.

Chandler's sweet round face lights up like the Fourth of July, Ethan and Arden exchange smug "I knew it" expressions, Hayes rolls his eyes like an eighteen-year-old boy with better places to be, and Mom's eyes widen with shock and maybe a little hurt, too. Conrad's new wife is as clueless as ever, blinking rapidly and pouting her lips. And Conrad? Well, he's the only one I can't read.

"Hi, everyone," I say, my voice more high-pitched than I intended. "Thanks for coming. We obviously have something to tell you."

Cooper holds up our joined hands, brushing my knuckles against his lips for a quick kiss. "We're dating," he announces. No apologies or explanations and no room for negotiation.

There's a pause, like everyone is taking a collective breath.

Arden is the first to break the silence, literally squealing and clapping her hands. "Perfect!"

Chandler jumps from his chair, knocking it over in the process. I think he's about to jump into my arms, but he goes for Cooper. "Brother!"

Cooper chuckles but doesn't correct him. Chandler started calling Ethan "brother" the second he found out Arden was our sibling. The way Cooper hugs my brother is incredibly endearing. Cooper knows there could come a day when Chandler will live with me and rely on my help. If Cooper wants to stay together for the long run, he knows I'm a package deal.

We find our seats, and Conrad leans across the table. "How long has this been going on?"

"Not long," Cooper answers. "Only about a week."

There's a tightness in his jaw as he nods and reclines slightly, whispering something under his breath to his wife. My mother gives them both the scathing side-eye. Mom is clearly annoyed to be in his presence, especially with his young wife fawning all over him like he's some sort of billionaire god.

"Well, congratulations," Mom says to us. "A little sudden, but I hope it works out for you two."

Does she mean that?

Honestly, I kind of doubt it. It's not that Mom wishes for our demise, but we're another couple tying her to Conrad.

"It will work out," Cooper says, not the least bit ruffled by her comment.

My heart swells. I wish I had his confidence.

"Thought you two hated each other," Hayes gripes. He takes a bite of bread, chewing and swallowing. "Last I heard, you're still fighting over the company shares."

Cooper gives Hayes a tight smile. "I don't think we need to worry too much about that. If Top of the World does well, the shares will revert. With how well things are going on set, the show will be successful."

Conrad steeples his hands together. "We've got a date set to air the first episode. September Twelfth."

Two more months and the product of all our hard work will accumulate to one fateful evening. If the premier tanks, I'm screwed, but I feel in my bones that won't be the case.

This thing is going to be huge.

"When do the promotions start?" Mom asks.

"Three weeks ahead of airing," Cooper replies with a curt smile. "Enough time to get the word out, but not too long that the excitement wears off."

I snort. "Oh, there is going to be plenty of excitement, no matter how early we market."

The conversation gets easier from there.

Nobody brings up Dad or Victoria or the past. We may all be thinking about it—there's an obvious undercurrent of distrust. It will probably always be present. I just hope we can let go of whatever distrust lingers between me and Cooper.

After dinner, I want to go home with Cooper, but I need to catch up on work. I missed a lot while on Nantucket. So I give Cooper a kiss outside the restaurant and promise to meet up with him later. He doesn't protest. Like me, he values his work, so he understands why I sometimes slip away on weekends to go to the office.

Laurence International's New York headquarters is like a second home to me, and the hum of the city follows me into the building, lingering as I push through the glass doors and take the elevator up to my floor. It's late, and the office is quiet— exactly the way I like it. Planning the October gala looms over my head, and I've barely scratched the surface of what needs to be done.

Balancing an emergency coffee in one hand and my purse in the other, I stop short at a faint light spilling out from underneath my office door. Strange. There's rarely anyone else here on Saturday evenings, and why would they be in *my* office?

The sound of a keyboard drifts out, and I speed walk to find Jonathan, my assistant, sitting at my desk. His dress shirt is untucked at the sides, and his sleeves are rolled up. There's a notebook open next to him and as he relays information off my computer. My heart pounds, equal parts irritation and confusion swirling through my chest.

What the hell is he doing at my desk? We set him up with his own cubicle, so there's no reason for him to be in here.

"Can I help you?" My voice comes out sharper than intended as I barge into my own damn office.

Jonathan Vale looks up, startled. He's in his mid-twenties, with gel-styled blond hair and wire-rimmed glasses that he adjusts as he stands.

"Oh, Ms. Laurence! Good evening. I didn't expect you until

Monday." He flashes a snake-oil smile, entirely too comfortable for someone who has no business being in here.

"Why are you at my desk?" I told him *not* to touch anything until I could train him properly. If he's going to be my assistant, then I should be the one to tell him what to do.

"I wanted to get ahead of things," he says. "The donor call sheets are ready." He gestures to a neat pile of documents on the corner of the desk. "And the RSVPs for the gala have been updated in the system. Oh, and the seating chart? All done."

I stare, my coffee growing cold in my hand. The seating chart alone would have taken me hours, but it's an incredibly important task and something I like to do with Miriam.

"You did all of that?" I raise a brow, pushing down my annoyance. Maybe he was trying to help. Maybe this job is important to him, and he's a good kid, and I'm unfairly holding his uncle against him.

"Yes, ma'am." He beams.

"Don't call me ma'am." I sigh, and he blanches. Fuck. How do I handle this properly?

Part of me wants to bark at him, tell him it's not his place to make those decisions without consulting me, let alone infiltrate my office. But another part is begrudgingly impressed he did so much work with so little delegation.

I set my bag and coffee down and circle around to my chair as he steps out of the way.

"When you were hired, did HR not issue you your own computer?" I ask, already knowing the answer.

"They did, but I needed the notes you saved in your files, and you were too busy to get back to me—" He quickly backpedals. "I mean... you were on holiday, so I wanted to help."

I wouldn't call my two weeks on Nantucket a holiday.

My eyes narrow. "How did you get access to my computer?

Everything is password protected. There is *sensitive* information on here."

Many of the emails I receive aren't for anyone in the company to read. I have board meeting communications in there.

His eyes widen. "Password protected? I don't think so." He motions to the computer. "Here, check for yourself."

With a huff, I open it, first logging out and then moving my mouse to prompt the login screen. I expect a prompt to enter my password to pop up, but the computer just asks me to hit enter.

"What the hell?" My body prickles with a deep sense of unease. "Someone messed with this."

"It wasn't me," Jonathan says, but do I believe him?

My gut says no.

That said, I don't have proof. I'll have to talk to my boss on Monday and see if she knows anything. Maybe the tech department did something while I was gone.

"I hope you'll understand I'm just trying to do my job," Jonathan continues, his tone shaky.

I nod. "Very well, but please don't use my computer again without my permission. It's a violation of my privacy."

His face pales. "I'm so sorry, Ms. Laurence."

I wave him off. "I appreciate your enthusiasm. I'll need to review all the work you've done. The seating chart especially."

"Of course. It's all here." He slides the papers toward me.

I glance at them, then at him. He's standing there like a puppy waiting for a pat on the head.

"Thank you for your hard work," I say warily. "Next time, don't assume you can tackle something as critical as the seating chart without checking with me first. You're meant to be my assistant, not take over my job."

"Understood," he replies with a nod, but there's a smug

glint in his eye that unsettles me right to the bone. I'm suddenly very suspicious that taking over my job is *exactly* what this man intends to do. He is Lance Vale's nephew, after all, and while this company has Laurence on the door, Vale has made it clear he doesn't mind making as many adjustments to the company as needed to assert his power.

Shit. I need to watch out.

I smile as big as I can; two can be fake here. "Go home, Jonathan. Get some rest. First thing Monday morning, we have a lot of work to do. I'm pleased you're my *assistant.*"

When I emphasize the word, he winces, and I know my suspicions are correct.

This is not a man who wants to be anyone's assistant, and I highly doubt he believes he'll have to wait long until he can move into my office permanently.

Jonathan is gunning for my job, and I'm sure his uncle was the one who is helping him do it.

FIFTY-TWO

S ybil
    Present - Age 27

The dim bluish light casts a glow across the cramped screening room. It smells like stale popcorn and sweat in here, byproducts of late-nights and rushed decisions. Cooper sits next to me on the long couch that's pushed up against the window, Perry on my other side. Everyone else is gone for the evening, but we're reviewing some footage from Nantucket.

Perry crosses his arm and leans back, clearing his throat.

"What is it?" Cooper asks. "You gonna lecture us again about PDA?"

As soon as we decided to give this thing a go, Perry was the first person we told. He took it better than expected, claiming he was happy for us but also asking us to keep PDA to a minimum.

"About that," Perry releases a long-suffering sigh, voice tinged with forced optimism. "This is... delicate."

Damn. I thought he was going to complain about the audio glitches from yesterday that made us lose half a day of content. Apparently, this is about me and Cooper. I sit forward and Cooper removes his arm from my shoulder, opting for my knee instead.

"There's been an anonymous complaint," Perry continues. "About you two."

My stomach lurches. "Us?"

Cooper's voice hardens. "What kind of complaint?"

Perry clasps his hands together like he's about to deliver a sermon. "The complainant suggested your relationship is interfering with your professional judgment."

"Are you kidding me?" I stand quickly, needing to move, pace the room or something. I've never had a complaint lodged against me in my entire career.

"We may not have made the best decisions on Nantucket," Cooper says. "But we've been professional since we made things official."

"Someone obviously feels differently," Perry counters.

Cooper's jaw tightens. "Who filed it?"

Perry sighs. "The network has an anonymous complaint submission form for cast and crew to use without fear of retaliation."

"The network?" Coop tsks. "I *am* the network."

"Then maybe you should know about this," Perry points out. "As much as I'd love to sweep this under the rug, we have to take it seriously. Last thing we need is negative attention before we launch."

"What do you suggest?" I ask.

"Fact is, you've gone public, and that's not changing."

"Fucking right," Cooper mutters.

Perry holds up his hands. "While I'm happy for my friends, I'm also invested in my career. We need to control the optics.

Call me the bad guy, but we only have a few choices to handle this properly."

I tilt my head. "What do you have in mind?"

"One, you guys don't come to set at the same time. If you're not seen together while you're here, there's no room for anyone to claim anything unprofessional is happening."

I press my lips together. It's not a terrible idea. Doesn't mean I like it.

"Nope. Not doing that," Cooper growls. "What's option two?"

"Glad you're keeping your sense of humor about this, Coop," Perry jokes.

Cooper doesn't laugh, but I crack a smile.

"The network has offered to hire an ethics consultant."

"A what?" I question.

"An ethics consultant," Perry repeats, leaning casually against the couch. "Someone to come in, observe you two, and ensure everything is above board."

"I'm sure this was my father's idea," Cooper chides.

"You mean spy on us?" I ask, my voice flat and unsurprised.

"*Spy* is an ugly word," Perry says, but doesn't refute that's exactly what's happening. "I can't say if your father is behind this, Cooper, but I wouldn't put it past him."

"I don't think we have a choice." I look eyes with Cooper. "We have to do the professional thing and agree."

"Fine, bring in the consultant," Cooper relents. "I guess a spy is a necessary evil. I'm not willing to avoid my girlfriend at work."

"Are you sure?" I ask.

He gives me a weak smile. "Think you can keep your hands off me?"

Perry rolls his eyes and fakes a gag.

I *can* keep my hands off Cooper at work, and it's fair

someone could be uncomfortable with us, but we've been really good about keeping things professional since we returned to the city.

This whole thing is annoying.

"I'm renting a third apartment," Cooper announces. "Whatever is vacant in the building. I don't care. This show has taken all my personal spaces, and I'm over it."

"There's only a handful of weeks left of filming."

"Don't care. I want privacy for me and Syb."

"Well, I know what your trust fund looks like." Perry gives him a knowing look. "You should've done this from day one."

Cooper smirks. "Yeah, well, I was invested in being here when a certain someone came to set."

The look he gives me is so hot that my insides practically burn up. Suddenly, I understand why someone might be uncomfortable. I want to rip his clothing off, and considering his bedroom is steps away, I plan to do that once everyone leaves.

"Rent something. Buy something. Whatever. But figure your shit out." Perry grabs his things. "I'm going to go check on my sister."

Madeline's been home recovering, improving little by little each day. I'm sure having her family check on her often helps.

One minute later, and it's just me and Cooper.

"Don't give me that look." I laugh. "This is your fault."

He jumps up and wraps me in a hug, pulling me flush against his body. Dropping his mouth to the shell of my ear, he whispers. "How is this my fault?"

"You started it." My voice is husky and untamed. Cooper's body reacts, growing hard between us.

"Are you talking about eating you out on Nantucket?" he asks boldly. "As I recall, we were in a locked bedroom when that happened."

Locked bedroom *on* location.

"Or maybe it was fucking on the beach that did it?" I ask, teasing him.

"My beach," he growls. "My house. My woman. What's wrong with that? If people want to complain, they can complain to my face, not some fucking anonymous form."

I chuckle. "I'm sorry, baby, but who is going to do that? You're the boss. That's kind of intimidating."

"Do I intimidate you?"

Yes.

"No." I sigh. "But we *are* at crew headquarters right now and probably shouldn't be touching."

He doesn't like that.

FIFTY-THREE

S ybil
    Present - Age 27

"My bedroom isn't technically crew headquarters," he says, scooping me into his arms. He walks us across the family room to the primary suite.

The idea that he's going to rent another place to have more privacy for us makes so much sense. He can come to my place, of course, but Soho is not the most convenient spot with so much work happening in this midtown building.

We need somewhere we can sneak away when the looks between us grow too heated to ignore.

He closes the door and presses me against it, taking my lips and instantly deepening the kiss. His hands are frantic as they travel across my body, sliding under my shirt and bra, fingers pinching my nipples before softening with gentle caresses. He repeats the motions, sharp and soft, sending waves of desire through me.

"Do you really think your dad is sending a spy?"

"Maybe, or maybe someone at work is jealous," he whispers against my mouth. "Do you think it's because they want me?" He presses his hard-on into my core, and I buck against him. "Or do they want you?"

My brain is mush, but I manage a whimpered, "Yes."

"I think it's you, pretty Valentine. You're more gorgeous than any of those stars upstairs." He sneaks his hands around my leggings and slips them down my thighs. "As they should be. Too bad for them, this perfect woman only belongs to me."

"Perfect, you say?" I tease.

"Perfect heart, perfect personality, perfect body." His fingers push into me, and I cry out as his palm presses on my clit. "And a perfect tight cunt."

His filthy mouth drives me wild, fueling my desire. I grab his wrist, reveling in the cords of muscles as they work me. "What about it is so perfect?" I breathe.

He chuckles, stripping off the last of my clothing and carrying me to his bed. "Do you want me to show you?"

I nod eagerly. I don't think I've wanted anything more.

When I reach out to help him with his shirt, he brushes me off. "Oh no, you don't move. Tonight, I'm in charge. Do you think you can handle that, Valentine?"

"Yes, sir."

I'm not the most submissive person, but in the bedroom, I love it. I'm so in charge and in control in my regular life, especially at work, that giving into this side of myself feels like letting go.

He strips for me, and I practically whimper at the sight of his ready cock. I want to do unspeakable things to him, and I'd just as soon let him do whatever the hell he wants with me, so long as I get to touch him.

Leaving me naked and panting on his bed, he goes to his

closet as if we have all the time in the world. I want to scream at him to get back here, but I wait on the bed, my eyes widening when he returns with a handful of silky black ties.

"Have you ever been tied to bedposts before, Sybil?" he asks.

He sounds like a businessman in a conference room, not like a boyfriend about to fuck his girlfriend.

I shake my head. "I've been asked before, but... I declined."

"Are you afraid?" He pulls a silk tie through his hand, and my mouth waters. "You don't have to do anything you don't want to, honey, but you know I'll take care of you, right?"

I do know that. I trust him. Maybe too much. That's the problem.

"Okay." My voice is breathy.

His grin is wicked as he gets to work, leaving trails of tender kisses on my flesh while he ties my wrists above my head and my legs stretched open. I don't think I've ever been so exposed. He retreats to admire his handiwork, hooded eyes roaming my body, taking extra time to gaze upon my bare pussy. I ache to cover myself, to be shy, but I also ache to have this experience with him more.

We lock eyes.

"Are you going to show me why I have a perfect cunt, or are you going to stand there?" I demand.

He chuckles. "So impatient. Remember what I said, Valentine? *I'm* in charge tonight. You agreed. Do you still want this?"

My enthusiastic "*yes*" borders on embarrassing.

Removing his prosthetic and leaving it on the floor, he crawls onto the bed. He positions his mouth at my entrance, his warm breath tickling my skin.

"You don't come until I say, got it?"

I hesitate. "Wait... what?"

He presses his mouth to my center, swirling his tongue

around my aroused bud, opening me up even more for him. I practically come undone right then and there.

"Do you trust me?" he asks.

"Yes," I breathe.

"Then relax. Don't come yet."

My hands fist, and I force my breathing to slow. "I'll do whatever you say. No coming until you tell me to."

"You tell me if you're too close?"

I nod vigorously.

He chuckles, satisfied. "That's my girl."

He gets to expertly eating my pussy, and I ride his mouth as much as I can under the restraints. I climb toward orgasm quickly.

"I... Cooper, I'm—"

He pulls back. "Not yet, baby."

God, I need to relax. I'm *not* going to beg—that's not my style, no matter how fun this game is.

He crawls on top and enters me quickly, the fullness of his erection so incredible that stars flash behind my eyes. Bucking against me, we move in tandem, him so deep inside I can't tell where he even begins. Right when I'm about to come by penetration, not something so easily done for me, he stills his body, slowly removing himself inch by torturous inch.

"Tell me what you need, baby. Beg for it."

Nope, not begging. "You know what I need," I hiss in frustration.

"Oh, honey..." He smiles wickedly. "You're making this hard for me."

"I'm not going to beg."

He kisses me, long and slow, and then whispers against my ear. "You'll beg when you're ready to come. Until then, I can go all night."

Honest to God, I don't know how he can hold back. I've

never been with a man capable of holding off his orgasm as long as Cooper is right now.

But as frustrating as this is, I love it.

This game goes on several more times until we're panting for release. Doesn't help we're both stubborn as hell.

I know how much he wants this; I can see it in the glazed look in his eye, in the tenseness of his jaw, and in the speed of his breathing, but he doesn't give in. He won't. Not until I beg.

Cheeky little shit.

"Submit to me," he commands, pumping into me hard and fast, then going still when as my inner muscles clamp around his cock.

I arch into him, and he groans.

"Cooper..." I can barely speak. I'm at my breaking point. He's got me tied up in more ways than one.

"Say it, baby. Please, say it," he rasps.

Now he's the one begging, which is exactly what I needed. This is how we both win.

I nip at his neck, then retreat and thrust my hips upward as hard as I can.

"Fuck me, Cooper. Make me come. *Please*," I groan. "I need you. Please. Please. Please let me come."

"Are you sure?" He smirks and pumps once. "You did say please. Four times."

"Shut up." I laugh, but we're fucking hard, and I'm so, so happy.

"You're ready?"

"Yes," I gasp. "Go as hard you can, Coop. It won't hurt me. I need all you can give me. I've wanted you for so long."

That sets him off in a way I have yet to experience. He grinds down with each deep thrust, our bodies furiously pounding, the sound of skin slapping and our moans loud.

This is, without a doubt, the most animalistic and erotic sex

I've experienced in my life. All I can do is feel him inside me, moving, pumping, fucking, loving.

Again.

Harder. Faster.

More.

Our orgasms hit at the same moment, surges of explosive pleasure with such force I can't help but scream his name. He lets out a similar roar as the moment between us intensifies, and the slapping of our bodies continues. The moment builds and builds and builds, as if all the orgasms he'd made me wait for come together in rapid succession. I lose myself as he pumps every last ounce of passion from my body.

Never in my life have I had an orgasm last that long—so long that my entire body tingles with pleasure. I lose my breath, and my mind floats away.

He falls onto me, equally sated. He stays inside me until he's no longer hard, and there's nothing left to do but separate. The second it happens, I miss him, aching for him to fill me all over again.

I'm sore and satisfied in the most wonderful way. Knowing I'll get to experience that again and again has a grin plastered on my face.

"Guess I'd better expedite the new apartment thing, huh?" he says sweetly, and I laugh. If anyone with a key had happened to walk into crew headquarters tonight, they definitely would have heard us, and we'd be in even more trouble. Right now, I don't care about that. All I care about is this man and the amazing way he handles not only my body, but also my heart.

FIFTY-FOUR

S ybil
    Present - Age 27

"Between Cooper's father's spy—I mean *the network's ethics consultant*—and my new assistant, who *happens* to be Vale's nephew, I feel like I can't do anything without being scrutinized," I complain to Miriam as we navigate the busy Manhattan crosswalk. We're going to an important vendor meeting, and now that we're out of the office, I finally feel like I can properly whine.

"I think you *are* being scrutinized," she laments, her white bob swishing as she walks. "I didn't want to say anything, but while you were gone, Vale and his nephew had a *lot* of questions about your job and mine. It seems pretty obvious Vale hopes to get his minion into the position that is rightfully yours."

Despite the late July heat, my body runs cold. "That is exactly the feeling I get about it, too."

"Don't worry. I told Vale off, and let's just say he didn't like that very much," she gripes. "Invited me to retire early, the ass."

I grit my teeth. "And what did you say?"

"I told him the last thing he needed was an ageism lawsuit. I will retire when I'm good and ready."

Which is only three months away. October has been her plan all along, but given this new information, she might want to hang on. I hate that for her; I know she's been planning on this next stage of life for a while.

She squeezes my hand. "Don't you worry. My job is yours. You've earned it. But I do wish I was the one filling my replacement and not the hiring committee."

So Lance Vale and I are similar in that respect—we both are fighting for the roles we want within this company. Maybe it's entitled of me, but I feel like I have a right to Laurence International. There's nothing else I want to do more, but I don't know if I can do it under Vale's leadership. If they put him in as official CEO, I'm going to have to move on, which is hard to fathom.

"Here we are," Miriam says as we enter one of the city's finest hotels. We're here to discuss some of the details regarding the event we've got booked for October's charity gala. It's coming up quick, but at least we're doing all the catering and decor through the hotel, which simplifies things.

The second we enter the hotel lobby, a flutter of unease swirls in my stomach.

Miriam, the driving force behind The Laurence Foundation, steps ahead of me, her high heels clicking against the polished marble. She's the picture of confidence, and I wish I felt the same.

The front desk manager greets us with a polite smile.

"Your appointment is for today?" He frowns, clicking on his computer. "I don't have anything for you two."

I let out a huff. "I confirmed earlier this week. Please go get Evelyn. I'm sure it's on her calendar, and she's expecting us."

Evelyn is the events planner for the hotel.

The manager leaves us, concerned hesitation in his normally polished expression. It sends my anxiety into a tailspin.

"Good afternoon, Sybil and Miriam." Evelyn approaches us. "I wasn't expecting you."

We've done a lot of business with Evelyn over the years. I give her a friendly smile, burying the unease in my stomach. "I confirmed our appointment, so I don't know why it's not on your books. We have to finish planning the details for our gala in October."

Evelyn's face falters—a crack in her usually professional exterior. After a quick glance around the busy lobby, she motions for us to follow her to her office.

Sitting across from her, I expect her to pull out familiar books with options for the event, but she turns to us with a frown. "I don't know how to tell you this, but I think there's been a misunderstanding."

My lungs burn. "What do you mean?"

Evelyn's eyes bounce between me and Miriam. "Your event was canceled. Two days ago. Don't you remember?"

"Canceled?" I shake my head slowly. "We never canceled anything."

"We *wouldn't* cancel," Miriam adds sternly. "We have this same event on the same weekend every year at your hotel. It's been this way for nearly two decades."

Evelyn winces. "Which was why I was so surprised you canceled it." She gives me an apologetic look. "We received a call from you a few days ago, Sybil. If it wasn't you, it was a woman using your name. They said the event was canceled due to unforeseen circumstances."

My pulse pounds in my ears. "I never would've made that call. You didn't think to confirm with me personally?"

Evelyn pales. "I told you, I mean *them*, whoever they were, we require written confirmation as per the terms of the contract. They sent an email from your work address." She turns the screen to face me. "See for yourself."

Miriam grips the arms of her chair like she's on a roller-coaster, about to make the big drop. "There's obviously been a mistake or someone trying to sabotage our event."

"I'm afraid it's the latter," Evelyn says. "Look here, this is your email address, correct?"

Sure enough, in black and white, is my email address attached to a brief request to cancel the event.

Bile churns in my stomach, and I immediately picture Jonathan sitting at my computer, typing away, clearly doing *something* more than a seating chart.

I'm going to kill that little weasel.

"I understand your frustration," Evelyn says, her customer-service voice trying to de-escalate the tension. "We verified both over the phone and in writing. I'm so sorry someone hacked into your email and pretended to be you on the phone, but unfortunately, the ballroom has already been rebooked."

"Rebooked?" I gape at her. "You've got to be kidding me. This is a charity gala for Laurence International. We can't move it to another day. This event has been on the first Saturday of October for years. What would you have us do?"

Miriam places a steady hand on my arm. "Take a breath, Sybil." Her eyes narrow to death-slits at Evelyn. "Are you certain there's nothing you can do to get us our date back?"

Evelyn shakes her head. "I'm so sorry. I can't cancel an event after they've already booked and paid, but I can return your deposit, given the unfortunate situation. We really hope to do business with you again."

I blink rapidly, anger giving way to confusion, trying to make something fit that isn't quite making sense. "Wait. You said *I* called you, right? It was a woman who spoke with you?"

"Yes, I was surprised you'd wanted to cancel the event, and I distinctly remember a woman's voice insisting upon it. I'm sorry, I really thought she was you, and when the email came in, I proceeded."

I stare at Evelyn for a long moment, mind reeling. Maybe Jonathan sent that email, but there's no way he would've made the phone call. He and Vale must have recruited someone.

Miriam crosses her arms, expression darkening to match my own internal turmoil. "This wasn't Sybil. Someone impersonated her. I want you to make note that for future events, any cancellations with Sybil must be done in person."

Evelyn bobs her head vigorously. "Of course. I'll make a note of it in your file. I'm so sorry."

Miriam lets out a long breath through her nostrils. "I want you to figure out what phone number called you."

Evelyn places her hand over her heart. "I will do everything in my power to find answers for you. This is... unprecedented in my career. I've never seen such sabotage before."

My teeth grind together. I'm determined to get to the bottom of this, but first I have to start making phone calls. I've got to find a new venue, which will be next to impossible for a Saturday. I'm afraid it won't matter how much money and connections I throw at this problem.

I laugh bitterly. "Yeah, me too, but given the last year of my life, this doesn't even surprise me."

Fuck Jonathan Vale, and fuck Lance, too. They're sick for being willing to let innocent people get hurt in their scheming. While I'm upset about my job, I'm more upset about the possibility that those disabled kids and their families won't get the funding they're counting on. I won't let that happen.

FIFTY-FIVE

Sybil
Present - Age 27

As much as I want to march into Lance Vale's office and demand answers, and as much as I want to fire Jonathan's scheming ass, I decide to go a different route.

I'm going to kill them with success.

Not kindness, as the saying goes.

Kindness is the last thing I feel toward those men. Rage is a more appropriate word. I'm sure I could kill them with that. Gladly. But I'd rather not spend my life behind bars.

It's been two weeks, and I haven't said a word about the venue cancellation to either of them. I've also asked Miriam to keep it to herself. I'm proving my worth in this job, like I've done time and time again.

In the last two weeks I've pulled off the impossible—securing a new venue at a large modern art gallery with enough space to fit our guests and calling in favors with my favorite vendors who love me as much as I love them. All for the first Saturday in October.

All that, and I still kick ass producing *Top of the World*.

I've been extra careful, changing my passwords but still using my personal phone, computer, and email address to handle vendor communications, as well as stressing that any cancellations must be done in person. I'm not about to make the same mistake.

Mom has called an emergency meeting with the board on my behalf. We're going to explain everything that's been going on with Lance Vale and his nephew, and if we're lucky, they'll be gone by tomorrow.

The board comprises nine members, but the bylaws require a supermajority for big decisions, which is seven out of nine votes. Lance Vale hasn't been able to get seven yet, and I'm determined he never will.

Mom is only one vote, representing our family. Her vote used to belong to Dad. One day, it will go to us kids.

I'm greeted with the sharp scent of polished wood and the faint aroma of expensive cologne. Ten faces stare back at me, some icy, some curious, and others friendly. Mom sits at the far end of the table. Her hands are folded neatly over her lap, and her hair and makeup are done to perfection. She's a mirror to me, exactly what I'll look like in twenty-five years, and I use her natural sophistication as a boon to my nerves.

I can do this.

I *have* to do this.

Lance Vale is also at the table—the tenth face here. He sits to Mom's right and watches me with sharp understanding, his smirk twitching. He knows what he did, so I'm certain he knows what this emergency meeting is all about.

"Ladies and gentlemen," I start. "Thank you for taking the

time out of your busy schedules to be here. This matter is important. We need to talk about Mr. Vale."

I motion to Lance, and his face hardens. "What do you have to say, Sybil? I'm curious."

The room shifts, a ripple of unease moving through the group like falling dominoes. When Lance leans in his chair with smug confidence, I focus on why I'm here.

"I've hired an outside law firm specializing in cyber security and IT to do an internal investigation," I state. "Two minutes ago, I emailed all of you the results of that investigation. In it, you will see I have undeniable proof that Lance Vale has been illegally accessing my company computer and phone, reading private emails, and more alarmingly, attempting to sabotage the foundation work."

Gasps punctuate the room, but Lance doesn't even flinch. He glares at me, loathing in his eyes, then his face clears, making room for a look of shock.

"What is this you're accusing me of? I have done no such thing."

I ignore him. "I have timestamps of the unauthorized access, as well as emails sent to outside contacts, sharing confidential information meant to undermine my role and my family's legacy of Laurence International."

Vance shakes his head. "This is a setup. What she's claiming is not true." He gives me a pointed look. "After all my mentoring? I guess it's true that nepotism breeds incompetence. You're not as good at your job as you think you are, Sybil. That's what this is really about."

The comment stings, but I refuse to let it bother me for long. I've got him, and he knows it.

"Enough." Chairwoman Crandall holds up her hand. She turns to me. "You've made some serious accusations. What of this sabotage against the foundation that you speak of? Where is your proof?"

I chronicle what happened with the hotel cancellation and how I've worked overtime to make the changes necessary.

Vale shakes his head. "That wasn't me. How prosperous to assume I'd even care about such a thing."

Mom finally speaks up, her eyes narrowed and her tongue sharp. "If it wasn't you, Lance, then it was your nephew you forced on Sybil as her new hire. Either way, it would've been under your direction, and it's obvious you're a hypocrite who wants your nephew in Sybil's spot."

Lance has the audacity to look hurt. "I've known you for decades, Amelia. The fact that you are betraying me now is not only shocking, it's hurtful."

Mom's eyes narrow. "Then you must know how it feels to be a Laurence. Ever since my husband was killed, you've stopped at nothing to secure your place as CEO and push my family out of our namesake. There's a reason you haven't been able to gain a supermajority. You will never live up to Gregory's legacy. He was twice the CEO you'll ever be."

Vale glares. "I'm twice the man he was. I don't cheat and lie and endanger others."

The room goes silent.

Vale turns his attention to the other board members. "As I have emphasized, this wasn't me. Maybe it was my nephew—maybe he's gunning for Sybil's job. I don't know the answer, and I will support an investigation. But it wasn't me."

So he's going to throw his henchman under the bus. I know he's lying. I can feel it in my bones.

"We'll put it to a vote," Chairwoman Crandall suggests. "All in favor of Vale staying on as interim-CEO, with our own internal investigation into this matter, say yay."

The quiet thickens with anticipation, as one by one, the nine votes are cast. With every nay, I'm flooded with relief, but every yay makes me sick.

It's over quickly. Five to four.

Lance will stay on.

I can't believe it, but I remind myself this is only the beginning. Once a second investigation reveals the truth, he'll be out for good.

My heart pounds in my ears as Vale rises to his feet, the picture of false humility. "Thank you for the confidence. I will prove my worth to this company, as I have been doing for many years."

With that, he stomps from the room.

Mom and I lock eyes. I want nothing more than to get the hell out of here, and I can tell she feels the same. Ever the politician, she'll stay and converse with the other board members. Diplomacy is her strong suit, and she'll hold our family name up after this failed coup.

It's not right. They need to get rid of Vale. He's out to make Laurence his own and doesn't care what he has to do to get there. Sure, it would be a pain for the board to hire someone else, but they've been interviewing candidates for months, so there's bound to be someone.

This has gone on long enough.

Dad died over a *year* ago.

I can't take much more of this flaky shit. All the politics and games? It's exhausting.

What about Dad's legacy? What about the future of my family?

I don't wait for Mom; I'm barely paying attention when I step into the elevator, and Lance Vale slides in behind me.

He's the picture of calm indifference as the doors close us in, and he hits the button for the ground floor, but I'm sure he's seething inside.

"You think you've won something here, don't you Sybil?" His voice is low, dangerous even.

I don't say a word.

"I've been patient with you, but now I'm done. You think because you're a Laurence you can get whatever you want? You are in for a rude awakening. You are a spoiled girl."

"I'm not afraid of you," I snap. "I am proud to be a Laurence, and you can't stand that I'm good at my job. Just like you can't stand that my little brother is as brilliant and charismatic as my father was and will one day step into the role you think is yours. You've failed to gain the supermajority for over a year because the board wants to find someone who doesn't play your childish games. You're the spoiled one here."

He chuckles. "Next time you come for me, you'd better bring more than Mommy's vote. You made a joke out of yourself today, proving exactly why you shouldn't be here."

The elevator opens, and he storms out.

I don't mind. He's scared; Mom and I came close to toppling him down, and he knows it. The vote was only five to four in his favor, and Mom is still up there, working her magic. We may have declared war, but we're Laurences, and we'll be damned if we let anyone take this company away from our family.

Fifty-Six

Sybil
Present - Age 27

Cooper and I lay in bed, our bare limbs entwined, the calm silence settling between us after a frenzy of passion. The light from the lamp pools across the ceiling of my bedroom.

Almost every night, we sleep and wake up together. It's not something either of us are used to. It's nice, but maybe a little too nice. I'm still waiting for the other shoe to drop.

Cooper is burrowing deep into my heart. It scares me but makes me feel safe all at the same time.

"You've been quiet," Cooper points out. "Is everything okay?"

I sigh. "Lots on my mind at work."

"The show or the foundation?"

I debate on how much to tell Cooper about my problems with Lance. I'm pretty good at compartmentalizing my life, even consider it one of my strengths, but this situation has gotten out of hand. The stress is starting to get to me. And if I'm being honest, it would be really nice to have a man to talk to about my problems.

I roll to my side so our faces are inches apart and gaze into his coppery-brown eyes, searching for something I can trust.

"Sybil," he continues, running a thumb along my cheekbone. "You don't have to carry everything on your own. Letting me in doesn't make you any less strong." He kisses me softly on the lips. "In fact, it makes you even stronger."

My throat tightens, voice shaking. "I don't know where to start."

He runs calloused fingers up and down my arm, igniting goosebumps. "Just start with one thing. One worry. Let me carry something for you, however big or small."

A wobbly laugh escapes. "Do you realize what you're signing up for? My life isn't simple."

He raises an eyebrow. "I'm well aware. My life is complicated, too. It's a good thing I'm not looking for a simple girl."

The weight of his words sinks in, breaking down my walls little by little. "Most men don't want to deal with messy. What makes you different?"

His lips curve into a handsome smile, so sweet and pure it almost hurts. "Because I care about you. I always have."

For a moment, I imagine the word *care* is actually *love*, and everything fits into place. I've never been as comfortable with a man as I am with Cooper. He was my best friend for so many years for a reason. I know him, inside and out, and he knows me, too.

Is this what love feels like?

I have to bite my lip to keep from crying. God, when did I become so emotional?

"Okay," I relent, "I'm in the middle of a feud with Lance Vale."

His jaw tightens, but he stays silent as I carefully explain the situation. With each word, my chest tightens with rising anger, but it also feels nice to let someone else carry this weight with me. Cooper's neck twitches and his jaw clenches. He's holding back churning thoughts.

"That's a lot to carry," he says when I'm finally done.

"I know. Sorry." It's a bunch of work drama, and he's busy enough as it is. I shouldn't put this on him. "It's not your problem."

"I'm not saying it's a lot for me to carry; it's a lot for *you* to carry. I fucking hate that guy, so I can't say I'm surprised he's pulling this shit." His voice is clipped. "But it pisses me off the board hasn't fired him. You made it perfectly clear he doesn't deserve to be there. It's like they think since Gregory passed, they can walk all over the rest of you."

Relief swells—he gets it.

"Exactly. It's fucked up. What kills me is that Vale's been interim CEO for over a year. Does it really take that long to hire someone?"

Cooper thinks on it. "There's strategy here. A long game. Remember when we were in undergrad and the president of the university left, so they brought in an interim? They didn't rush to fill that position, either. The new guy was there for a year before they'd officially given him the job. It was a trial run."

I frown. "That guy ended up with the title."

"Unfortunately, it's not uncommon to happen that way. Someone brand new can make the shareholders nervous. People want what they already know, want to keep the status quo, even if it's not perfect. They like to feel like they're in control."

I swallow hard. "Must be why some of the board members keep fighting for him to stay on."

He shrugs. "Because he's the known thing, or maybe they actually like him." A crease forms between his brow. "Or maybe he's got dirt on them. Who knows, really? This stuff is political, and it's even harder when you're a publicly traded company. That's why my father refuses to go public and has made me and Ethan swear to never take it public, either."

"Way to rub it in," I tease, elbowing him in the side.

"Hey…" He kisses me again, long and soft, and suddenly I don't want to talk anymore. My body is ready for round two. "I care about you, and I care about your future. I own shares in Laurence, remember? I care about that, too."

I nip at his lips. "Not for long. Top of the World will be successful, and you'll be returning those shares. Mark my words, King."

He kisses me, his hand sliding between my legs. "I'm sure you're right. You always are."

"No fair. You know I have a praise kink."

The kiss deepens, and we don't talk. Everything we have left to say, we say with our bodies.

FIFTY-SEVEN

Sybil
     Present - Age 27

We wrap filming, and for the next month, life gets a little easier. I work closely with Perry and the network as the editing packages come together, but it's not the same time suck as being on set.

Marketing started last week, and now I'm *certain* the show will be a hit. People are excited, and they have every right to be. Post-production is going to edit together one of the most entertaining reality television shows in modern history. That might be wishful thinking, but my gut says this is going to be huge.

When it's time for the premier party, I'm ripe with anticipation as I step onto the red carpet, Cooper at my side. My heart pounds in tandem with the flashing lights of the cameras.

We stop for photos and then make our way inside the theater.

We're nobodies compared to the stars, and I don't expect us

to end up in print, but this moment is thrilling, nonetheless. This is it. The premier of *Top of the World*.

We did it.

I'm dressed in a long fitted red gown, my hair professionally styled in swooshing curls, and my makeup smokey and glam.

Cooper wears a perfectly tailored black tux, and he looks amazing. He's easily the most handsome man here tonight. I can't take my eyes off him.

"You're the most beautiful woman here," he whispers against my ear. "You know that, right?"

I laugh. "I literally had thought the exact same thing about you seconds ago. Are you reading my mind?"

He grins. "Maybe."

We make our way to the large theatre lobby that's been transformed into a party venue. The room is packed with both familiar and unfamiliar faces, several of Hollywood's and Manhattan's elite, and of course lots of influencers who we are expecting will jump on the live social media feed aspect of the show once they see how it works.

A young woman stops me and Cooper. "You're the producers, right? Congratulations."

"Thanks," I say, introducing myself to the woman who turns out to be from the network's marketing department.

"This is going to be huge," she gushes. "The buzz has been incredible. You made my job easy."

We thank her and continue on, soaking in the cumulation of our hard work. It's fun to see it coming together, to celebrate.

I search the crowd for Benton, certain he's going to be a breakout star after what's airing tonight, but a little nervous for the rest of the season. He never should've hooked up with Gloria, and I'm pretty sure he knows that now.

"There you are." Perry approaches, his smile brighter than I've seen it in months.

"This is kind of insane," Cooper remarks, looking around the party. "I see the appeal of your career now."

Perry chuckles, and it reminds me of when we were young, his joy almost childlike. "I know, right? Pretty amazing. What will be even better is when we're ranked number one for rating."

I give him a hug. "You should be so proud."

"I am, and you should, too. Enjoy it. If you'll excuse me, I've got to go mingle."

By *mingle*, he means network. He's about to become the talk of the town.

Despite all the stress I've been under lately, I can't let this magical moment slip away. I take Cooper's hand, prepared to enjoy every second of tonight, and not worry about how it looks that we're together. We've followed all the rules given to us by the network, but tonight, rules be damned.

He pulls me to him, one arm around my waist and the other on the back of my neck. Our eyes meet for a long moment before he dips his head forward, claiming my lips. We don't care who's watching. We kiss like we're the only two people in the room.

All too soon, Perry interrupts us with an announcement over the microphone.

"Thank you all for joining us tonight, and many thanks to our cast, crew, sponsors, and the network for making the dream of Top of the World come true." Cheers ripple through the crowd. "Without further ado, please turn your attention to this sneak peek of our pilot episode. You'll notice something special for the show—a live social media feed on the right side of the screen, highlighting real-time reactions from at-home viewers."

A projector lights the screen on the far wall, and the house lights dim.

The promo opens with a sweeping drone shot of the Manhattan city skyline at sunrise, hazy golden light bouncing off glass and steel. The camera speeds up, zooming in on one of those buildings. I instantly recognize it as Cooper's, and my heart soars. Cooper squeezes my hand and gives me a boyish grin.

The floor to ceiling window is shaded, the viewer unable to see inside, but the drone passes through an open door, revealing six young New Yorkers——our inaugural cast.

A deep and catchy voice speaks over ambient music. *"Some people live on top of the world. Their lives, careers, relationships, and futures are brighter than most. Who are these people? They're the rich and the famous, the privileged and elite, and for one hot summer, six of them will live together under this roof."* The voice deepens. *"Who are they underneath the fame and money? For these six lives, everything is about to change."*

The image flashes to Justin, smirking as he runs lines in front of a mirror. *"Everyone loves him on the silver screen,"* the voice over narration says, *"but can they handle the real Justin Mercer?"*

Then on to Gloria, working out in the gym. *"Her looks made her a millionaire, but perfection comes at a high price. And her love life? That's anything but perfect."*

Onto Audra Mason, strumming her guitar, sitting cross-legged on the rooftop. *"She's spent her life being the good girl pop star, but is she actually a bad girl looking to reinvent herself?"*

Cut to the siblings, playfully arguing with each other over the dinner table. *"These siblings are political royalty, but are they tired of playing it safe?"*

Finally, a shirtless Benton dips into the hot tub, sending a ripple of feminine giggles through the crowd. *"And what about the playboy who scores on more than just the ice? Is he ready to take a shot at true love?"*

A montage of footage flashes across the screen, from dinner

parties, to wine glass clinks, steamy hookups, tearful confrontations, and the carefree bonfire on Nantucket.

The promo ends with the six of them standing on the penthouse roof, overlooking the city, and the title flashes across the screen.

The voice over finishes with, *"Top of the World, where the dreams are big, but the egos are bigger."*

The screen goes dark, and the crowd explodes into thunderous applause. Not for the first time, I know what we've done here is going to work. Clearly, I'm not the only person who can't wait to watch the first episode.

FIFTY-EIGHT

S ybil
Present - Age 27

Perry made sure to prep me and Cooper for what to expect. After the red carpet arrival, where everyone would be dressed to the nines, the cast would give interviews while the rest of the guests enjoyed themed cocktails and conversation. After the initial announcements and promo trailer, there would be an early viewing of the pilot.

Everything tonight is meant to create buzz for the show, so cameras are expected to be everywhere, especially the cellphone cameras of all the social media influencers. We're counting on them to spread the word even more, and gaging their reactions so far, they're already salivating at the content possibilities.

"Who's ready to view the first episode?" Perry asks into the microphone, and everyone cheers. "Remember, when the show airs in two days, it will be paired alongside a real-time social media feed. Viewers can comment and like or dislike what's happening as America watches together."

I'm not sure if I'm going to like that, but Perry insists it's going to make our numbers better. The social media influencers seem excited, at least.

We shuffle into the large theatre for the premier, and as expected, the cast and most important crew members get to sit in a sectioned off clump. That's how I end up behind our cast and their dates. I finally spot Benton.

He and Gloria are *not* each other's dates for tonight.

They broke up in dramatic fashion on the last day of filming. Their drama will be the final linchpin of the season. Until then, they have to pretend to be civil with each other, not that Gloria is even trying. She keeps shooting him scathing looks.

Benton does *not* seem happy about it, but I know for a fact he's happy to be rid of her.

I catch his eye and give him a thumbs up. He only shrugs. I've assured him it's all going to work out, but he's convinced he's going to be the most hated man in America. I feel guilty about that, and I promised to go to bat with him in post editing.

I turn my attention to the screen as the pilot starts, one hand firmly clasped in Cooper's. He rubs his thumb along my palm, and I lean over to kiss his cheek. In my other hand is a champagne flute, filled with crisp, sweet, bubbly deliciousness. Cooper's chosen to stay sober, and I offered to skip the drinks, but he insisted I have one.

I'm proud of how much he's matured. The old Cooper would've never said no to a drink.

The buzz from earlier hasn't died down, but the audience quiets when the cast gets introduced on-screen. The forty-five minutes that follow are filled with typical reality television antics, but elevated because of the status of the cast, and then elevated even further with the feed of comments.

These are example comments made up by the network, but I see Perry's vision. The algorithm has been built to feature the most liked comments. It reminds me of watching a live tv show finale while simultaneously scrolling on my phone to see what people are saying about it.

It's wild and fun, completely on-pulse with current trends, but I have to admit, I'm glad I'm not on the show. If they want more fame, well, they've just landed in a heaping pile of it. Is it a pile of gold or a pile of trouble?

The episode ends with Benton and Gloria making out in the hot tub, his voice over explaining how he's not looking for anything serious and only here to have fun, which is great, considering Gloria had told him she wants the same thing. Then we've got her voice over, gushing about how she's looking for marriage and babies, and she thinks Benton might be the one to make her dreams come true.

The screen goes black, and the crowd erupts into applause.

On our way out of the theater, we're stopped by people wanting to chat with us about the show or congratulate us. I lock eyes with Benton, knowing exactly how he feels. He's practically being mobbed, and while he's smiling, his eyes are tense.

My stomach flips. There's a narrative arc within the season that temporarily makes him the villain before it turns around and shows the truth of him being manipulated the entire time by Gloria. She never got to know the real him; she wanted airtime and drama. He's just got to stick it out for the next few months.

But it's going to get worse before it gets better.

"You ready to go?" Cooper asks, and I nod.

With his hand on the small of my back, he leads me out the front doors. We're not the only ones leaving; a crowd spills out after us.

New York City at night glitters, and I'm floating on a high.

Cameras are still out here, capturing every move, searching for famous faces, but the crowd has multiplied exponentially, and Cooper's hand slides into mine.

"Stay close," he murmurs.

We're swallowed, weaving through the sea of bodies, and I realize why it's gotten so crowded. The security can't do a good enough job when most of these people aren't guests from the event. Word got out, and fans showed up, here to catch a glimpse of famous people.

Several of them call out names, and some of them start crying.

"What the fuck?" Cooper curses under his breath, and my anxiety grows.

People shout, cars honk, and the neon glow from the cinema creates a dizzying effect.

"It's Justin!" someone screams, and the crowd shifts violently. A sharp jolt sends me sideways, and I lose my grip on Cooper's hand as a group of teenage girls pushes me. I'm not about to be trampled, so I shuffle to the edge of the crowd, my eyes frantically scanning for Cooper.

He's taller than most men and women, but it's loud and crowded, and he's got a prosthetic leg. He needs to be extra careful.

"Cooper?" I yell into the crowd.

A few people look at me weird, but for the most part, I'm ignored. My pulse quickens. Where is he?

"Cooper!" My voice cracks as I yell again, but it's drowned out by the sudden surge of noise from the crowd. The cast has come into view.

I need to get in there, but before I can take a step, someone grabs my arm. Hard.

"Spare some change?" The voice has a jagged edge that scrapes my nerves.

I turn and freeze. The man looming over me has a dark look in his sunken eyes. His clothing is filthy and tattered, and he grins with broken, yellowed teeth.

"I don't carry cash," I say. "Sor—"

The apology sticks in my throat as the man yanks me closer, his street-stench slamming into me.

"You do," he hisses, fingers digging into my arm while his other hand darts yanks at my designer purse.

"*Stop.*" I twist away from him, panic rippling up my spine. He shoves me hard to the ground, pain exploding through my tailbone.

"You Hollywood creeps think you're better than me?" he screeches. His dirty hands reach for me, and I almost throw my bag at him just to get him away. But his fingers lock around my throat.

He squeezes my windpipe, locking my scream in my chest. I claw at his wrist, kicking like a maniac.

"Shut up, stupid bitch." He lands a punch to the side of my face, the crack like a gunshot in my ears. My head snaps to the side. White-hot pain blooms from cheek and jaw.

I choke on my sobs, not understanding why this man doesn't just take my purse and go. He punches me again.

My vision goes white, then black, then clears. I'm crying so hard I can't breathe. Or maybe it's because he's still choking me.

There's a flash of movement, and Cooper's rage-filled voice fills the air. "Get away from her!"

The pressure on my neck releases, and I gasp for a much-needed breath. The sound of fists, knuckles against bone, barrels toward me. I blink my tears away, begging my eyes to focus.

"Cooper!" I scream. His fists are bloody, his back arched, his arm a continuous pendulum. I barely see the man on the ground underneath him.

"Stop, Cooper. Please," I beg, panic gripping my heart. He

can't get caught in a media shitstorm. He can't beat this man to death.

Cooper's arm stops mid swing. His chest heaves as he meets my gaze with tortured eyes.

"Let's get out of here," I ask, setting a hand on his shoulder. "Please."

He releases his hold, and the man scrambles away, disappearing into the crowd.

Cooper watches his retreat, darkness shadowing his face. "We need to report that asshole for assault."

All I want to do is get out of here. People are starting to stare, a few pointing their cellphones our way.

"Please take me home." I climb to my feet and straighten my dress.

"Are you okay?" a nearby girl asks.

"I'm fine," I lie. "Crazy person attacked me. He's gone. Be careful out here."

The girl nods, and her friends look at me with equal parts horror and disgust.

I really need to leave.

Cooper turns me to him, his fingers trailing across my face. I wince. The pain is spreading.

"Fucker," he growls. "I'll fucking kill him."

"Yeah, you might, but we're not doing that," I say firmly. "We're going home."

Cooper shakes his head. "You need to see a doctor."

I want to argue, but when I touch my forehead, my fingers return dripping with blood.

"I've got you," he whispers, voice breaking. "Let's go."

He wraps his arm around me, anchoring me away from the chaos.

FIFTY-NINE

S ybil
  Present - Age 27

The scent of the antiseptic stings my nose, and the thin sheets feel all wrong. My forehead throbs in time with my heartbeat, the pain dulled by the treatment I've received over the last few hours.

I hate hospitals. Hospitals felt safe to me until they couldn't save someone I loved, and I wonder if Cooper hates being here as much as I do. Is he thinking about his mom? Or maybe losing his leg? He didn't have to come with me, but he did.

Cooper demanded the best plastic surgeon on call look at the cut instead of the general surgeon. Luckily, it's not deep enough to need more than typical wound care, but the bruise that blossomed around the cut and the accompanying pain prompted further testing. I got lucky. No concussion.

We're waiting for the discharge nurse to sign me out so we can go home. Cooper sits in the chair beside me, his elbows resting on his knees, his hands clasped in a tight lock. His eyes are hard, and his mouth is set in a thin line.

"I'm fine," I reiterate for what feels like the thousandth time. The lie is heavy as it leaves my mouth. "No stitches. I'm all fixed up with glue and the bandage. I'll be okay. I *am* okay."

Coop's gaze flicks to my forehead, eyes narrowing. "Sybil, you were attacked. That fucker could have…" His voice trails off, his face punctuated by a haunted look.

We're both imagining the same thing. What if that guy had a weapon on him? What if Cooper hadn't pulled him off me when he did? We filed a police report, but there's not much else we can do.

Cooper shakes his head, running his hands through his already disheveled hair. "I should've been there with you. If not for my fucking leg, I—"

"Stop," I cut him off. "This is not your fault. It's an awful thing that happened, but it's over now, okay?"

He heaves out a long sigh, and I know he doesn't want to stop blaming himself, making my chest feel like it's being ripped open. It's not my head that hurts—it's the possibility that my heart might not be able to survive this relationship if we don't work out in the end.

When I was on that cold hard ground, it was Cooper I wanted, Cooper I thought about. I needed him in ways I didn't think my heart could need anyone.

I'm in love with him.

"I think we should hire private security for you," he blurts, and I balk, immediately hating the idea.

"This was a fluke thing, Cooper."

"What if it's not?"

"Don't say that."

His brows furrow, and he pauses as if considering his words carefully. "There have been times when your dad hired security for your family, right? Maybe we should hire some again."

I swallow hard, considering his offer. "I mean, yeah, Dad hired security a few times, but only when we were getting active death threats over things happening with Laurence. Nothing like that has happened in years. Our family keeps things pretty private, and I've never needed a personal bodyguard."

"It would make me feel better, and wouldn't it make you feel safer?"

He's being a little ridiculous. It would be one thing if we were stars on the show, but what happened was unfortunately me being in the wrong place at the wrong time. It could've happened to anyone.

I shake my head. "Private security would make me feel weird, like I have something to fear, and I don't. You know how much I value my privacy. I don't want some random dude following me around."

I can tell he wants to argue, but he holds it in, thank goodness.

"How about *you* be my bodyguard for now, and if something else happens, or if I get a weird feeling about my safety, I'll hire a professional?"

He doesn't like it, but he agrees with a curt nod.

Suddenly, tears well up in my eyes again. I hate this so fucking much. What was supposed to be a dazzling night of celebration has turned into a nightmare.

I glance at my fingers as they squeeze the thin sheet over my legs. Closing my eyes for a moment, I command myself not to cry, promising I'm going to be okay.

Cooper's chair screeches across the linoleum as he scoots closer, covering my hand with his own and sending calming warmth through my body. He's grounding in a way nobody and nothing else is.

He kisses my temple below the cut, then he whispers into my ear, "Just so you're clear, what happened is not your fault, either."

My mouth pops open, and I let out a choking sob. "I-I know that... but it still *feels* like it is. Where was my sense of self-preservation? I should've handed over the damn purse, but it all happened so fast."

I blink, momentarily dazed by the intensity of Cooper's gaze.

"You did nothing wrong."

"I feel stupid," I confess.

"Don't." His grip on my hand tightens, and the pain in his eyes sharpens. "You don't blame yourself, and I won't blame myself. Deal?"

I nod. "Deal."

"That guy was a coward, but you're the bravest person I know."

The lump in my throat swells. What did I do to deserve this man? He's the most remarkable person and an incredible boyfriend, lover, and friend. He's showing up as the partner I've wanted but didn't believe existed for a type-A control freak like me.

I want to kick myself for not seeing this potential in him before. What if it had been me and him in college instead of me and Ethan? Would we have worked out? It's hard to know... so much has changed, but I want to believe we would've found a way to make it work. How I felt for Ethan pales in comparison to how I feel for Cooper.

Ethan was like the sunset—beautiful and vibrant but fades fast. Cooper is the sunset, sunrise, sunshine, moonlight, and everything in between. He's *every* source of light. I'll never be in darkness again.

"You think I'm brave, huh?" I joke, trying to lighten the mood.

"Yes," he says simply, as if it's the most obvious thing in the world. "You've been through so much, more than most people will ever have to go through, and you've not let it break you. You always come out stronger."

"I could say the same thing about you."

He stares at me for a long moment, the energy between us charging. My pulse quickens, and his thumb brushes over my knuckles.

"I love you," he says.

Those three little words are so big... big enough to change everything.

"Maybe this isn't the best time to say it," he says, hanging his head but keeping our eyes locked. "But I can't *not* say it, not anymore. I love you, Sybil. I have loved you for as long as I can remember, and I will love you until I cease to exist. Loving you is a part of me that can never be removed."

My body buzzes, happiness squashing fear until all I can feel is joy and gratitude.

"I love you, too."

He lets out a breathy sigh, pressing a gentle kiss to my lips, his mouth lingering against mine.

"Say it again?" he whispers.

"I love you, Cooper."

He grins. "You have no idea how long I've wanted you to say that to me."

"Oh, really?" I tease.

He nods against my forehead. "I've kind of had a crush on you since we were kids."

"Only kind of?"

"Okay, more than a crush."

We kiss again, and I feel safer than I have in as long as I can remember. This is *right* and good and inevitable and meant to be. Now that I've got him, I'm never going to let him go.

Sixty

S ybil
Present - Age 27

The High Line stretches ahead of me and Arden, the autumn leaves beginning to show off their colors. There are so many things to love about Manhattan in the fall, and this spot is one of my favorites.

"What's on your mind?" Arden asks, her voice soft as we walk side by side. "Is it the attack?"

I shake my head, fingers involuntarily jumping up to the bruises I've covered with makeup. "It's the gala," I admit. "I'm trying to keep everything on track, but it's... a lot."

Arden nods. "That's not surprising. You're basically running the show, right?"

I let out a dry chuckle. "Feels like it. The prep is endless, and the stakes are high, but at least there's Cooper to come home to."

She waggles her brows. "Tell me more."

"It's good with him," I say, grinning despite myself. "Better than good. I've never felt this way about anyone before."

Arden bumps my shoulder. "You deserve it, Syb. It's about time."

I'm grateful, but the moment fades as my thoughts shift. "It's not just the gala... Lance Vale has been cold as ever."

"What do you mean?"

That's right, she only knows Lance from the brief internship she did last summer.

"Oh, if only you knew what a psycho he's become."

"*What*?"

I laugh, even though it's not funny, then spend the next ten minutes bitching about what a horrible boss he's turning out to be. When I get to the part about the email hack and someone canceling the first gala venue, she's in total shock.

"And the board really didn't fire him?"

I shake my head.

"Assholes."

Arden rarely swears so when she does, it makes me laugh, but right now I'm too worked up.

"At least he moved his nephew to another department," I finish with a huff, "but now I'm scrambling, and I really want the promotion when Miriam retires."

"You're literally a Laurence. The job is as good as yours."

I shrug. "If Vale secures the official CEO gig, I might as well pack up my desk now."

Her face pales. "That's scary."

"I love The Laurence Foundation with my whole heart. I want to continue building the vision."

Arden smiles. "You will. You've got the heart and the brains for it."

I'm grateful for the reassurance, but my mind is already drifting. "Then there's Top of the World..."

She laughs knowingly. "I've been watching the episodes, and don't forget, I live in the building. People do know the stars aren't living there anymore, right? Fans keep showing up, and our doorman is about to lose his mind. Poor Pauly."

I wince, and she loops her arm through mine as we pause by a stretch of flame-colored maples. The city hums around us, but in this garden, it feels like we've found a sanctuary. "You care so much about everyone else, Syb. When was the last time you let someone take care of you?"

I laugh lightly, but there's no real answer to her question. I guess I let Cooper take care of me to a degree, and I've definitely let him into my heart and my life, but that doesn't mean I'm willing to rely on him for anything I can do myself. It's the same reason I have had such a hard time bringing on an assistant, even though I tell myself I'll hire help.

I trust myself way more than I trust others.

Arden and I walk in comfortable silence, and our ability to be silent together is how I know Arden is one of my best friends. We get each other. It's still crazy to think that she's actually my sister, but I'm grateful too, even if the circumstances that brought her into this world came with a lot of heartbreak. Truth is, I love my brothers with my entire heart, but I always wanted a sister, and I feel so lucky to have her.

How often do I tell her that?

"You know I love you, right?" I elbow her gently.

She pulls me into a side hug. "Aww, I love you, too."

"For real, though," I say. "I'm lucky to have you. I'm glad you're my sister."

She beams, and we continue on.

The crunch of fallen leaves beneath our boots is almost rhythmic, and the air smells damp and earthy. The sky above blends into gold and pale blue as the sun dips lower. It's truly the perfect autumn evening.

The closer we get to sunset, the more crowded The High Line becomes. Soon we're surrounded by New Yorkers and tourists, and while I don't mind crowds and thrive around large groups of people, Arden is the exact opposite. I can see the panic creeping into her eyes as her cheeks turn blotchy.

"Let's go," I say, and we weave our way toward the nearest set of exiting stairs.

"Top of the World?" someone says, catching my attention. "It can't be canceled already."

"That's what the news is reporting," another young woman replies in a screeching tone. I find her as she holds up her phone. "Look here, TMZ says so, and everyone else is reporting the same."

What the fuck?

I stop abruptly, no longer caring about the crowded sidewalk. Arden and I share a glance before pulling out our phones.

"It's all over the entertainment news," she whispers.

I go to my email first. Sure enough, there's something waiting for me from King Media. I read through it quickly, the words *regrettably not moving forward with a second season* clear as day.

Denial. Shock. Rage. They all hit me at once.

"This doesn't make sense," Arden hisses, scrolling through her phone. "Why would they cancel the most popular show of the year?"

Oh, they'll have a bullshit reason.

Numbers. Money. Talent. Lawsuits.

Who knows, but the real truth, the one that won't be revealed, is this is a way for King to get revenge on Laurence? Our success was never going to be good enough.

"I need to speak with Cooper," my voice comes out as coarse as sandpaper. "Can you get home on your own?"

"Of course," she replies with a grim look. "Go get this sorted, and let me know if I can help."

I give her a quick hug and then get the hell out of there.

My instinct is to call Cooper, but I want to see his face when I confront him about this. Does that mean I don't fully trust him? Maybe so, but I'll know if he knew about this ahead of time and didn't warn me.

Maybe he planned this all along?

No, don't think like that. I chastise myself. *Give him a chance to explain.*

I know Cooper, and I know he loves me. There's no way he's the one behind this. It has to be his scheming father.

Even though it's Friday, Cooper isn't at home. He told me he was going to be in the office a bunch this weekend, so I'm going straight to King headquarters. If I'm lucky, maybe I'll run into Conrad, so I can give him a piece of my mind.

It doesn't matter what kind of excuses the network has; they're wrong for this. Laurence invested money in this show, too, and King can't pull the rug out from under us. We deserve an explanation, and I'm sure our contract protects us from this kind of betrayal.

I head into King headquarters, and security stops me before I can go upstairs.

"Sorry, you'll have to wait until you have an appointment. You're not on the approved list."

I frown. I've been on that list for months.

"Even on a weekend? My boyfriend's upstairs."

The security guard shakes his head.

"She's with me," a familiar voice says, and my chest tightens. I know that voice, and as unsettling as it is, as much as I hate the person attached to it, at least he can let me accompany him upstairs, and we can figure out what's going on.

Reluctantly, I turn to face Lance Vale.

SIXTY-ONE

S ybil
    Present - Age 27

"Hi, Lance." I sigh. "Are you going up there to talk to them about Top of the World?"

He nods sharply, and together we stride toward the bank of elevators. My pulse is already pounding in my ears, a warning drumbeat.

We step into the modern elevator. It reminds me of this man beside me, cold and clinical. His suit cuts a sharp line against the minimalist backdrop, a complete opposite of my casual evening clothing of jeans, sweater, and puffer jacket.

"Do you know what's going on?" I ask. "Top of the World is a viral sensation."

"Yes, it is."

As much as we've come to hate each other, I think Vale actually cares about this.

"King can't do this to Laurence. We all stand to make a great deal of money on our investment in Top of the World. We have contracts in place that explicitly state the Laurence shares will be returned if the show makes it to a season two. Canceling it is an expensive and unnecessary legal battle waiting to happen."

He hums in agreement. "And meanwhile, Top of the World will lose momentum."

"Yeah, exactly. We don't want that."

Lance releases a slow methodical breath and turns on me, peering through his spectacles as if I'm the most vapid and stupid person he's ever done business with. "Did you really think Conrad King would let a Laurence win?"

My mouth pops open.

"I'm on Laurence International's side," he says smoothly. "You'll see."

I fold my arms over my chest and try not to panic, but I feel like everything is falling down around me. What am I supposed to do here? Who am I supposed to trust?

The elevator doors open, and my heels click against the floor as I lead the way. Cooper's office is next door to his brother's and father's, and my stomach knots tighter and tighter with each step, but I want to stop by Cooper's first.

Except, he's not here.

His office is empty.

I pull out my phone to see a dozen missed calls from him.

Lance strides right past me to Conrad's office, pushing open the heavy door and striding inside as if he's taken meetings here before.

My heart shatters to the floor when I catch the conspiratorial look Lance and Conrad share.

They planned this... and I'm the idiot who fell for it.

"Sybil," Conrad says, spreading his arms in a mock gesture of welcome. "What a pleasant surprise to see you here."

"Where's Cooper?" I demand, voice coming out louder than I intended.

"Cooper is tied up with some important business matters at the moment, but I'm sure Lance can bring you up to speed."

Lance is already sitting down, appearing relaxed and smug. He pats the seat next to him like he's calling a child to come get a talking-to, and I want to scream.

"You did this?" I glare, stepping fully into the room but not sitting down. Fuck that. "You agreed to the cancelation? Why would you do that? Top of the World is successful. There are contracts in place. Just wait until the board hears about *this.*"

Lance sighs. "Calm down."

"Don't tell me to be calm."

He raises an eyebrow and turns to Conrad. "This is why I don't think she has what it takes to run the foundation. She's too emotional."

He wants to sit here and berate me about emotions when he fucking screwed me over?

Conrad holds up his hand. "The show isn't canceled," he announces, giving me a sympathetic look.

I blink, taking his words to heart. A seed of hope plants in my chest, and I feel like I can breathe again.

"What do you mean?" I whisper. "Is this a misunderstanding? Because if so, you need to alert the media. The news is everywhere."

Conrad shakes his head. "The show's been sold to another network." He nods toward Vale. "Lance and I already signed the necessary paperwork. Perry gets to stay on as creator, though I can't say what the new network will do with it. That's their prerogative."

My skin crawls at their smug grins.

It doesn't make sense that they'd sell something so special

before it reaches its value. There's so much money to be made here, especially for King Media. The advertising offers coming in are insane. The show was expensive to produce, but we're blowing our projections out of the water.

This is only the beginning. We could do *Top of the World* shows in different cities with different casts. Then there's merch. Reunion shows. Maybe even meet and greet tours.

"Why...?" I ask, but before they can answer my question, the truth slaps me across the face. "This was all about the shares?"

"Now she's got it," Lance says with a laugh, his tone smooth as silk. "The terms of the deal stipulated we couldn't outright cancel the show if it was successful, but it also stipulated it must air on King's network for a second season in order for you to get your shares back. There was nothing that said the show couldn't be sold to another network if both Laurence and King agreed to it, which we did."

Conrad gives me a little wink. "The deal was lucrative, and all investors will be happy. Well, except maybe *your* family."

I blink rapidly, turning on Lance. "The investors won't be happy we lost five percent of our ownership to King. This will make you look worse than ever. You're never going to be voted in as CEO now."

Lance points to Conrad, who doesn't even flinch. "Oh, the shares *are* returning to Laurence, just not where you think. Lance Vale will be taking them off King's hands."

"That's right," Lance says. "My extra shares will certainly help me get my rightful spot as CEO. I'm not worried."

My knees weaken, and acid builds on the back of my tongue. "This is sabotage."

Vale shrugs. "It's called strategy."

I shake my head. "Cooper would never agree with this."

Conrad chuckles, low and condescending. "Oh darling, you

always were so naïve, weren't you? I thought maybe you'd grown out of that, but I guess not."

"What are you saying?"

"Cooper *already* agreed to this," he says with finality. "Signed on the dotted line and everything."

Shock is a cruel bitch. "He wouldn't do that."

"He did. Unlike your family, my son knows the importance of loyalty."

My world tilts, everything falling into sick and twisted place.

Lance stands from his seat and approaches me. "Your family's grip has been slipping on the company for years. Your father was a good leader, I won't deny that, but even he couldn't get Laurence to where it needed to be, and your childish little brother will certainly run it into the ground. With me in charge and nepotism out of the way, Laurence will become one of the most profitable conglomerates in the world."

Betrayal sears, hot and painful. My mind races, trying to make sense of it all, but there's one thing I can't understand.

Cooper.

The man I love and trust did this. I've brought him into my life and my body and my heart.

I stumble away. "This isn't over," I say, voice trembling with rage and cracking with betrayal.

"Oh, but it is," Lance confirms. "Let me give you one last piece of business advice, Sybil. Learn when to give up."

I turn and flee, the door slamming shut behind me. I gasp in short and shallow breaths. My chest tightens as if it's collapsing in on itself. The tears finally break through, proof I've been played, that I'm as weak as those men think I am.

I've let my family down. The man I love isn't who I thought he was. I can't even go to Arden because she's married to a King.

I open my phone to see more missed calls from Cooper as well as a slew of unread texts, but I'm not ready to talk to him.

The only thing I can do is pull off an incredible gala in two weeks and pray the hiring board sees the value I bring to Laurence.

I'm not very optimistic.

SIXTY-TWO

C ooper
Past - Age 26

I used to be a party person, but I lost that side of myself when I lost my leg. I didn't want to come tonight, but Ethan insisted. It's New Year's Eve, what used to be a favorite night of the year, but Ethan doesn't understand the old me is gone.

It's not like a prosthetic is one and done. I learned that the hard way. Six months in, and I'm already on my second leg. The thing about prosthetics is that not only do they wear down over time, but my stump changes over time as well. If I lose weight or gain muscle, I'll need an adjustment. If something is misaligned, I'll need an adjustment. If I develop neuroma or bone spurs, same thing. Don't even talk to me about friction and pressure points.

The fact that I'm even doing as well as I am is nothing short of a miracle, and that's mostly thanks to having been born into a rich family. Lots of people with limbs like mine aren't so lucky.

Not that I consider myself lucky. I'm still angry, but at least I'm channeling that anger into an actionable plan.

Tonight, however, the plan is to get wasted.

The hotel ballroom is a glittering nightmare, packed shoulder to shoulder with twenty-somethings who belong at this party more than I do.

The chandeliers sparkle like they know it's their night to shine, and so do all the dresses. It's a sea of silver and gold. Even the ice cubes have edible glitter. The whole thing screams opulence and wealth.

Ethan is busy with his arms around Arden, the two already lost in their love-bubble. His laughter is lighter than it's been in years, and I'm happy for him. They're like a vision out of a holiday romance, while I'm their misplaced plus one, nursing my second whiskey and trying to make myself invisible.

Hard to do when everyone at this party knows about the prosthetic. They also know about the drama between the King and Laurence family.

I note that I've slept with many of the women here at one point or another and take another drink. Not that I'm sleeping with anyone anymore. I can't.

Every time I try to hook up with someone, I panic about my leg. It's fucking ridiculous. Even the hot nurse at the rehab didn't do it for me, though I played it off like we were fucking, so Ethan didn't worry any more than he already was.

I can feel eyes on me—curious, pitying eyes. They're coming from every corner of the room, heavy and scrutinizing.

I adjust in my seat at the bar, the prosthetic leg awkward beneath me. The marble floor isn't made for comfort or subtlety. The last thing I need is to fumble on that dance floor, so I stay right here with my ass in this chair and plan to stay here all night.

A familiar laugh breaks my thoughts. I turn to find at the

woman who ruined my life flirting with a man farther down the bar. Now *she* belongs here, with her shimmering dress, her striking auburn hair, and her sultry green eyes. She always looks like she belongs everywhere she goes while simultaneously standing out, like she's better than everyone else. It's a Laurence thing.

I used to love that about her, but now I hate it. I hate her. For everything. For the accident. For breaking my heart. For hurting my family. Even for being here right now and not looking my way while everyone else stares at me like I'm fragile and broken.

Taking another drink, I turn from Sybil to take inventory of the bottles behind the bar instead. I need something stronger. I drain the rest of my whiskey and order vodka. Mixing these is a bad idea, but I don't care.

I drink, and I drink, and I drink.

Midnight closes in, and the crowd grows rowdy. The old me would've been out there feeding off that energy, but the new me is still planted in this chair.

Not for the first time—maybe not even for the hundredth time—I find Sybil and the man she's been flirting with all night. He's tall and wearing a cheap suit and looks like a bank-teller. She's practically rubbing her breasts against his arm as they talk.

Her hungry eyes flick to me, and I snap.

In my mind, I stride over confidently, but in reality, it's more of a drunken shuffle.

"We need to talk," I tell her and although her expression darkens, she gives me a reluctant nod.

We leave Mr. Bank Teller, and I get a little smug at the fact that he looks pissed off.

I lead her to the edge of the crowd. It's so loud we can't really talk. Not that I'm even sure what I'm going to say.

"What do you want?" she asks, and I stare at her mouth for a little too long. "Cooper?"

"Are you going to kiss that guy at midnight?" I ask, words slurring.

Her eyes narrow. "Yeah, that's what people do. Speaking of which, I need to get back there. The countdown is about to start."

I stare at her. No words. Drunk off my ass.

She turns to leave, but I snatch her wrist. "You don't even know that guy. Did you just meet him tonight?"

Her cheeks go pink. "So what? You sleep with women you barely know all the time, and don't pretend otherwise. We went to college together, remember? I know how you are."

That was a long time ago.

That was *before*.

I chuckle darkly. "I've grown up, Sybil. It's called maturing. Maybe you should consider it."

Her eyes round, and I instantly feel like the world's biggest asshole, but I'm so fucked up and can't seem to stop myself from arguing with her. Anything to get her attention.

"Why do you have to do this? Every time we try to have a conversation, you're a complete jerk. We used to be friends."

"You broke up with me," I say. "Not the other way around."

"Broke up? We weren't together."

"You know what I mean."

"You're drunk." Her voice goes quiet, edged with disappointment. "It's really not good for you, Cooper. It makes you... different."

"Different?" Yeah, a lot of things made me different.

She frowns. "And difficult."

"So you're perfect?" The words spill out. "I'm a drunk because my life is a fucking mess, thanks to your fucking family.

You're out here partying and letting anyone stick his dick in you."

The countdown starts, *ten, night, eight...*

She stares at me like she can't believe me, like she doesn't know who I am anymore.

Her eyes narrow, and she steps closer. "Maybe you still have some growing up to do, Cooper. Losing your leg fucking sucked, I know, but I lost my *dad* that day. You're not the only one who has suffered a loss, but you are the only one drinking like a fish and acting like a fucking victim."

Three, two, one. Happy New Year!

For a split second, everything is frozen.

The noise of the crowd fades, and her pretty green eyes stare at me, those lips parted. I foolishly imagine a universe in which I kiss her, but that's quickly replaced by the reality of her words.

I *am* a fucking victim. I didn't do shit to cause my leg to get destroyed by that boat. She did. She told Gregory about Arden and Ethan. She spurred her father on during his tirade. After everything went to shit, she didn't take responsibility for her actions.

She turns away, clearly scanning the crowd for the man she was flirting with, but he's already locked lips with someone else. They're practically dry humping on the dance floor. Classy.

"That's the guy you wanted to fuck tonight?" I chuckle. "Looks like he thinks you're pretty replaceable. Your taste in men has really gone downhill since you left Ethan. You should raise your standards."

"Leave me alone," she practically screams, and I know I've pushed her to the edge. A twisted satisfaction stirs in me, but it's overshadowed by guilt. Am I the world's biggest asshole, or is she? It's hard to tell these days.

The rest of the night is a blur. Flashes of Ethan's concerned face, of Arden's voice, the taste of that vodka threatening to come up my esophagus. A car taking us home. And then nothing.

Blissful sleep.

I wake the next morning with a pounding headache and a mouth that feels like it's full of sand. I really need to stop drinking; nothing good comes of it anymore.

The sunlight streaming through the window is clearly a punishment for my behavior, and my stomach twists.

I will never stop hating her. I love Sybil, but I hate her because I love her—one feeds the other. Something's got to break.

I stare at the ceiling, realizing what I need most.

I need to go to my father.

I'll go and ask for his help. Conrad King is the master of games, and if there's one game he knows best, it's revenge.

SIXTY-THREE

S ybil
    Present - Age 27

I keep my phone on silent. I'll call Mom later and tell her everything that happened, but for now, I'm too embarrassed that I didn't see this coming.

I go straight home, change into pajamas, then fall into bed. How could I have been so stupid? I still can't believe this is happening, that Cooper betrayed me, but then again, everything Lance and Conrad revealed makes sense.

I let my stupid heart fall in love instead of allowing my logical brain figure out I was clearly being set up. Of course I was. My gut knew something was off the minute Cooper wanted me to work on *Top of the World*.

I turn on some music, trying to drown out my thoughts. Eventually, someone knocks on my front door.

Gathering myself together, I splash cold water onto my face

in a pathetic attempt to de-puff and de-redden, then head to the door.

"I didn't know they were going to sell the show to another network," Perry blurts the second I open it, holding his hands in surrender.

I sigh and widen the door, letting him inside.

He steps through and tries to give me a hug, but I dodge him.

"I don't want anyone to touch me right now."

"That's fair."

I follow him to the couch, and we sit on opposite ends.

"What do you know?" I ask, studying him carefully, trying to gauge if I can actually trust him.

"I know King and Laurence sold the show, but I only found out today. They did it behind my back as much as they did it behind yours."

My stomach hardens. They were willing to hand over *Top of the World* to a competitor because it would mean my family would be screwed? Wow, that's great.

"No amount of money is worth what they did," I say, deadpanned.

"Especially since both companies stood to make more money over time as Top of the World grows into a franchise."

All the excitement I've had about the show deflates at once. "I'm so sad I won't be working on it anymore."

While nonprofit fundraising is my passion, I loved my time on set.

Perry goes quiet. He'll stay on as the show's creator, but everyone from King and Laurence will be gone.

"Did you get a payout?" I ask carefully.

His lips thin, and he nods.

"How much?" I'm sure it was a fair offer, but since he's

staying on with the show, I have no idea what that number would even be.

"A lot." Which tells me it's got to be in the multiple millions.

"Enough that you're not *that* sorry, right?" I joke, but it comes out harsh.

"Don't do that. You and Cooper are my best friends. I wanted to do this with you guys by my side. Of course I'm happy about the success of the show, but it's bittersweet now."

"Cooper knew about this all along, just so you know. He made a deal with his dad well before he brought me in. He played us both, or maybe he played me, because you didn't really lose anything."

Perry looks away, shaking his head at the floor.

"You say you had no idea this was going to happen, but you don't look that surprised."

He takes a deep breath and peers at me through strained eyes. "Unfortunately, I'm not surprised he did this."

My stomach clenches as if I've been punched in the gut.

"Explain?"

"Not to make excuses, but he's been through a lot."

Enough to pull this shit? No, there's got to be more.

"Please tell me the truth, Perry. I can take it."

"He loves you, but he also... hates you."

I swallow hard, my throat dry as sandpaper. "How does that work?"

How can you claim to love someone while hating them at the same time? My heart beats for Cooper, and I never would've done this to him had the roles been reversed.

"Cooper's wanted you for years, since you were children. He tore himself apart loving you." He pauses, running his hands over his knees. "But you hurt him. You have to own that."

"Because I dated his brother first? That was years ago, and

everyone moved on. So tell me, what did I do to deserve a betrayal this fucked up?"

"You know." His tone is sharp.

I bark out a laugh. "You're kidding me with this, right? I know he's your boy, but I thought I was your friend, too."

Perry throws his head back in exasperation, raking his hands through his short black curls. "I'm not talking about years ago. I'm talking about the accident last summer."

I blink rapidly, my brain trying to catch up. "What does the accident have to do with me?"

He gives me a pointed look, like I should be able to read his mind.

"Are you saying Cooper blames me for what happened? Sorry, but I don't blame Cooper for the horrible crap his parents have done, and also, have we forgotten that my dad was the one driving, and he was the one who died that night?"

"I'm not talking about Gregory's mistake. I'm talking about *you*, Sybil. You never took accountability for what you did to contribute to the accident."

I'm completely at a loss. "What did I do?"

He shakes his head. "Wow, really?"

My mouth falls open. Is this what being gaslit feels like?

"Look, you need to talk to Cooper about this."

I stand up, my arms folded over my chest and blood whooshing in my eardrums. I don't think I've *ever* felt more frustrated. "I'm sick of all this cryptic shit. It would be really nice if someone would be straight with me."

Perry tilts his head up. "Fine. You really want to do this?"

"Obviously."

"*You* told your dad about Arden and Ethan. *You* set off his temper. Maybe it doesn't make sense, but Cooper didn't have anyone left alive to be mad at for losing his leg, so he blamed you."

The weight of his words crashes down on me. I never even considered the idea that Cooper would blame me for his leg. Not once did he say a word about it.

"I'm sorry," Perry continues. "It's not fair or logical to blame you for your father's actions, but I was with him during recovery, and he wasn't in a good headspace. It messed with his psyche, but you wouldn't know that, because you never came to check on him."

A decision I still regret.

Tears blur my vision, and Perry pushes to his feet. I don't know what to say or think or even feel. I never imagined my mistakes would cost me so much—my legacy with Laurence International, but more importantly... my heart.

"I'm going to leave now." Perry steps back. "You and Cooper should talk about everything. If it's any consolation, I think he loves you."

Even though he also hates me? No, that's not any consolation.

Perry leaves me with a storm of emotions. I'm angry, devastated, ashamed, frustrated, but most of all, I'm completely heartbroken. I can't simply turn my feelings off, and I'm still hopelessly, desperately in love with Cooper. But there's a part of him who hates me enough to hurt me like this, so there's no way he's hopelessly, desperately, in love with me, too. That's not love.

I crawl into bed, letting the minutes turn into hours, feeling my emotions so I can begin to process them.

I should call my mom, and I will call my therapist, and eventually, Cooper and I will have to talk, but right now, all I can do is pick apart every tiny detail about the accident. Even though the pain of losing Dad is fresh, the memories are hazy.

I force myself to replay those moments again and again,

trying to resurface anything I might have missed, hoping to see things from Cooper's point of view.

The whole family was out on Dad's boat. There was a gorgeous pink sunset, and the Nantucket sound was lapping gently at the boat. Dad asked Arden if she's been talking to the Kings.

"She's been doing a lot more than talking," I said.

I didn't understand why Dad had lost his temper so badly. I realize now he was trying to hide his deep, dark, shameful secret—he was Arden's birth father.

Did Dad drive into them on purpose?

When I play it back, I remember the way Dad swerved at the last second, but he lost control. I really think he was trying to scare Ethan away from Arden. He never would've wanted to hurt anyone.

The moments after the boat crash are still murky, and I've let them stay that way.

I force myself to clear the details, let them hit me as hard as they did that day. Tears stream down my face and leak into my ears.

Dad hit Cooper.

Arden flew overboard.

Ethan went after her.

Cooper was in the water, and nobody could find him.

Dad and Ethan went in to look for him, and Ethan got him out.

I made a tourniquet for his leg.

But Dad...

Dad never resurfaced.

The sobs come harder. I could never blame Cooper for my father going into the water. He died trying to save him, and he wouldn't have gone in if he didn't care about Cooper in the first place.

And now Cooper hates me. How is that fair?

The accident was an accident—but what Cooper did to me was on purpose.

Wiping away the tears, I roll over and retrieve my phone, not letting myself read his texts or listen to his voicemails. I delete them all. If he really wanted to talk, he could've come here.

Right before I block his number, I send him a final text, my fingers shaking with every letter I type.

Sybil: You got your revenge, Cooper. I hope it was worth it. I'm truly sorry about what happened to your leg. I wish I would have known you blamed me for it. We should have talked about this a long time ago, and I regret not coming to the hospital when it happened.

Regarding Top of the World, I know you were involved in screwing me over. It makes me sad for both of us, but it happened. I've decided it's best to cut off contact. You and I are toxic, and there's too much bad blood. Please respect my decision, and let me move on. I'm blocking your number and banning you from my building. I hope you have a happy life and find the healing you deserve.

I realize it's a long text—a big blue chunk he might not even read, but it doesn't matter. I didn't write it for him. I wrote it for me.

Sixty-Four

C ooper
Past - Age 27

I'm standing alone, eyeing the bar. I shouldn't be, but being at Ethan and Arden's wedding reception is testing my resolve. As if sensing my unease, my father strides over, gripping my shoulder.

"How long have you been sober?" he asks.

I turn on him, and he releases me. "How did you know?"

"I make it my business to know what my sons are up to. As far as I can tell, you haven't had a drink in months. You also removed the bar cart from your office. I'm impressed."

I guess I wasn't inconspicuous, but I don't want this to be a big deal. "Thanks. I haven't had a drink since New Year's Eve."

It's March. It's the longest I've gone in a decade.

He nods slowly. "Do I want to know what happened on New Year's Eve?"

My eyes shift to where Sybil is chatting with some friends across the room. Excusing the fact that we're here to celebrate

Ethan and Arden's elopement, it's obvious Sybil is responsible for this party.

"No," I tell my father, embarrassment coloring the back of my neck. Now that I haven't touched a drop for a few months, I realize how much alcohol controlled me. Not anymore. The only thing I want controlling me from now on is myself.

"Well, I'm proud of you," he says, and I shouldn't care that he's proud of me, but I do. I've been programmed to seek his approval. "It takes strength to give up a vice like that." He turns so we're shoulder to shoulder, his gaze also flicking to Sybil. "You've given up two vices, it seems."

The comment makes me pause. Doesn't matter that I think she's the most beautiful person I've seen in real life. I don't want her anymore.

It feels good to be free of her.

Ethan and his new wife dance nearby, the two lost in their own bubble of love, and a pain of guilt twists my gut. I don't want to use their engagement party as part of my plan, but once I let Dad in, he helped me plot the whole thing.

Tonight is, unfortunately, an important element of the story we're creating here. The first reveal has to come publicly, with all the Kings and Laurences, so they can't bury it with lawyers.

Ethan's going to be pissed, and Arden will be hurt, but I don't see another way. There are casualties in war.

"We should speak in private," Dad says, and I follow him from the ballroom and into an empty hallway.

"This is your last chance to back out," he warns, looking me dead in the eyes. "Once this is in motion, there's no stopping it."

I motion to my right pant leg. "I think I understand lasting consequences better than most."

Dad's face clears of any hesitation. "Okay, then."

We stare at each other for a long moment, communicating without words.

When I went to him pissed off at the Laurences and asking how we could get revenge, he told me about Arden's true parentage and the old contract he and Gregory had drafted years ago. I asked him why he hadn't brought all this up sooner, and he said he was waiting for things to align, but he wasn't sure he was willing to put Ethan through the truth. I wasn't sure I was willing to, either. I thought about it for a while and came to the conclusion that I needed this.

What happened with the Laurences—at Sybil—eats me up every day.

And what will Ethan care? He's going to stay married to Arden no matter what happens. Their love won't be shaken by this.

Besides that, Arden deserves to know who she really is.

Doesn't mean I'm not uneasy about it.

Doesn't mean I'm not worried.

"Are you going to make the announcement, or am I?" Dad questions me.

"You are," I remind him. For this to work, he has to be the bad guy.

Nobody can know my involvement with any of this until it's over.

Tonight is step one of many.

It's going to suck to see people I care about get hurt, but it's a necessary evil when love and hate belong to opposite edges of the same knife.

Dad encourages me to befriend Sybil again. That's going to be the hardest part, but I can do it knowing that in six months, this will all be over.

Step one, reveal Arden's true parentage and the marriage contract.

Step two, use the company shares to leverage Laurence into working with King.

Step three, befriend Sybil, and get her to trust me.

Step four, screw over the Laurence family, making them look incompetent in front of their board, essentially ending their rein.

That last step I'm still not sure about, but Dad has assured me he has the right contacts to make it happen.

Dad leaves, and I stay to gather myself for a moment, wondering if this is worth all the trouble. Do I really want to go through with this?

Once it's done, Sybil will hate me. Any possibility with her will be destroyed forever.

I never saw myself as the kind of person who'd go to such lengths to hurt someone else, even if it's someone who hurt me.

This isn't a choice I can unmake.

There's still time to stop Dad from the announcement. We can take the secret of Arden's parentage to our graves.

I lean against the wall and groan.

Shit, I think I'm getting cold feet. I don't know if I can do this.

My phone buzzes in my pocket, the perfect excuse to give me one more minute to hide in this hallway.

I quickly read a text from one of my old flings. My heart drops with each word, a sourness filling my stomach.

Roxanna: Hey, I've missed you. Wanna have some fun? By the way, the leg thing doesn't bother me one bit. You're sexy no matter what.

I stiffen, considering my options. Since the accident, I've tried to hook up with several women and haven't been able to follow through. It's like a different person takes over, and I freeze up. It doesn't matter if I'm into it or if she's the most seductive creature on the planet. I can't seem to go there with anybody.

It's been months and nothing.

I think of Roxanna's sultry curves and raven hair, and my

cock twitches. I'd love to try again with her, and I will, but I'm going to have to reclaim some of my masculinity first. Even if it's the toxic-masculine part. Even if it changes who I am.

I'm permanently changed, anyway. The Laurences can feel some of this pain for once.

"Fuck it," I mutter, slipping my phone into my pocket and striding into the party like I don't have a care in the world.

Instead of finding my father like I had intended a minute ago, I zero in on where Sybil is dancing with Perry.

Perfect, exactly the people I wanted to see together.

Two seconds later, I tower over her with a rakish smirk and a devil-may-care attitude. "Mind if I cut in?" I ask, secure in the knowledge she would very much mind if she knew what I've planned for the two of us.

SIXTY-FIVE

S ybil
      Present - Age 27

I'm tempted to spend the entire weekend rotting away in my bed and feeling sorry for myself, but that's not my style. I already cried myself to sleep, and I'm sick of it. It's a beautiful Saturday morning, and there's so much I could be doing, but first I need to brush myself off and make a plan for my future.

A future that *might* not include working at Laurence International is hard to swallow. If I only have one gala fundraiser left, I'm going to make sure it's the best one I've ever hosted. After that, I'll figure it out. As devastating as it is to be pushed out of my own legacy, I'm not going to let it ruin my life. Nonprofit fundraising is my passion, and I'll keep doing it no matter what.

First, I need to talk to Mom. She came to the city first thing when she got the news about the show. It's nice that she has my back, but I doubt she knows the full extent of this betrayal. As

440

tempted as I am to call her and vent, I think this is a conversation we should have in person.

I shower, give my hair a blowout, and apply a full face of makeup, then I put on my favorite black high-heeled boots and a brand-new cashmere white sweater-dress, pairing the look with my black Birkin bag. Even though I feel like shit, I'm going to look good.

Stepping onto the busy SoHo sidewalk, my heels click against the pavement, and I tug my bag close under my arm, searching for a cab. A gust of early-autumn air blows my hair off my shoulders, but I barely feel it.

Cooper leans against a sleek black town car that's parked on the curb, his hands shoved into the pockets of a fitted wool coat. His jaw is tight, his expression is unreadable, but the second his midnight eyes lock on mine, I know exactly what he's feeling.

Exhaling sharply, I attempt to walk past him. If I pretend he isn't there, then he can't stop me. I don't want to deal with whatever lies he came here to spew. I already know he was involved with my career ruin.

Right as I pass him, he pushes away from the car and steps directly into my path.

"We're not breaking up," he says sharply.

I falter. "Excuse me?"

"You don't get to end it with a text and then block me."

I jut my chin up. "It's already over, Cooper. What does it matter if it's through text or in person? You lied and screwed me over. What did you think was going to happen?" I shake my head. "Actually, I don't want to know."

His eyes narrow. "You're a bad liar."

"Well, you're a good one," I snap, and he winces. I can already feel my eyes burning, and I fucking hate it. I *will not* cry in front of him.

"You didn't give me a chance to explain. You know me,

Sybil. Does this bullshit sound like something I would want for you?"

Hope can be the cruelest of the emotions; it's there one second and gone the next. "I thought I knew you... but I need you to answer one question. Did you know this might happen?"

His lips thin, and a moment of hesitation passes over his gaze. He doesn't even need to say it, but he does. "Yes."

"That's all I need to know."

I brush past him, intent on leaving him in my past, but he's not giving up so easily. He walks alongside me.

"I fucked up and set us on a path I never should've even considered, but I wasn't thinking clearly."

I scoff. "Yeah, Perry told me all about how you blame me for your leg. It breaks my heart, Cooper. It really does. I'm so sorry for my part in that day, but that was an accident, and what you did to me was purposely malicious."

He reaches for my arm, but I shove him off.

"Don't touch me."

My eyes scan the street for an open cab, but so far, no luck. I need to get out of here. I should've called a car. I'd take the nearest subway, but Cooper would just follow me down there.

"I can fix this," he says. "I *will* fix this."

My voice wobbles. "Cooper, you cost me The Laurence Foundation."

He knows how much it means to me.

Sometimes broken things can't be fixed.

"This is you and me, Sybil. This is us. We're Sybil and Cooper. We'll be okay. We have to be."

He tries to touch me again, and I stop, turning on him, my hands balled into fists at my sides. "You were my *best friend*."

"You were my best friend when you hurt me," he says, "but I forgave you."

"Don't—"

"We're *together*, you and me. I never thought I would be so lucky to have you, but it happened. I went to my dad to stop all this as soon as we returned to the city. He said he would. I didn't know he had already involved Vale or the full extent of their plans."

That gives me pause.

Cooper sees that as an in. "You love me. I know you love me."

I can't deny it, but I won't confirm it, either.

"And I love you," he presses. "There's a lot I need to explain, but right now, we're short on time, and you're going to have to trust me."

I laugh. "Trust you?"

"Yes. I swore to myself long ago that if I was ever lucky enough to win you over, I would *never* lose you." His voice is raw with emotion, and I desperately want to believe him. "You think I'd let you leave me without a fight? No, Sybil. We're *not* breaking up. I'm not my brother. I can't let this be over."

I turn away, lost for words.

"I have a plan to fix this, but we need to go. We're already running late."

I close my eyes for a second, just long enough to breathe through the mix of pain and love pulsing in my chest. "Cooper, I don't know if I can do this."

"Come with me." His voice is softer this time, and there's a desperate edge I've never heard from him before. "Please. If you want to be done with me when this is over, then we can have a conversation about that, but right now, you've *got* to let me fix this. I need you by my side. I need you, Sybil, in every way. Always. But especially today."

He's earnest, his eyes open and begging. A little seed of hope grows in my heart. He watches me—waiting—not touching me. Against my better judgment, I nod.

Sixty-Six

S ybil
    Present - Age 27

Before I know it, we're riding up the elevator of Laurence International. Cooper stands close. "You may want to know… I've already spoken with your mother. She's aware of what's about to happen."

I blink at him. "You did what?"

"I was at home and deep in my work last night. I obviously missed a lot. As soon as I realized what went down, you had already blocked me." He raises an eyebrow. "I called your mother, and she helped me set up this meeting."

My mouth dries, and I just stand there, scrambling to find a response. The words are caught somewhere between my heart and my brain.

"I'm never going to let you down again, Sybil." He squeezes my hand. "I promise. Even if you *did* block my number. I almost bought another phone solely so I could call you."

444

I frown. "It was hours before I made that decision. I went to your office, but you weren't there."

Dark shadows pass over his face. "You must have come by when I stepped out. I never would've ignored you."

"Your dad and Lance were there—"

"I know," he cuts me off, his tone angry again. "Believe me. My *father* already got an earful about the shit he pulled."

I want to ask for more information, but the elevator doors open, and he leads me to the large boardroom.

Several faces I know well turn to us at once.

My thoughts spiral in a million directions, and I swallow hard. My cheeks prickle with embarrassment—they all know I lost *Top of the World*. I wasn't ready to face the Laurence company board, let alone my mother, his father, and Lance Vale. Even the tv-screen is lit on the far wall, with people who've video-conferenced in. What could Cooper have to say to all these people?

"Cooper," I whisper under my breath, but he steps forward, immediately taking control of the room.

"Thank you for meeting this morning. We are busy people, so I'll keep this brief."

"Son, what is this about?" A crease forms between Conrad's eyebrows. He's sitting next to Lance Vale, and I can barely look at them without wanting to scream obscenities.

"We've already done the emergency-coup meeting thing," Vale adds, his glare heavy in my direction. "It didn't work, remember?"

Mom stiffens, turning on the two men. "Shut your mouths for once."

"As I was saying..." Cooper continues, trying to hide his grin. "I'm going to make this brief. A few months ago, you were given proof Lance Vale had hacked into Sybil's work computer and was trying to sabotage her, but most of you choose to sweep that under the rug."

One of our most Vale-sympathetic board members clears his throat. "That investigation is ongoing."

The corner of Coop's lips rise. "Your investigation is a joke."

The board member moves to stand up. "I don't have to be here for this. I'm late for my tee-time."

"Sit your ass down, Kristof," Mom chastises, and the man's face turns pink.

Oh wow, Mom is *on* one. I've never seen her so pissed.

"Thank you, Amelia," Cooper says, turning to Kristof and the others. "Your investigation didn't prove Vale's guilt, since your investigation was biased from the start. Too many of you are in Vale's pockets, and I would wager to bet he's either blackmailed you or paid you off to get his way. If he hasn't done those things yet, trust me, he's working on it."

"Excuse me?" Vale jumps to his feet, index finger pointing at Cooper. "This is baseless slander."

"You better be able to prove these claims, son," Conrad adds.

"Oh, I can, and sorry, I didn't mean to say I would bet. I meant to say I *can prove* Lance Vale has paid off or blackmailed half the people in this room, and he's working on the rest. If he hasn't gotten you under his thumb, watch out. He'll sabotage you the way he's done to Sybil."

"You have a lot of nerve—"

"I took it upon myself to start my own investigation weeks ago, and I have definitive *proof*."

The room goes dead silent, and several pairs of eyes widen in Vale's direction. The tone shifts completely.

"When I learned how you all failed Sybil weeks ago, I took it upon myself to hire the best hacking and private detective team in the business. I spared no expense, because I was certain they'd find something, and I was right."

"That's illegal," Vale hisses.

Cooper chuckles. "You want to talk to me about illegal? Everything you've done and all the shit you've pulled on these people?" He surveys the group. "Things I'm sure you all would hate to be made public. What would the investors think? Let alone your friends and families."

Murmurs of outrage ripple through the room, and I lock eyes with Mom, who offers a playful wink. She's eating this up.

Cooper yells over the noise, and the group silences. "God, you people really need to learn active listening."

"Cooper," his father growls. "Be careful."

"I'm done being careful," he replies. "I gave you a chance to change directions, and you didn't, so here we are."

"What do you want from us?" the chairwoman asks.

"Either you release Lance Vale from his position at Laurence International and never allow him to return, or all your dirty little secrets and bribes with the man will be made available to everyone else in this room. Who knows what could leak." He pauses for dramatic effect, and I stare at him in awe. "The choice is yours."

SIXTY-SEVEN

S ybil
    Present - Age 27

Less than a minute after Cooper's ultimatum, the board unanimously votes to remove Lance.

"Do this, and *I'll* be the one to share all your secrets," Lance fumes.

Cooper lets out a sardonic laugh. "You're admitting to blackmail now? Don't worry, I've got plenty on you, too. Don't think my investigators didn't do a *thorough* job. I'm sure your financial crimes alone would be enough to send you to prison. How about we all agree to keep our mouths shut, huh?"

Vale's lips press together, his face turning purple. When security is called, nobody comes to his defense. He leaves on his own accord, a few obscenities thrown our way at the last second.

For the first time today, I laugh.

The meeting disperses, and Cooper asks me, my mom, and Conrad to stay behind. My emotions are spinning in every

448

direction, racing through me one after the next. I'm shocked that this happened, elated Lance is gone, thrilled I still have a place at Laurence, but hurt that Cooper and his father took me down in the first place.

"There's more," Coop says with a little frown. "I think we should sit."

I assumed the exchange of ownership equity is what Cooper wanted to talk about, but his voice is thick with regret, and my stomach drops. We all take a seat at the far corner of the conference table, eyes on Cooper.

"Vale was willing to do anything to get what he wanted. He blackmailed, bribed, and fabricated lies to claw his way to the top. He had his sights set high for a long time. I'm sure he was elated when Gregory passed away."

Mom looks stricken. "Gregory trusted him."

Cooper shakes his head. "I'm not sure he did."

"What do you mean?"

"It wasn't just some of the people in this room Vale blackmailed. I have proof he did it to your husband as well."

Conrad and my mother exchange a glance, then Conrad turns on his son with a scowl. "What did Vale do?"

Cooper sighs. "Lance found out about Arden and used the information for his benefit."

"How?" Despite her rigid posture and stoic face, Mom sounds absolutely wrecked.

"I'll email you the proof, and it takes a bit of logic to put it all together, but it's pretty clear Vale wanted to weaken the partnership between King and Laurence. What better way than to reveal a deep, dark secret?"

"Like an affair," I whisper, my stomach immediately souring.

Cooper nods. "Your father was willing to agree to some

pretty awful things in order to keep the truth about Arden's paternity a secret."

Mom sighs. "He must have harbored a lot of shame for having children with me while simultaneously getting my sister pregnant."

My heart hurts, knowing our past and everything Dad tried to keep hidden. He loved someone he couldn't have, and the consequences eventually took his life.

"Where are you going with this?" Conrad asks, but his usual bravado is gone. He's a husk of his normal self.

Cooper turns to his father. "Mom *never* had an affair with Gregory Laurence."

Shock—pure and utter and complete shock.

We blink like goldfish, our mouths hanging open.

"The whole thing was fabricated by Lance Vale to get Laurence and King to stop doing business together," Cooper explains. "It helped him leverage his position within Laurence and get to COO faster."

"Oh God," Mom whispers. "We were played."

Cooper nods. "What do you think would it take to get someone like Gregory to agree to such a damaging lie? To give up his best friend and business partner? To jeopardize his family?"

"Arden," I whisper.

Arden was the pawn used by powerful men that none of us knew was even on the game board.

"Lance Vale did a lot of digging on Gregory, looking for a pain point to exploit, and he found exactly what he needed."

Conrad drops his head into his hands. I wonder what he's thinking. For years he believed his late wife had cheated on him with his best friend, and now Cooper is saying that never actually happened.

"Here was this girl in foster care, living in Massachusetts

that Gregory had fathered with his wife's late drug addicted sister," Cooper says. "As hard as the fabricated affair with my mother was on his family and marriage and business, Gregory knew the *Arden* secret getting out would have much harsher consequences, so he let Lance manipulate him into going with the lie."

Mom nods, her voice hollow. "I forgave him for Victoria. It was hard, but I forgave him..." She wipes a stray tear from her face, her wrinkles deepening, as she continues. "But after he'd kept my sister's only child a secret from me, I've been angry. It's been over a year, and I still haven't forgiven him for that."

Dad willingly allowed Arden to grow up in poverty without a family—something Mom *never* would have accepted had she known. I'm sure he felt deep shame about his actions later in life. Either way, he was going to get revealed for having an affair, but I guess the real one carried more risk than the lie. I wonder if he regretted his choices?

"He was right to assume I would never forgive him for it," Mom goes on, her voice sharp. "Even though he's dead, I don't think I can, and I don't think I have to."

I take Mom's hand, my vision blurring with unshed tears. I know exactly how she feels.

"I don't think I can forgive him for that either, but I can move past it. We both can."

I'm not going to let any of this ruin my life, and I hope she won't let it ruin the rest of hers. Mom squeezes my hand, and I know she gets it. She's in the same place I am—angry with someone we desperately miss.

Conrad's head is still in his hands. This is a lot to process, and I think the man might be in shock. As far as I know, he was a devoted husband. Now he's on wife number three, not seeming to care about his love life the way he did with Victoria.

He's a hard-ass businessman in every sense of the word, and

I'm livid at him for what he pulled with *Top of the World*. But I can recognize the pain written all over his face.

I feel sorry for him. Nobody deserves this.

"You're sure she didn't cheat?" He finally looks up, watery gaze on his son.

"I have plenty of proof. I'll send everything over." Cooper's voice cracks. "She never lied."

"I'll kill him." Conrad flies out of his chair, his face blotchy and his eyes wild.

"I felt the same when I found out," Cooper replies. "I thought you might beat the life out of him right here in front of a dozen witnesses, which is why I had him sent away before I told you."

Conrad strides from the room, presumably to hunt Lance down and beat the shit out of him. Or maybe he's done showing vulnerability and needs privacy. Either way, I think I know exactly how he's feeling.

Duped.

Stupid.

Exposed.

Angry.

But mostly... *relieved*.

Mom squeezes my hand again and stands. "I'll leave you two to talk," she says, slipping out the door.

Even though Cooper is sitting right next to me, I can't look at him. A heavy, all-consuming silence falls on us, and I stare at my empty hands, wondering what in the world to do with them.

"I'm so sorry, Sybil."

I force myself to look at him, to search his gaze for answers, hoping for something I can trust and hang onto, but I don't even know what I'm looking for. My trust has been tested and shaken again and again, and I don't think I can take it anymore.

"Why didn't you tell me what was going on?" I demand. "You let everything happen without warning."

His chest rises and falls with a shaky breath. "I was afraid. You've left me before. You make walking away look so easy, and I... I can't handle that."

"So that gave you a right to lie to me?" I shake my head. "You broke my trust, Cooper. And I'm expected to forgive you and get over it? Just like that? How can I be with someone I can't trust? I don't know how to do that."

Fear ripples across his features as he awkwardly slides to his knees in front of me, gripping my thighs tightly between his large palms.

"I'm so fucking sorry. I don't want to lose you." His face falls into my lap, and he growls in frustration before gazing up with adoring eyes. "I love you so fucking much. Please give me another chance. This is me begging."

Tears fall, hot and wet. "Don't do this," I respond. I'm so tired of being emotionally manipulated by everyone and can't handle much more, especially not from the man I love.

He swallows hard, looking at me like I'm something to be worshipped. "Last night I almost slipped up and went to the liquor store, but I didn't. I have to be sober for you. I'll do anything for you."

"That's not fair. I can't be responsible for your sobriety."

He shakes his head, dark hair falling across his devastating eyes. "I'd *never* put that on you. That's not what I'm saying. If you want to end things with me, I'll respect that, and my choices with my addiction are mine alone, and I can't promise anyone I'll never make mistakes with it again. But I can promise to always do my best." He lets out a long sigh. "Between the release that alcohol can give me and the life I can have with you, I picked *you* last night, and I'll pick you every time."

My heart cracks, and I want so badly to let him in, to kiss

him, to love him unconditionally and accept every flaw. But I'm not sure if I'm ready, and if there's one thing I have to have with Cooper, it's authenticity.

"We should take a break. I'm not saying we're over forever, but I need some space to think about what I want to do next. Can you give me that?"

His face crumbles, and I can tell he wants to argue, but eventually, he nods. "I'll give you anything you want."

What I want is him, but what I need is to be alone. If I decide to stay with Cooper, I'm going to have to trust him fully. Right now, I'm not ready to give him that.

Sixty-Eight

C ooper
     Present - Age 27

"If you love her, let her go, and if she really loves you, she'll come back."

That right there is the shit advice my father gave to me when I went to him, begging not to go through with our plan. At first, he told me it couldn't be undone, then he said that garbage about letting her go, and finally he realized I was dead serious about making Sybil my wife one day. He told me not to worry. He *claimed* he would handle it.

I should've fucking worried.

I ache to follow Sybil home, demand we work things out, but I respect her enough to give her the time she's asked for.

She'll come back, right? I don't even want to think about what it will feel like to lose her again. The idea of it is soul-crushing.

I head to Arden and Ethan's penthouse and fill them in. They take it as well as can be expected. It's not every day you find out your mother never actually had an affair, and it's certainly not every day you learn you were a pawn in a large blackmail scheme because your uncle who was actually your father was willing to go to great lengths to hide your existence.

Ethan and Arden are pros at handling the drama, which makes sense given their history. I shouldn't be surprised they don't let this news rattle them.

"So you're pretty pissed at Dad right now, huh?" Ethan asks.

"Obviously," I drawl. "He fucked me over. I confronted him as soon as I found out what went down, and he said he was already too far down the path with Vale."

"Do you think your dad would be willing to make some changes to make it up to you?" Arden asks, and Ethan gives her the side-eye.

"Probably... Do you have something in mind?"

She locks eyes with Ethan, who shakes his head. "They'll never go for it."

"Go for what?"

Arden lifts a shoulder. "It can't hurt to ask."

"Have you met our father?"

"Want to clue me in?" I say, waving my hand for attention.

Ethan sighs. "I'm pretty unhappy with my career. I want to pursue something else without losing access to the trust fund."

I blink. Is he for real? "You don't want to be CEO of King Media?"

Ethan shakes his head. "I think you'd be better at it. You actually like the job."

I mean, it's true that I love our work, but I had no idea Ethan felt differently.

"What other career are you wanting to pursue?" It's hard to

wrap my mind around him doing something else. This has been the plan since birth.

His cheeks go pink, and I swear my jaw actually drops. When I have ever seen my confident and broody brother ever look so sheepish?

Arden's smile is beaming. "You can tell him."

"I was thinking medicine. Maybe oncology. I couldn't save Mom, but maybe I could save someone like her, ya know?"

"That's amazing, Ethan. We should talk to Dad about it, for sure."

They both visibly brighten, and even though getting our father on board might be next to impossible, this feels like it's going to happen.

We end up eating Chinese takeout at their place, and then I slip over to my penthouse next door. It's getting dark, and I should be exhausted after the day I've had, but I'm buzzing with energy and end up pacing the length of my family room, my mind whirling with thoughts of Sybil.

It's only been half a day, but I miss her already. I want her here with me. I want to kiss her and hold her and be secure in the knowledge that she loves me as much as I love her.

Something tickles the back of my mind—an itch I can't seem to scratch. I feel like there's something I'm missing.

Something important.

I veer toward my office, sliding into my chair and loading up my computer. It's strange being home in my penthouse after it was taken over by *Top of the World,* even stranger seeing my house on national television every week.

All my things have returned to their rightful places, but I feel like a completely different person. I recognize this house, but the man I was six months ago is unrecognizable.

My private investigator sent me a massive document about

Lance Vale, complete with the numerous files Lance kept on people, and I load it onto my computer screen. I have no doubt I'll have many demands to delete any possible blackmail fodder I could have over board members. I'm more than happy to do that. Never have I, and never *will* I, operate like Lance Vale.

I scroll through the endless documents, my mind quickly categorizing everything, searching for something still unknown.

I'm missing something. I know I'm missing something.

Then I see it.

My mouth goes dry, my heart races, and my stomach completely flips. How could I be so stupid? I cannot believe I didn't see this before, didn't realize the obvious.

Fuck!

I jump from my desk, not even bothering to turn off my computer, and sprint out of the penthouse, texting Sybil as I ride the elevator downstairs.

Cooper: Are you okay? I need to know you're okay. There's something we need to discuss asap.

The text returns as green instead of blue, indicating she's still got my number blocked.

There's not a lot of traffic tonight, and it only takes ten minutes to drive to her loft in SoHo. I bribe her doorman to call her down to talk to me.

She's not home.

Double fuck.

I pace outside her building, my mind racing in a million different directions, picturing every worst-case scenario. I need help—*she* might need help. I yank out my phone, about to call Arden to see if she can get in touch with Sybil on my behalf, when a text pings through from an unknown number.

Unknown: You really think I would let you ruin everything I've worked for?

The moment I read it, I clock what this is: a threat. Another message quickly follows with a location. It's a private residence, not far from the city.

I jump into my car and race to the location. On the way, another text comes through from the same number.

Unknown: Don't inform anyone where you are if you care about Sybil's life.

At the next red light, I quickly respond.

Cooper: I won't, and I'm on my way.

I screenshot the text and send it to my father and Ethan, along with a message.

Cooper: Sybil's in trouble. I'm on my way to help her. If you don't hear from me in half an hour, then send the police.

I put my phone on *do-not-disturb* after that. They'll try to talk logic into me, and this doesn't call for logic—it calls for action. At least I thought to bring my handgun before I left the penthouse. I never thought I'd have to use this thing, but after Sybil got attacked by that creep, I renewed my license and have been bringing it when we're in public. Not to mention, I haven't been letting her out of sight when we're not at work.

Except I did let her out of my sight, and now she's in trouble.

I arrive at a grand home surrounded by a large wall and a gated entrance. A security guard lets me through, and I race up the driveway, parking and shoving my gun under my belt.

I step out, and a second security guard approaches. The first one looked more like a rent-a-cop, but this one has some serious military energy. "I'm going to pat you down for weapons, so if you've got something, better remove it now. Also, you're going to need to leave your phone with me."

With a frustrated sigh, I remove the gun and hand it over with my phone, hoping he doesn't notice how badly my hands are shaking. If something happens to Sybil, I'll never forgive myself.

"Mr. Vale will see you now."

I should've known I was dealing with a dangerous man when Sybil got attacked at the premier. The whole thing was planned. He wanted to hurt her then, and my gut says he intends to hurt her again.

SIXTY-NINE

S ybil
Present - Age 27

I shouldn't have come here, but when I got that text from Jonathan Vale with the video message attached, I knew I didn't have a choice.

I thought I was going to Jonathan's house to speak with him alone, but turns out, that was a setup. Now, I'm sitting across from Lance Vale and his nephew *at Lance's house*, with a gun casually pointed at me.

We're sitting in Lance's home office like this is some kind of business deal and not a hostage/blackmail situation. He's on one side of the desk, and I'm on the other. His nephew lounges on a loveseat to my left, like he doesn't have a care in the world.

"We only wanna work something out," Jonathan says, flashing a sickly smile. "Don't be so obstinate. You don't have a lot of choices, honey."

He winks, and I grimace. "If you think I have that kind of sway with the board, you're delusional."

Lance leans back in his chair, voice cold, the butt of his gun tapping against his desk. "They will listen to you because you're a Laurence, and if they won't listen to you, they'll listen to your mother."

"Why?" Jonathan snorts. "They're just trophies. She needs a man to speak for her."

I give him a dark glare. "I don't need a man."

"You need Cooper," he challenges. "You're a slut who sleeps around and had an affair with your co-producer. Pretty sure you'd like to keep that private, wouldn't you?"

Lance grins and nods at his nephew. "She's always cared about her privacy."

And therein lies the problem...

The video message that got me here contained far more than I expected. It's a mix of moments I want to keep private, starting with the day on Nantucket when Gloria confronted me about Benton, and ending with footage of me and Cooper having sex on the beach. In between are lots of stolen kisses between the two of us.

I want to scream, knowing someone was filming those private moments. "You guys are sick for filming those things."

Jonathan and Lance both roll their eyes, and I'm forced to bite my tongue. They had someone on the crew working for them, and I want to know who.

The sharp edge of desperation hangs in the air like a battle ax about to fall.

I'm desperate for my private life to stay private, and they're dead set on using me to fix their mess. How the hell am I supposed to convince the board to reinstate Vale? Cooper already revealed Vale's true colors. These men will never work at Laurence International again.

And my private moments will end up on some disgusting porn website for public fodder.

Fucking fantastic.

My thoughts return to the night on the beach. Not only was it my first time with Cooper, but it was the first time he'd had been with a woman since getting his prosthetic leg. That was a special moment and not something for anyone else to know about, let alone watch.

I fucking hate these men.

"I have a great idea," Jonathan says, smiling like a viper. "If threatening you and your little boyfriend isn't enough to convince you to do the right thing, how about we add someone else to the mix? Hmm, maybe your other boyfriend, Benton?"

I straighten and swallow hard. "What do you mean?"

"Well, it's simple," Lance says. "We got our hands on the full, unedited footage from *Top of the World*. Since you wrongfully removed me from my position with the foundation, I've spent weeks combing through the footage. I think America would love to see exactly how much of a jackass New York City's favorite hockey player really is."

My stomach twists.

"It's at a new network," I say carefully.

Lance grins. "Yes, thanks to my connections. As I recall, you're the one who said sex sells. We have all the footage ready to go. All I have to do is send one email, and I guarantee we'll twist everything needed to make Benton public enemy number one within the month."

I wince. I want to help Benton, but not at the price they want me to pay. I can't call another board meeting, and I can't change the outcome of the last one. Despite everything they have on me, their time for blackmail is over. They don't know it yet, but I'm not going to change my mind. If they want to share my sex life with the world, so be it. If they want to screw over

Benton, it's out of my control, and I'll do everything in my power to help him rehab his image when this is all over.

My eyes flick to the gun, and I swallow hard. It's got to be for show, right? Lance wouldn't actually *hurt* me.

He'd end up in prison, because while he may have wealth and influence, so does my family. It's not like he could kill me and get away with it. My phone was on me when I drove over here, pinging off cell phone towers.

"I'm curious," Lance says, "why did you even come here today if you have no intention of negotiating? Did you think you could cry your crocodile tears and expect me to feel sorry for you? I'm not your daddy. You have no influence on me."

Coming here was obviously a mistake, but I was hoping to protect not only my future at Laurence International but the privacy of my intimate moments with the man I love.

"I thought you'd be reasonable," I try. "I don't have enough sway to change the board's mind after everything that's happened. Ask for something that's within my capabilities to give you."

Lance's tone drips with condescension. "You were never the brightest crayon in the box, were you? The idea that you did as well as you did boggles my mind."

Jonathan laughs. "It's because she's a rich white woman."

"And you're rich white guys, so what's your point?"

Lance's smile turns razor sharp. "We didn't actually bring *you* here to negotiate. We already know you don't have any power. We only brought you here, because we need Cooper."

My stomach drops.

If there's one person Lance King wants revenge on right now, it's got to be Cooper.

Maybe the gun's not for me after all.

I grit my teeth, hating that I fell for this trap.

"Speaking of which," Lance says smoothly, "he just arrived."

My heart slams against my ribs, and tears prick my eyes. It doesn't matter that I'm mad at Cooper—I love him, and I don't want him to get hurt.

Lance grips his gun tighter, like he knows damn well he might have to use it.

A security guard deposits Cooper into the room, closing us inside, and those eyes I love so much sweep over the scene—first going to me, then to the gun, then back again.

In less than a second, we have an entire conversation without saying a word. He's telling me to stay calm and not to do anything stupid, and I'm telling him he never should've come here, that this was a mistake.

A big one.

Cooper, still standing in the doorway, turns on Vale. "What do you want?"

"Cutting right to the chase, I see. Alright. I want my rightful and well-earned position at the top of Laurence, but if that's not possible, then I want your father to step aside and give me King as my consolation prize."

He's out of his mind. I'd laugh if I wasn't so scared.

"And if you don't get your way?"

"You don't want to know," Jonathan interjects, and Cooper shoots him a glare.

"Don't interrupt the grownups," Cooper snaps.

Jonathan's eyes go wide. "How dare you speak to me that way."

"Shut up, Jonny," Lance says. "For the love of God, let me handle this. I promised you'd walk into a high-power job after graduation, so let me make that happen."

Jonathan sinks into himself, pouting like a child.

"And if I don't get you into a position I have no authority over?" Coop barks out a laugh and strides farther into the room, sitting in the chair next to me.

"Hey, baby," he says, leaning over and dropping a quick kiss to my lips, leaving me completely speechless. "Missed you."

Vale slams his fist onto the desk, grabbing the gun. "Is this a joke to you? Pay attention."

Cooper turns on him with a raised eyebrow. "Put that gun down if you want to talk. You think I'd be stupid enough to come here without informing someone first? The police will arrive soon if my father doesn't hear from me. So why don't we get this over with, so I can take my girl home?"

Vale's eyes bulge. "You don't think I'll hurt her? I warned you I would if you—"

"I know you'd hurt her," he growls, leaning across the desk, seemingly unaffected by the gun pointed at his chest. "I know you hired muscle the night Sybil got attacked. Tell me, were you trying to kill her, or are you a sick fuck who enjoys battering women?"

A jolt of shock collides with memories of that night. Vale hired that man to hurt me? "Oh my God," I whisper. "You tried to have me killed."

Vale frowns. "Of course not."

Cooper's voice doesn't waver. "Don't lie. I know it was you. I saw the transaction and—"

Jonathan interrupts with a cackle. "Sorry guys, but I have to take credit for that one. I used my uncle's contact and account."

"You what?" Lance glares at his nephew.

"I thought Sybil deserved a little roughing up after she fired me." He gives me another wink, and Cooper's hands ball into fists. "I was there, you know. In the crowd. You should've seen your face. Hilarious."

Cooper looks like he's two seconds away from jumping onto Jonathan and strangling him.

"Jonny, are you kidding me?" Lance demands. "I gave you

access to my resources, but that doesn't mean you get to do whatever you want."

"I'm your heir and prodigy."

"Not if you don't keep your ass in line."

Jonathan raises a mocking eyebrow. "You're surprised I'd resort to violence? Don't be." He pulls a gun from a holster under his lapel and points it right at me. "I learned a long time ago you have to be willing to resort to any means necessary to get what you want. You taught me that, Uncle. Don't look so surprised."

My heart rockets. Is this how I die?

Boom!

The gun fires followed by a thud.

But I'm fine, and so is Cooper.

Lance's body slumps on his desk, crimson blood pooling around his head.

A scream rips from my throat.

SEVENTY

S ybil
Present - Age 27

"Well, shit. I may have underestimated this situation," Cooper deadpans.

Jonathan's sharp laugh cuts through the room. "*Shit* is right. Didn't think I had it in me, did you?"

I definitely didn't.

"Don't move," Jonathan orders, stepping toward his uncle's body.

I know what he's looking for before he even moves. The confirmation comes when he crouches and snatches up the gun, never taking his eyes off us.

"I'm going to tell you exactly how this is gonna go," he says, voice steady, almost amused. "One wrong move, and one of you is getting a bullet in the brain. Got it?"

"Are you sure you want to do this?" Cooper's voice is even

and controlled. "You just killed a man. Now you're threatening to kill two more people. I already told you the cops are going to show any minute."

Jonathan shrugs, unfazed. "The cops won't hurt my plan."

Cooper looks impressed, but I know he's faking it. "Alright then, you sound like you're pretty smart. Let's hear it."

Cooper's calm is a facade. I know him better than anybody, and he's terrified. My body is shaking, shock ripping through me in sickening waves. Cooper sits perfectly still, but his hand—the one closest to me—trembles slightly.

"You're going to give me exactly what I want," Jonathan says, his eyes burning into Cooper. "Or your girlfriend dies. Got it?"

Cooper nods. "I got it. You want a job, is that right? Well, I gotta warn you, working for the man sucks sometimes, but if you really want it, you can take mine."

Jonathan laughs, full of scorn. "You think I want to work at your stupid company? That I want to 'work for the man,' as you say? I never wanted that. My *uncle* wanted that. He didn't have the vision I have. He didn't get it."

Jonathan's eyes gleam as he continues. "I never looked up to my uncle, you know. He's a corporate bootlicker. I look up to people like your father, who built King Media from nothing and became a billionaire. That's what I'm gonna do."

There it is. The delusion. The goddamn podcast-fueled fantasy so many young men these days easily adopt, thinking that becoming a billionaire is simply something they can work hard for. Extreme wealth doesn't work that way. A billion dollars takes more than work—it's like winning the lottery, only harder and rarer.

Jonathan thinks that because a handful of powerful and well-connected men have struck gold and built empires, he's destined to be next. I'd love to burst his bubble, but I know better than to taunt the man holding two guns.

"How exactly do Sybil and I factor into your plans?"

"One of you is going to take the fall for my dear uncle's death, here."

Okay, so he really is crazy. We'll tell the cops the truth later, after the threat is gone.

Jonathan tilts his chin. "Who's gonna take the blame?"

Cooper's hand shoots up. "That would be me."

I shake my head. "Cooper, don't—"

"Do you have a fucking death wish?" Jonathan sneers at me. "Let your man be a man and protect you for once. God, I'm so tired of all this feminist-woke-bullshit. You're infected, do you know that? You're fucking infected. You don't even have to work, you're already filthy rich, and yet you want to work rather than accepting the role you were bred for? You think it's okay to take jobs from deserving men like me who actually have real skills?"

He shakes his head, heat rising in his cheeks. "Be grateful for Cooper. He's doing the right thing. I don't want to hear another word out of your pretty mouth. Let the men take care of business, and shut the fuck up."

He's completely unhinged. Cooper's face is turning blotchy, and I know he's feeling everything I'm feeling, punctuated with rage.

I nod at Jonathan, secure in the fact that we'll handle this with the police later. Once we explain everything, they'll believe us over this lunatic, won't they?

"I'm gonna hand you the gun now," Jonathan continues, looking at Cooper. "You know, the one you used to kill my uncle who was threatening your girlfriend."

Cooper's eyes brighten in anticipation, and Jonathan snorts.

"Don't worry, the gun only had one bullet in the chamber,

so it's useless now. When the police get here, you'll both confirm Cooper tackled me, took my gun, and killed my uncle. He was going to kill me, too, but, lucky me, with only one bullet in the chamber, I was able to get away and retrieve my uncle's weapon to defend myself."

My mouth falls open.

Jonathan is smarter than I thought.

His lies might actually be believable.

"I have proof you two are a couple and very much in *love*," he says, drawing the word "love" out like it's a joke. "So, of course, you'll say whatever you had to say to protect each other. The truth is—according to the police—you came here to talk to us, you got mad, you took it too far, and you're ultimately responsible for my uncle's death."

Jonathan dangles the gun in front of Cooper's face like a carrot. When Cooper takes it, my heart drops. He's really going along with this. He could spend the rest of his life in prison for a crime he didn't commit.

"Prison is better than watching him kill you," Cooper says, looking at me like the sun rises and sets in my face. "I love you, Sybil. I'll do anything for you."

I'd do anything for him, too, and I shake my head with tears running down my face. "Please don't."

A commotion sounds outside the door, and the security guard knocks, then speaks through the panel. "The police are here. What should I do?"

Jonathan's grin is barely contained, but his voice shakes with distress. "Send them in! Hurry, my uncle's been shot!"

The guard shuffles off.

"I can't wait to get my hands on the Vale fortune. I'm the sole heir, you know. Auntie and Uncle never had any children. I stand to end up with millions in seed money for my company."

He takes his eyes off us for a second to smile fondly at his uncle's body—that's when Cooper lunges, tackling Jonathan to the floor.

Boom!

The other gun fires.

"I'll kill you for this," Cooper growls, pinning Jonathan to the floor. "You think I'm taking the fall for you? That you can hurt my woman? You're out of your goddamn mind!"

I scramble to my feet, searching for guns and more blood—God, please, no blood.

Jonathan struggles, but Cooper has him locked down right as the police burst in.

"Did you hear that?" Cooper calls out to them. "You hear how excited he is about that 'seed money' he's getting as his uncle's only heir? He fucking killed the guy not five minutes ago!"

They move quickly, apprehending both men.

The security guard from before walks in the room. "I heard it all. It's the truth. He killed my employer," he says, pointing at Jonathan.

Thank God he's able to corroborate on our story. The tension that's wound tight around my lungs slackens, and I can breathe again.

"No," Jonathan tries, color draining from his face. "They're lying!"

Conrad King sweeps into the room, his eyes wild with fear as he takes in the scene, and my breathing relaxes even more. As much as I can't stand Conrad and as angry as I am at him, I know he'll take care of Cooper.

"Are you okay, son?" he asks between desperate panting breaths.

Cooper shrugs from between the cops who are holding him down. "Yeah, the mother fucker killed his uncle and then shot me in the leg. He just shot an expensive hunk of metal." He gives me a rakish smile, complete with a trickle of blood on his lips. "But Sybil's okay, so I'm okay."

A wave of relief washes over me, and I burst into tears.

SEVENTY-ONE

C ooper
Present - Age 27

"I'm taking you home," I tell Sybil the second we're finished giving our statements to the police. She doesn't protest, only nods numbly and lets me guide her outside to my car.

She must've taken a cab to get here, so at least I don't have to worry about getting her car back to her place. She's in no state to drive. Her tears have dried up, but a traumatized storm cloud hangs over her face.

Jonathan Vale is lucky the police showed up when they did. I was two seconds away from ending him. I've never taken a life before, but I wouldn't hesitate to end that psychopath. Nobody hurts Sybil and gets away with it.

I help her into the front seat, then swing around to the driver's side and get us the hell out of there, turning the radio on low and the air conditioning on high. It's hot out today, and she's still sweating from what happened.

"I can't believe Lance is dead," she whispers, her voice shaky.

I reach for her hand, relieved when she lets me thread my fingers through hers. "The guy made a lot of enemies over the years, and now you don't have to worry about either of those men ever coming after you again."

She swallows hard. "Wait, what about the sex tape? They had footage on us, and if the police get it—"

I shake my head. "Don't worry. I talked to my father on the way out. His people will make sure everything is deleted. Nobody will see that footage, but just in case, I'll contact my hacker to get Jonathan's computer wiped."

Illegal, but shit if I care right now.

She visibly relaxes, closing her eyes and breathing in long and slow breaths until she falls asleep.

I take my time getting her home, going the long way and being careful not to wake her. I want her to get a little extra rest. I'd carry her upstairs if she'd let me, but I know Sybil. Maybe one day she'll let me carry her over the threshold of our place after we get married, but I have to convince her of marriage first. As far as I know, she still wants space from me. I almost lost her once today, and I can't lose her again, not in any capacity of the word.

I pull up to her building, and when I stop, she startles.

"No," she gasps, sitting up straight.

"Hey, it's okay." I take her hand again. "You're home."

She blinks rapidly as everything returns. She's about to get out of the car, taking my heart with her, when she turns back. "Will you come upstairs?"

"Yes," I reply immediately.

"I... don't want to be alone right now."

"I don't want you to be alone right now, either." I clear my throat. "And I'd very much like to be the one upstairs with you."

She rolls her eyes. "I'm not talking about sex, Cooper. I'm talking about comfort. Friends?"

Friends. The word hollows my stomach and drops a big rock right in the middle.

"I'll be whatever you want me to be."

She directs me into her building's parking garage and a vacant space set aside for her unit, then leads me upstairs.

I want to hold her, touch her, kiss her, make love to her—to tell her how much she means to me and then show her without words.

But she wants a friend right now.

We step inside, and she turns on me with a lost expression.

"Cooper, are we going to be okay?"

"I know I told you I'd be whatever you want me to be, but that was a lie. I only know how to be the man who's desperately in love with you. That's all I've ever been when it comes to you. Since we were kids, even then, I loved you."

Her lips part, and her reply is featherlight. "I know."

We stand there, silence stretching between us, and she looks me up and down like she's still deciding what to do with me.

"Maybe... maybe we could take a bath?" she asks sweetly.

I smile at the idea of Sybil naked in the bathwater.

Friends don't take baths together.

I follow her to the large clawfoot tub, thanking the interior-design gods for this win. A bathtub is hard to find in the city, let alone one that can fit two people.

She turns on the water, and with her back to me, slowly strips off her clothing. Her shirt goes first, tossed to the side, then come the jeans that cling to her perfect ass. She does her bra next, adding it onto the pile and shaking out her long hair as it flows down her pale body. When she bends and slips her panties down her long legs, I nearly lose it.

She peers over her shoulder at me, a playful twinkle in her eye, and I feel like I've won.

"I'm tired of being sad," she says at last. "I want you naked."

I'm wearing my heart on my sleeve with this next question, but I have to ask it. "Do you want more than my body? Do you want me?"

She smiles. "Yes, I want you."

"As more than friends?"

"As friends *and more*."

Joy sweeps through me, and I waste no time removing my clothes. In one long stride, I go to her, wrapping my arms around her waist and letting her sway into me. Even with the damaged prosthetic, I hold her up. I don't care if my weight distribution feels off, or that it sends nerve pain through the right knee. I'll take all the pain for Sybil. Hell, I'll take a bullet for this girl. Today proved that.

"I'm so sorry, Sybil. I messed up, and I almost lost you."

"I almost lost you, too." Her voice breaks, and my heart shatters, but she puts it right back together with her next confession. "I love you. I don't ever want to be apart from you again. Love is more important than anything else, Cooper. And you're the man I'm choosing to give my heart to."

Heat flares low, and I clutch at her hips, bringing my mouth down on hers, kissing her like it's our last kiss but secure in the knowledge that it's not. She loves me. She doesn't want to be apart from me. And loving me is more important than being angry.

She's seen my shadows, my darkness, my pain and broken pieces—and she wants me, anyway.

Sybil Laurence is finally mine.

She loves me.

I work her knees wider with my thigh, and when I feel her

slick heat rubbing against me, I consider taking her right here, right now.

She pulls away with a giggle. "I think the bath is ready now."

Sure enough, the water is at the perfect height. How she was able to keep an eye on that while I was ravishing her simply won't do. I need her so completely turned on she can't think about anything else.

"Get in, baby," I say, helping her in first and following quickly after I remove the prosthetic.

She maneuvers so she's sitting on my lap, her ass pressing into my erection, and I bite down a groan while grazing on her neck.

"You're killing me," I whisper.

"Is that so?" She deliberately wiggles her ass, teasing my cock and driving me wild.

I need her desperately, but she wants to play games first, so I slip one hand around her waist, dipping my fingers between her folds. The other hand slides up to her breasts to pinch her wet nipples. My mouth closes over her tilted neck, nipping and sucking.

She lets out a breathy sigh that I match with my own needy growl.

"What do you want, baby? Let me take care of you."

"I... I... want you inside of me."

I plunge my finger into her core and hook it against her g-spot. "Like this?"

"No," she breathes. "I want to ride your dick."

I laugh, and then she arches seductively, and I'm not laughing anymore.

I flip her around, sliding her onto my cock inch by inch. We're a perfect fit. My thoughts dim as she rides me. I snap my hips up to meet each thrust. The hot water rocks with us, some of it splashing over the edges of the tub.

She's got her head thrown back, the sheen of water like condensation all over her body. Her pink nipples are peaked, and the ends of her beautiful auburn hair clump together as it sways in the water. She's a goddess, and I'm a mere man, here to worship, and when I lean forward and swirl my tongue around the altar of her breasts, the moan she releases sounds like heaven.

Hooking my hand on her neck, I bring her lips to mine and kiss her deeply while she rocks, her inner walls gripping my cock. She's tight and perfect, and it doesn't take long before we climb the mountain together, about to fling ourselves over the edge.

To fall or fly? I think both.

"Please," she begs against my mouth. "I need this. Harder. Please."

I give my goddess what she needs and thrust upward. "I know, Valentine. I got you, baby."

Thrust.

"And I know…"

Again.

"Exactly…"

Harder.

"What. You. Need."

Again. Again. Again.

She groans my name, and we jump together, a rush of pleasure racing through our veins like pure adrenaline.

We burn for each other.

Burning hot.

Coming undone.

Our connection is soul-deep, and I don't know if I believe in past lives or future ones, but I do know I never ever want to love another woman.

This is it for me. Sybil Laurence is the one, and I've always known that to be true.

She's my past, my yesterday, my now, my tomorrow.

She's my forever.

EPILOGUE

Sybil
Two Weeks Later - Age 27

The industrial art gallery gleams with polished concrete floors and soaring ceilings, every inch alive with chatter and laughter. String lights crisscross overhead like twinkling constellations, casting a soft glow over the crowd. I step back for a moment, taking it all in—the children and families mixed with the clusters of sharply dressed benefactors, everyone either marveling at the art on display, chatting, or dancing. The air is rich with the aroma of hors d'oeuvres and champagne and my heart is full.

This is my night—I pulled it off.

After pouring over every detail and dealing with the Vales' sabotage, I can't believe it's come together so perfectly. From the intricate floral centerpieces to the local jazz quartet playing in the corner, to the elegant guests, and the families we invited to join us at the event.

Everything is perfect.

It's all been made more perfect by Cooper. Despite all the trauma we've endured, we've both grown so much. We've killed the toxic parts of ourselves, broken the patterns that were hurting us, and healed so much pain along the way.

A server passes by with a tray of champagne, and I grab a flute.

My fingers tremble slightly, not from nerves, but from the sheer magnitude of our donations tonight. We've always done a lot, but after a record-breaking night, we can do so much more than before. We're going to change so many more lives.

I glance at Cooper standing near the bar in his tailored suit. His dark wavy hair is a little tousled, and when he turns to catch my eye, my heart swells. A warm, private smile curves those lips I love so much, and I smile right back.

Everything about him is something to love.

Miriam's voice pulls me to the party. She's holding a microphone up front, her silver hair catching the light as she calls me over. Anticipation races to my nerve endings. I wasn't expecting this. I'm happy behind the scenes, moving in silence, making things come together without needing praise.

Weaving through the crowd, I join her under the spotlight, beaming at the crowd. I'm so damn grateful for all the donations we've collected.

"Before we wrap up tonight's program, I have a couple of announcements to make," Miriam says, and my heart flutters. I know it's coming, but the moment is so surreal. "First, we have to thank Sybil Laurence for this incredible night." She pats me lightly on the shoulder. "It wouldn't have been possible without her tireless dedication, creativity, passion, and perseverance in the face of adversity." *If only they knew.* "And I'm excited to announce we've beat all previous records, having raised over fifty million dollars that will go directly to deserving children and families all across this country."

The crowd erupts into applause, and my cheeks flush. I scan the room, searching for Cooper, to find him standing next to my family and watching me with so much pride it makes my chest ache.

"And second," Miriam continues, her voice softening, "as many of you know, I'll be retiring at the end of this month. I couldn't be prouder to announce that Sybil will be stepping into my shoes and taking on the role as President of The Laurence Foundation."

The room blurs as the crowd breaks into applause again, louder this time. I cover my mouth with one hand, over-whelmed by the wave of emotions crashing over me. This is what I've been working toward, and I know I had a head start. I know I had privilege and help, but I worked hard for this.

Damn it, I'm going to do an amazing job.

Chandler stands next to Mom with his hands over his head as he claps and cheers louder than anyone else. Did my parents know that having a child with down syndrome would one day lead to all this? That Chandler would inspire so many people and be the catalyst for one of the country's biggest special needs nonprofits to receive much needed funding? I'd do anything for that kid. I'm so damn lucky to have him in my life for so many reasons, not only this one, though this one is pretty great.

Miriam leans in, whispering, "You've earned this, Sybil. Every bit of it."

I blink away tears as I step forward to say a few words of thanks, and then my time in the spotlight is over.

The music plays, and after chatting with a few people offering their congratulations, Cooper swoops in.

"Let's dance," he says, and I gladly let him lead me away.

I rest my head on his shoulder and smile, feeling happier than I've felt in ages. This night couldn't be more perfect.

"Hey you," I say, leaning to look him in the eyes. "How much of that fifty million did you contribute?"

He smirks. "It's a secret."

I roll my eyes. "Is that so?"

"Yup. Anonymous donation."

I snort. "Well, I heard we got our largest anonymous donation in foundation history tonight. You wouldn't happen to know anything about that, would you?"

"All I know is the woman I love is building something extraordinary, and I'm a very wealthy man who intends to support her."

I tut, but I can't be mad.

"I have something else to tell you," he says, his tone not so light anymore. "It's about Ethan."

I turn to look over at where Ethan and Arden are dancing. "What is it?"

"Ethan has expressed unhappiness working at King Media. Frankly, he doesn't want this career."

I cough on a gasp. "What?"

I was with Ethan all through college and saw how hard he worked, how intent he was on being the best, on making his father proud and becoming a force of business.

"Arden really changed him for the better," Cooper explains. "You know our dad had that dumb clause in our trust fund contract stating we had to work for him or else we would lose everything, right?" *Oh boy, don't I know it.* "Long story short, Ethan and I went to our father and told him I'll be taking over as CEO for King Media when the time comes, and Ethan is leaving the company next year to attend medical school."

"Wait, medical school?" I practically squawk. "I had no idea Ethan had any interest in medicine."

Cooper nods. "That makes two of us. Apparently, it's been Ethan's secret dream since he was a kid. Losing our mom has made him want to get into it more." He grins. "Guy wants to cure cancer, so who am I to tell him no?"

"Wow. How did Conrad take it?"

Cooper laughs. "Not well at first, but when I explained that I'd fund Ethan's schooling and life for as long as necessary, Dad realized he was outnumbered and relented on the trust fund issue. He signed an addendum for Ethan, so my brother can pursue his dreams and not lose a dime."

I tilt my head, studying Cooper. "And what about you? What's your dream?"

"You're my dream," he says simply, eyes locked on mine.

"You know what I mean. Do you want to stay at King?"

"I think I'll do as well as CEO as I would've done as COO." He winks. "When the time comes, of course. I've got some other life goals to get to first."

He doesn't say it, but I already know he's thinking about marriage. I'm thinking about it, too. I can't *not* think about it with this man. With Ethan, it felt like we had to get married to check off an item on a list, but with Cooper, it's something I want badly.

He's my forever person.

I want forever with him.

"Is that right? What did you have in mind first?"

"Move in with me," he says. "Or we can get our own place. Or I can move in with you. I don't care. But I want to live together."

I pretend to think on it. "Hmm... I guess I wouldn't mind living in such proximity to Arden again."

He laughs. "Remind me to thank her."

"For what? Luring me into your clutches?"

"Pretty much."

"Aw yes, nothing like a long-lost cousin-sister to shake things up."

He winks. "Exactly."

I laugh with joy, although joy is not a big enough word to hold what I'm experiencing. Tonight feels like the beginning of something new and special, like the best years of my life are starting right now.

Cooper - Two Months Later - Age 28

Carrying grocery bags in both hands, I hurry into the penthouse, the anticipation killing me. I can't wait to spill the news. I'm pretty sure she's going to be excited, but a little part of me worries she won't. Guess there's only one way to find out.

I push the door open with my shoulder, deposit the food on the counter, then find Sybil curled up in our bed watching reruns of *The Office*. Her hair is tied in a messy bun, and she's wearing my sweatpants, complete with a ratty Nantucket hoodie she's had for years.

"Honestly, you've never looked so beautiful," I say, and she laughs.

"Hardy-har-har."

"I mean it." And I do.

"Well, I did say we were having a fat-dog night."

A fat-dog night means staying home and eating so much junk food that we have to lie around like fat dogs until we eventually fall asleep.

It's Valentine's Day and her twenty-eighth birthday, so she gets to choose what we do tonight. We've both been pulling overtime at work, so I'm not surprised she wants to be lazy, which sounds perfect to me.

She points a socked foot in my direction. "What flavor of

Doritos did you get? Because your answer could make or break our relationship."

I snort. "Don't worry, baby, I know you hate the cool ranch, which is crazy since it's the best one, but I got you the salsa verde."

"In the green bag?"

"And gummy candy and a pepperoni pizza and... your favorite cheesecake."

Her grin is magnificent. "Taking the reins from Ethan, I see."

I sit on the edge of the bed and begin massaging her socked feet. "Why would you say that?"

She shrugs. "He's had my favorite cheesecakes flown in from Boston for years on my birthday."

I shake my head. "Valentine... that was me."

Her mouth falls open with an audible pop. "What the fuck? Why didn't you tell me?"

I shrug. "As I recall, we didn't talk for several of those years."

She pouts, her eyes welling with happiness. "Good point. Thank you, Cooper. I wish I would've known."

"I didn't do it for recognition. I did it because I loved you, and I wanted my girl to have her favorite cake on her birthday."

Even before she was my girl, she was my girl.

"Hey, there's something kinda cool I have to tell you," I say, dropping her foot. She senses the change in my tone and sits up straight.

"What's up?"

"I just got off the phone with Perry."

"Oh?" Her eyebrow rises.

"First of all, his sister is cancer free."

She yelps and pumps her fist. "Hell yeah!"

"And there's news about Top of the World. As you know, season one ended with record ratings." It also ended with her friend Benton not looking so good, something she's felt extremely bad about ever since.

"They're renewing it for a second season?" she guesses correctly.

"Yes, they are... and Benton has agreed to return."

"Wow. Okay. I bet his publicist told him he needs to rebuild his name."

I make a mental note to warn him that someone working on that set who can't be trusted. Despite an investigation, we never did figure out who took footage of me and Sybil together for the Vales to use against us. That mystery has become one of those things we've had to let go as we've moved forward.

"Exactly, but there's more."

"They can't have the penthouse," she deadpans. "They can pry my cold, dead body out of here before I'll move willingly."

I bark out a laugh, agreeing completely.

"Never. They know they have to find a new location. That's not it. The new network has decided to run a nationwide sweep-stake, and one lucky woman will get to join the show, living among the rich and famous for three months."

"You're telling me some ordinary, everyday woman is going to get to be on Top of the World?"

"That's *exactly* what I'm telling you."

She pumps her hands in the air, cheering. "That's fucking brilliant. We're going to watch it together, right?"

"Of course, but right now, I'm hungry and you're hungry and what I want to watch is you eat."

I help her off the bed, leading her toward one of many normal evenings together. Sure, this isn't the set of a glamorous reality tv show anymore, but I still feel like I'm on top of the world.

THE END

*"Cowards die many times before their deaths;
the valiant never taste of death but once."*

William Shakespeare's Julius Caesar

Acknowledgments

Thank you for supporting my work. If you enjoyed this book, please leave a review and tell a friend.

Would you like to read some hot Devious Delights bonus novellas? Join my Facebook Reader Group titled Nina Verona's Reader Room or sign up for my newsletter to get free access. You can also find me on socials at @Author.Nina.Verona.

Many thanks to my beta readers, arc team, cover designer Natasha Snow, editor Cassie Mae, book club friends, and my incredibly supportive husband. I couldn't do this without you!

Writing romance as a full-time career is my dream, and while I still have a long way to go, I'm so hopeful because of you wonderful readers who champion my books and the supportive people in my social circles who believe in me.

We're just getting started!

All The Love,
Nina Verona

SWIMMING
LESSONS
A Crushed By Love Novella
NINA VERONA

His
Valentine
A
Collateral Damage
Bonus Novella
NINA VERONA

About the Author

Collateral Damage is Nina Verona's second spicy contemporary romance. There's more to come! In her free time she enjoys books and television, spending time with friends and family, hiking and traveling, cuddling with her cats, drinking a good spicy-sweet chai tea, reading tarot cards and star charts, and can usually be found under a cozy minky blanket or out for a walk.

@Author.Nina.Verona